"I WON'T SEE
YOU AGAIN . . .
I MUST LEAVE."

As the carriage rolled away with its lovely inhabitant tucked safely inside, Damon felt more restless than he had ever been in his life. His mind was filled with her. He relived every moment of the past few hours and craved more.

He wanted her. He wanted her with an unreasoning, blind insistence that raged through every nerve. And he resented her for it.

She was married. So was he. Moreover, they occupied separate worlds.

He should put her from his mind, now. It was the only rational choice. But something in him rebelled at the thought. He had never felt so confined and curtailed, his choices limited by a past that weighed on him like a mile's length of iron chain.

He was married to a woman he didn't even know.

LISA KLEYPAS

Somewhere I'll Find You

AVON BOOKS
An Imprint of HarperCollinsPublishers

Special thanks to Mary Jo Putney
for her kindness and generosity to me

AVON BOOKS
An Imprint of HarperCollins *Publishers*
10 East 53rd Street
New York, New York 10022-5299

Copyright © 1996 by Lisa Kleypas
Front cover and inside front cover art by Victor Gadino
Inside cover author photo by Larry Sengbush
Library of Congress Catalog Card Number: 96-96171
ISBN: 0-380-78143-3
www.avonromance.com

First Avon Books printing: October 1996

Avon Trademark Reg. U.S. Pat. Off. and in Other Countries, Marca Registrada, Hecho en U.S.A.
HarperCollins® is a trademark of HarperCollins Publishers Inc.

Printed in the U.S.A.

20 19 18 17 16 15

To Griffin, with love,
from your mother

Prologue

Warwickshire, 1824

The music of the May Day celebration filled the air, drifting from the village to the honey-colored castle on the lake. One of the occupants of the castle, Damon, Lord Savage, the Marquess of Savage, wandered along the road to the village, lured by the music in spite of himself.

He was not a frivolous man, nor did he enjoy taking part in large gatherings. For the past two years Damon had devoted his life to rebuilding his family's fortunes, and looking after his younger brother and ailing father. The responsibilities he had assumed did not allow time for entertainment. He was drawn to the village by a mixture of curiosity and loneliness, and the need to be out of doors.

A multitude of girls in white dresses were gilded in the mauve light of sunset as they danced around a tree that had been hung with ribbons and garlands. Laughing, drinking, and singing, the villagers gathered to celebrate the pagan festivities of May Day, which would continue through the night.

Unobtrusively Damon stood at the edge of the crowd while the evening darkened. Torches and lamps were lit, throwing flickering shadows across the grass. Although he had seen the May Day ritual many times before, Damon was still struck by the picturesque sight of the maidens twining long streamers around the maypole. Gracefully they skipped in a circle, their hair crowned with circlets of flowers, their white skirts billowing around stocking-clad legs.

Like the other men present, Damon took note of the particularly attractive girls. It had been a long time since he'd had a woman. Later, he had promised himself, he would take a mistress and enjoy the pleasures he had forsworn, but for now there was too much to be done. If only he could rid himself of the inconvenient desire for a woman's touch, for the soft perfume of feminine skin, and the feel of slender arms wrapped around him. During the days he was too busy to dwell on the subject, but at night . . .

Damon's chest moved in a taut sigh. He watched the revelry for a few minutes more, conscious of an emptiness inside that refused to abate. Deciding to return to the castle and indulge in a large snifter of brandy, he turned away. All of a sudden, his attention was caught by a group of strolling players that had arrived to take part in the festivities. Raising their voices in boisterous song, they joined the crowd and clapped their hands in time to the music.

A few friendly villagers encouraged the newcomers to join the dancing maidens. Two of the women complied, but the third, a slender girl with blond braids pinned to the crown of her head, shook her head adamantly. The revelers persisted in spite of her refusal, pulling and pushing the girl toward the maypole. Someone placed a circlet of flowers on her head, making her laugh reluctantly as she followed the other maidens in their path around the garlanded tree.

Damon watched the girl in fascination. She was easily distinguishable by her dark dress and the grace with which she moved. She seemed like a sprite who had suddenly appeared from the forest and would vanish at any moment. It was strange, the effect she had on him, his body turning hollow with yearning, every sense focused on the sight of her and the high, sweet sound of her laughter.

She's just a girl, he told himself silently, trying in vain to rid himself of the urges that consumed him. *She's a girl like any other.* But that wasn't true. The strength of his reaction to her alarmed and electrified him. He would give all he owned for one night with her. He was never vulnerable to sudden impulses, had never been ruled by anything but logic and reason. It seemed that all the recklessness he had never allowed himself to feel had come over him in one moment.

Damon moved around the edge of the crowd with the deliberateness of a predator, his gaze locked on her. He wasn't certain what he intended to do, only that he had to be near her. She was dancing faster now, driven by the music and the impatient tugging of the girls who had joined hands with her. Laughing, gasping for breath, she managed to break free of the circle and stumble away. The garland of flowers flew from her head and landed near Damon's feet.

He bent and closed his fingers around it, unconsciously crushing some of the fragrant petals.

Blotting her perspiring face with her sleeve, the girl wandered away from the crowd. Damon followed her, his heart driving hard in his chest. Although he didn't make a sound, she must have sensed his presence. She stopped and turned to face him, while the May Day crowd continued its revelry. Damon ventured closer to her, stopping a scant foot away from her.

"I believe this is yours," he said thickly. She looked up at him, the color of her eyes indistinguishable in the darkness. The hint of a smile appeared on the tender curve of her lips.

"Thank you." She reached for the flowers, her cool fingers brushing his for a split second. He felt the shock of it all through his body.

"Who are you?" he blurted out.

The girl laughed, perhaps as startled by his bluntness as he was. "I'm no one of importance. Just an actress with a traveling company." She hesitated briefly. "And you?"

He remained silent, unable to answer while the heady scents of crushed flowers, wine, and perspiration filled his nostrils and made his blood rush through his veins. He wanted to tear her away from the crowd and carry her to the woods, bear her down to the damp leaf-covered ground . . . He wanted to press his mouth against her pale skin, and unbraid her hair until it rippled between his fingers.

The girl regarded him curiously, tilting her head to the side. "You must be from the castle," she said. All at once her expression became wary. "Are you one of the Savages?"

Damon shook his head, denying who he was, wanting to detach himself from everything in his past and future. "I'm a visitor here," he said, his voice slightly hoarse. "Just as you are."

She looked skeptical but seemed to relax.

"Where are you from?" Damon asked.

Her teeth flashed in the darkness. He had never seen anything as beautiful as her smile. "I don't choose to think about my past." She pushed back the stray locks of gleaming blond hair from her forehead. "Why did you come outside, sir? Was it to take the air or watch the dancing?"

"To find you."

A quiet laugh escaped her, and she tensed like a bird ready to take flight. Sensing that she was about to slip away, Damon found himself acting without conscious thought. His hands came to either side of her head, holding her securely in spite of her startled protest. "Let me," he whispered, a tremor running through his fingers as they pressed against her downy cheeks. He pressed his mouth to hers, and she became very still. Her breath rushed hot and fast on his skin, while the taste of her spilled through his senses in an intoxicating rush. He felt her response, and the moment was suspended in time, magical, unlike anything that had ever happened to him before.

She turned her face away, making a sound of confusion. Damon was intensely aware of the velvety touch of her cheek against his, the nearness of her body. They were both silent, motionless as they drank in the sensation of standing close together.

Chapter 1

London, 1825

She was late. Julia quickened her pace, trying to keep her skirts from dragging along the muddy ground, and at the same time shield her face from the persistent drizzle of cold autumn rain. If she didn't reach the Capital Theatre soon, her hair and clothes would be soaked. "My audition," she muttered despairingly, shouldering past the people on the broken, slippery sidewalk. A once-jaunty yellow feather drooped down from the brim of her small hat, and she pushed it back impatiently.

Today was one of the most important days of her life. If all went well, she might become part of the most successful acting company in England. However, if she failed to impress Logan Scott with her talents, she would have to return to the grimy little Daly Theatre in the Strand. The manager there, Mr. Bickerston, regarded the actresses as if they were prostitutes, turning a profit for himself by arranging for them to meet wealthy men. He was furious with Julia for refusing to associate with a lecherous old baron who had been willing to pay an exorbitant fee for the privilege of bedding her. "You'll obey my rules," Bickerston had spat at her, "or you're no longer in the company. The next time I find a man for you, you'll accept him or be damned!"

To make matters worse, Bickerston had a gambling problem, and he often couldn't pay the actors the full amount of their salaries. If Julia didn't make money soon, she wouldn't be able to afford the terrace room she had rented. And she couldn't resort to what the other actresses did, selling their sexual favors to supplement their income. For her that would never be a choice, even if she starved.

Julia sighed, her skin crawling at the thought of returning to the Strand. She had to find a better place to work. Tightening her grip on the damp sheaf of paper in her arms, she lowered her head and walked faster. All of a sudden she rammed into a hard object that nearly sent her sprawling backward. The stack of papers cascaded from her arms. Only a man's quick grab at her shoulders kept her from falling onto the muddy pavement.

"Are you all right, miss?" the man inquired, steadying her.

Julia bent to scoop up her sodden papers. To her dismay, the hem of her skirts dragged through a dirty puddle. "You should watch where you're going," she exclaimed.

"I might say the same to you, miss." The man's voice was as dry and rich as a glass of red wine. He helped her to retrieve the fallen papers, pausing to glance at them.

Julia took them from him before he had the

chance to read anything. "I'm on my way to an audition," she said crisply. "I'm very late." She began to walk past him, but he stopped her with a light touch on her shoulder.

"Which theater do you want?"

She looked up at him, blinking as a rain-laced breeze swept over her face. He was tall and well-built, his wide shoulders covered with a heavy black coat. Through the veil of rain dripping from the brim of his dark hat, she could see blunt, attractive features and a pair of intense blue eyes. "I'm trying to find the Capital," she said.

"You've reached it." He indicated a nearby doorway. "That leads to the greenroom, where auditions are usually held."

"How do you know that?" she asked suspiciously.

A smile pulled at the corner of his wide, mobile mouth. "I'm a member of the company."

"Oh." She was taken aback, and a touch envious. Lucky, lucky man, to be a part of such a prestigious group.

His smile remained as he contemplated her. "If you wish, I'll show you the way."

Julia nodded and cautiously preceded him through the doorway into a quiet, dim hallway. Relieved to be out of the rain, she brushed at her damp skirts and tried to straighten them. Politely her companion waited until she removed her dripping hat and cloak, and he took them from her. "We'll leave these in a spare dressing room to dry," he said, opening a door and hanging the articles on the large brass hooks affixed to the wall. He removed his own hat and coat, and ran his fingers through his disheveled hair, trying to bring order to the short, wavy mass.

Julia smoothed her own dark hair, wishing she had a mirror to help restore her appearance.

"You look well enough," the man said, as if reading her thoughts.

For the first time, Julia smiled at him tentatively. "I was hoping for something better than that."

He shrugged. "Your looks won't matter as much as your acting skill."

"Yes, of course." She followed him down the hallway, past dressing rooms, offices, carpenter shops, and wardrobe rooms. The Capital Theatre was a large place, comprised of a main theater with four satellite buildings. It had never been regarded in the same light as the Theatre Royal in Drury Lane until Logan Scott had taken over its management. Under his brilliant direction, and driven by his powerful performances, the Capital had become one of the most respected theaters in town.

Although Logan Scott was still a young man in his twenties, he had already achieved a legendary status in the theater. The thought of actually meeting him made Julia's stomach flip-flop violently. If he decided that she had no talent, her career would be finished.

"How long have you been with the company?" Julia asked, her nervousness increasing as they went deeper into the building. They passed workmen in the hallway, and turned a corner where actors' voices could be heard in the practice rooms.

"Since it began four years ago," her companion replied.

"You're very fortunate to be working with Mr. Scott."

"Am I?" he asked dryly. "He has quite a temper, you know."

"That can be forgiven in such a brilliant artist. Mr. Scott is the greatest actor in England. Everyone calls him the new David Garrick."

A sardonic snort escaped him. "I think that's an overstatement."

Julia glanced at him in surprise. "Aren't you an admirer of Mr. Scott?"

"Occasionally, yes. I just don't happen to think he's comparable to Garrick. Not yet, at any rate."

Julia shrugged. "Since I've never actually seen him on stage, I'll have to reserve judgment."

They reached the greenroom, which was not actually green, and Julia clutched her papers tightly as she stepped inside. The large cream-painted room was filled with well-worn chairs and settees, battered tables, and a tray piled with bread, smoked meats, and cheese. Two women were seated in the corner, while a girl and a young man were rehearsing a scene on the other side of the room, pausing to laugh at some bit of awkward choreography. A portly older gentleman sat off to one side, reading a play and mouthing the lines silently.

At the sight of the new arrivals, they all looked up. Immediately they came forward to Julia's companion, crowding around him until Julia was nudged aside. He fended off a torrent of questions and demands with upraised hands.

"Later," he informed them. "For now I have some business to attend to—an audition."

Julia stared at him with wide eyes. Now that they were in the well-lit greenroom, she could see many of the details about him that had escaped her before. He was dressed in expensive, perfectly tailored clothes: dark trousers, a rich emerald vest, and a black silk cravat. She had never seen such beautiful hair on a man, unruly waves of brown that gleamed with burnished mahogany highlights. It was cut short and brushed back, but it had a rumpled appearance that practically begged a woman to smooth it.

His air of authority was unmistakable. That, and the compellingly deep timbre of his voice, and most of all those riveting blue eyes, convinced Julia of who he was. She felt her heart plummet to her feet, and she knew the color had left her cheeks. "You're Logan Scott," she murmured. "You should have told me."

His eyes gleamed with mischief and challenge. "You should have asked."

She nodded in rueful acknowledgment, wondering if she had managed to ruin all chances of creating a favorable impression.

"And your name is . . . ?" he prompted.

"Mrs. Jessica Wentworth," Julia said, using the stage name she had invented for herself. The half-dozen people in the room stared at her curiously. She wanted to crawl away into some dark corner and hide.

"Very well, Mrs. Wentworth," Logan Scott said softly. "Let's find out what you're capable of." He held out one broad hand for the audition pieces she had brought, and casually riffled through the damp pages. "I see you've prepared a scene from *Mathilda*. Excellent. We had a long run of that play last season. Charles is quite familiar with it." He gestured to the tall blond man a few feet away. "Would you mind taking the part of Lord Aversley, Charles?"

The young man obeyed with alacrity.

Scott seated himself comfortably, and the others followed suit. "If you don't mind, Mrs. Wentworth, we'll allow the other members of the company to watch your audition."

Julia did mind, actually. It was much more difficult to play a scene in front of a very small group than a large one. And these people were *actors*, the most critical audience of all. They would mock her for wanting to be part of the Capital—they would see immediately that she'd had no training, and precious little experience. But she had come too far to retreat now. Julia forced a smile to her face, and unlocked her knees in order to join the young man at the center of the greenroom.

In appearance, Charles was not the ideal Lord Aversley—he seemed rather too bland and handsome for the role of a consummate villain. On the other hand, he possessed an air of self-assurance that impressed Julia. She had no doubt of his ability to play convincingly any character he chose.

"Mathilda is a tricky role to choose for an audition," Logan Scott remarked. It was unclear if he was speaking to Julia or the others in the room. "The part of a long-suffering heroine is usually tiresome."

Julia nodded gravely, staring at his imperturbable face. "I shall endeavor not to be boring, Mr. Scott."

There was a twitch of amusement at the corners of his mouth. "Begin when you're ready, Mrs. Wentworth."

Julia nodded and stared at the floor in concentration, preparing herself for the scene. The story of *Mathilda* had brought fame to its author, S. R. Fielding, two short years ago, first in the form of a novel and then as a smashing success on the stage. The public was fascinated by the tale of an ambitious country girl's descent into prostitution, and her eventual redemption. The scene Julia had chosen was a pivotal one in which Mathilda, still a virgin, was seduced by the diabolical rake Lord Aversley.

Julia glanced up at Charles, and she began to speak in a rough country accent. He responded in the pure, aristocratic tones of Aversley. With each line, Julia felt herself sinking deeper into the character. She became half-flirtatious, half-fearful, advancing and retreating as Aversley slowly pursued her around the room.

Logan concentrated on the girl, all his senses arrested. Although she was a small woman, a little below average height, her slenderness gave her the illusion of being taller. With her ash-blond hair, brilliant blue-green eyes and delicately angled face, she was too pretty, actually. It was rare to find a woman of such unassailable beauty who was also a proficient actress. Truly beautiful women never seemed to have the emotional depth or drive to play anything other than an ingenue.

Less than a minute after the scene had begun, Logan realized that Jessica Wentworth had a remarkable presence, the kind that made the hair on the back of his neck prickle. She had the gift of transforming herself into the character she played. He knew without vanity that he possessed the same ability, and that on occasion one or two of the players in the company could achieve it. But such a talent was rare in a girl who couldn't be more than twenty.

Jessica Wentworth interpreted the character of Mathilda with seeming effortlessness. She was strangely touching, with a child's curiosity and a pitiable fascination for the man who would ruin her. And there was a thread of calculation in her manner, a smart and subtle understanding of Mathilda's misguided ambition to have a wealthy man in her power. Logan shook his head slightly, appreciating the fluid quality of her performance. He glanced at the other actors and saw that they were staring raptly at the newcomer.

Julia began to relax and enjoy the pleasure of working with an actor as accomplished as Charles. He made it surprisingly easy for her to believe he was Aversley as he sneered and stalked her from one side of the room to the other. However, she faltered and stopped in dismay as she heard Logan Scott's voice cut through the exchange of dialogue.

"I'll finish the scene with her, Charles."

Startled, Julia watched as Scott stood from his chair and approached her. He motioned for Charles to sit down, and assumed his place. Julia was momentarily transfixed by the change that came over Logan Scott, the sudden crackling tension in the room, the flicker of blue fire in his eyes. He smiled at her slightly, and began speaking as Aversley. It was thrilling. Julia wanted to take a seat and just listen to the suppressed power of his voice. He gave the character of Aversley a catlike quality, a preposterous self-importance, and an unexpected hint of bitterness.

Adjusting the pitch of her performance to his, Julia responded as Mathilda, and for a few moments it was easy to lose herself in the role, forgetting who she was. Aversley toyed with Mathilda, lunged for her, promising pleasure and torment with his silky voice and his hot blue eyes. He gripped her arms, and Julia was startled by the genuine feeling of being trapped. She tried to wrench away, but he held her near, and spoke close to her mouth until his warm breath fanned her lips.

They were at the part of the play when Aversley kissed Mathilda and carried her offstage, leaving the rest of the action to the audience's imagination. Julia tensed in Logan Scott's arms, feeling utterly possessed by his hard grip. She thought briefly that he would kiss her, and was relieved when a mask dropped over his face and he released her carefully. The scene was over.

The others in the room were silent. Julia felt their gazes on her as she stepped back and rubbed the places on her arms where Scott had held her.

Noting her action, Scott turned toward her

with an arched brow. "Did I hurt you?" he inquired with mild surprise.

Immediately Julia shook her head and let her hands drop. His hold hadn't been painful in the least, but his touch had seemed to linger even after he had let go.

There was a long pause after that, while the members of the company continued to stare at Julia, and Scott pinned her with a speculative look. Was he pleased, disappointed, uncertain? Did he think she had any merit as an actress? Julia was driven to break the silence. "Shall I try another scene?" she murmured. "Something from a different play?"

"That won't be necessary." Suddenly he seemed impatient, glancing about the room like a leopard in a cage. One of his elegant hands lifted in a gesture for Julia to leave with him. "Come, Mrs. Wentworth. I'll give you a tour of the theater."

None of the others seemed to find that surprising. The portly older man in the corner gave Julia an encouraging smile as she passed. A pretty young girl with curly brown hair and vivid sea-green eyes approached her at the doorway. "That was the best Mathilda I've ever seen," the girl said.

Julia smiled in thanks, heartened by the remark. But Logan Scott's opinion was the one that meant life and death, and so far he hadn't volunteered a single word.

"You've had little, if any training," he remarked, taking her through a maze of administrative offices.

"No," Julia said quietly.

"And not much experience."

"I've done some touring around the provinces with a traveling company. Most recently I've worked at the Daly Theatre in the Strand."

"The Daly," he repeated, sounding far from impressed. "You deserve better than that."

"I hope I do, sir."

He paused and showed her the theater library, filled with shelves of books on costume, scenery, and acting technique, as well as innumerable copies of different plays. Pausing at one stack of paper, he selected a worn edition of *Much Ado About Nothing,* and handed it to her. Clutching the copy tightly, Julia followed him from the room.

"What I ask from the actors in my company is that they strive for the most naturalistic style possible," Scott remarked. "I can't abide the posturing and studied manners I've seen in the majority of London theaters. Most actors are overtrained fools who substitute extravagant gestures and pauses for real acting."

Filled with an admiration that bordered on awe, Julia nodded in agreement. "They say you've revolutionized the stage in England and Europe—" she began, but he interrupted her sardonically.

"I don't like to be flattered, Mrs. Wentworth. It only serves to inflate my opinion of myself, and that's a dangerous thing. I'm already too arrogant by far."

A surprised laugh escaped her. "I'm sure that's not true."

"Wait until you know me better."

A bubble of hope rose in her chest. "Will I?" she dared to ask, and he smiled. Strange, how a man could smile and seem so warm, and yet there was still something unreachable about him.

"Perhaps," he replied. "You have great potential as an actress, Mrs. Wentworth. You wouldn't be a bad addition to the company."

They reached the theater, walking past the rear drop and side wings. Julia accompanied Scott to the footlights at the edge of the stage, and stared out at the auditorium. It was dim and handsome, seating approximately fifteen hundred people, with tiers of side boxes that rose to dizzying heights. Julia had never been inside the place before. It was a gorgeous theater, painted white, salmon, and forest-green. The walls were lined with columns that were covered in gold and inlaid with green glass, while the interiors of the boxes were lined with rich flowered paper.

The stage itself was built on a slant, so that the actors in back were elevated a few inches higher than the ones in front. Standing on the scarred floor, Julia could almost imagine what it was like to play to an assembly of a thousand people or more.

"There are matters that need to be discussed," Scott remarked abruptly. "Your salary, the number of performances required, the demands I make of the players . . . rehearsals, for example. I insist that all actors and actresses be present for every rehearsal, no matter how well they know their parts. You may run your personal life in any manner you wish, but if anyone misses a rehearsal or a performance, they take the risk of being fined or even dismissed. The same goes for drunkenness, tardiness, pregnancy, affairs with the other players, or anything else that interferes with the theater schedule."

"I understand," Julia said, a faint blush rising in her cheeks.

"I have a particular system for managing the company," he continued. "If you have a grievance, there is a proper time and place for airing it—you'll be informed of the particular channels later. I never receive calls at my home concerning theater business. I place a high value on my privacy."

"Naturally," Julia said, her heart beginning to beat fast with excitement. The way he was talking, it sounded as if he was planning to hire her.

"There is something else that must be made clear," Scott said. "Beyond any artistic merits it may possess, the Capital is a business enterprise. I make all my decisions according to the need to bring in a profit—and I've made no secret of it. If I decide to hire you, it is because you will bring money to the theater. All of the players, including myself, understand that we're here because of our profitability."

Julia stiffened, all her hopes draining suddenly. Was he suggesting that he wanted her to become a prostitute to further the good of the theater?

"I have no desire to pimp for anyone," Scott murmured in amusement, apparently reading her thoughts. "I'm only pointing out that one of your responsibilities—as well as mine and everyone else's—is to attract sponsors for each new season. You can use your talent and charm to accomplish that. There's no need to sleep with anyone . . . unless you wish to, of course."

"I don't wish to," Julia said fervently.

"That's entirely your concern," he assured her. A frown crossed his broad forehead as he contemplated her. "It occurs to me . . . I don't recall having arranged an audition for anyone today."

The question caught her off-guard, and she answered hastily. "I believe it was done with the assistance of one of your managers—"

"No one does anything around here without my permission."

Julia nodded, her face turning scarlet. "I lied," she admitted. "I would never have gotten to see you otherwise."

There was a touch of annoyance in his laugh. "You'll do well for us, I think. Tell me, Mrs. Wentworth . . . are you actually married?"

Although she had prepared herself for the question, Julia felt herself flush in discomfort. She couldn't tell him the truth, yet she knew he was too talented an actor to accept a lie easily. She wandered aimlessly across the stage, her arms folded over her chest. "Not really," she said without looking at him. "I thought that posing as a 'Mrs.' would give me protection against unwelcome advances."

"Very well."

When no further questions seemed forthcoming, Julia glanced at him in surprise. "Aren't you going to ask about my family? My background?"

He shook his head, tugging absentmindedly at a lock of mahogany-red hair. "I assume you're like most people in the theater, who have a past they would like to escape."

"Even you?" she dared to ask.

Scott nodded. "There are events in my life from which I've run for a long time. But I never seem to get farther than here." He glanced around the empty stage and seemed to relax. "I never feel entirely comfortable anywhere as I do at the Capital. It's home to me . . . as I hope it will become home to you, Mrs. Wentworth."

A smile broke out on her face. "Yes," she murmured, sensing a little of why he so clearly loved the place. She could easily imagine the thousands of stories and personalities that had filled this stage, the air ringing with music and voices, the audience feeling the players' emotions; fear, hope, love . . .

In the theater a person could forget who he or she was, at least for a while. Actors could turn themselves into anyone they wished to be. That was what she wanted for herself. She would live as Jessica Wentworth, and bury all traces of Julia Hargate—and the secret that had haunted her all her life.

"I told you so," Nell Florence said, her wrinkled face breaking into a rare and beautiful smile. "It was the right choice to approach Logan Scott. I admire his work at the Capital. Despite his youth, he's a capable manager. You'll profit far more by joining Scott's acting company than you would have at Drury Lane." Her frail shoulders moved in a shudder, and she made a face of disdain. "Drury Lane is being ruined by that American impresario Stephen

Price and his freakish taste for spectacle. You should have been born a half-century ago and worked for David Garrick—he would have known exactly what to do with a girl of your talents. To think of how you could have played opposite him in *The Wonder* . . ."

"Then you approve of Mr. Scott?" Julia asked, gently prodding her back to the subject before Mrs. Florence could lapse into one of her long reminiscences.

"Oh, yes. His productions have wonderful style, and his devotion to the art of acting is unquestionable."

They sat together drinking tea in Mrs. Florence's parlor, with its musty furniture upholstered in rose silk, and walls covered with ancient theater mementos. Julia had met the elderly woman only a few months before, when Mrs. Florence had accepted a small part in a production at the Daly Theatre. Normally an appearance at the Daly would have been beneath such a great actress, who had acted at Drury Lane for more than thirty years. However, Mr. Bickerston had paid Mrs. Florence a fortune, knowing that her name would fill every seat in the theater.

After a successful month-long run of the play, Mrs. Florence had left Bickerston and the Daly—but not before she had taken Julia aside and given some well-intentioned advice. "Your gifts are being wasted here," she had told Julia. "You must find another theater, a reputable one, and get some proper training."

Julia had been flattered almost to the point of speechlessness. She greatly admired the elderly woman and the success she had made of her life. Born to a large and impoverished family on the east end of London, Nell Florence had profited from her considerable talents on the stage and also from a few discreet love affairs with wealthy men. Although her legendary beauty had faded with age, her rich red hair now streaked with silver, she was still a handsome woman.

Several years ago Mrs. Florence had retired to a London townhouse with a small staff of servants to look after her. If an aspiring actor or actress took her fancy, she would occasionally give acting lessons. Although Julia couldn't afford to pay her high fees, Mrs. Florence had decided to take her under her wing regardless.

"I can afford to teach for pleasure, if I wish to," she had said. "I believe our association will do us both some good. I will help you to achieve the success you deserve, and you will brighten my days with your visits. Old people must always have young ones around . . . and you are very much like I was at your age."

Once a week Julia would visit Mrs. Florence in her cluttered parlor, drinking tea from painted china cups as she paid rapt attention to the elderly woman's instructions. Now that Julia had been hired as a member of the Capital Theatre, Mrs. Florence seemed as pleased by Julia's success as if it were her own.

"I knew Scott wouldn't hesitate to hire you, once he saw you act," she remarked. "You have a quality, my dear, which he couldn't fail to see. You seem to give everything of yourself when you're onstage . . . but you withhold just enough to make them want more. Never give everything, Jessica, or you'll be taken for granted." Settling back in an overstuffed chair, the elderly woman regarded Julia with bright eyes. "Now tell me . . . how was it to play a scene with an actor of his caliber?"

"Thrilling," Julia said instantly. "He almost made me believe it was really happening. I've never met anyone who could make a scene from a play seem more real than life."

"So it is with the great ones," Mrs. Florence replied reflectively. "But beware, Jessica . . . after reaching the heights that are possible in the theater, real life can seem rather disappointing. You may awaken one morning to find that your profession has stolen precious years from you. And you'll be no better off than I, surrounded by faded artifacts and portraits, with nothing but memories to sustain you."

"I would love to be exactly like you," Julia said fervently. "You've made your mark in the theater, you're respected and comfortable and *independent* . . . I could hope for nothing better than that."

For a moment Mrs. Florence's eyes were filled with sadness. "I haven't always made the right choices, child. I've had to live with the consequences for a very long time."

"Do you mean . . ." Julia stared at her, perplexed. "Is it that you regret not having married?"

"I only wanted to marry one man in particular," the elderly woman informed her, with a wry twitch of her lips. "Unfortunately he didn't mix with the theater. He wanted me to leave it entirely, and so . . ." She spread her hands in a gesture of helplessness. "I let him go. How I envied other women who didn't have to make such a choice!" She stared at Julia in a faintly pitying way, as if it were a certainty that Julia would someday face the same painful dilemma. Julia wished she could tell Mrs. Florence the truth . . . that she would never need to choose between love and her profession . . . that she was in fact already married, and her husband was no obstacle at all.

Quietly Julia made her way to her mother's bedroom, located in the darkened east wing of Hargate Hall. The luxurious gothic estate was dark and stalwart, with tall chimneys and long, narrow windows. Set in the midst of the chalky Buckinghamshire hills, it was connected to the market town a mile away by old, sunken paths that hadn't changed for decades. Hargate Hall was dim and quiet, with heavy mahogany furniture and ceilings covered with webbed fan vaulting.

Being inside the home she had left two years ago gave Julia an uncomfortable, closed-in feeling. Resolutely she climbed one of the long flanks of stairs leading from the first floor to the second, half-fearing that at any moment she would hear her father's knifelike voice commanding her to get out.

Aside from several discreet greetings from a few servants she had known since childhood, no one dared speak to her. It was known to everyone at Hargate Hall that she was not a welcome visitor—her father had forbidden her to set foot on the property—yet no one would stop her from visiting her ailing mother, Eva.

Wrinkling her nose at the stale air in Eva's bedroom, Julia went to the curtains, drew them apart, and opened a window to admit a breeze from outside. There was a stirring beneath the covers on the bed, and Eva's weak voice.

"Who is that?"

"Your prodigal daughter," Julia replied lightly, and went to the bed, bending over to kiss her mother's pale brow.

Eva blinked rapidly and tried to sit up, her face stiff with consternation. She was a small, slim woman, with ash-blond hair streaked with silver, and large brown eyes. She seemed to have aged a great deal in the past two years, her colorless skin etched with tiny lines and the bones of her face more prominent than ever. "Julia, you shouldn't be here. It's dangerous!"

"It's all right," Julia said quietly. "You wrote to me and said that Father would be gone today. Don't you remember?"

"Oh, yes," Fretfully her mother rubbed her forehead. "Things slip from my mind so easily of late." She sighed and let her shoulders press back into the pillow. "I've been ill, Julia . . ."

"Yes, I know." Julia was tight-lipped as she stared down at her mother, who had always been slender. Now she appeared birdlike in her frailty. "You shouldn't be closed in this dark room, Mama. You need light and fresh air, and a walk outside—"

"You mustn't stay long," her mother said weakly. "If your father comes home unexpectedly . . ."

"He would throw me out," Julia finished for her, her mouth curling sarcastically. "Don't worry, Mama. I'm not afraid of him. There's nothing he could say or do that matters to me now." Her face softened as she saw her mother's distress, and she sat carefully on the edge of the mattress. Taking one of Eva's thin, cool hands in her own, she pressed it carefully.

"I've made a new life for myself. I'm an actress now, a fairly good one." She couldn't help smiling as she saw her mother's expression. "*Actress*, not prostitute . . . though I'll admit most people don't seem to understand the difference. This season I'll be working at the Capital Theatre, training under Logan Scott himself. I'll have a handsome salary, my own carriage, a house . . . and I've chosen a new name for myself. Jessica Wentworth. Do you like it?"

Eva shook her head. "It's not what you were born for," she said through dry lips. "It's not who you are."

"Who am I, Mama?" Julia asked softly, although she knew the answer. Her chest tightened with sudden unhappiness.

"You're the Marchioness of Savage."

Julia shot off the bed, unable to bear the sound of the name. "Only because I had no choice in the matter. I'm married to a man I don't know, all to satisfy Father's social ambitions. It's an absurd situation. I don't know Lord Savage by sight, I've never even corresponded with him. Sometimes I wonder if he exists at all!"

"It appears that Lord Savage has no more desire than you to acknowledge the marriage," her mother admitted. "Neither your father nor the Duke of Leeds could have expected that both children would resent the marriage so greatly."

"Not resent having our futures stolen?" Julia strode around the room as she continued heatedly. "I was sold for the price of a name, and Lord Savage for a fortune. Father secured a title for his daughter, and the Savages were saved from financial ruin. And all they had to do was sacrifice their firstborn children."

"Why must you bear such ill will against your father?" her mother asked sadly. "What he did was no different than what other parents of our position do. Marriages are arranged all the time."

"It was different. I was only *four years old*, and my so-called husband wasn't much older." Julia went to the window and stared through the parted drapes, filtering the silk-fringed velvet through her fingers. "That first time I found out, I was twelve and fancied myself in love with a village boy . . . until Father took me aside and said I would never have the right to love any man because I was already married." She shook her head and laughed without humor. "I couldn't believe it. I still can't. For years I've been haunted by thoughts of my 'husband,' wondering if he's grown up to be a half-wit, a bore, a skirt-chaser—"

"From what we have heard of him, Lord Savage's reputation is that of a quiet and responsible man."

"I don't care what he's like," Julia said, knowing that her mother would think this pure stubbornness on her part—and perhaps that was partly true. But it was also because of the awareness that if she accepted the life her father had chosen for her, she would fade into the same kind of docile, unhappy creature that her mother had become. "It doesn't matter if Lord Savage is a saint. I never intend to become the Duchess of Leeds. I won't agree to the plans Father made for me. He controlled every day, hour, and minute of my life until I finally gathered the courage to run away."

"He wanted to shelter and protect you—"

"Father kept me cloistered on this estate, never allowing me to go anywhere or meet anyone. From the day I was born, he was determined that I should marry a man with a great title. I wonder, did it ever occur to him that I might someday have landed a duke or an earl without his interference? Or did he even once consider that I might not have wished that for myself? I suppose it was too much to expect that he might have wanted me to be happy—"

Julia broke off, realizing that her fingers were clutched in the folds of velvet. She loosened her grip and took a calming breath. It pained her to know that even though she had escaped her father's domination, Eva was still under his control. Her mother's only recourse was to take refuge in illness, gradually turning herself into an invalid. It was Eva's only defense against an autocratic husband who manipulated the lives of everyone around him.

Edward, Lord Hargate despised illness of any kind. He was actually rather afraid of it, for it was so completely alien to his robust nature. He was a strong man whose relentless drive led him to dismiss anyone's feelings but his own. He could be cruel at times, denying people the things they wanted most in order to demonstrate his wealth and power. The rest of the Hargate family—cousins, brothers, uncles, and aunts— all avoided him as much as possible. Yet even when he was at his worst, his wife defended and supported him, as was her duty.

"There must be something else you can do," Eva murmured, "other than turn to a life in the theater. The idea of my daughter living among those people, working on the stage . . . It sounds very sordid."

"I'll be quite safe at the Capital," Julia said firmly. "It's a reputable company. And acting is the perfect occupation for me. After being se-cluded so much of the time when I was a child, I developed quite an imagination."

"I remember how I worried," Eva murmured. "You seemed to live in a fantasy world most of the time, always pretending to be someone else."

Julia returned to the bedside and smiled down at her. "Now I'm being paid a very good salary for it."

"And what about Lord Savage?"

Julia shrugged. "For the time being, he doesn't seem to want to acknowledge the marriage. I can't see any other choice except to lead my own life." She grimaced uncomfortably. "How odd it is, knowing that I belong to a stranger . . . that legally he has more rights over me than I do over myself. The thought of it makes me want to run

to the ends of the earth. I'll admit that I'm afraid
to find out what kind of man he really is. I'm not
ready for that—I may never be."

"You won't be able to hide the truth forever,"
Eva murmured. "Someday Lord Savage will find
out that his wife has been working on the stage.
How do you think he'll feel?"

"No doubt he'll want an annulment." Suddenly an impish grin crossed Julia's face. "And
I'll be glad to oblige him. I'm certain to make a
far better actress than a duchess."

Chapter 2

1827

As soon as the hired detective left the room, Damon abandoned all pretense of calm. Although he never allowed himself to lose his self-control, this was too much frustration to bear. The urge to shout, hit someone, break something, was unbearable. He wasn't aware that he had been holding a glass until he heard it shatter in the library fireplace with explosive force. "Dammit, where is she?"

A few moments later, the door opened and his brother Lord William peered gingerly around the edge. "Apparently the detective had no luck in finding our mystery marchioness."

Damon was silent, but the uncharacteristic flush on his face betrayed his emotions. While the two brothers were strikingly similar in appearance, in temperament they couldn't be more different. They both had the black hair and the striking, sharp-hewn features common to the Savage clan. But Damon's gray eyes, the shade of smoke and shadows, rarely revealed his thoughts, whereas William's gaze was usually filled with mischief. William possessed a charm

33

and happy-go-lucky air that Damon, the elder, had never had the time nor the inclination to cultivate.

So far in his short life of twenty years, William had managed to land himself in a large number of scrapes and predicaments. He had sailed through them all with the youthful conviction that nothing bad would ever happen to him. Yet Damon seldom rebuked him, knowing that at heart William was a good lad. What did it matter if he indulged his high spirits for a while? Damon intended for his younger brother to have all the freedom and advantages that he'd never been allowed—and he would protect Will from the harsh realities that he himself had not been spared.

"What did he say?" William prompted.

"I don't want to talk now."

William sauntered into the room, heading to the mahogany pedestal side cabinet that held rows of opulent cut-glass decanters. "You know," he remarked casually, "it's not necessary that you find Julia Hargate in order to get rid of her. You've been searching for three years, and there's no sign of her here or abroad. It's clear that the Hargates don't want her to be found. Her relatives and friends are either unwilling or unable to divulge any information. You could obtain an annulment, I daresay."

"I won't without Julia's knowledge."

"But why? God knows you don't owe her anything."

"I owe her a fortune," Damon said grimly. "Or rather, the family does."

William shook his head as he handed a fresh glass of brandy to his brother. "You and your damned sense of responsibility. Any other man in your position would cast off Julia Hargate like unwanted ballast. You don't even know her!"

Taking a deep swallow of brandy, Damon stood from his desk and wandered around the room. "I need to find her. She was a victim in this as much as I. The agreement was made without our consent, but at least we can dissolve it together. Besides, I don't want to take any steps without making some kind of settlement on her."

"With her family's fortune behind her, she has no need of a settlement."

"There's a possibility she has broken with the Hargates. I won't know until I find her."

"I hardly think Julia is destitute, brother. More likely she's amusing herself at some French or Italian seashore and living quite well off her papa's money."

"If that were true, I'd have located her by now."

William watched as his brother went to stand at the window. The view was spectacular, as it was from nearly every room in the modified medieval castle. It was built on a lake, with great stone arches that rose from the water and supported the ancient building as it reached toward the sky. Many of the once impenetrable honey-colored walls had been replaced by spectacular windows filled with diamond-shaped panes of glass. Behind the castle stretched the endless green countryside of Warwickshire, lush with pastures and gardens. Long ago the castle had served as a staunch defense against invaders of England, but it had now settled into a mellow and gracious old age.

The Savage family had nearly lost possession of their ancestral home—and everything else they owned—because of the present duke's bad investments, not to mention his taste for gambling. Only Damon's marriage to Julia Hargate, and the dowry her father had provided, had saved the family from ruin. And now they owed her the title of duchess, which wouldn't be long in coming, judging by their father Frederick's failing health.

"Thank God I wasn't the firstborn child," William said in a heartfelt tone. "It was a damned strange bargain Father struck, marrying off his son at age seven in order to secure money for his gambling debts. And it's stranger still that you've never met her since."

"I never wanted to see Julia. It was easier to pretend she didn't exist. I couldn't acknowledge that she was—*is*—part of my life." Damon's fingers clenched tight around the glass.

"Is the marriage legal?" William asked.

"No—but that's not the point. Father made a promise all those years ago, one involving me. It's my responsibility to honor it, or at least reimburse the Hargates for the money we accepted from them."

"Honor . . . responsibility . . . " William shivered and grimaced playfully. "My two least favorite words."

Damon swirled his drink and stared moodily into the glass. Although it wasn't Julia's fault, each letter of her name was a link in the invisible chain that bound him. He would never be at peace until the matter was resolved.

"I've imagined Julia a hundred different ways," Damon said. "I can't stop wondering about her, and what drove her to disappear like this. God, I'd like to be free of her!"

"When you do locate her, Julia may want to hold you to your obligation. Have you considered that? You've tripled the family's wealth since you've taken charge of the Savage finances." There was a teasing glint in William's dark blue eyes as he added, "And women seem to find you attractive, in spite of your gloomy character. Why would Julia be different? She wants what every woman desires—a titled husband and a fortune to go with him."

"I don't know what she wants from me." A bitter laugh escaped Damon. "Nothing yet, apparently, or she wouldn't still be in hiding."

"Well, you'd better do something about the blasted situation soon, or Pauline will make a bigamist of you."

"I'm not going to marry Pauline."

"She's told everyone in London that you are. Good God, Damon, don't you think you should tell Pauline the rumors are true, that you are in fact married?"

The subject of Pauline, Lady Ashton caused Damon's scowl to deepen. The sultry young widow had pursued him ardently for a year, invading his privacy and cornering him at every social event he attended. Pauline was the kind of woman who knew exactly how to please a man.

She was beautiful and dark-haired, completely uninhibited in bed, and possessed a dry sense of humor that appealed to Damon.

In spite of his better judgment, he had begun an affair with Pauline about six months ago. After all, he was a man with the same needs as any other, and he had little taste for prostitutes. Neither did he have an interest in the flocks of marriage-minded virgins being brought out each season. They were forbidden to him, though the fact of his marriage was not known for certain by the public.

Recently, however, Pauline had begun a campaign to become the next Marchioness of Savage. So far she had been wise enough not to pressure him or make demands. In fact, she hadn't yet dared to ask him if the gossip was true, if he already had a wife.

"I've told Pauline many times not to hope for a future with me," Damon said gruffly. "Don't pity her—she's been well-compensated for the time she's spent with me."

"Oh, I don't pity Pauline," William assured him. "I have a fair idea of the jewels, gowns, and credit accounts you've given her." A sly grin curved his mouth. "She must be damned entertaining in bed to deserve all that."

"She's good at many things. Beautiful, charming, and intelligent. All things considered, she wouldn't make a bad wife."

"You're not seriously considering . . ." William frowned and stared at him in surprise. "Talk like that alarms me, Damon! Pauline may like you, may even be fond of you, but in my opinion she's not capable of love."

"Perhaps I'm not either," Damon murmured, his face inscrutable.

A quizzical silence passed, and William appeared nonplussed. Then he gave a short laugh. "Well, I can't say that I've ever seen you fall madly in love—but having a wife since age seven is something of a handicap. You haven't let yourself feel anything for a woman because of some obligation to a girl you've never known. My advice is, dispose of Julia . . . and you may be surprised at how quickly your heart thaws."

"Always the optimist," Damon accused ruefully, and motioned for his brother to leave the room. "I'll consider your advice, Will. In the meantime, I have work to do."

Julia suppressed a yawn of boredom as she surveyed the ballroom. The dance was an elegant affair with sprightly music, a grand display of refreshments, and a sophisticated assemblage of rich and titled guests. The room was too hot, even though the towering rectangular windows had been opened to admit cooling summer breezes from the garden. Guests dabbed surreptitiously at their perspiring faces and drank cup after cup of fruited punch in between dances.

In spite of Julia's objections, Logan Scott had insisted that she accompany him to the weekend party at Lord and Lady Brandon's Warwickshire country house. Julia was fully aware that it was not precisely her company Logan desired, although they had developed a friendship of sorts over the past two years. The real reason he had wanted her to attend was her ability to attract donations to the Capital Theatre.

Julia stood with Logan in the corner of the ballroom, sharing a discreet conversation before they would mingle separately with various guests. Idly she smoothed the skirts of her ice-blue silk gown, a simple design with a wide, straight neckline that almost bared the tops of her shoulders. Aside from the four blue satin bands that molded the dress to her slender waist, the only ornamentation on the gown was a subtle pattern of satin cord and banding at the hem.

Logan spoke close to Julia's ear while his keen gaze swept the room. "Lord Hardington is ripe for the picking. He has a fondness for the theater, and a weakness for beautiful women. And most importantly, he has a private income of ten thousand a year. Why don't you go discuss the upcoming season with him, and our need of more sponsors?"

Julia smiled ruefully as she regarded the portly, red-cheeked older gentleman. She glanced back at Logan, who was striking in a black evening coat, an emerald silk waistcoat, and close-fitting cream trousers. His hair shone like polished mahogany beneath the light of the chandeliers. Although everyone else was here for social reasons, Logan regarded the event as an opportunity for business. He would use his good looks and charm to solicit funds for the Capital—and as always, he would be successful. Almost everyone wanted to associate with a man who was perceived as one of the greatest artists the London stage had ever known.

To Julia's surprise, she had quickly achieved

her own popularity in the theater, giving her a social standing that was considered significant for an actress. She commanded a high salary, which had enabled her to purchase a house on Somerset Street, only a few doors away from her former teacher Mrs. Florence. The elderly woman took a personal pride in Julia's success and welcomed her eagerly whenever Julia had the opportunity to visit for tea and a long chat.

Wishing she were with Mrs. Florence right now, rather than wasting her time mingling with people who considered themselves superior to her, Julia sighed softly. "I don't like these large gatherings," she said, more to herself than to Logan.

"It doesn't show. You move among these people as if you were born to it." Idly Logan brushed a bit of lint from his sleeve. "You would do well to recruit Lord Lansdale—the short one by the refreshment table . . . and Lord Russell, who's recently come into a handsome patrimony. A warm smile and a little encouragement might convince him to become a patron of the arts."

"I hope this is my last weekend party for a while. It makes me uncomfortable to flatter rich old men in hopes of attracting their money to the theater. Perhaps the next time you could bring Arlyss or one of the other actresses—"

"I don't want one of the others. You're as effective at these gatherings as you are on stage. In two years you've become the Capital's greatest asset—aside from me, of course."

Julia smiled impishly. "Why, Mr. Scott, if you continue to praise me, I may ask for a higher salary."

He snorted. "You won't get another shilling from me. You're already the highest paid actress I know of."

His glowering expression made her laugh. "If only people knew that the man who wooed me so passionately on stage—and won me a thousand times as Romeo, Benedick, and Mark Antony—only concerns himself *off*stage about shillings and business matters. You may be quite a romantic figure to the ladies of London, but you have the soul of a banker, not a lover."

"Thank God for it. Now go and charm the gentlemen I pointed out—oh, and don't forget that one." Logan nodded toward a dark-haired man standing in a small group only a few yards away. "He's managed his family's estates and investments for the last few years. At the rate he's going, he'll someday be one of the richest men in England. You would do well to persuade him to take an interest in the Capital."

"Who is he?"

"Lord Savage, the Marquess of Savage." Logan gave her a brief smile and left to mingle with some acquaintances.

Lord Savage, the Marquess of Savage. Julia was still and silent with confusion. Her brain was suddenly slow to work. She wondered if she had heard correctly. It seemed odd to hear the name and title fall from Logan Scott's lips, odd to know that after all her fearful and outraged imaginings, the object of her resentment was a living, breathing man. Her past had finally come crashing headlong into her present. If only she could find a way to disappear . . . but instead she could only stand there, trapped out in the open. She was afraid that if she did move, she wouldn't be able to keep from bolting like a hunted fox.

Somehow she hadn't expected her husband to be handsome, as splendidly dark and elegant as a foreign prince. He was a tall man with a quietly powerful presence. Beneath a black coat, an amber-and-gray-striped waistcoat, and charcoal trousers, the broad, sloping spread of his shoulders tapered to a slim waist and hips. His features were austere and perfect, his gaze devoid of emotion. He was a startling contrast to the men she usually associated with, men such as Logan and the other actors in the company, who earned their salaries with their expressive faces. This man seemed utterly inaccessible.

As if he sensed her presence, he glanced in her direction. A questioning frown touched his brow, and his head tilted slightly in concentration. Julia tried to look away, but he wouldn't let her, his gaze locked steadily on her face. Filled with sudden panic, she turned and began to walk away in controlled strides. However, it was too late. He cut across her path and reached her, forcing her to stop or risk bumping into him.

Julia's heart thumped painfully in her chest. She lifted her gaze and stared into the most extraordinary eyes she had ever seen, cool gray and ruthlessly intelligent, framed by black lashes so long that they had tangled at the outside corners.

"You look familiar to me." Although his voice

lacked the rich, winelike clarity of Logan Scott's voice, it held a pleasantly husky undertone.

"Do I?" Julia could barely force the words from her numb lips. "Perhaps you've seen me on stage."

He continued to stare at her, while all she could think was *You're my husband . . . my husband . . .*

Damon was puzzled by the young woman who stood before him. The music and colorful profusion of the ball seemed to recede in the background as he studied her face. He knew they had never been introduced—God knew he would never forget a woman like her—but there was something disturbingly familiar about her. She was slim and cool in her pale blue gown, holding herself with a regal poise that would not admit any hint of uncertainty. Her face seemed more like an artist's creation than something belonging to a real woman, hauntingly lovely with cheekbones angled deeply over the soft curves of cheek and jaw. Most remarkable of all were her blue-green eyes . . . they could have belonged to a fallen angel, virginal, soft, and yet sadly familiar with the ways of the wicked world.

Perhaps you've seen me on stage, she had said.

"Ah," he said softly. "You must be Mrs. Wentworth." She was far younger than he had expected of the popular actress, whose image had been spread all over England in paintings, prints, and engravings. The public was wild over her, as were the critics, lauding her attractiveness and skill. She had undeniable talent, but more than that, it was her warmth that had endeared her to audiences, making her instantly familiar and appealing.

But that creature was a world apart from the wraithlike young woman who stood before him now. It seemed that her neck was almost too slender to support the weight of the heavy blond braids that were twisted and pinned at her nape. He wasn't aware of reaching for her hand, nor of her offering it, but suddenly her gloved fingers were in his. As he raised them to his lips, he became aware that she was trembling.

Questions raced through his mind. Was she frightened of him? Why had she been standing here alone? Unconsciously he made his voice softer than usual, as if he might frighten the wary creature before him. "May I be of service, madam? I'm—"

"Yes, I know. You're the Marquess of Savage." All at once her face had changed, a social smile coming to her lips. She withdrew her hand. "My theater manager, Mr. Scott, desired me to make your acquaintance. He seems to believe I might be able to convert you into a patron of the Capital."

Surprised by her directness, Damon didn't return her smile as he replied. "You're welcome to try, Mrs. Wentworth. But I never waste money on frivolous pursuits."

"Frivolous? Don't you believe that people need to escape into the world of the theater every now and then? A play can make the audience experience something they've never imagined before. Sometimes they find that their feelings and opinions have changed afterward, and they regard their lives in a new way . . . that's hardly frivolous, is it?"

He shrugged casually. "I have no need of an escape."

"Don't you?" She stared at him even more intently, if that was possible. "I don't believe that, my lord."

"Why not?" No woman had ever dared to speak so boldly to him. First she had been trembling, and now she was challenging him. If she did want money from him on behalf of the Capital, this was a novel approach to getting it.

A flush crept over her neck and up to her cheeks, as if she were struggling to suppress some powerful emotion. "I've never met a person who is comfortable with his or her past. There is always something we would like to change, or forget."

Damon was very still, his head inclined toward hers. She seemed tense and restless, like a bird poised for flight. He had to fight the urge to reach out and take hold of her, and keep her with him. Something vibrated in the air between them . . . some elusive awareness that tantalized him. "And you?" he murmured. "What is it you would like to forget?"

A long silence passed. "A husband," she whispered, her lashes veiling her blue eyes.

Julia didn't know what had driven her to say such a thing. Horrified by her recklessness, she gave him a quick curtsy and slipped away into the crowd before he had a chance to react. "Wait—" she thought she heard him say, but she ignored him and fled the ballroom.

Damon stared after her, while recognition seared across his brain. He remembered the May evening in Warwickshire, the bewitching girl dancing in the torchlight. She had been an actress with a company of strolling players, and he had stolen a kiss from her. There was no doubt it was she, and that somehow his premonition of meeting her again had finally come true. "My God," he said under his breath.

Stunned by the stroke of good fortune, Damon stared at the place where she had stood before him. Before he could gather his wits, he became aware of Lady Ashton's approach. Her hand drifted possessively across his sleeve. "Darling." Her smooth purr caressed his ear. "Apparently you've made a new acquaintance. She hurried away before I could reach you. You must tell me what was said between you and Mrs. Wentworth! Oh, don't frown like that—you know I'm aware of everything you do. You have no secrets from me, darling."

"I may have one or two," he muttered.

Pauline's dark eyes were questioning, her red lips arranged in a pout. "Did she make a play for you?"

"She asked if I would become a sponsor for the Capital this season."

"And naturally you refused."

"Why do you assume that?"

"Because you never part with a shilling unless it's absolutely necessary."

"I'm generous with you," he pointed out.

"Yes, which is absolutely necessary in order to retain my affections."

Damon laughed. "And well worth it," he

replied, his gaze sweeping over her voluptuous figure. She was dressed in a sea-green gown molded tightly over her round breasts, pushing them high in an opulent display. Her full hips were outlined by a skirt ornamented with lavish silk flowers and jade beading.

"Tell me about Mrs. Wentworth," Pauline coaxed, reaching up to smooth his dark hair, aware that the proprietary gesture would be noticed by everyone around them. "What was she like?"

Damon searched in vain for an appropriate word to describe the woman he had encountered. Finding none, he shrugged helplessly.

Pauline's lips gathered in a petulant frown, and she tossed her head until the emerald plume fastened in her dark curls bobbed merrily. "Well, I've no doubt she's like every other actress, willing to lift her skirts for every man she meets."

Wryly Damon thought that Julia Wentworth's behavior was likely no different than Pauline's, except that Pauline believed her bloodlines made her superior. "She didn't appear to be promiscuous."

"It's said all over London that she's having an affair with Logan Scott. One only has to see them act together to know for certain." She gave a dramatic little shiver for emphasis. "The air fairly smolders! But Mr. Scott would have such an effect on any woman, I'm certain."

Damon knew little about the world of theater, but like everyone else he was aware of Logan Scott's accomplishments. Scott championed a more natural style of acting than had ever been attempted before. His powerful yet vulnerable Hamlet was legendary, but he was equally talented at comic roles in light fare such as *The Frustrated Husband*. Although Damon was far from qualified to be a critic, he had recognized Scott's extraordinary gift of drawing the audience into the thoughts and emotions of a character.

Even more impressive was the flood of money Scott had brought to the Capital Theatre, making it a worthy rival of Drury Lane. He was an adept manager of both people and profits. A man of such talents should be courted by the cream of society—and indeed, Scott appeared to have many well-born and prominent friends. But he would never be fully accepted by them. He was a self-made man, and the peerage believed he had aspired to a position he had never been meant for. Men and women in the acting profession existed to entertain both the masses and the aristocracy, belonging nowhere but in their own half-world of art and illusions.

The image of Jessica Wentworth's beautiful face came unbidden to Damon's mind. What would become of her when she was no longer able to earn her living on the stage? An actress had few choices, except to take her chances as a wealthy man's mistress, or if she was fortunate, marry some aging widower or humbly endowed member of the peerage . . . but of course, Mrs. Wentworth was already married.

What would you like to forget?

A husband.

What kind of man had she married? Who was he, and why—.

"Darling, what are you thinking about?" Pauline tugged imperiously on his arm. "I'm not accustomed to seeing a man's attention drift so far away when *I'm* close by."

Damon shook the thoughts of Jessica Wentworth from his mind and looked down at Pauline. "Then give me something else to think about," he murmured, and smiled as she leaned up to whisper provocatively in his ear.

By the time Julia reached the marble staircase that led to the upstairs rooms, her throat had tightened and her eyes were stinging with tears. She paused at the first landing, her fingers clenched on the banister.

"Jessica." She heard Logan Scott's unmistakable voice, and his feet on the stairs as he approached her. She waited without turning around, not wanting him to see her face. "What happened?" he asked with a touch of annoyance. "I happened to glance in your direction, and saw you running from the ballroom like a scalded cat."

"I'm tired," she managed to say thickly. "I can't go back in there tonight."

"Has someone said something to upset you?" Logan took hold of her arm and forced her to face him. His breath caught as he saw her tears. "Tell me what happened." There was a glint of fury in his gaze. "If some bastard dared to insult you, I'll knock his arse from here to—"

"No," she murmured, pulling away from his hard grip. "No one said anything to me. I'm perfectly all right."

Logan frowned as she brushed her fingers

furtively over her wet cheeks. "Here." A quick search in his green coat, and he produced a linen handkerchief.

Julia accepted the offering and blotted her eyes, trying to control her emotions. She wasn't certain how she felt . . . afraid, angry, sad . . . perhaps even relieved. She had finally met her husband, spoken with him, looked into his eyes. Savage seemed like a cold, self-controlled man, a man she wanted nothing to do with. And he felt the same—he didn't want her, had never written or tried to find her, and was perfectly content to ignore her existence. Although it was unreasonable, she felt betrayed by him.

"Perhaps I can help in some way," Logan commented.

A wry smile twisted her lips. "You've never offered to help me before. Why now?"

"Because I've never seen you cry."

"You've seen me cry hundreds of times."

"Never for real. I want to know what happened tonight."

"It has to do with my past," she said. "That's all I can tell you."

"Is it?" His blue eyes gleamed with a smile. "I've never had the time or patience for solving mysteries—but I am curious about you, Mrs. Wentworth."

Julia blew her nose and wadded the handkerchief in her fist. In the two years since they had met, Logan had never made such a personal comment to her. His interest in her was the same as in all of the players in the company, to elicit the best stage performances he could from them. Julia had become accustomed to his friendly bullying, his bursts of impatience, the way he sometimes changed his personality to get what he wanted. But to admit that he was curious about her past . . . it wasn't like him.

"My secrets aren't all that interesting," she said, picking up her skirts and ascending the stairs slowly.

"I wonder," Logan murmured, watching until she disappeared from sight.

To Julia's relief, she saw nothing of Lord Savage the next day. The guests at the weekend party occupied themselves with various outdoor pursuits. It was a fine day; the rich blue sky was streaked with lacy white clouds. The ladies strolled about the manicured gardens, tried their hands at archery, or went driving in fine carriages to view local points of interest. The men went shooting in the woods, fished in the nearby stream, or gathered in groups to drink and talk.

Although Julia felt melancholy and restless, she did her best to carry on animated conversations with the other guests. It was easy to entertain Lady Brandon and her friends with tales of the theater. The women were fascinated by the details of a world that was so foreign to them. Any mention of Logan Scott, especially, was guaranteed to provoke a great deal of feminine interest.

"Mr. Scott plays the lover so well onstage," one woman remarked in a sultry purr. "One can't help but wonder if he is equally amorous offstage. Can you enlighten us, Mrs. Wentworth?"

There were scandalized gasps at the outrageous question, and then the group of women all leaned forward imperceptibly to hear the reply. Julia smiled at the beautiful dark-haired woman, whom the hostess had earlier introduced as Lady Ashton. "I believe Mr. Scott is amorous toward a great many ladies . . . but he has a policy never to become involved with an actress, for reasons he has never explained."

"I saw the two of you in *Romeo and Juliet*," another woman exclaimed. "There seemed to be such *genuine* feeling between you! Wasn't some small part of it real?"

"Not really," Julia admitted frankly. "Except for a moment every now and then, when the acting seems so real to me that I can let myself believe in the characters we're playing."

"And for that moment, do you fall in love with your leading man?"

Julia laughed. "Only till the curtain falls."

After teatime, everyone retired to change into elaborate dinner outfits. The women eventually emerged in gowns of thin crinkled silk or ribboned gauze, the men in gleaming linen shirts, patterned waistcoats, and narrow trousers strapped under the insteps to keep them straight. Julia donned a gown of champagne-colored silk with a low-cut bodice sewn in tiny flat pleats. A narrow swath of delicate blond lace covered but didn't entirely conceal the shadowy vale between her breasts. The short, puffed sleeves were made of gauze and trimmed with more blond lace.

Dinner was a spectacular array of roasts and game, puddings in fancy molds, flavored jellies, and innumerable dishes of vegetables in sauce.

An army of servants moved in a dignified bustle to serve the two hundred guests seated at the two long tables in the center of the dining room. Near the end of the feast, meringue baskets filled with creams and pastries were brought out, as well as platters of berries and fruit.

In spite of the temptations set before her, Julia ate sparingly. She knew that as usual, Logan would be asked to entertain the guests after dinner, and she would be called upon to assist him. She was never able to perform well on a full stomach, which made her sluggish and sleepy. Tonight of all nights, she wanted her wits about her.

Julia caught glimpses of Lord Savage at the next table, as he conversed with the women to his right and left. Both ladies seemed to find his company enthralling. Frequently they reached up to rearrange their own dangling curls or toy with their jewelry, like fluttery birds preening themselves in hopes of gaining his admiration. Julia wondered if all women reacted to Savage in such a manner. Perhaps it was inevitable. Whatever his character, his wealth and good looks were indisputable. Moreover, his air of reserve would provoke any female to try to attract his attention. Julia was relieved that he didn't so much as glance in her direction. Apparently he had forgotten all about her, his interest diverted by other, more approachable women.

When the meal was concluded, the ladies retired for tea and gossip, leaving the men to enjoy a selection of cigars and glasses of rich port. Later they all rejoined in the large salon, where a multitude of chairs and settees had been arranged in groups.

Walking into the salon on Logan's arm, Julia was not surprised when Lady Brandon approached them with a look of anticipation on her round face. It wasn't every hostess who had the opportunity of providing her guests with the likes of Logan Scott as the after-dinner entertainment. "Mr. Scott," Lady Brandon murmured, her ample cheeks flushed, "perhaps you would honor us with a recitation, or some characterization from a play?"

With an elegant flourish, Logan took the lady's plump hand and bowed over it. He had a way with women, no matter what their age, appearance, or circumstance, that made them swoon with delight. Boldly he stared into Lady Brandon's eyes until she must have felt as if she were drowning in the rich blue depths of his gaze. "It would be my great pleasure, madam—and hardly enough to recompense you for such magnificent hospitality. Is there anything in particular you would prefer?"

"Oh," Lady Brandon breathed, her hand trembling visibly. Her rosebud lips parted in a helpless smile. "Oh, *anything* you choose would suffice, Mr. Scott. But . . . something romantic would be very nice!"

"Something romantic," Logan repeated, smiling at her as if she were the most clever woman alive. "We'll do our best, madam." He glanced at Julia and quirked his ruddy brows inquiringly. "Shall we undertake a scene from my new play, Mrs. Wentworth?"

Julia murmured her assent with a demure smile, knowing that he had been planning on it. Once or twice a season, Logan launched a play he had written, always a social satire loaded with wit and charm. If not a genius, Logan was a clever writer with a sure instinct for what the audience desired. His newest creation, *My Lady Deception*, was the story of a nobleman and a well-bred woman who, through a set of implausible but amusing circumstances, found themselves posing as their own servants; he as a footman, she as a housemaid. Naturally they met and fell in love, and their subsequent efforts to maintain their deceptions and stay true to each other produced many comical results. The play gently teased the aristocracy for its narrow views and suffocating social rules.

It was hardly original material, but Logan had a way of shaping it into something fresh and entertaining. Julia liked the story of two people discovering each other without the constraints of their usual lives. Logan hadn't yet decided to give her the leading role in the stage production. It was clear that he would choose between Julia and Arlyss Barry, another young actress in the company. Julia wanted the part for herself, but she knew it depended on whether Logan liked Julia's romantic approach, or Arlyss's more broadly comic one. Perhaps if all went well this evening, it would sway his decision in her favor.

When the group had settled around the room, leaving a cleared space in the front, Logan stepped forward and introduced himself and Julia. Briefly he described the scene they were about to perform for the guests' entertainment, and mentioned that if they cared to see the entire play, it would be shown at the Capital Theatre later in the season.

As Logan spoke, Julia sorted through lines of dialogue in her mind. But there was a strange shiver of nerves all across her back, and her concentration was ruined as she sensed the dark presence of Lord Savage nearby. Like a magnet, her gaze was drawn to the corner, where he was seated in the company of Lady Ashton.

Savage seemed relaxed and comfortable, his long legs stretched before him as he appeared to listen to Lady Ashton's light chatter. But his gaze was fastened alertly on Julia. Her heart pounded as she realized that he was as unwillingly fascinated by her as she was by him. Perhaps he was somehow able to sense the link that had been forged between them since childhood, changing the course of both their lives.

Julia had never imagined that someday she would be acting while *he* watched. She had performed such drawing room scenes before, either with Logan or the other actors. There was a far more intimate quality in playing to such a small audience. Because of the close range, there was less need for voice projection, and she could use a more finely tuned array of gestures and facial expressions. Usually she enjoyed situations such as this . . . but not now. It seemed that every trace of her ability, and every word she had memorized, had completely vanished.

Logan motioned for Julia to join him at the front of the room. She tried to obey, but for the first time in her life, she froze. Her feet had no sensation, save for an icy prickling around her ankles, and her chest was filled with panicked drumming. She couldn't do it—she couldn't go on with the scene. She knew Logan could see the color drain from her face. He showed no reaction except for a pleasantly encouraging smile. Walking over to her, he took her hand in a painful grip that had the effect of restoring her senses somewhat.

"Do you want some wine?" he murmured, leading her to the front of the room.

It took all her strength to manage a whisper. "I-I don't know."

Logan murmured to her *sotto voce,* making it appear to the others in the room as if he were offering her advice. His words, however, were anything but soothing. "Listen to me. I don't give a damn about how you feel or what's going through your blasted mind at the moment. All I care about is the play and my theater. If you value your career, you're going to do the damned scene as we rehearsed it. You're an *actress.* Do what I've hired you to do."

Julia nodded stiffly, feeling the warmth come back to her cheeks. She must get through the scene, no matter that her long-lost husband was watching her. Logan's quiet bullying reminded her of all the work she had done to become Jessica Wentworth. She couldn't ruin it all now.

"Tell me my first line," she whispered unsteadily.

"For God's sake . . ." Logan muttered, giving her a dark look. "I'll start the thing. Just try to follow along."

Julia went to a spot a few yards away from Logan and concentrated on him fiercely, waiting for his first words. The scene depicted the moment at which the two lovers discovered the other's true identity. As she stared at Logan, she saw his face change, and he began to speak to her as if he were a man in love. She felt herself slide into the role without effort, almost without thought. She was more focused than she had ever been in her life. Dimly she sensed the thrill of excitement in the room, but she was too engrossed to dwell on it.

As the characters uncovered their mutual deception, they went through a lightning-fast chain of reactions; disbelief, outrage, defensiveness, relief, and helpless passion. Logan's antics sent the small audience into fits of laughter, but only with the balance of Julia's sweetly romantic yearning did the scene reach a startling depth of tenderness.

Damon watched without blinking, almost without breathing. It seemed as if each word were spontaneous, as if the actors were living the scene rather than performing a piece that must have been rehearsed many times before. They made the art of acting look effortless. It was clear that Jessica Wentworth was an actress of extraordinary talent.

"My God, they're both wonderful," murmured Pauline, who was never moved to praise anyone unless she could somehow include herself.

Damon didn't reply. Despite his admiration, an unpleasant feeling crept over him as he watched the two actors. Was it genuine, the undercurrent of emotion that seemed to flow between them? How could such smoldering intensity be merely an illusion? He wondered if Logan Scott had ever held Jessica in his arms and kissed her for real, if he had ever crushed her exquisite body beneath his. Surely any normal man would find her an unholy temptation. Damon imagined what Jessica Wentworth was like in her passion, shivering and abandoned as she gave herself to her lover.

A trickle of sweat ran beneath Damon's starched cravat. He took a deep breath, suddenly feeling as if his lungs would explode. It was insane, but he wanted to rush to the front of the room and tear her away from Logan Scott. It shocked him, his piercing awareness of her, the maddening craving to touch and smell and taste her. He had always been in control of himself and his circumstances, had *insisted* on it for as long as he could remember. No one had been allowed to have any power over him . . . not since he had realized long ago that his future had been sacrificed for his family's well-being. He had never wanted anyone with such unthinking desire, a feeling that engaged him body and soul and left no choice but pursuit.

The scene ended as Logan Scott bent over Jessica and gave her an impassioned kiss. Damon's hands curled into fists, while jealousy filled him in a poisoned rush. Applause resounded through the room as the guests exclaimed in delight. Smiling broadly, Logan Scott declined pleas for another scene, a monologue, something else to entertain them. Soon he and Jessica Wentworth were surrounded by admirers.

"A handsome pair," Pauline observed, plying

a fan of silk and lace to cool her face and throat. "This afternoon Mrs. Wentworth claimed that their relationship is strictly professional . . . but only a fool would believe that."

Before Damon could reply, his younger brother William approached them, and obediently bowed over Pauline's gracefully proffered hand. "You look ravishing this evening, Lady Ashton—as usual."

Pauline smiled flirtatiously. "How charming you are, Lord William."

William turned to Damon, his blue eyes alight with enthusiasm. "Quite a good scene, wasn't it? I never thought there could be such a thing as a female Logan Scott—but Mrs. Wentworth is as superb as he is. I want to meet her, Damon."

"She's a married woman," Damon replied flatly.

"I don't care."

Pauline laughed at William's youthful passion. "For a lad of your looks and blood, it shouldn't be difficult, dear boy. She's an actress, after all. Just be forewarned—she'll probably demand a fortune in jewels in return for her favors."

"It would have to be a fortune to exceed *your* price, darling," Damon said softly. Pauline gave him a haughty frown, while William smothered an impudent laugh. "Excuse me," Damon continued, rising to his feet, "I want to have a word with Mr. Scott."

"What for?" Pauline asked sharply, but he ignored her, making his way to Logan Scott, whose ruddy head was just visible over the crowd around him. Damon was filled with the most biting impatience he had ever known. He wanted to make everyone in the room disappear except for Jessica Wentworth.

As busy as he was, Scott didn't fail to notice him standing nearby. His blue eyes met Damon's, and though they had never been introduced, there was a gleam of recognition in them. Skillfully he managed to disengage himself from two or three simultaneous conversations, and approached Damon. Although he wasn't quite as tall as Damon, he was broad-shouldered and solid. Scott appeared to be a prosperous, supremely cultured man, his well-heeled image belying the rumors that he had been born as the son of a common fishmonger on the east side of London.

"Lord Savage," Scott said, transferring a glass of wine from his right hand to his left in order to exchange a firm handshake, "I regret that we've never had the opportunity to meet before now."

"Mr. Scott." Damon returned the handshake. "I've long admired your talents."

"Thank you, my lord." Scott's mobile features arranged themselves in an expression of mild inquiry. "I hope you enjoyed the scene tonight. It is a small sample of the many worthy productions that will be shown at the Capital this season."

"Yes, I did. In fact, I enjoyed it so much that I feel moved to make a contribution to the theater."

"Ah." A flash of satisfaction appeared in Scott's blue eyes, and he took a long sip of wine. "That would be very much appreciated, my lord."

"I hope that five thousand pounds will be of help."

At the mention of the sum, Scott nearly choked on his wine. Quickly regaining his composure, he regarded Damon with frank surprise. "As I'm certain you're aware, Lord Savage, that is an unusually generous donation. You have my deepest gratitude, as well as that of all the Capital players." He paused, his gaze speculative. "However . . . I can't help but suspect you would want something in return for such a large sum."

"I have one small request."

"I thought so." Scott raised his brows inquiringly.

"I would like Mrs. Wentworth to have supper at my estate one evening."

Scott seemed unperturbed by the statement. Undoubtedly many men had shown such interest in Jessica Wentworth before. "And if she refuses?"

"The money is still yours."

"That's a relief to hear, Lord Savage. Because Mrs. Wentworth is not a woman who can be bought, nor is she easily wooed. I can tell you about the scores of gentlemen who have failed with her. She doesn't seem to care about wealth or social position, and to my knowledge she has no desire for a man's protection. To be blunt, I would lay very steep odds against her accepting any kind of invitation from you."

"Perhaps you have some influence with her," Damon suggested softly. "I trust you will use it on my behalf."

Their gazes met, blue eyes staring into steely gray. It was impossible for Damon to tell whether Scott was motivated by some fatherly feeling for Jessica Wentworth, or if his feelings crossed the threshold of actual jealousy. Scott spoke tonelessly. "I will not be responsible for urging Mrs. Wentworth into a situation that could be compromising or difficult for her—"

"All I want is to spend a few hours with her," Damon said smoothly. "I give you my word that she will not be offended in any way. I would like you to persuade her to accept my invitation. If she doesn't, my donation to the Capital will still be given as promised."

Scott hesitated for a long moment, then took another sip of wine. Being a worldly man, he understood that some concession was expected—necessary, in fact, regardless of Damon's assurances to the contrary. One supper was hardly too much to ask in return for five thousand pounds. "Very well. I'll discuss the matter with her."

"Thank you." Damon kept his face blank, but he felt as if he could draw a full breath for the first time since Jessica Wentworth had cast her spell over him. It would be done—Scott would convince her to meet with him, and he would have a few hours alone with her.

He must have gone insane. He wasn't behaving like himself at all. He was never moved by impulse—he calculated and planned his every action. But he would allow himself this temporary lapse, if only because he didn't seem to have a choice.

As he and Logan Scott parted company,

Damon caught a glimpse of Jessica, who stood several yards away with her own group of admirers. Her accusing gaze was fixed on him as if she already knew what he had done.

"What did you say to him?" Pauline asked as soon as he returned to her and William. Clearly she was annoyed at having been abandoned even for a few minutes.

Damon shrugged and gave her a bland look. "I've decided to become a sponsor for the Capital."

"*You?*" She gave him a skeptical glance.

"You never go to the theater unless you're knocked over the head and dragged there," William commented. "Why the sudden interest in the Capital?"

"Yes, why?" Pauline asked, her mouth tight with suspicion.

"I want to broaden my interests," Damon replied, the look in his eyes warning them both not to question him any further.

"What did he say to you?" Julia demanded as soon as she could separate herself from the guests and take Logan Scott aside for a private word.

Logan's eyes were pools of innocent blue. "Who?"

"Lord Savage," she said between her teeth. "What did the two of you talk about? I saw the expression on your face—the look you always wear when someone offers you money."

"Well, there you have it." He smiled and opened his hands in an appealing gesture. "He's going to make a handsome donation to the

Capital. Quite a generous fellow. Pleasant, gentlemanly—"

"Stop praising him and tell me what he wanted!"

"We'll discuss it later."

Driven by fast-rising frustration, Julia caught his sleeve, her fingers digging into the fine, dark amber cloth of his coat. "Did he mention me?"

"Why do you ask that?" Logan's gaze delved into hers. "He did, as a matter of fact. What is going on between you?"

"Nothing," she said immediately. "And nothing will. I have no interest in him at all."

"That's unfortunate. Because I made him a promise of sorts."

"You have no right to make any kind of promise involving me!" she said hotly.

"Quiet," Logan murmured, mindful of the other guests nearby. "No one is going to force you to do anything. We'll talk later, when you've managed to control your emotions."

Julia willed herself to stay calm, and released her clutch on his sleeve. "Tell me now, or I'll go mad."

"Savage wants to have supper with you one evening."

"No!"

"Before you refuse, let me remind you of a few facts. I pay you a higher salary than anyone in the company except myself. I spare no expense having costumes made for you of the best silks and velvets, and real jewels for you to wear. I surround you with some of the finest casts ever put on stage, and choose plays tailored to display your talents to the best advantage. I don't think that having one platonic dinner with Lord Savage would be too much of a trial for you, in return for the five thousand pounds he's donating to the theater."

"Platonic dinner?" she sneered. "If you're going to become a pimp, Mr. Scott, you may as well be honest about it. I'm hardly naive."

"No, merely ungrateful," he said smoothly. "I've worked hard for you the past two years—that is all my contract requires."

"Any other actress in the company would accept Savage's invitation with pleasure."

"Then send one of them in my place. Send them all!"

"Damn you," Logan said softly. "Refuse Savage, if you must. But there will be a price to pay. You proved tonight that you deserve the leading part in *My Lady Deception*—but you won't get it, or any other parts you want this season, unless you accept Savage's invitation. And before you cry 'unfair,' remember that without the training I've given you, and my close attention to your career, you would probably be touring the provinces with a group of strolling players."

Julia shot him a look of impotent fury and walked away from him, brushing by the gentlemen who were attempting to gain introductions to her.

Standing before the closed door of one of the second-floor bedroom suites, Julia lifted her hand to knock, then hesitated and let it fall to her side. The hour was late, everyone having retired to his room for the evening. Behind this door, and many of the others, there were sounds of drawers and armoire closets opening and closing, as well as the murmurs of servants as they helped guests change into their sleeping attire.

After bribing a servant to tell her which room the Marquess of Savage was staying in, Julia had come here with a mixture of fear and resolution. She had never visited a man's room before, but this seemed to be the only way she could talk to Savage in private. She had to confront him, and make it clear that whatever his intentions were, he would get nothing from her. Perhaps then he would withdraw his dinner invitation.

She was terribly nervous, almost as panicked as she had been earlier in the evening. Taking a deep breath to restore herself, she forced herself to knock. Her shaking knuckles barely grazed the panels. As slight as the sound was, it had been noticed. Julia blanched as she heard a muffled inquiry from within. Seconds later the handle turned, and she found herself staring up into Lord Savage's shadowy gray eyes.

Julia tried to speak, but her throat had closed, and all she could do was stand there silently. Her heart beat frantically, until her ears were filled with the sound of rapid drumming. She had seen the actors at the Capital in various stages of undress, when quick costume changes made privacy impossible—but it was far different to be confronted with Lord Savage wearing only a burgundy silk dressing robe. In the confines of the suite, he seemed much larger than he had in the spacious ballroom downstairs, his broad shoulders looming over her, his bare golden throat level with her eyes.

Savage inclined his head an inch or two, his gaze not moving from her face. She sensed that she had surprised him by appearing here, and at this hour. Good—she wanted to appear bold and confident.

"May I come in?" she asked, her voice miraculously steady.

Instead of replying, he opened the door and gestured for her to enter. Julia complied, then paused as she saw a valet gathering linens in the corner.

"That will be all," Savage murmured to the servant, who nodded and left at once, quietly closing the door behind him.

They were alone, in a room filled with yellow brocade, mahogany furniture, and paintings of harmonious pastoral scenes . . . alone and facing each other, after all these years. There was no way Savage could know who she was, but still she felt exposed and in danger, with only her secrets to protect her.

Chapter 3

S avage continued to stare at her until Julia began to wonder if there was something amiss with her appearance. Self-consciously she smoothed her hair, then jerked her hand away. It didn't matter if every lock on her head were sticking straight out—she hardly cared about his opinion of her.

Glancing down at his own lack of attire, Savage tightened the belt of his silk robe. "I hadn't planned on receiving visitors," he said.

She folded her arms before her, a gesture that was both militant and self-protective. "I won't stay long."

He stared at her once more. It seemed that he was as uncomfortable as she was with the silence between them . . . but he appeared to be equally powerless to break it. Julia tried in vain to read his thoughts, but he revealed nothing. What kind of man was he? Usually it was easy for her to discern someone's character, to sense if a person was intrinsically kind, selfish, shy, or honorable. Savage betrayed nothing of himself.

His face was austerely beautiful, with its long

nose, the distinctive angles of his cheeks, and the aggressive jut of his jaw. There were appealing, surprising touches of softness in the wide curve of his mouth and the long-lashed gray eyes. It must be unbearable temptation for many women to make Savage smile, look at them with desire, to arouse any sort of emotion in those enigmatic features. It even provoked *her* imagination, the thought of what it must be like to earn his hard-won trust, to hold his dark head in her lap and fondle the thick locks of black hair—

"Why are you here, Mrs. Wentworth?" he asked.

Julia felt a scowl pinching between her eyebrows, and she answered in a crisp tone. "I think you already know, my lord."

"Scott has spoken with you."

"Yes, he did. And now I've come to correct an impression of yours. You seem to think that your money can buy anything you want."

"Most of the time it can."

"Well, you can't buy *me*." She had been sold once in her life, for the price of a title she had neither asked for nor wanted. It would never happen again.

"There seems to have been a misunderstanding," he said quietly. "If you object to the idea of having dinner with me, you're free to refuse."

"You've made that impossible. If I don't accept, I'll lose all the choice parts at the Capital this season—parts I would have otherwise had!"

He seemed perturbed, a frown drawing his

dark brows together. "Would you like me to speak with Mr. Scott?"

"No! You'll only make the situation worse."

Savage shrugged, and infuriated her with a matter-of-fact reply. "I suppose you'll just have to make the best of it, then."

"What about the woman you were seated with in the corner tonight?" she asked. "Lady Ashton, I believe. She seems quite attached to you."

"Lady Ashton has no claim on me. She and I have an understanding."

"How sophisticated of you," she said acidly. "Let me pose a question to you, Lord Savage. If you were a married man, would you still desire to have dinner alone with me?"

"Since I'm a bachelor," he said evenly, "the question is irrelevant."

A *bachelor!* The realization that he had decided to ignore their long-ago marriage, pretend she had vanished from the face of the earth, filled Julia with outrage. To be truthful, she had done the same thing—but their situations were hardly comparable. After all, she had spent the past years struggling to make a new life for herself, whereas he had enjoyed himself playing lord of the manor with *her* dowry at his disposal!

"Does it bother you in the slightest that I have a husband?" she asked. "That I belong to someone else?"

He hesitated for a long moment. "No."

Julia shook her head slowly, staring at him with disdain. "I know what you think of me, my lord . . . the same thing most men in your position think of actresses. But let me assure you, I'm not a prostitute—and I certainly can't be had for the cost of dinner and a few promises—"

"That's not what I think." Savage unnerved her by taking a step forward until she could almost feel the warmth of his breath on her skin. She was aware of the latent strength in his body, the intimidating force of him, but when he spoke, his voice was gentle. "I'm not going to take advantage of you, Mrs. Wentworth. All I want is an evening with you. If you don't enjoy my company, you can leave at any time . . . but you won't want to."

She laughed unsteadily at his arrogance. "You're damned certain of yourself, aren't you?"

"I'll be waiting at the Capital on Friday, after your performance."

Julia's mouth tightened as she considered him silently. Savage was a perceptive man. If he had attempted to force her outright, she would have fought him to her last breath. But he had sensed that, and had left her the ability to refuse, if she chose.

Savage waited for her reply with the expectancy of a cat stalking some small creature it fancied. For some reason his patience touched her. With a flash of intuition, Julia thought that perhaps he secretly feared and desired the same things she did. He had been shaped by the same manipulations that she had . . . and in his own way, perhaps he had rebelled against them also.

How could she help but be curious about him? How could anyone resist the opportunity to find out more about the stranger she was married to? And he had no idea who she really was. Why not spend a few hours with him? What harm could it do? Most evenings after a performance she went straight to her small house on Somerset Street, and either read a book or stared pensively into the fireplace. This would be an interesting diversion, to say the least. And she need never tell him that she was Julia Hargate.

The irony of the situation almost made her smile. What a rich joke it would be, although no one but she would understand. If only her father knew that after all the years of rebellion, she was going to have dinner with her husband. He would have apoplexy!

"All right," she heard herself say in a businesslike tone. "I will see you on Friday."

"Thank you, Mrs. Wentworth," Savage said, a flicker of satisfaction in his gray eyes. "I guarantee you won't regret it."

"He sounds quite dashing," Arlyss said, drawing her short legs beneath her as she sat in a worn chair in the greenroom.

"No," Julia replied thoughtfully. "'Dashing' implies a devil-may-care quality, which Savage hasn't got. There is something very controlled and intense about his manner."

"Fascinating."

The two women sipped cups of tea and talked languidly as they waited to be called for rehearsal. Logan Scott, Charles Haversley, a handsome blond actor in his twenties, and two other players were currently occupied on stage with a complicated bit of blocking. The rehearsal was for *The Taming of the Shrew*, a production that Julia was particularly enjoying because it was her first opportunity to play the part of Katherine. Arlyss had been cast as the younger sister, Bianca.

Although Julia and Arlyss were often in competition for the same roles, they had become friends during the past two years. Each had come to recognize that the other had talents different from her own. Some roles were better suited for Arlyss's comic abilities, while others required Julia's more versatile range. In between rehearsals and performances, they talked about their personal lives, their fears and ambitions, although Julia was careful never to reveal too much about her past.

"Why don't things like that ever happen to me?" Arlyss complained, stirring more sugar in her tea. The possessor of an incurable sweet tooth, she battled constantly to keep her short, shapely figure from becoming too plump. "I would *adore* being pursued by an attractive marquess who happens to be as rich as Croesus. Instead, I get the fat old men who only want a quick roll in bed, and then point to me while I'm on stage and boast to their friends."

Julia gave her a sympathetic glance. "You allow men to take advantage of you, Arlyss— and there's no need for that. You're beautiful, talented . . . you're one of the most popular actresses on the London stage! There's no need to give away your favors so easily."

"I know," Arlyss said with a glum sigh, toying with her mop of brown curls. She pulled a few hairpins from her untidy coiffure and stuck them back in haphazardly. "I just can't seem to help myself where men are concerned. I'm not like you, Julia. It's hardly natural for a woman to be so iron-willed. Aren't you ever lonely? Don't you crave a man in your bed sometimes, if only to remind you that you're a woman?"

"Sometimes," Julia admitted. She stared into her own cup of tea, her gaze fixed on the amber depths. "But I usually manage to save those feelings and use them on the stage."

"Maybe I should try that," Arlyss said. "After all, the men I entertain are merely substitutes for the one I really want."

Julia gave her a half-pitying, half-amused glance, knowing exactly whom Arlyss was referring to. "You know Mr. Scott's rule about actresses. Besides, I don't see the reason for your infatuation with him."

"It's more than infatuation! It's undying love. I can't believe any woman *wouldn't* feel that way about him!"

"Mr. Scott is far from the perfect man," Julia said sourly. "Good heavens, I just told you about the way he's forced me to have supper with Lord Savage! Mr. Scott may seem like a man of grand principles, but at heart he's nothing but a money-grubber."

Arlyss airily waved the comment away. "All men have flaws. Besides, he was right—five thousand pounds is nothing to turn up your nose at." She chewed thoughtfully on a slice of dry cake, and followed it with more tea. "I've heard that there is a woman living at Mr. Scott's house this very moment—his latest paramour. She'll last no longer than six months . . . they never do. There must be some reason Mr. Scott is so opposed to the idea of marriage! Something must have happened in his past . . . something dark and painful . . ."

Julia snorted at her friend's dreamy expression. "Really, Arlyss, you have too many romantic illusions. I would think that a life in the theater should have cured you of that."

"No, it only makes it worse! When you spin romantic illusions for other people all the time, you can't help but be caught up in them."

"I don't."

"You're made of iron," Arlyss said. "I don't know whether to envy or pity you." She leaned forward, her green eyes sparkling with interest. "Tell me . . . what are you going to wear when you dine with his lordship?"

"Something plain and unbecoming."

"No, no, no . . . wear something to make his eyes drop out! Something to make his mouth turn dry and his head spin and his heart pound—"

"As if he had some horrible disease," Julia said with a laugh.

"You must wear your black and pink gown," Arlyss urged. "I won't *allow* you to choose anything else."

"I'll consider it." Julia looked up as a member of the house staff appeared at the greenroom door to inform them that Mr. Scott desired their presence onstage.

After days of exacting rehearsal, the Friday performance of *Taming of the Shrew* went superbly. As Logan had directed, Julia threw all her energy into the boisterous production. In previous adaptations the story had been watered down to something resembling a drawing room comedy, with much of the ribald humor removed. Logan Scott had restored all of that, and added a robust physicality that both startled and pleased the audience. It was a lusty, vigorous play that made some critics howl with displeasure and others with delight.

With Logan playing the dashing Petruchio to Julia's devilish Katherine, the audience roared with laughter at their volcanic battles, and sat spellbound during some of the quieter, tender moments. Unfortunately, at the end of the production, Julia was battered and sore. The play called for many physical antics, including one bit in which Katherine tried to attack Petruchio, and he swung her off her feet like a rag doll. In spite of Logan's efforts to be careful with her, Julia was not surprised to find a few faint bruises on her arms and torso.

Ignoring all entreaties for her attention, Julia locked her dressing room door, washed the sweat and paint from her face, and used two pitchers of water in a thorough sponge bath. After dabbing perfume on her throat and inner elbows and between her breasts, she turned her attention to the gown she had brought with her. As Arlyss had insisted, she had decided on her favorite evening gown. It was fashioned of jet-black Italian silk, the surface glossy and finely corded. One deep pink silk rose adorned each short, gathered sleeve. The gown's only other adornments were the vertical slashes of pink at the hem, opening and closing rhythmically in billowy swaths as she walked.

After dressing carefully, Julia left the back

fastenings undone and regarded herself in the mirror. A faint smile came to her face. No matter how she felt inside, it was reassuring to know that she looked her best. The black silk provided a dramatic contrast to her pale skin and ash-blond hair, while the touches of rose-pink echoed the color in her cheeks.

"Mrs. Wentworth," came her maid's voice through the door. "May I come in an' see to your things?"

Julia unlocked the door to let the plump, dark-haired girl inside. Betsy was an efficient servant, taking care of her costumes, keeping the dressing room orderly, and assisting her with a multitude of small tasks. "Will you fasten my gown, please?"

"Yes, Mrs. Wentworth. I've brought some more flowers."

"You may keep them if you like," Julia said nonchalantly. The dressing room was already filled with floral arrangements and their cloying perfume.

"Oh, but these are so beautiful! Just have a look," Betsy coaxed, bringing forth the massive arrangement.

Julia exclaimed in pleasure as she saw the profusion of lush roses ranging from palest pink to crimson-red, interspersed with exotic orchids and tall spikes of vivid purple and white del-phinium. "Who sent them?" she asked.

Betsy read the card. " 'Savage,' it says."

So it was from Lord Savage. Julia reached out and pulled one of the pink roses from the arrangement. She toyed with the petals, and brought the flower with her to the dressing table.

As Betsy fastened the back of her gown, Julia expertly twisted and pinned her hair into a loose, thick coil at the top of her head, leaving a few curls to dangle on her temple and neck. After a moment's hesitation, Julia broke off the blossom, wrapped the end in a bit of paper, and anchored it in the coil with a large pin.

"That looks lovely," Betsy said, breaking off another blossom and pinning it to Julia's small black silk reticule. "He must be a special man for you to take such pains, Mrs. Wentworth."

Julia pulled on a pair of sleek black gloves that covered her elbows. "One could say I've been waiting for him all my life."

"How grand . . ." Betsy began. She stopped, her round face wrinkling in a frown as she saw the shadowy fingermarks on Julia's upper arms, and another on the tip of her bare shoulder. "Dear me, those won't do at all."

Julia regarded the bruises ruefully. "I'm afraid they can't be helped. After the bouts Mr. Scott and I had on stage, I'm only surprised there aren't more."

Reaching for a cake of flesh-colored facepaint, Betsy moistened her fingertips with water, rubbed them across the surface, and then dabbed the color sparingly over the bruises. Julia held still, surveying the maid's handiwork with a pleased smile. "They're hardly noticeable now. Thank you, Betsy."

"Will there be anything else before I put your costumes away?"

"Yes . . . would you find out if there is a carriage waiting for me outside?"

Betsy returned soon with the news that there was indeed a vehicle behind the theater, a fine black carriage trimmed with silver, a pair of outriders beside it, and two footmen dressed in dark red livery.

Julia felt her heart quicken with painful force. She put her hand on her chest, as if she could calm the violent thumping, and breathed deeply.

"Mrs. Wentworth? All of a sudden you look rather ill."

Julia didn't reply. What could have possessed her, agreeing to spend a few hours alone with Lord Savage? What could they possibly say to each other—what mad impulse had driven her to this? Summoning her courage, she relaxed her shoulders, which seemed to have climbed up to her ears. Betsy helped to settle a hooded black silk pelisse over her head and shoulders, and fasten the garnet clasp at the throat. Murmuring good night to the maid, Julia left her dressing room and made her way through the labyrinth of theater facilities.

As she passed the back entrance, a small crowd of theatergoers pressed forward to meet her, a few daring to touch her cloak or her gloved arms. A towering footman helped to usher her through the crowd to the waiting carriage. Deftly he pulled out an extra step for her easy ascent into the luxurious vehicle, and closed the door behind her. It was all accomplished so swiftly that Julia barely had time to blink before she was settled in a soft velvet-and-leather-covered seat.

She stared at Lord Savage, who sat opposite her, one side of his handsome face lit to knife-blade sharpness by a carriage lantern, the rest left in shadow. He smiled with the dangerous charm of Lucifer himself. Hastily Julia lowered her gaze to her lap. Her hands lay perfectly folded and still, when she wanted to knot her fingers together in agitation.

Lord Savage belonged to a world from which she had been running for years. It was her right—some might even say her duty—to assume the title and position her parents had procured for her. She had resisted it with all her might, out of willfulness and resentment, and most of all fear at the discovery of what kind of man she had been given to. She didn't want to stop fearing Savage, didn't want to weaken her defenses in any way. But her own curiosity had led her to this . . . as well as the troubling pull of attraction between them.

"You were extraordinary tonight," Savage said.

Julia blinked in surprise. "You watched the play, then? I didn't see you in the audience."

"It was a demanding performance for you."

"Yes, it's quite exhausting." Briefly she wondered what he had thought of the ribald interplay between herself and Logan Scott—if he had been amused along with the rest of the audience, or if he had disapproved. Something must have shown in her face, because he leaned forward and pinned her with his disconcerting silvery gaze.

"What is it?" he asked.

Deciding she had nothing to lose, Julia told him what she had been thinking.

Savage replied slowly, considering his words with care. "It's not my right to disapprove of what you do on stage. Acting is your chosen profession."

"And you had no personal feelings?" she asked idly. "During the part when Mr. Scott kissed me, or chased me across the stage and—"

"I didn't like it." The words seemed to escape him before he could prevent it. His mouth twisted with self-derision. "You and Scott were rather too convincing in your roles."

Julia had the feeling that he was as surprised by the admission of jealousy as she was. Alarmed and flattered, she retreated until her shoulders dug into the plush upholstery. "It's only a play," she said.

"I've seen actors in plays before. The two of you seem . . . different."

Julia frowned at her reticule with concentration. She had heard the popular opinion that she and Logan Scott were lovers, and she also knew why. They had stage chemistry, she and Logan, the kind that made it possible to act together so convincingly that illusion and reality were temporarily joined together with seamless perfection.

However, that rare harmony in their acting would never, could never, extend beyond the stage. Not once had the thought seriously crossed Julia's mind. She turned to Logan as everyone else did, for direction, guidance, praise, and criticism . . . but not for anything that wasn't directly related to her career. There was nothing comfortable about Logan, nothing that invited trust or even the barest hint of safety and warmth. It was clear that Logan would never love a woman as he loved his theater, or sacrifice for a living person what he would for his twin gods of art and ambition.

Perhaps that was why he and Julia had chemistry on the stage, because each of them sensed the other's inability to surrender to another person. There was safety in that, knowing there was no risk of love, pain, or disillusionment between them . . . that whereas their emotions on stage seemed to run deep, nothing would remain after the curtain fell.

Since attaining adulthood, Julia had tried to find contentment in the independence she prized so highly. If only she could stop herself from wanting more. She longed for someone to understand and cherish her, a man to whom she could give all of herself with no fear or doubt. It was her most private dream, one she hated to acknowledge even to herself.

At times she felt as if she were divided into two selves, one part of her wanting isolation from the rest of the world, and the other aching to be possessed and loved as she had never been in her life. Her father, with his dominating nature, had precious little love to offer anyone. Her mother had always been too timid, too lost in the shadow of her husband to give Julia the attention a child required. And the constant inflow and outflow of servants from the Hargate household had prevented Julia from forming a close attachment to any of them. Love was something to be feared more than desired.

Realizing that she had been silent for an unaccountably long time, Julia glanced warily at Lord Savage, worrying that her thoughts might have betrayed themselves.

"We're almost there," was all he said, in a murmur that somehow relaxed her.

The carriage traveled along Upper Brook Street and turned to ascend the long drive leading to a massive white and cream-colored house. The building was cool, beautiful and perfectly symmetrical, with towering Grecian columns and a wide portico adorning the front. Two graceful white wings fitted with rows of gleaming Palladian windows stretched out from the central structure. It was entirely different from the dark, gothic estate Julia had grown up in.

Savage preceded her from the carriage and reached in to assist her. Their gloved fingers caught firmly until she reached the ground, and he offered her his arm. Walking with him up the wide marble steps and into the house, Julia was intensely aware of the hard muscle in his forearm, and the way he checked his long stride to match her shorter ones.

A narrow-faced butler welcomed them inside, taking Julia's hooded pelisse and Lord Savage's hat and gloves. Julia was amazed by what she saw of the entrance hall and the rooms beyond, the forty-foot-high ceilings and antique columns, the exquisite floors tiled in green, blue, and amber. "How beautiful," she exclaimed.

"Yes." But Savage was staring at her instead of their surroundings.

"Show me around," she urged, eager to see more.

Obligingly Savage escorted her through several rooms, pausing to describe the history of certain painted panels or furnishings. It was clear that the Savage family had a great appreciation of art. Many of the ceilings were studded with medallions of delicately painted angels, clouds, and mythological figures, while nearly every corner featured a piece of rare sculpture. There were walls decorated in gold and white to display portraits by Van Dyck and Rembrandt, and landscapes by Gainsborough, Marlow, and Lambert.

"I could stare at these for hours," Julia said, regarding a wall of paintings with delight.

"I don't often have the time to enjoy them."

"What keeps you so busy, my lord? Supervising all your investments and business interests, I suppose."

"There is a lot to be managed," he admitted, staring thoughtfully at the Van Dyck before them.

All of a sudden Julia was mortified by the indiscreet growling of her stomach. She placed her hand over her midriff. "How unladylike. I'm afraid I haven't eaten since this morning."

The corners of his mouth twitched with a smile. "Shall we go in to dinner?"

"Yes, I'm famished." Taking his arm once more, Julia accompanied him through more gleaming, art-filled rooms. Though it would have been best to find a neutral topic, she couldn't resist prying. "Surely you could hire estate agents and managers to take care of your business, my lord."

"I prefer to handle most of it myself."

"You don't trust other people very easily," she observed.

"No," he said quietly. "Particularly when my family's finances are at stake."

Julia glanced at the uncompromising line of his profile, her brows lifting in mild surprise. Why would he admit such a thing to her? Without exception, all members of the aristocracy pretended that their money sprang from limitless sources, to be squandered without a trace of worry.

Savage continued without a change in inflection. "My father insisted on managing the family's affairs by himself until he fell ill several years ago. When I assumed control of everything, I discovered that the Savages were heavily in debt, and all our financial dealings were in shambles. The duke had a taste for gambling. If he ever made a sound investment, it was purely by accident."

"You seem to have done very well for the Savages since then. Your father must be pleased that you have righted the situation."

Savage shrugged. "The duke never admits that he was wrong about anything. He doesn't acknowledge that he made mistakes."

"I understand." The words came out almost in a whisper. But Savage couldn't know exactly how well she *did* understand. As Julia had always suspected, their fathers were two of a kind. Like Lord Hargate, the Duke of Leeds had

tried to control his family with an iron hand.
When it had become clear that he was a poor
manager of property and people, he had sacrificed his son's future in exchange for a large
settlement from the Hargates.

Julia suspected that long ago Lord Savage had
decided that he would never be controlled by
anyone again. She felt a touch of sympathy for
him, even kinship . . . but she suspected that as
a husband, he would be inflexible, untrusting,
and remote. A highly undesirable mate, at least
for her.

The sumptuous dishes at dinner would have
satisfied a dozen people. Julia sat to Savage's
right at a long table laden with silver trumpet-
shaped vases filled with orchids and trailing
nasturtium. The first course consisted of vegeta-
ble consommé, followed by salmon rillettes covered with cream and dill. Afterward the servants
brought steaming trays bearing pheasant stuffed
with truffles and hazelnuts, and veal scallops
swimming in Bordeaux sauce.

Julia protested as more dishes arrived; puddings, open tarts, sweetbreads, and vegetables.
"This is far too much. I can't possibly do justice
to it!"

Savage smiled and coaxed her to try a quail
egg stuffed with cream and lobster. Indulging
herself as she hadn't in a long time, Julia drank
from a selection of French wine and applied
herself to the feast with pleasure. Savage proved
to be a charming dinner companion when he
chose, conversing agreeably on a variety of
subjects.

"Why become an actress?" he asked near the end of the leisurely meal, leaning back as their plates were removed and tiers of pastries and fresh fruit were set before them.

Julia toyed with a scarlet strawberry on her plate. "It was a desire of mine since childhood. I left my family's home when I was eighteen, worked in a company of traveling players, and then performed at a theater in the Strand until I was fortunate enough to be hired by Mr. Scott."

"Does your family approve of your career?"

Julia snorted at the idea. "Decidedly not. They wanted me to remain at home . . . but only if I abided by certain conditions which I found unacceptable."

"When did you marry?" he asked. "While you were at the Strand?"

She frowned at him. "I never discuss my marriage."

A half-smile played on his lips. "I'm not convinced your husband actually exists."

"He does," she assured him, sipping her wine. *He exists as much as your wife does*, she was tempted to say, but kept her silence.

"Will he ever want you to leave the theater?"

"He would be a bloody hypocrite if he did," she said pertly. "He's an actor himself." She suppressed a smile as she saw the spark of interest in his expression, knowing that he took her meaning literally. It was the truth, however. Lord Savage was undeniably skilled at hiding the truth and presenting a false facade. He was as accomplished an actor as any of the Capital players.

He seemed about to ask something else, when

suddenly his eyes narrowed, and he stared at her bare upper arm.

"My lord?" Julia asked, puzzled by his expression.

Before Julia could react, Savage had grasped her arm in his warm, broad hand, and turned it upward toward the light. The smear of paint over the bruise-mark was clearly visible. Julia tried to twist away, spluttering in confusion. "It's nothing . . . I-I'm perfectly all right . . . the performance, you see—"

"Hush." He turned to an approaching servant and brusquely requested a tin of salve from the housekeeper's supply.

Julia watched in dumbfounded silence as Savage dipped the corner of a napkin into a glass of cool water. She stiffened with surprise as the damp cloth passed carefully over the bruise. Savage found another dark fingermark, and a shadowy blotch on the tip of her shoulder. He wiped away the dabs of concealing paint with exquisite care.

A warm rush of color spread over Julia's skin, rising past her throat to her face. No man had ever touched her like this. His face was so close that she could see the grain of dark whiskers in his closely shaven skin, and the thick fan of his lashes.

A pleasant smell clung to him, the scents of cologne and warm skin mingled with starched linen. His breath was laced with the sweetness of after-dinner wine. Julia's heart began to thunder as she thought of smoothing her fingertips over his black hair, the neat curve of his ear, the bold sweep of his eyebrow. She'd had too much to drink. She was dizzy, flushed . . . she wanted to pull away, and yet . . .

The servant returned with a small tin of salve, handing it to Lord Savage. As he departed, he closed the door and left them in seclusion.

"There's no need . . ." Julia began unsteadily. Her voice faded as Savage uncovered the waxen pink salve, which held a strong herbal odor.

Savage's gray eyes lifted to hers. For the first time she noticed the subtle hints of blue and green in their depths. When he spoke, his voice was a shade deeper than usual. "Scott should be more careful with you."

"He is," she whispered. "It's just that I bruise very easily."

His gaze remained fixed on hers as he touched his fingers to the salve and leaned forward. It seemed as if he was waiting for her to object. A denial trembled on her lips, but somehow she couldn't make a sound. She felt his fingers on her arm, smoothing salve over the bruises. He touched her as if she were made of porcelain, the brush of his skin barely perceptible against hers. Julia had never guessed that a man could be so gentle.

He moved to her shoulder, tending to the bruise there while she held absolutely still. Wild impulses flooded her . . . she wanted to lean against him, to feel his entire hand against her skin, to guide his long fingers over the curve of her breast. She held her breath, willing the feeling to go away, but the craving grew until her nipples drew tight beneath the smooth silk of her gown. Helplessly she waited for him to finish, staring fixedly at his downbent head.

"Are there any more?" he asked.

"None that I'd care for you to see," she managed to say.

A smile flashed across his face. He covered the tin and gave it to her. "My gift to you, Mrs. Wentworth. Apparently you'll need more of it before *Taming of the Shrew* completes its run."

"Thank you." Julia picked up her black gloves, discarded at the beginning of dinner, and used them to fan her burning face. "It's very warm in here," she said lamely.

"Shall we walk in the garden?"

She nodded gratefully and left the dining room with him, crossing an anteroom to a pair of wide French doors that led to a paved garden path. It was dark and cool outside, crisp breezes rustling the leaves of fruit trees and whispering through the hedges.

They walked in silence past dense yew hedges and a line of flowering plum trees. Near the center of the garden was a large fountain filled with sculpted angels. Julia paused to admire the scenery, and became aware of a chest-high rose hedge bordering the path. The blossoms were familiar to her, large bursts of pale pink with an indescribably sweet perfume.

"Summer Glory roses," she murmured. "My mother's favorite. She used to spend hours in her garden tending them. The most beautiful and by far the most thorny, she told me."

Savage watched as she leaned close to a rose and inhaled its heady fragrance. "That particular variety is quite rare, especially in England. It was given to my family a long time ago from . . ." He stopped, a strange alertness infusing his expression. "A friend," he finished. The two words seemed to hang between them, punctuating the air with a question.

All at once the air left Julia's lungs, and she struggled for a replenishing breath. Summer Glories were indeed a unique variety. Now that she thought of it, her family's estate was the only other place she had ever seen them. She realized that in all likelihood her mother Eva was the one who had given the cuttings to the Savages all those years ago. Before turning into an invalid, Eva had prided herself on her skill at cultivating exotic roses . . . she had often made gifts of plants to friends and acquaintances.

Rapidly Julia considered ways to cover up the blunder, and decided to change the subject as quickly as possible. She walked past the shrub with feigned indifference. "Is Lady Ashton aware that I'm here with you tonight?" she asked abruptly.

"Lady Ashton," Savage repeated, sounding bemused at the unexpected question. He followed her along the path. "No, I haven't told her."

"If she finds out, will it cause a problem for you?"

"She has no claim on me."

"Oh, yes . . . your 'understanding' with her . . ." Julia winced as a bit of gravel slipped inside her silk shoe. She paused and removed the shoe, shaking it to remove the unwanted bit of stone. "Does Lady Ashton entertain hopes of marrying you, my lord?"

"You're asking very personal questions, Mrs. Wentworth."

"I'm certain she does," Julia said in answer to her own query. "You're quite an eligible man . . . aren't you?"

Savage took the shoe from her and bent to replace it on her foot. "I have no intention of marrying Lady Ashton."

Hopping a step or two, Julia reached for his shoulder to steady herself, making the discovery that there was no padding in his coat. His muscles felt like oak beneath her palm. "Why not?" she asked, looking down at the seallike gleam of his hair in the moonlight. "Doesn't she suit your high standards?" Her breath caught as she felt his fingers on her ankle, gently guiding her foot back into the shoe.

His voice was slightly muffled as he replied. "I intend to marry for love."

A pang of empathy mingled with Julia's surprise. So underneath his practical, self-controlled exterior there was a private dream, the same dream that had been stolen from each of them. "I wouldn't have expected such a romantic notion from a man like you, my lord."

"What would you expect of me?"

"That you would marry for convenience and search for love elsewhere."

"That's precisely what my father did. I'm certain my mother, being a sensible woman, expected nothing else of him, but I believe it hurt her all the same. I swore to myself that I would have something different."

"That isn't always possible, though."

"It will be for me."

How would it be possible? He must have an annulment in mind. He would have to be rid of her before he could consider marriage, unless he thought there was nothing wrong with bigamy.

"How can you be certain?" she asked. "You have no guarantee that you'll find your soul mate."

"No guarantee," he agreed, releasing her ankle. "Only hope."

He stood until he gazed down at her from his full height. His head was above hers, his face cast in shadow. Julia should have let go of his shoulders, but she felt peculiarly off-balance, as if that would mean releasing her hold on the only solid thing in the world.

"We've met before, you know," he said softly.

The words sent a chill of alarm through her. "You're mistaken."

"I've never forgotten that night." His hands were firm on her waist, holding her steady as he stared into her upturned face. "It was three years ago in Warwickshire. I had walked from the castle to watch the village May Day celebration. I saw you dancing." He was silent then, watching as her expression changed from bewilderment to recognition.

"Oh," Julia said faintly. "I didn't realize . . ." At first she had thought he was referring to their marriage. Good Lord, so he was the stranger who had kissed her that night! She lowered her gaze to the center of his chest, remembering how the kiss had haunted her for months afterward. It was incredible that fate had drawn them together yet again. "I asked you that evening if you were one of the Savages, and you denied it. Why didn't you tell me who you were?"

"I had no way of knowing how you would

react. You might have assumed I would try to take advantage of you."

"You did—you kissed me against my will."

A reluctant smile crossed his face. "I couldn't help it. You were the most beautiful woman I had ever seen. You still are."

Julia tried to pull away, but he kept her anchored against him. "What do you want from me?" she asked unsteadily.

"I want to see you again."

She shook her head vehemently. "You can't buy another evening with me, even if you purchase the entire Capital Theatre."

"Why not? Because your husband would object?"

"I've told you I won't discuss him."

"I won't let you refuse without explaining why you won't see me."

"Because I have no interest in an affair with you . . . and given our respective situations, that is the only thing you would be able to offer me." Julia's blood drummed in a volatile rhythm. His body was so close to hers, she could hear his breathing, sense his heat, and she was drawn to him like a moth blundering toward a flame. She wanted to tilt her head back and feel his mouth on hers, and press herself against him. There had never been temptation like this, a promise of something extraordinary within reach. But she would not give in to the self-destructive urge. It would be disastrous.

"I won't see you again," she said, twisting until his hands dropped away and she was set free. "I must leave." She hurried back to the fountain, and paused at the juncture of two paths.

Savage's voice was just behind her. "This way." They walked back to the house in silence, seized with a tension that neither seemed able to break.

As the carriage rolled away with its lovely occupant tucked safely inside, Damon wandered alone across the marble floor of the entrance hall. He felt more restless than he had ever been in his life. His mind was filled with her; he relived every moment of the past few hours and craved more.

He wanted her. He wanted her with an unreasoning, blind insistence that raged through every nerve. And he resented her for it.

Slowly he went to the long staircase leading to the top two floors of the house. He stopped at the first landing and sat on the steps. Bracing his forearms on his knees, he stared without interest at the luminous medieval tapestries that covered the wall.

Jessica Wentworth was committed elsewhere. So was he. They occupied separate worlds. She was right, there was little he could offer her except an affair. And there was Pauline to consider. She didn't deserve to be betrayed and abandoned. What they had together was comfortable and easy, and it had been enough for him . . . until Jessica Wentworth.

He should put Jessica from his mind, now. It was the only rational choice. But something in him rebelled at the thought. He had never felt so confined, his choices limited by a past that weighed on him like a mile's length of iron chain. He was married to a woman he didn't even know.

If only he could find Julia Hargate, damn her to hell, and cut her from his life once and for all.

Chapter 4

❦ ❧

The moment Julia entered the greenroom, she found a half-dozen expectant gazes pinned on her. The assembled actors, the principals of *Taming of the Shrew*, were unabashedly curious about what had occurred during her evening with Lord Savage.

Only Logan Scott seemed too preoccupied with rehearsal notes to notice her entrance. "You're late, Mrs. Wentworth," he finally said without looking up.

"Forgive me, I overslept," Julia murmured as she made her way to an empty chair. It was the truth. After she had returned to her small house on Somerset Street, she had stayed awake for a long time, drinking wine and staring pensively at nothing. Even after going to bed, she had found sleep elusive. It seemed that when she finally dozed off, it was already time to awaken and face the day with bleary, dark-circled eyes.

She hadn't been able to stop thinking about Savage. Last night had been the culmination of all the fear and curiosity that had plagued her for years. Now all her imaginings about her un-

known husband were gone. He was real to her,
and more dangerous than she had ever
dreamed. Savage was a magnificent man, intelligent, powerful, driven, the kind who could
dominate a woman's life so completely that she
would lose herself in his shadow. He was very
much like her father in that regard. Julia didn't
want to be the wife of a strong man—she had
worked too hard to become Jessica Wentworth.

It would have been easier to disregard Savage
if not for the disarming hint of vulnerability she
had seen . . . the gentle way he had touched her,
the startling admission that he wanted to marry
for love someday. Was there more to be discovered beneath his guarded exterior? She could
never take the chance of finding out. It filled her
with a strange despair, thinking of what had
transpired between them. She had made it clear
that she would not see him again, and she knew
in her heart that it was for the best. But why did
it feel as if she had lost something infinitely
precious?

"Here you are," came Arlyss's murmur, and
the petite actress passed her a cup of hot tea.

Julia accepted it gratefully and sipped the
sweet, bracing liquid.

"He didn't let you sleep a wink, did he?"
Arlyss asked in delight. "I've never seen you so
exhausted. Was he very good, Jessica?"

Julia gave her a weary scowl. "I wasn't with
him—not in that way."

"Of course not," said Mr. Kerwin, a portly
actor in his sixties who considered himself a
sophisticated man of the world. He excelled at
playing anxious fathers, harassed husbands,

drunkards, and buffoons, always with a lopsided charm that endeared him to the audience. "Never admit a thing, my dear—your private life should remain just that." He punctuated the comment with a friendly wink.

Logan's voice, dripping with sarcasm, intruded on the budding conversation. "Mrs. Wentworth, would you care to join us? I have a page of notes concerning your mistakes of last night's performance. I'm certain you'll want to hear them."

Julia nodded and sipped more tea, wondering why Logan seemed so tense this morning. He should be pleased—the performance had been well-received by the audience and critics, and she had done her part for the Capital by attending the promised dinner with Lord Savage. What more did he want?

Before Logan could proceed with his reading of the morning's notes, the greenroom door opened and the hesitant face of one of the company's property-men appeared. "Begging pardon," he said apologetically to the room at large, and his gaze flew to Julia. "A parcel was just delivered for you, Mrs. Wentworth. The boy who delivered it said it should be brought to you right away."

Intrigued, Julia gestured for the small, plainly wrapped box in his hand, and he brought it to her. Mindful of Logan's gathering scowl, the property man vanished quickly. Julia was sorely tempted to open the package, but she set it aside to be unwrapped later, knowing it would annoy Logan to have further interruptions of the meeting. The assembled company stared intently at the mysterious box, completely ignoring Logan's impatient rustling of his notes.

"Well?" Logan finally said to Julia, his mouth twisting sardonically. "You may as well open the damned thing. It's apparent that no one will pay attention to the work at hand until you do."

Arlyss leaned over Julia's shoulder, her eyes bright with interest, her brown curls fairly dancing with energy. "It's from *him*, isn't it?"

Cautiously Julia unwrapped the box and discovered a folded note inside. Everyone leaned closer, as if they all expected she would read it aloud. Defensively she held the note close to her midriff and scanned it silently.

Madam—

I am told this once belonged to the gifted actress Mrs. Jordan. It deserves to be worn by someone with the grace and beauty to display it properly. Please accept this token with the understanding that no obligation comes with it, save that you enjoy it.

> *Your servant,*
> *Damon, Lord Savage*

Cautiously Julia lifted a small blue velvet pouch from the box, and dropped its contents into her hand. Arlyss gave an audible gasp, while Mr. Kerwin made a rumbling noise of approval in his throat. Unable to resist, the group of actors gathered around to view the offering.

In the center of Julia's palm was the most

exquisite brooch she had ever seen, a tiny bouquet of roses with glittering ruby petals and emerald leaves. She could well believe that Mrs. Dora Jordan, the consort of the king's brother so many years ago, would have owned such a magnificent piece. Although Julia had been offered jewelry and gifts from many would-be suitors—and she had refused all of it—no one had ever given her something so elegant. Dumbfounded, she stared at the small treasure in her palm. "I . . . I'll have to return it," she said with difficulty, and there was an immediate chorus of disapproval.

"Why should you?"

"Keep it, lass, there's your future to consider—"

"With his fortune, the marquess could buy you a thousand more and never miss a shilling!"

"Don't be hasty," Arlyss urged. "Before you do anything, think about it for a day or two."

"All right, that's enough," Logan said, tugging impatiently at a lock of his burnished russet hair. "There are far better things to occupy us than Mrs. Wentworth's conquest."

Obediently the players returned to their seats. Julia closed her fingers over the jeweled pin, her mind racing. Of course she must return it—she had never accepted a gift from a man before. In spite of his words to the contrary, she knew that Lord Savage would expect a favor in return. He was not the kind of man to give something for nothing. But a strange thought came to mind. He was her husband; why shouldn't she take it from him? Their long-ago marriage had deprived her of so many things. Surely she deserved this small compensation. The brooch was so beautiful, so enticing, and it suited her perfectly.

Mrs. Wentworth's conquest, she thought, flushing in dismay and delight. She shouldn't be pleased that Lord Savage had taken an interest in her. She should be alarmed. What an astonishing twist of fate, to be courted by her own husband! This flirtation with disaster must end before it went any further.

Sliding the brooch back into the velvet pouch, Julia forced herself to pay attention to Logan's notes. She was quiet and subdued while the others asked questions and made their own suggestions concerning the play. When the meeting was concluded, she went toward her dressing room, wanting a few minutes of privacy to think.

"Mrs. Wentworth," Logan murmured as Julia passed, and she stopped with an inquiring glance.

"Yes, Mr. Scott?"

Logan wore a matter-of-fact expression, but there was a pinched look between his ruddy brows that betrayed some inner turmoil. "It appears the dinner with Lord Savage wasn't a great hardship after all."

"No," she said evenly. "It was quite pleasant."

"Will you see him again?" Suddenly a self-mocking smile hovered on his lips, as if he felt like a fool for asking.

"No, Mr. Scott." Julia wondered why his expression seemed to smooth out. Perhaps he was concerned that a relationship with Lord

Savage might interfere with her career? Or was there possibly some personal motive in his question?

"Then it's all over," he said.

Her hand tightened on the brooch encased in velvet. "Most certainly, Mr. Scott."

Pauline, Lady Ashton lounged on the embroidered ivory silk counterpane of her bed, her voluptuous body covered in a slightly transparent pink dressing gown. She murmured a languid greeting to Damon as he entered the bedroom of her elegant London townhouse. They had been apart for the weekend, while she had visited her sister's family in Hertfordshire.

Immediately upon her return, Pauline had sent a brief note, perfumed and sealed with gold wax, to Damon's town address. From the demanding tone of the message, Damon guessed that Pauline had already heard of his latest activities. God knew how she kept such a close eye on him—it appeared as if she had employed a network of spies to watch him.

"Hello, darling," Pauline said, gesturing him close with a slender white hand. Pulling his head down to hers, she kissed him ardently, holding him to her with surprising strength. Damon jerked his head back and stared at her curiously. There was a look on her face that he didn't like, a mixture of excitement and triumph, a glitter of anticipation in her dark brown eyes. It seemed that she was preparing for battle . . . and that she possessed a weapon that would guarantee her victory.

"Pauline, there's something I want to tell you—"

"I already know," she interrupted calmly. "It's rather humiliating, you know, enduring the sneers and false pity of the *ton*, while they're all trying to be the first to tell me that you've developed an infatuation for some cheap little actress."

"I didn't intend to embarrass you."

"How clever of you to plan it for an evening when you knew I would be visiting my sister's family in the country! How was she, darling? It must have been thrilling to have such a celebrated tart in your bed—"

"Nothing happened between us."

She laughed skeptically. "Really? So she's playing that game. I've used that tactic myself . . . remember? I made you wait a full month before allowing you to have me. Waiting makes the victory so much sweeter, doesn't it?"

Until that moment, Damon hadn't been certain of what he wanted from Pauline, or what his obligations to her might be. She had been an entertaining companion for several months. He had never lied to her, had never taken anything that wasn't willingly offered . . . and he had paid handsomely for the privilege of being accepted into her bed. Although he hadn't come here with the intention of breaking off their relationship, he knew now that his liaison with Pauline had grown stale. They had never shared anything but physical pleasure. No deeper understanding or intimacy had developed beyond that, and it never would.

"Why did you send for me?" he asked.

She stiffened at the new note in his voice, a cool disinterest he had never shown to her before. "I want to discuss your intentions, darling. Are you planning to make Jessica Wentworth your new mistress?"

"That isn't your concern."

"You're going to leave me for a creature like *her*? She's nothing but a new toy, a pretty bauble that you'll soon tire of . . . and when you do, you'll return to me."

Pauline's arrogance annoyed him. He had never allowed anyone to take him to task for anything he did, and he was hardly going to give Pauline that right. "If I do visit another woman's bed," he said softly, "I'll be damned if I require your approval."

"Very well, my lord. Am I at least allowed to ask what will become of me?"

Damon raked her with an appraising glance. As beautiful and desirable as Pauline was, she would find a new provider within a week. He had no illusions that she loved him—she showed no symptoms of that particular malady. Ending their relationship would hardly leave her brokenhearted and destitute.

"You'll do very well," he said. "I doubt a man has ever looked at you and found you wanting, Pauline." He softened slightly as he continued. "I've enjoyed being with you these past months. I'd like to end things on an agreeable note, without spoiling the memories. I'll make certain all your bills are settled. I want to leave you with a parting gift . . . a new carriage, more jewelry, a house . . . just tell me what you'd like."

Her brown eyes locked with his. "You've already left me a parting gift," she said without blinking. Her voice contained an edge of irony that he didn't understand. Slowly her hand crept to her slightly rounded stomach, and slid over the smooth surface in a meaningful caress.

Uncomprehending, Damon watched the movement of her white fingers. His mind would not accept what she was trying to tell him.

"What should I ask for?" Pauline murmured idly, keeping her hand clamped protectively over her abdomen. "A little extra money, I suppose, and then I should promise not to trouble you about my condition after that. That's the usual arrangement, isn't it? Men in your position have illegitimate children all the time, and they feel no obligation to the mothers of their bastard offspring. But I know you, darling. You're not like most men."

"We took precautions—" he said hoarsely.

"Sometimes precautions fail."

"I want you to see a doctor."

"I already have. You're welcome to meet him, of course, and have him confirm the news." She paused and added with a sudden flash of vulnerability, "You may disbelieve me, or claim that the baby isn't yours, but at least I've told you the truth."

If it was a bluff, it was a masterful one. Pauline spoke without blinking, without the telltale flush or heightened pulse of a woman who was lying. She was supremely calm and clear-headed.

A child . . . his, and Pauline's. Every part of him rebelled against the idea. For his entire adult life, he had never overindulged himself where women were concerned. He had chosen his partners carefully, and to his knowledge he hadn't sired bastards by any of them. Pauline was right; men seldom felt they owed anything to their pregnant mistresses except financial support for the children. This didn't have to be a trap . . . but for him it was. He felt cold all over. He turned away from the bedside so that Pauline couldn't watch the sickening realization sweep over his face.

He couldn't abandon her now, no matter what he felt for her personally. He was linked to her forever through this child. Pauline knew him well enough to understand that he couldn't live with himself if he didn't take care of her and the baby. From now on his life would be entwined with theirs.

He knew that Pauline wanted to become his wife, she expected it of him . . . and he would have expected it of himself, if not for one obstacle. A bitter smile twisted his lips, and he heard himself say aloud, "I can't marry you."

"I understand your reluctance, darling. However, there are some facts to consider. You have need of an heir, or your brother will have the title after you. And there is the welfare of the child—"

"I'm already married." It was the first time Damon had ever admitted it to anyone except his brother. He closed his hands into fists, while impotent rage swept over him. Damn his father to hell for bringing him to this!

Silence descended over the scene, so absolute that he finally turned to look at Pauline. She was gray-faced, whether from shock or fury he couldn't tell.

"*What?*" she wheezed. "The rumors are true? I

never would have believed it—not of a man like
you—"

"It happened a long time ago. I was a boy of
seven. My father arranged it."

"If this is a trick—"

"It's the truth."

The gray left Pauline's complexion, replaced
by a rush of crimson. "My God . . . why has it
been such a bloody secret? And where have you
kept your *w-wife* all this time?"

"I haven't seen her since the day we were
married. The families agreed that we would be
raised separately, and 'introduced' when we
were of suitable age." Damon took a deep breath
and forced himself to continue. "But that never
came to pass. I don't know how the facts of the
matter were told to her. My father chose to
emphasize how fortunate I was, being tied to a
wealthy family and never having to go through
the trouble of choosing a wife for myself. I hated
him for what he had done, no matter what his
reasons were. I resisted my family's attempts to
bring the two of us together, and Julia—"

"Julia," Pauline repeated blankly.

"—she appeared to be equally reluctant to
meet me. By the time I had finally decided to
take the matter in hand and confront her, she
had disappeared. That was three years ago. I still
haven't been able to find her."

"What do you mean, disappeared? Doesn't
anyone know where she is? Her family?"

"If any of her friends or relations know,
they're not going to admit anything. I've hired
detectives who have searched all through Europe without finding a trace of her."

"But why would she vanish like that? Something must have happened to her." A hopeful note entered her voice. "Perhaps she's dead! Yes, that or disfigured by an accident . . . or perhaps she's taken her vows and is hiding in a convent—"

"All of those possibilities have been considered—but there's no evidence to support any of them."

"If she were alive, she would come forward to take her place as the next Duchess of Leeds."

Damon shrugged. "It's possible that the idea of me as a husband doesn't appeal to her," he said dryly.

There was a visible struggle on Pauline's face, anger and desire making small blue veins prominent on her temples and throat. "What will you do about Mrs. Wentworth?" she asked in a voice that shook. "Or must you have an entire collection of women at your disposal?"

"She has nothing to do with Julia Hargate, or with you."

"She's to be my replacement," Pauline snarled. "Regardless of what you've done to me, and what you owe me!"

As he gazed at Pauline's enraged features, another image appeared in Damon's mind . . . Jessica Wentworth's clear turquoise eyes, and the gleam of moonlight on her skin. *I have no interest in an affair with you,* she had said, *and that is the only thing you would be able to offer me.*

"I'm not going to see her again," Damon said quietly. "She deserves far more than I can give her."

"What about me?"

"You'll be taken care of. You and the child. But it won't be the same between us, Pauline."

She relaxed visibly, evidently choosing to ignore his implication. "Naturally," she said in a much softer voice. "I knew you wouldn't abandon me, darling." She reached out for him beseechingly, her red lips parting in invitation. Damon shook his head and walked toward the bedroom door. It took all his self-control to keep from running away from the perfumed prison. "Damon, we must talk!"

"Later," he muttered, grateful for every step he put between them. He didn't want to make love or talk . . . he wanted to stop thinking and feeling, at least for a while.

Madame Lefevrbre's shop was filled with the acrid scents of dye, fabric, and steaming amber tea. There were other, more lavishly appointed dressmakers' shops in London, with furniture upholstered in velvet and walls covered in gold-framed mirrors, but none attracted the kind of wealthy and discriminating clientele that Madame Lefevrbre did. Julia loved the enterprising Frenchwoman's simple, flattering designs, as well as the beautiful silks, muslins, and soft wools she used.

Pausing in her consultation with another woman, Madame Lefevrbre came to personally welcome Julia into the shop. She valued Julia's patronage not only because of her growing celebrity, but also because Julia always paid her bills promptly, unlike the scores of women who had to coax reluctant husbands or paramours to pay for their newest gowns.

"Mrs. Wentworth, you have arrived early for your fitting," Madame Lefevrbre exclaimed, guiding Julia to a chair by a table laden with stacks of designs, fabric swatches, and dolls outfitted with miniature versions of the latest fashions. "If you wouldn't mind waiting here for a few minutes—"

"Certainly, Madame." They exchanged a smile, regarding each other with the mutual respect of two women accustomed to providing for themselves. Julia sat in the well-worn chair, declined a cup of tea, and began to browse through the stack of fashion prints.

"I will return for you soon," the dressmaker said, disappearing behind the muslin curtains that led to the back of the shop.

As Julia lingered over a particular design, a morning gown with a slim silhouette and satin ribbon that crossed over the breasts, she realized that the nearby chair was occupied.

The attractive dark-haired woman picked up a doll and toyed with the tiny frilled ruff around its neck. She glanced at Julia and smiled slightly.

Julia's answering smile dimmed as she realized that the woman was Lady Ashton. She groaned inwardly, wondering why such an unlucky coincidence would happen to her. Without doubt, Lady Ashton had found out about her clandestine meeting with Lord Savage by now. A guilty flush began to creep over Julia's skin, but she reasoned with herself valiantly. She had done nothing wrong in having dinner with Lord Savage . . . and besides, after all these years she was entitled to at least one evening with her own husband!

Lady Ashton possessed a formidable self-composure, seeming not at all perturbed by their chance meeting. "Mrs. Wentworth," she said in a velvety voice, "how pleasant to see you again."

Julia managed an agreeing smile. "It's rather a surprise to find you here," she commented.

"Not so much of a surprise. I insisted that Madame schedule my appointment close to yours. I hoped we would have the opportunity to chat."

Refusing to let her discomfort show, Julia stared at her with a perplexed arch of one tawny brow.

"How many people admire you, Mrs. Wentworth," Lady Ashton remarked, setting aside the doll and picking up another. She slid an appraising glance over Julia's slender form. "Lovely, talented, and desired by most of the men in London. I've seen engravings and paintings of you everywhere . . . why, you're the most admired actress on the English stage. I'm positive you could have any man you set your cap for. Who would be able to resist you?"

A tense silence followed, while Julia marveled silently at the woman's acting skill. If Lady Ashton was outraged, hurt, or humiliated, she wasn't revealing a trace of it. "I'm not certain what you mean," Julia said with a questioning lilt in her voice.

The other woman shrugged. "I suppose I'm trying to say that any other female—myself, for example—would be poor competition for one as celebrated as you."

Julia looked at her without flinching. "I have no desire to compete with anyone."

Lady Ashton gave a light laugh, although there was no amusement in her brown eyes. "That's very reassuring. I certainly hope that a woman with all your advantages would never attempt to lure away a man who belongs to someone else."

Unspoken messages were transferred in their shared gaze. *Don't try to take what is mine,* Lady Ashton's eyes warned, while Julia replied silently, *You have nothing to fear from me.*

Eventually Lady Ashton looked away, turning her attention to the lace trim on the doll in her arms. She replaced it carefully on the table. "This is my first visit to Madame Lefevrbre's," she remarked. "I will require a great many new gowns, I'm afraid."

"No doubt you'll look very well in anything she designs," Julia replied mechanically. With a trim, voluptuous shape like Lady Ashton's, she could probably wear sackcloth and make it look fashionable.

"Not for long, I'm afraid." Lady Ashton patted her flat stomach and glanced down at it fondly. "I'm expecting some significant changes in a matter of months."

The fashion prints trembled in Julia's hands, and she set them in her lap. The information struck her like a bolt of lightning, scattering her thoughts into chaos. My God . . . a baby . . . Lord Savage's child. Aware that Lady Ashton was watching her intently, she recovered enough from her confusion to pretend a great interest in a particular design. She wondered if Lord Savage had known about the pregnancy before, if he knew now, how he felt about it . . .

Angry, perhaps. And trapped. And most of all, responsible. He would not callously abandon a woman who was carrying his child. He had said he had no intention of marrying Lady Ashton . . . he wanted to marry for love. That dream was impossible now. Julia was almost, *almost* tempted to pity him, but there was no denying that the situation was of his own making. He and this calculating woman would make a handsome pair, both of them dark and exotic, both possessing an apparently ruthless drive to obtain what they wanted.

Well, Lord Savage would have to deal with the circumstances he had created . . . and Julia would make doubly certain that she stayed far away from him. Let him and Lady Ashton resolve their own problems . . . she had her own life to attend to.

To Julia's relief, Madame Lefevrbre's pleasantly chattering voice intruded on her thoughts, bidding her to come to the back of the shop for her fitting now. She stood and forced herself to smile faintly at Lady Ashton. "Good day," she murmured. "I wish you well." The other woman nodded, evidently satisfied with her morning's accomplishments.

Having recently received a letter from her mother, Eva, Julia knew exactly when her father would be absent from Hargate Hall. He often went to London to attend club gatherings or meet with his financial advisers. Julia managed to visit her mother every month or two, seldom missing an opportunity to make the hour-long carriage drive to her family's home. She was never certain what Eva's condition would be— her health was uneven, sometimes fair, sometimes poor.

Today Julia was gratified to find her mother sitting up in her private receiving room with a light embroidered blanket across her knees. Eva's complexion was brighter than usual, her expression serene. A basket filled with half-finished needlework rested on the floor near her feet. Eva reached out her arms in welcome, and Julia rushed to embrace her.

"You take my breath away," Eva exclaimed, laughing at Julia's hard squeeze. "My goodness . . . it seems that something has happened since the last time you came."

"I've brought a present for you."

Opening her drawstring reticule, Julia removed the small jewelry pouch and let the glittering ruby pin fall into her palm. "It was a gift from an admirer," she said casually. "I've decided it will suit you far better than me." She couldn't keep the piece, much as she loved it. She wanted to dispose of all reminders of Lord Savage.

"Oh, Julia . . ." Eva exclaimed softly at the sight of the jeweled bouquet.

"Try it on," Julia urged, pinning the brooch to the white ruffles at her mother's throat. "There . . . now you'll always have roses with you, no matter what the season."

"I shouldn't accept this from you," Eva said, reaching up to touch the delicate pin. "It's much too valuable—and if your father should see—"

"He never notices such things. And if he does, tell him it was left to you by a recently departed friend." Julia smiled brightly into her mother's worried face. "Don't refuse my gift, Mama. It suits you perfectly."

"Very well," Eva said, her expression smoothing out, and she leaned over to kiss her daughter. "You must tell me about this admirer of yours. Is he the reason you seem so animated? Or is it that Mr. Scott has given you the role you desired in his new play?"

"Neither of those things." Julia stared at her steadily, feeling her cheeks turn pink. "I . . . I've met him, Mama."

Eva stared at her uncomprehendingly . . . and slowly the realization dawned. There was no need to ask who "he" was. Her lips moved soundlessly. "How?" she finally asked in a whisper.

"Purely by chance. I was at a weekend party. I heard his name and turned around, and there he was. He doesn't know who I am. I couldn't tell him."

Eva shook her head slowly. A visible pulse fluttered at her fine-skinned temple. "Oh, Julia," she breathed, her voice thin and bemused.

"He invited me to dinner," Julia continued, finding it an indescribable relief to tell someone what had happened. "Actually, 'coerced' is a better word. He promised Mr. Scott a large donation to the theater in exchange for my company, and so I agreed."

"You *dined* with Lord Savage?"

Julia nodded jerkily. "Yes, at his London estate, a week ago."

"And you never told him . . ." Eva's voice drifted into silence.

"No, I couldn't. And he doesn't suspect a thing. To him I'm merely an actress he's taken an interest in." She gripped her mother's slender hands more tightly. "He claims to be a bachelor. It appears that he refuses to acknowledge the marriage."

Inexplicably, a guilty look came over Eva's face. "What do you think of him, Julia? Do you find him appealing?"

"Well, I . . ." Uneasily Julia pulled her hands away and toyed with a fold of her skirts, pleating the soft aqua muslin with her fingers. "I suppose anyone would say that he's handsome. And he certainly is a fascinating man." A reluctant smile came to her lips. "We have many of the same flaws, I think. He's guarded and untrusting, and he seems determined to control every aspect of his life, so that no one can do to him what his father did all those years ago." She shook her head and laughed shortly. "It's no surprise that he never wanted to find me! I doubt he ever gives a thought to Julia Hargate, except to hope that I've somehow disappeared from the face of the earth."

"That's not true, Julia." Eva sighed and looked away, seeming to cringe in discomfort at what she was about to reveal. "Three years ago Lord Savage came to Hargate Hall, demanding to know where you were. We told him nothing, of course, except to say that you were abroad and unreachable. Ever since then we have received occasional visits from people in his employ, making new inquiries about you. Lord Savage has most definitely been trying to find you."

Julia stared at her in bewilderment. "Why . . . why wasn't I told that he was looking for me?"

"I didn't believe you were ready to face Lord Savage. I wanted the choice to be yours. If you had ever desired to meet him, you could have gone to him of your own volition. And your father didn't want Savage to find you, for fear that you would act impetuously, and lose the title and position he had gained for you."

Julia made a sound of frustration and leaped to her feet. "Will the two of you ever tire of manipulating me? I should have been told! I didn't know that Savage wanted to see me!"

"Would it have made a difference?" her mother asked softly. "Would you have wanted to see him then?"

"I don't know. But I should have had the choice!"

"You've always had a choice," Eva pointed out. "You could have met him long ago, but you chose to avoid him. Just the other night you had the opportunity to tell him who you were, and you chose to keep silent. How can I tell what it is you want, my dear, when even you don't know?"

Julia paced wildly around the room. "I want to be free of him! My marriage to Savage should have been dismissed a long time ago. I'm positive he wants it to end as much as I do, especially after what Lady Ashton told me."

"Who is Lady Ashton? Why do you mention her?"

"She's his mistress," Julia said sourly. "And she claims to be pregnant with his child."

"Pregnant," Eva repeated in shock, although she usually shrank from such indelicate words. "Oh . . . what a terrible complication."

"Not at all. The situation is very simple. I'm going to end all ties with Lord Savage."

"Julia, I beg you not to act rashly."

"*Rashly?* It's taken me years to make this decision. I don't think anyone would claim I've rushed into anything."

"You've spent so much time avoiding the consequences of your past . . . avoiding *him*," Eva said earnestly. "You must face your husband at last and tell him the truth, and deal with the situation together—"

"He's not my husband. I've never accepted him as such. That so-called marriage was nothing but a sham. I can easily find a lawyer to confirm its validity and notify Lord Savage."

"And what then? Will it be like this for the rest of our lives? Must I see you in secret for the rest of my days? Will you never try to make peace with your father, and bring yourself to forgive him?"

The mention of her father made Julia's jaw harden. "He doesn't want my forgiveness."

"Even so, you must give it to him, not for his sake but your own." Eva's eyes were filled with love and pleading. "You're not a rebellious girl any longer, Julia. You're an independent woman with a strong spirit—much stronger than my

own. However, you mustn't lose the gentle part
of your nature, the part that is tender and
compassionate. If you nurture this bitterness in
yourself, I'm afraid of what will become of you.
In spite of everything, I still have the same
dreams for you that every mother has for her
daughter, to have your own husband and home
and family—"

"I won't have that with Lord Savage," Julia
said stubbornly.

"Will you at least talk to him?"

"I can't—" Julia began, but she was interrupted by a hesitant knock at the door. It was
Polly, a housemaid who had been in the Hargates' employ for almost twenty years. She was a
humorless but kind woman with a small, owlish
face. Julia had always liked her for her utter
devotion to Eva.

"Ma'am," Polly murmured to Eva, "there is a
visitor asking to see Lord Hargate. I told him the
master wasn't at home . . . and then he asked
for you."

Eva looked perturbed. She rarely received
impromptu visits because of her poor health. "I
don't want to interrupt my time with my daughter," she said. "Please ask him to call later."

"Yes, ma'am, but . . . it's Lord Savage."

"Lord Savage is in the entrance hall?" Julia
asked numbly. At the housemaid's nod, she
uttered a string of curses that caused the other
women to stare at her in astonishment. "He
mustn't know I'm here," she said, striding toward the adjoining room, another sitting area in
Eva's private suite. "Mama, have him brought

up here and find out what he wants . . . but
don't tell him anything about me."

"What will you do?" Eva asked, clearly bewildered.

"I'm going to hide nearby. Please, Mama,
don't say anything to him . . . I can't make any
decisions now." Julia blew her a kiss before
disappearing into the next room.

Damon had set foot on the Hargate estate only
twice in his life before now. The first time had
been on the day of his wedding, when he was
seven. The second was three years ago, when he
had first approached the Hargates about their
daughter's whereabouts. He had found Lady
Hargate to be a quiet and pale woman, subdued
in voice and appearance. Predictably, Lord Hargate was a cold man, the kind who considered
himself superior to everyone he encountered.
Since that day Damon had often wondered
which one Julia Hargate favored more, her timid
mother or her overbearing father. Neither possibility was appealing.

Damon waited patiently in the entrance hall.
The interior of the house was luxurious, intimidating, almost churchlike, with its intricately
vaulted ceilings and the smell of polished wood.
What had it been like for a little girl to grow up
in such surroundings? Had Julia Hargate filled
the halls with boisterous shrieks and sent her
childish voice echoing up to the lofty ceilings?
Or had she played quietly in some private corner, lost in her own imaginings? His own childhood, with all its faults and uncertainties, was
infinitely preferable to this.

Where was Julia now? Where would she escape to after being brought up in a place like this? *Escape* . . . Briefly he thought of Jessica Wentworth on the night they had met at the weekend party, and what she had said to him. *I've never met a person who is comfortable with his or her past. There is always something we would like to change, or forget—*

The housemaid returned and interrupted his thoughts. "Lady Hargate will see you, my lord. But not for long, if you please, sir, as her health is delicate."

"I understand."

The housemaid led him from the entrance hall to the upstairs, along thickly carpeted hallways and endless stretches of carved woodwork. Damon wasn't certain what he would say to Lady Hargate. He would have preferred to meet with Julia's father, and do whatever was necessary to force him to reveal his daughter's whereabouts. Unfortunately it wasn't possible to threaten or browbeat a sickly woman.

A mother with poor health . . . it occurred to Damon that this was another similarity he and Julia Hargate shared. Years ago his own mother had died of consumption, her body pitifully frail and her mind occupied with constant worry over the fate of her family. How unjust it had been for a woman who craved stability to be married to a gambler. If only Damon had been able to protect her from his father, and give her the peace and security she had deserved. The awareness that he had failed his mother would haunt him all his life.

He wouldn't abandon Julia Hargate and have

her on his conscience as well. His own sense of honor demanded that he help her in any way possible.

He owed a responsibility to Pauline as well, but there was a difference between the two situations. Julia was a victim of circumstances she had been helpless to control. Pauline, on the other hand, was doing her best to manipulate him, and there was no doubt that her pregnancy was anything but an accident.

Entering a receiving room decorated in pale pink and salmon, he saw Lady Hargate seated in a large chair. There was something oddly familiar in her unyielding poise as she held herself upright and straight-backed, in the way she extended her hand to him as she remained sitting. She seemed exactly as he remembered, like a bird that infinitely preferred the shelter of its luxurious cage to the beckoning world outside. Once, she must have been a lovely woman.

Damon kissed her thin hand respectfully.

"You may sit beside me," she said, and he obeyed at once.

"Lady Hargate, I apologize for the inconvenience of my call—"

"It is a welcome pleasure to see you," she interrupted gently, "as well as an overdue one. Tell me, how is your family?"

"My brother William is well. Unfortunately my father has had a series of brain hemorrhages which have left him very weak."

"I am sorry." Her voice was filled with sincerity.

Damon was silent for a moment, debating on how to proceed. He didn't want to make small talk, and from the way she was looking at him, it was clear that she expected him to bring up the subject of Julia. "Have you heard from your daughter?" he asked abruptly. "You must have had some news of her. It's been three years."

She was evasive but not unfriendly as she replied. "Have you continued your search for her, Lord Hargate?"

Damon nodded, staring at her intently. "Yes, without any luck. Julia Hargate doesn't seem to exist anywhere in the civilized world."

In the next room, Julia pressed her ear close to the door, embarrassed to be eavesdropping but unable to stop herself. She was unbearably curious to find out what Savage would say to her mother, what tactics he would use to try to discover the truth.

"And if you do eventually find my daughter?" Eva inquired. "What are your intentions toward her, my lord?"

"From all indications, Julia is either afraid or unwilling to take her place as my wife. God knows I don't blame her. We're complete strangers. All I want is to know that she is well, and that she has everything she needs. Then I intend to resolve the matter in any way Julia prefers."

"What if she wants to remain your wife? She may desire to become a duchess someday."

"Then let her tell me so herself," Damon replied grimly, his tension suddenly whipping out of control. "Let me see it in her eyes, and hear it in her voice. Damn her, I'd like to know what she desires, so I can stop looking for her and be done with this!" Instantly he regretted the outburst, fearing he had offended the delicate creature. "Pardon—" he muttered, but she waved the apology away and looked at him with disconcerting understanding.

"More than anything," she said, "my daughter wishes to make choices for herself . . . and she has always rebelled against the fact that one of the greatest choices of all was stolen from her. Of course you must feel the same way."

Suddenly Damon's emotions rushed within him like a river battering against a crumbling dam. There was no one in the world he trusted enough to confide in, not even William. His problems, his feelings, had always been his own burden, and he alone had been responsible for them. But at this moment the need to tell them to someone was one of the most powerful compulsions he had ever known.

Damon flexed his hands and spread his palms on his knees. "Yes, I feel the same way," he said, his voice raspy. He couldn't bring himself to look at her. "I know why Julia rebelled, and why she's unable to face the consequences of what Lord Hargate and my father arranged. Although I've always known it wasn't her fault, I still blamed Julia for things she had nothing to do with. For years I hated her, almost as much as I hated my father for being a spendthrift and a gambler. I tried to forget her very existence. My mother's death and my father's ill health enabled me to bury myself in a world of new responsibilities. But Julia was always there in the back of my mind. I've never been able to love anyone, never felt I had the right to, because of

her. I realized I could only be free of her by
facing her."

"I never realized how the marriage would
affect the two of you," Eva murmured. "At the
time it seemed to make a strange sort of sense.
Two families of good blood, ensuring that their
children would each have a suitable life's
partner . . . I felt relief, knowing that my daughter's future was taken care of, and that she would
someday have a title that everyone would
respect. Perhaps it would have been an accept-
able arrangement for any other child but Julia.
Unfortunately, I didn't know that my own family would be torn apart by the decision I acqui-
esced to. I didn't understand what a strong will
she had . . . *has*," she corrected with a rueful
smile.

"What is she like?" Damon heard himself ask
thickly.

"Julia doesn't resemble me, or her father . . .
it seemed that even as a child she relied on her
own opinions and judgment rather than defer to
ours. I wish she weren't quite so independent—I
don't believe that is a particularly useful quality
for a woman. But there is another side to her,
fanciful, passionate, and vulnerable. She has
infinite moods and interests. I've never found
her to be the least bit predictable . . ."

As Damon stared at Lady Hargate, his attention was caught by the glitter of jewels amid the
ruffles at her throat. She kept talking, but the
meaning of the words was suddenly elusive, all
sound muffled by the startled drumming of his
heart. He glanced away to keep from betraying
his thoughts, but an image burned brightly in

his mind, and sudden knowledge exploded inside him. He fought to keep his breathing steady.

She was wearing the ruby pin he had given Jessica Wentworth.

There was no other like it in the world, and no possible way Lady Hargate could have received it except . . .

It had been a gift from her daughter . . . Jessica Wentworth . . . Julia Hargate.

Chapter 5

It was difficult for Damon to keep from staring at the ruby pin. He had bought it for Jessica Wentworth, and he had taken pleasure in the idea that she might wear something he had given her. So many things were beginning to make sense . . . her elusiveness, her mysteriously absent husband, her instant recognition of the rare roses that had been a gift from her mother to his all those years ago.

Questions seared through his mind, followed by conclusions that made his mouth harden bitterly. Why hadn't she told him who she was? What kind of game had she been playing? He had thought she felt the same attraction for him that he had for her, but perhaps it was all an illusion. She was an actress, a skilled one. She must have planned to make him fall in love with her, while she laughed inwardly because he didn't know she was his wife.

His blood raced with anger and hurt pride. He could hardly wait to get his hands on her and throttle her for what she had put him through. Three years of fruitless searching, while she had been hiding in the most public place of all—the theater. He had imagined Julia Hargate as a fragile dove seeking refuge from the unbearable circumstances of her marriage, and instead she was a successful actress with a talent for deceit.

No wonder her family hadn't wanted to admit what had become of her. It was unheard of for a young woman of her fortune and breeding to turn to a life on the stage. Most of Lord Hargate's peers would sneer and call Julia a disgrace. All the same, Damon was aware of a sneaking admiration for her boldness. It had taken courage to accomplish what she had, surviving—no, prospering—with nothing but her own talent. She had made tremendous sacrifices and undertaken serious risks to attain her goal. Her disdain for the arranged marriage, and her desire to thwart her father's wishes, must have been formidable.

He had battled with the same feelings all these years—it was only that they had reacted differently to their circumstances. Julia had relinquished everything, her reputation, her security, and even her name. He, on the other hand, had assumed his father's position as head of the family, determined to control not only his own life but the lives of everyone around him.

Keeping his gaze on Lady Hargate's face, Damon felt an unwilling touch of pity for her. She seemed to be a kind woman, but ill-equipped to deal with her domineering husband and willful daughter. Lady Hargate stared at him questioningly, seeing that something had changed in his expression.

"I realize that Julia doesn't want to be found,"

Damon said with forced calm, "but this has gone on for too long. I have obligations that you aren't aware of. There are important decisions I must make, and soon. I've waited years for Julia to appear. I can't wait any longer."

Lady Hargate seemed flustered by his direct stare. "Yes, I understand. Lord Savage . . . if I can manage to send word to Julia, I will try to convince her to come to you."

Before Damon could reply, a new voice entered the conversation. "You will not!"

They looked up in unison at the man who entered the room . . . and Damon stood to confront his father-in-law, Lord Hargate.

"Edward!" Eva said, her complexion turning chalky with dismay. "I-I didn't expect you to return so early."

"How fortunate that I did," her husband replied, his face wreathed in brittle hauteur. "You should have refused to receive Lord Savage, my dear, until I was available to see him."

"I couldn't turn away Julia's husband . . ."

Edward Hargate ignored his wife's feeble protests and exchanged a long stare with Damon. The past two years had aged him greatly, turning his iron-colored hair into a distinctive silver-streaked mane. A web of fine lines had not softened his lean face, but had given it the appearance of time-weathered granite. His eyes were as small and black as olives, shaded by thick, unruly brows. He was a tall man with not an ounce of fat to spare, a man who clearly made stringent demands on himself as well as others.

"To what do we owe the pleasure of your

unexpected visit?'' he asked Damon in a voice saturated with sarcasm.

"You already know," Damon said curtly.

"You shouldn't have come. I believe I've made it clear that you will learn nothing about my daughter from us."

Damon kept his face inscrutable, in spite of the growing fury that spread through him. He wanted to leap on the older man and wipe the smug superiority off his face. Obviously Hargate felt no remorse for anything he had done, no matter whom he had hurt.

"This situation isn't of my making," Damon said in a low voice. "I have a right to know what has become of Julia."

The older man laughed harshly. "You don't want to know about the shame she has brought on all of us . . . herself, her family, and even you, her husband. Do what you wish about her—just don't mention her name in my presence."

"Edward," Eva said pitifully, her voice breaking. "I don't understand why things must be this way—"

"She chose this, not I," he said sharply, seeming unmoved by the tear that trickled down his wife's thin cheek.

Julia had been frozen in the next room, flattened against the wall by the door as she listened to the meeting between Lord Savage and her parents. Her instinct for survival prompted her to flee, she felt terribly vulnerable, as if one harsh word from her father would cause her to shatter. She was terrified to face him. But the need to see him, and force him to recognize her presence, drove her to act. Before she was aware of what she was doing, she launched herself through the doorway and strode into the receiving room.

At the sight of her daughter, Eva gasped in dismay. Lord Savage showed no reaction, save a sudden clenching of his jaw. Edward seemed thunderstruck by her appearance.

Coming to stand by her mother, Julia slid a hand over her mother's narrow shoulder. Perhaps it appeared to be a gesture of comfort, but in truth it was to give herself strength. The frailty of her mother's bones beneath her hand, and the knowledge that her father had contributed to Eva's unhappiness, whipped Julia's anger to new heights.

"How dare you show your face here!" her father exclaimed.

"Believe me, I wouldn't if there were any other way to see Mama."

"The two of you have been conspiring against me!"

Julia stared at him, noting the changes that time had made in him, the new lines on his face, the silver of his hair. She wondered if he could see that she had altered as well, that she had lost her sweet girlish softness and had now become a woman. Why had he been incapable of the fatherly tenderness she had always longed for? A few words of kindness from him, an expression of pride in her accomplishments, might have changed the course of her life. She wished to rid herself of the need for his love, had tried ever since she had left him . . . but something in her stubbornly refused to relinquish the last vestiges of hope.

The humiliating sting of tears rose to her eyes, and she willed them not to fall. "I was never able to please you," she said, staring at her father's stony face. "Is it any wonder that I finally stopped trying? No one is ever able to suit your high standards."

"You're claiming that I expected too much of you," her father remarked with a lift of his craggy brows. "All I ever asked was for your obedience. I hardly think that unreasonable. In return I gave you luxury, education, and, God forgive me, a well-titled husband."

"Do you know why I became an actress? Because I used to spend all my time imagining what it would be like if you loved me, if you cared a whit about what I thought and felt. I became so good at pretending that I couldn't live any other way."

"Don't blame me for your failings!" Edward cast a scathing glance at Damon. "I find it an amusing irony to see how perfect the two of you are for each other—both rebellious and ungrateful. Well, I won't interfere in your life again—and you will not interfere in mine. I forbid either of you to return here."

Instinctively Damon moved forward to stop the argument. But as he approached Julia, she jerked away with a startled sound and gave him a look of helpless appeal that stunned him. In that moment he realized that he understood her, perhaps more than anyone else ever would. She possessed the same futile combination of pride and longing that had driven him his entire life. She wanted to be loved, but she was terrified of surrendering her heart to someone else's keeping.

Damon's hand twitched at his side. He was on the verge of reaching for her, taking her away from the ugly scene. Words hovered on his lips, things he had never said to a woman before. *Come with me . . . I'll take care of everything . . . I can help you.* Before he could make a move, Julia turned and fled the room, her back straight and her fists clenched. After her exit, the room became eerily silent. Damon turned to observe that Lord Hargate seemed unmoved by the scene.

"Whatever my faults," Hargate said, "I never deserved a child like her."

A sneer pulled at Damon's lips. "I agree. She's far too good for you."

Hargate gave a disdainful huff. "Kindly remove your presence from my household, Savage." He gave a warning glance to his wife, indicating that the matter was far from over, and left the room in a few imperious strides.

Damon went to Lady Hargate, who had begun to look rather ill. He crouched by her chair. "Shall I call for a servant?" he asked. "Is there something you require?"

She responded with a bobbing shake of her head. "Please," she said in a faltering voice, "you must try to help Julia. She may seem very strong, but underneath—"

"Yes, I know," he murmured. "Julia will be all right. You have my word."

"How sad that it should come to this," she

whispered. "I always hoped that someday the two of you would find each other, and then . . ."

"And then?" he asked, his brows drawing together.

She smiled faintly at her own foolishness. "And then you might have discovered that you were right for each other, after all."

Damon repressed a sardonic snort. "That would have been a convenient resolution . . . but I'm afraid things aren't that simple."

"No," she said, looking at him sadly.

Julia entered her small house on Somerset with a mixture of panic and relief. She wanted to hide in her bed under the covers and find some way to erase today from her memory. As her housemaid Sarah approached, Julia instructed her not to admit any callers for the rest of the evening. "I don't want to see anyone, no matter how important it may seem."

"Yes, Mrs. Wentworth," the dark-haired maid said, accustomed to Julia's desire for solitude. "Shall I be helping you with your things, ma'am?"

"No, I'll undress myself."

After snatching a glass and a bottle of wine from the kitchen, Julia ascended the narrow flight of stairs that led to her bedroom. "My God, what have I done?" she muttered to herself. She should never have confronted her father—it had accomplished nothing, except that now Lord Savage knew who she was.

She wondered if Savage was angry with her. Yes, he must be . . . he must think that she had been trying to make a fool of him. What if he decided to retaliate? Julia sipped furtively at the wine. She would let several days pass before she faced Savage. By then his anger would have cooled, and perhaps they could have a rational discussion.

Moving like a sleepwalker, Julia entered the solitude of her bedroom. The walls were covered with a delicate print of sage and rose, complementing the large four-poster bed with its fluttering canopy of cool, pale green. The only other pieces of furniture in the room were a satinwood armoire and dressing table, and a chaise longue with a gilded frame and champagne velvet upholstery. A few framed engravings of actors and play scenes hung on the walls, as well as an original page of one of Logan Scott's plays, his gift to her after her first success at the Capital.

She moved around the room, taking comfort in the familiar objects, possessions she had provided for herself. No trace of her past was here, no unpleasant reminders . . . only the safety and privacy of being Jessica Wentworth. If only she could have the past day to live over! What self-destructive impulse had caused her to reveal her identity to Lord Savage?

She remembered the way he had looked at her just before she had left the Hargate estate. His gaze had seemed to pierce through her, and it had seemed that her every thought and emotion was clear to him. She had felt as helpless as a child, all her secrets revealed, her defenses destroyed.

Julia sat at her dressing table and finished the wine in a few gulps. She wouldn't let herself think about Savage anymore . . . she needed to sleep, and prepare herself to face the rehearsal tomorrow for Logan's new play. She couldn't let her professional life suffer because of her private problems.

She stripped off her clothes, dropped them to the floor, and donned a simple blue muslin dressing gown that fastened up the front with five satin ribbons. Sighing in relief, she pulled the pins from her hair and combed her fingers through the disordered ash-blond locks. As she picked up a copy of *My Lady Deception* and began to climb into bed, a sound disrupted the quiet of the house. Julia went still and listened alertly. The muffled tones of an argument filtered to her room from downstairs, and then she heard the housemaid's distant cry of alarm.

Julia flung aside the pages in her hand and rushed from her room. "Sarah," she called anxiously, hurrying to the stairs. "Sarah, what is it—"

She halted at the top step and saw the maid standing in the center of the entrance hall. The front door was wide open. Lord Savage had just forced his way inside.

Julia's mind was wiped clean with alarm as she stared at the menacing figure below her. His face was taut, his eyes narrowed dangerously as he stared back at her.

"Mrs. Wentworth," the housemaid stammered, "he . . . he just barged in . . . I couldn't stop him . . ."

"I've come to talk with my wife," Savage said grimly, still looking at Julia.

"Your . . ." the maid said in confusion. "Then you must be . . . Mr. Wentworth?"

A scowl settled over Savage's face. "No, I'm not Mr. Wentworth," he said with biting precision.

Somehow Julia managed to adopt a calm expression. "You must leave," she said firmly. "I'm not ready to discuss anything tonight."

"That's too bad." Savage started up the stairs. "I've been ready for three years."

It was clear that he would allow her no choice. Julia braced herself for battle and spoke to the frightened-looking maid. "You may retire for the evening, Sarah. I'll be all right."

"Yes, ma'am," Sarah said doubtfully, staring at the purposeful man who was ascending the stairs. Quickly the maid disappeared to her room, evidently deciding it was wiser not to interfere.

As Savage reached her, Julia lifted her chin and returned his gaze. "How dare you force your way into my home," she snapped, gathering the dressing gown more closely around herself.

"Why all the lies? Why not tell me the truth the first time we met?"

"You lied every bit as much as I did, telling me you were unmarried—"

"I'm not in the habit of telling intimate secrets to women I barely know."

"As long as we're on the subject of intimate secrets . . . does Lady Ashton know you're not the bachelor you claim to be?"

"As a matter of fact, she does."

"I suppose she wants you to get rid of your wife and marry her for her baby's sake." Julia had the satisfaction of seeing his features turn blank with surprise.

"How do you know about that?" he asked sharply.

"Lady Ashton told me when we were both visiting the dressmaker's. She tried to warn me away from you—but I could have told her there was no need. You're the last man I would ever choose to become involved with."

"Whom would you prefer?" he asked, his tone jeering. "Logan Scott?"

"Anyone except you!"

"Why?" His head lowered, and his breath was hot against her cheek. "Because I frighten you? Because you can't help wanting the same thing I do?"

Julia tried to step back, but his hands came to her shoulders. Although his hold was firm, she could have broken free if she chose. Something kept her there, some potent force that wouldn't allow her to pull away. "I don't know what you're talking about," she said unsteadily.

"You felt it the first time we met . . . we both did."

"All I want is for you to leave me alone," she said, and gasped as he urged her against his hard body.

There was a glow of heat in his eyes, turning the cool gray to molten silver. "You're still lying to me, Julia."

She trembled in confusion as she stayed against him, intensely aware of his scent, the warmth of his hands, the feel of his burgeoning arousal pressing against her abdomen. The rise and fall of his chest matched her own labored breathing. She had been held by men before, but always in the context of a scene from a play, always in the theater. The well-rehearsed words and movements had never been her own. The feelings had been skillfully manufactured for the benefit of an audience. Now for the first time it was real, and she had no idea what to do.

Savage moved his hands over the thin sleeves of her gown, his touch sending a sweep of warmth from her shoulders to her bare wrists. He spoke against her cheek, his lips brushing her skin with each word, his mouth tantalizingly close to her own. "The night you came to my room at the Brandons' estate, I would have given a fortune to touch you like this . . . anything just to be close to you. I promised myself that nothing would stand in the way of having you."

"Nothing except a wife and a pregnant mistress," Julia said, while her pulse throbbed madly.

He drew his head back, his thick lashes lowering over the bright gleam of his eyes. "I don't know for certain if Pauline is pregnant. I don't know if she's lying, or what I'll do if she isn't." He hesitated and added gruffly, "All I know is that you're mine."

"I belong to no one." She managed to pull back, stumbling a little. "Please leave now," she said desperately, heading to the protection of her bedroom.

"Wait." Damon caught her just inside the door and turned her to face him. "Julia . . ." All the convincing speeches he had rehearsed were locked in his throat. He wanted to make her understand that he wasn't the kind of man he had seemed so far. How had his well-organized life suddenly become such a mess?

He reached for a lock of her unbound hair, a golden banner that lay over her shoulder and trailed down to her waist. He sifted it gently through his fingers. She waited without moving or making a sound, seeming possessed by the same sense of inevitability that gripped him. Incredible, that he had resented and denied her for most of his life . . . and she had turned out to be what he wanted most.

Damon slid his hand beneath the fall of her hair to the nape of her neck, his fingers and thumb curving around the downy surface. He felt her muscles stiffen beneath his touch. A faint protest escaped her lips as he pulled her closer, degree by degree, until her body was caught against his.

"This isn't right," she whispered.

"I don't care." Nothing outside this room mattered to him . . . the life he had so carefully built for himself, the things he had fought against for years . . . he pushed them all to the back of his mind. He pressed a hand to the small of her back, molding her against him until she shivered and made an inarticulate sound.

He waited for her to move next. Gently her hands came up to his head, her fingers winding in his hair. He needed only the slightest urging of her touch, and his mouth came to hers. Pleasure swept through him, flooding his nerves and senses. She was delicious, the curves of her breasts plumping delicately on the wall of his chest, her hips soft and neat as they fit against his. The smooth river of her hair flowed over his arms and hands, and he broke the kiss to clench a fistful of the shining locks and rub them against his cheek.

A sob escaped her, and she shivered against him. "I want to hate you," she said in a muffled voice.

Damon stared into her face and drew his thumbs over the velvety edge of her jaw. "I'm no saint, Julia. I've lied to everyone, even myself, but it's no different from what you've done. You made the best life for yourself that you could. So did I."

Julia felt tears spill from her eyes, the warm droplets immediately swept away by his thumb. It was a relief to be able to talk to him truthfully for the first time. "I didn't know you were trying to find me all these years."

"Why didn't you tell me who you were, that weekend at the Brandons' estate?"

"I was trying to protect myself."

"You liked having an advantage over me."

"No," she said instantly, though she felt a betraying rush of heat in her cheeks.

A grim smile touched his lips. "You never wanted to tell me the truth about who you really are, did you?" He read the answer in her deepening color. His hands moved down her body in a proprietary caress. "You won't dismiss me that easily, Julia."

She tried to pull back, but she was held in place by his hand at the center of her back, the other closing around the nape of her neck. This time his kiss was blatantly sexual, his tongue searching the softness of her mouth. Julia couldn't help responding, a moan of pleasure rising in her throat until she turned her face away abruptly, pressing her cheek to his shoulder. She was fully aware, as he must be, of the disaster they were courting. "Nothing can come of this," she said against the fabric of his coat. "I could never be the kind of woman you want. And you have responsibilities . . ."

"I've always had responsibilities," he said, his voice vibrant with frustration. "I've approached every relationship with the understanding that it could never last, that I couldn't offer a woman my name or any permanent attachment. Now that I've found you, don't tell me you're not what I want."

"What are you saying?" she asked with a miserable smile. "That you might not want an annulment? What could possibly come of a relationship between us? I'm not Julia Hargate any longer. I've turned myself into someone who is completely unsuitable for you."

"That doesn't matter."

"It will," she insisted, trying to wedge her arms between them. "You would want me to give up everything I've worked for, everything I need to be happy. You're not the kind of man who could stand to see his wife on stage, being courted and kissed and held by other men, even if it is only acting."

"Damn you," he said softly, "I can't stand it now." He crushed his mouth over hers, urgently seeking entrance, devouring and demanding until she had no breath, no will, no thought except the driving need to take him inside herself.

His fingers tugged roughly on the satin ribbons of her gown, until the muslin sagged over her shoulders, revealing the high, pale curve of one breast. He traced the round shape with his fingertips, leaving trails of fire that made her nipple ache. She arched closer, pushing her breast into his hand, gasping as his thumb toyed with the hard tip.

Julia was filled with recklessness. What if she let him make love to her? She owed nothing to anyone except herself. Surely by now she had earned the right to make her own choices, especially this one. She had always masqueraded in some role or another, as Julia Hargate, as Mrs. Wentworth, as a thousand different characters created on the page. But in this moment those identities had been stripped away, and she stood before him without pretense.

"I never give in to temptation," she said, her trembling hands coming to the sides of his lean face. "It's something I can't afford. Work, discipline, self-reliance . . . those are the only things I can rely on. I don't want to fall in love. I don't want to belong to anyone. But at the same time . . ."

"Yes?" he prompted in the silence.

"I don't want to be alone."

"You don't have to be alone tonight."

"Would you accept just one night from me? And then walk away when I ask you to?"

"I don't know," he muttered, not wanting to admit the truth.

A hopeless laugh escaped her as she admitted to herself that she didn't care. Suddenly nothing was as important as the need to be with him, to know all the intimate secrets that had been denied her so long.

Reading the look in her eyes, Damon pulled the dressing gown from her shoulders. The garment fell to the floor in a rustling heap. Julia didn't move as his absorbed gaze moved over her. She had never suspected that the sight of her body could affect him so powerfully, bringing a flush to his face and a tremor to his hands as he reached for her.

With the backs of his knuckles, he stroked the tender skin beneath her breasts and the fragile lines of her ribs, and then his palm swept over her abdomen. Her breath caught as she felt him touch the curls between her thighs, his fingers gently searching until she pulled away with a stammer and a shake of her head.

He followed instantly, his arms sliding around her back, and she heard the sound of his low voice in her thunder-filled ears. His mouth sought hers, and she opened to him, surrendering her hard-won control for the first time in her life. He took her to the bed, pushing her back against the cool green silk, and she pulled at the layers of linen and broadcloth that covered him.

"Julia," he said, his voice a mere scratch of sound, "if you're going to stop me . . . for God's sake, do it now."

Feverishly she pressed her lips to his jaw and throat. "I want to feel you," she whispered. "I want to feel your skin against mine."

Damon responded with a ragged breath and an obliging flurry of effort, stripping off his coat, cravat and shirt. As he reached for the opening of his trousers, her small hands pushed his aside. He forced himself to wait patiently, his desire flaring hotly as he felt the pluck and tug of her fingers on his clothing. She was gravely intent on the task as she slipped the heavy buttons of his trousers through their neatly stitched openings.

When the last button was freed, Damon sat on the edge of the bed to remove his shoes, trousers, and linens. There was silence behind him, and then he felt the moist brush of Julia's mouth at the top of his spine. He stiffened at the sensation, every muscle locking as a long chain of kisses followed the first, working from his neck to the middle of his back.

Her arms slid around his shoulders as she held him from behind, her naked breasts pressed against his naked back. A silken lock of her hair fell over his shoulder. She seemed like a curious mermaid discovering a man for the first time, her body drifting against his, her hands gentle on his skin. She touched the contours of his chest and paused to feel the heavy thud of his heartbeat against her palm. Venturing downward, her fingers grazed the tightly bunched muscles of his abdomen. Damon's eyes shut hard as he felt the timid clasp of her hand on the aching length of his staff. His shaking fingers came over hers, tightening her grip until the pleasure threatened to overwhelm him.

Turning, he pushed her flat on the bed, lowering his body over hers. Eagerly she pulled his head down, tangling her fingers in his hair as she kissed him. Filling his hands with her breasts, he covered the peaks with his mouth, his tongue bringing the aroused nipples to even tighter points.

Julia lifted against him, lost in the communication of their bodies. In the last few silent minutes she had become a stranger to herself, shamelessly yielding her body and soul to someone else's will. She wanted more, to bring herself even closer to him, to forget her own existence in the consuming tide of ecstasy.

His hands and lips moved skillfully over her body, spreading currents of sensation wherever they touched. His knee pushed between hers, and she felt his fingers between her thighs, discovering the hint of moisture amid the tiny springing curls. Her eyes flew open at the intimacy, and she flinched at the glow of light coming from the bedside lamp. She wanted to be hidden in the darkness.

"Please," she said in a faltering voice, "the light—"

"No," he muttered against her stomach. "I want to see you."

Julia tried to protest, but the words were strangled in her throat as his head moved lower. She felt his mouth drift lower, lower, through the soft thatch of hair, licking deep to find the secrets beyond. His tongue was hot on her flesh, making her twist and groan as if in pain . . . but it wasn't pain she felt; it was a rapture too piercing to comprehend. Her hands descended to his hair, trying at first to push him away, then curving around his head in supplication. She was seized by an endless shudder of pleasure, her senses unraveling in a white-hot glow.

Damon lifted his head and slid his body over

hers. Julia arched and sighed, letting him do
whatever he wanted. She was far beyond virginal modesty now, pliant and open to his every
desire. There was a heavy push between her
thighs, a forewarning of pain. She bit her lip at
the intrusion and wrapped her arms around his
back, wanting him to take her with a primitive
urgency that would startle her in later moments
of reflection. But Damon paused and held back,
staring at her with dawning incredulity.

"You're a virgin," he whispered.

Julia's arms tightened around him, her small
hands working at the small of his back, stroking
and kneading in unconscious encouragement.

"Why?" seemed to be the only word he could
manage.

Her eyes glittered as she looked up at him. "I
never wanted anyone before you."

Damon kissed her taut throat, her cheek, her
trembling lips. It seemed that his entire being
was filled with all the blind yearning he'd felt in
his adult life. In a decisive motion he shoved
forward forcefully enough to rend her innocence. She tensed in his arms, drawing a quick,
shocked breath. Damon hated the pain he
caused her, yet he discovered a fierce satisfaction
in possessing her as no man ever had. She was
impossibly tight, her sleek depths holding and
wrapping him in intense heat. He pressed a slow
rain of kisses on her face, mingling words of
praise and desire as he tried to comfort her.

Gradually Julia began to relax as she adjusted
to the unyielding invasion. He was gentle with
her, his hands playing over her body in unhurried exploration. She quivered as she felt him

slide deeper, thrusting in a slow rhythm that drew currents of delight through her body. Somehow the initial pain had been banished, replaced by the urge to lift high against him and take him even deeper inside. He complied with the wordless demand, driving straight and sure within her until she was caught in another surge of delight. She felt him grasp her hips, his fingers clenching over the rounded flesh, and he made a low, tormented sound as he found his own release. Shivering, Damon pressed hard against her until it seemed that their bodies had melded into one.

Julia was intensely drowsy for a long time afterward as she rested in the crook of his arm. Damon had extinguished the lamp, leaving them in peaceful darkness. She was halfway in a dream, her head filled with idle thoughts, her senses drinking in the warmth and texture of the man beside her.

She was no longer the figure of mystery that teased the public's curiosity, or an actress reciting well-rehearsed lines from a play . . . she had been cut adrift from the past that had bound her. Turning her head, she gazed at the hard-edged profile of the man beside her. Lord Savage, her husband. He would take over her life if she allowed it. He would keep her safe and sheltered, and inundate her with so much luxury that she would hardly mind being confined in a golden cage. But she would never let anyone own her. She had spent most of her life under her father's thumb, and that had been enough.

She would not lose herself in her husband's shadow as her mother had done. She would

Chapter 6

Damon awakened slowly, puzzled at finding himself in an unfamiliar bed. The elusive scent of a woman's perfume emanated from the pillow beside him. Still half-asleep, he pressed his face into the fragrant cream linen. Memories of the previous night came back to him, and he opened his eyes.

He was alone in Julia's bed.

Julia . . . she had never been more than a name to him, a shadow from the past, and suddenly she had become stunningly real. He saw the flecks of blood on the sheet, and he was instantly riveted. Wonderingly his fingers moved across the crimson marks. He hadn't considered the possibility that Julia might be innocent. He had never been with a virgin before, only mature women who were fully versed in all the aspects of passion. Sex had always been a frolic, a casual pleasure, not the transforming experience of last night. Julia was the only woman in the world who had belonged solely to him.

Why had she allowed him the privilege she had given to no one else? Certainly he was not the first man to desire her. She was lusted after by every man in London. Logically he searched for all possible reasons she had given him her virginity, with so many unanswered questions still between them, and he could think of none.

He wanted her back in bed, now. She had been so incredibly beautiful, so artless and trusting. He wanted to tease and comfort and caress her, to make her feel things she had never thought possible. And afterward, to hold her for hours as she drifted into sleep, and watch over her dreams. It had come upon him so suddenly, this obsession with her, the need to see her every day and night, and yet he knew in every fiber of his being that it was permanent. He couldn't imagine a future without her.

Throwing aside the bed linens, Damon prowled naked around the room, scooping up his discarded clothes. He dressed quickly and pushed the muted green curtains aside to glance out the window. It was still early outside, the morning sun beginning to ascend over the steeples and high-crowned rooftops of the city.

The small house was quiet except for the footsteps of the housemaid as she crossed the front entrance hall. Upon seeing Damon halfway down the stairs, she flushed and glanced at him warily.

"My lord," she said, "if you would care for some tea and breakfast—"

"Where is my wife?" he interrupted brusquely.

The maid backed up a step or two at his approach, clearly uncertain if he should be considered a madman or not. "Mrs. Wentworth is at the theater, sir. They have rehearsals every morning.''

The Capital. Damon was annoyed that Julia hadn't awakened him before she had left. He considered following her, and confronting her immediately. They had many things to talk about. On the other hand, he had certain matters to take care of, not the least of which involved Pauline. He scowled at the nervous housemaid. ''Tell Mrs. Wentworth to expect me tonight.''

''Yes, my lord,'' the girl replied, skittering back as he headed for the door.

It had been a hellish morning at the Capital. Julia knew she was performing badly at the rehearsal, and frustrating Logan Scott to no end. She had trouble remembering her lines. It seemed impossible to concentrate on the character she was to play, or give the other actors their proper cues. In addition to a blinding headache, she was sore in every part of her body—and more than everything else, her mind was filled with thoughts of last night and what she had done.

In a moment of recklessness she had made a terrible mistake. It had seemed so right to be with Damon. She had been lonely, vulnerable, craving the pleasure and comfort he had offered. In the harsh light of day, however, everything was different. She felt a terrible heaviness inside—her secrets were slipping away, flying out of her reach before she could snatch them back. Even the familiar atmosphere of the theater failed to soothe her. Perhaps now Damon believed he had rights over her. She must make it clear that no matter what had happened, she belonged only to herself.

"Don't make the mistake of thinking I can't replace you," Logan warned tautly under his breath as she stumbled gracelessly through yet another scene. "It's not too late for me to give the part to Arlyss. If you don't begin to show some interest in what you're doing—"

"Give the part to her, then," Julia said, shooting him a simmering glare. "At the moment I don't care."

Unused to such rebellion, Logan tugged wildly at his dark mahogany hair until it nearly stood on end. His blue eyes gleamed with annoyance. "We'll do the scene again," he said through gritted teeth. He gestured imperiously to the other actors onstage; Charles, Arlyss, and old Mr. Kerwin. "In the meantime, I suggest that the three of you go to the greenroom and study your lines. At this point I wouldn't rate your performances more than a notch or two above Mrs. Wentworth's."

The little group obeyed with a few grumbles, evidently relieved to escape the tension-fraught theater. Logan turned back to Julia. "Shall we?" he asked coldly.

Without a word she moved to the left wing, from which she was to make her entrance. The scene was one in which the two main characters, Christine and James, found themselves in the first throes of love. As the sheltered Christine, she was supposed to be enthralled by the freedom of her masquerade, pretending to be a housemaid. She was also dismayed by her attraction to a mere footman, but unable to keep from throwing caution to the wind.

She made her entrance, trying to convey something of the character's mixture of eagerness and uncertainty . . . until she saw the tall, appealing figure of James waiting for her. With a laugh of excitement, she rushed to him and threw herself into his arms.

"I didn't think you'd come," he said, whirling her around easily, letting her feet touch the ground. He brushed a curl from her face as if he couldn't believe she were real.

"I didn't want to," she replied breathlessly. "I couldn't help it."

With apparent impulsiveness he bent to kiss her. Julia closed her eyes, knowing what to expect. She had been kissed countless times on stage before, whenever a scene required it, by Logan, by Charles, and even once by Mr. Kerwin, who had played an aging monarch married to a young and beautiful bride. Handsome though Logan was, his kisses had never affected Julia. They were both too professional for that. It wasn't necessary to feel something in order to convince the audience of it.

She felt his lips touch hers . . . but suddenly the memory of last night flashed through her mind . . . the heat of Damon's mouth, the pressure of his arms locking her against his long body, the passion that had swept over her—

Julia tore away from Logan with a muffled sound, staring at him dazedly while touching her lips with trembling fingertips.

The character of James dropped away, and

Logan's familiar expression appeared. He seemed confounded, shaking his head slowly. A vibrant note of anger pierced his voice. "What the hell is the matter with you?"

Julia turned away from him, rubbing her arms agitatedly. "Aren't I allowed to have a bad day like everyone else? You're never this harsh with the others when they're having difficulties with a part."

"I expect more of you."

"Perhaps that's a mistake," she said sharply.

His gaze bored into her back. "Evidently it is."

She took a long breath and turned toward him. "Would you like to try the scene again?"

"No," Logan replied sourly. "You've wasted enough of my time today. Take the afternoon off—I'll work with the others. And be warned, if you're not in perfect form tomorrow, I'll give the part to someone else. This play means a hell of a lot to me. I'll be damned if I'll let anyone ruin it."

Julia lowered her gaze, feeling a stab of guilt. "I won't disappoint you again."

"You'd better not."

"Shall I tell the others in the greenroom that you want them back here?"

He nodded and waved her away, his face set.

Sighing, Julia walked from the stage into the wings. She rubbed her temples and eyes, willing her headache to go away.

"Mrs. Wentworth?" A young man's hesitant voice intruded on her thoughts.

Julia paused and looked toward the speaker. It was Michael Fiske, a scene painter of exceptional talent. Armed with his paint and brushes, he had created some of the most beautiful and original flats, set pieces, and backcloths Julia had ever seen. Other theaters had recognized Fiske's talent and tried to lure him away, forcing Logan Scott to pay him an unusually large salary to retain his exclusive services. With his usual confident bravado, Fiske had informed Logan and everyone else at the Capital that he was worth his high wages. Most of them privately agreed.

But Michael Fiske's normally cocky expression was gone today, and his manner seemed unusually hesitant. He stood in a shadow, holding a small, bulky package, his warm brown eyes beseeching. "Mrs. Wentworth," he repeated, and Julia approached him.

"Yes, Mr. Fiske?" she asked with a touch of concern. "Is anything wrong?"

He shrugged his wide shoulders and clutched his package more tightly. "Not exactly. There's something I wanted to ask you . . . if you wouldn't mind . . ." He stopped with an explosive sigh, his good-looking face creased with doubt. "I shouldn't have bothered you. Please, Mrs. Wentworth, just forget—"

"Tell me," she insisted with an encouraging smile. "It can't be all that bad."

Looking tragically resigned, Fiske extended the paper-wrapped package to her. "Please give this to Miss Barry."

She took the object from him and held it carefully. "Is it a gift for Arlyss? If you don't mind my asking, why can't you deliver it yourself?"

A flush covered his lean face. "Everyone knows you're the best friend Miss Barry has. She likes and trusts you. If you would give this to her, and speak to her for me—"

Understanding dawned on Julia. "Mr. Fiske," she asked gently, "do you have a romantic interest in Arlyss?"

Hanging his head, he made a gruffly affirmative reply.

Julia was touched by his evident sincerity. "Well, that's no surprise. She's an attractive woman, isn't she?"

"She's the dearest, loveliest thing I've ever seen," he blurted out. "She's so bloody wonderful that I can't bring myself to talk to her. When she's near, my knees turn to jelly, and I can't even breathe. And she doesn't even know I exist."

Julia smiled sympathetically. "Knowing Arlyss as I do, I'm certain she would prefer it if you approached her yourself—"

"I can't. It's too important. I've thought about telling her how I feel, but . . . she might laugh or feel sorry for me . . ."

"No, I assure you she's not like that," Julia said hastily. "Arlyss is very fortunate to have a man like you to care for her."

He shook his head, crossing and uncrossing his arms. "I'm not a fine gentleman," he said glumly. "I don't have fancy clothes or a grand home—and I've got few prospects. She won't want me."

"You're a good man, and a wonderfully talented painter," Julia said reassuringly, but inside she worried that he might be right. Arlyss had always been easily swayed by glittering promises and tempting presents. In the past few years she had gone through a string of jaded men who used her for their own selfish pleasures, and then discarded her with no remorse. And then there was Arlyss's hopeless crush on Logan Scott, who would certainly never give a thought to a relationship with her. Arlyss had made no secret of the fact that she was attracted to powerful men. If only she would fall in love with someone like Fiske, an earnest young man who might not ever be wealthy, but who respected and loved her.

"I'll give this to her," Julia said decisively. "And I'll speak to her for you, Mr. Fiske."

He managed to look relieved and despairing at the same time. "Thank you—although it's a hopeless cause."

"Not necessarily." Julia reached out to touch his shoulder consolingly. "I'll see what I can do."

"God bless you, Mrs. Wentworth," he said, and walked away with his hands crushed inside his pockets.

Wandering to the greenroom, Julia found the other actors conducting their own rehearsal. She gave them all a shamefaced smile. "Mr. Scott wants you back on stage. I'm afraid I've put him in a royal temper. My apologies to everyone."

"No need for apologies," Mr. Kerwin assured her, his jowls swinging as he chuckled. "Everyone has a difficult day now and then, even a fine actress such as you, my dear."

Julia smiled gratefully, and gestured to Arlyss as the others filed from the room. "Come here for just a moment—I have a gift for you."

"For me?" Arlyss's brow puckered. "It's not my birthday."

"It's not from me—it's from a secret admirer."

"Really?" Looking pleased and flattered, Arlyss toyed with her mop of curls. "Who is it, Jessica?"

Julia held out the package. "Open this, and see if you can guess."

Giggling in excitement, Arlyss snatched the parcel and tore the paper with childish glee. After the layers of protective covering were demolished, both women stared at the offering in delight. It was a small, exquisite portrait of Arlyss costumed as the Comic Muse, with luminous skin, rosy cheeks, and a sweet smile curving her lips. The interpretation was idealized, her figure painted a bit slimmer than in real life, her eyes a little larger . . . but it was unquestionably Arlyss. The skill and talent of the artist were remarkable, resulting in a delicately shaded work that captured the joyous essence of its subject.

"How wonderful," Julia murmured, thinking that Michael Fiske could have a future beyond mere scene painting.

Arlyss scrutinized the portrait with obvious pleasure. "It's too pretty to be me! . . . Well, almost."

Carefully Julia touched the edge of the gilded frame. "Clearly it was painted by someone who loves you."

Thoroughly perplexed, Arlyss shook her head. "But who?"

Julia stared at her meaningfully. "What gentleman do we know who can paint like this?"

"No one around here, except for . . ." Arlyss sputtered with an incredulous laugh. "Don't tell me this is from *Mr. Fiske?* Oh, dear . . . he's not at all the kind of man I usually take an interest in."

"That's true. He's honest, hardworking, and respectful—completely unlike the debauched men you've been complaining about for so long."

"At least they're able to provide for me."

"What do they provide?" Julia asked softly. "A few gifts? A night or two of passion? And then they disappear."

"I just haven't found the right one yet."

"Perhaps you have now."

"But, Jessica, a *scene painter* . . ."

Julia stared into her friend's sea-green eyes. "Be kind to him, Arlyss—I believe he truly cares for you."

The petite actress frowned uncomfortably. "I'll thank him nicely for the portrait."

"Yes, talk to him," Julia urged. "You may discover that you like him. Judging by his work, he's a man of depth—and he is rather good-looking."

"I suppose," Arlyss said thoughtfully. She gave the portrait a lingering glance and handed it to Julia. "I mustn't keep Mr. Scott waiting. Would you be a dear and put this in my dressing room?"

"Certainly." Julia crossed her fingers as Arlyss walked away. An ironic smile spread across her face. She had thought herself to be worldly, even cynical, but there was a part of her that was still irrepressibly romantic. She hoped Arlyss would find love with someone who would appreciate her, no matter what her faults, no matter what her mistakes in the past. Wryly Julia acknowledged that it would make her feel better to know that even if her own situation was miserable, at least someone else could be happy in love.

Pauline looked up from the mountain of packages on the carpeted floor of her mauve and gold bedroom. She was a fetching sight, surrounded by frothy piles of ribbon and tissue, her dark hair falling in sensuous disarray over her bare shoulders. Her lips parted with an inviting smile as Damon entered the room.

"You're just in time to see my new purchases," she informed him. "I had a delightful shopping expedition this morning." She stood and held a garment up to her breasts, a sheath resembling a thin, spidery web of gold. "Look, darling . . . it's meant to be worn over another gown, as an adornment, but when we're in private I'll wear it just like this."

Gracefully she pulled it over her head and let the glittering woven fabric slip over her body, at the same time allowing the gown underneath to fall away. The web of gold enhanced the rounded beauty of her body, doing nothing to conceal the dark triangle between her thighs or the rose-brown points of her erect nipples. Excitement shone in her velvety eyes, and she licked her lips as she approached him slowly.

"Make love to me," she murmured. "It seems forever since you've touched me."

Damon stared at Pauline without expression, finding it difficult to believe that he could be unmoved by a woman he had once found so arousing. "I didn't come here for that," he said, keeping his arms at his sides even as she purred and rubbed against him. "I want to talk."

"Yes . . . afterward." She caught his hand and tried to bring it to her breast.

Scowling, Damon pulled away. "I want to know the name of your doctor. The one who confirmed your pregnancy."

The sexual interest faded from Pauline's face, replaced by a defensive, perturbed expression. "Why?"

Damon gave her an unyielding stare. "What's his name?"

Pauline went to the bed, draping herself across the thick brocade coverlet. With catlike languor, she traced a pattern on the fabric with a single fingertip. "Dr. Chambers. He's a very old, trusted physician who has attended my family for years."

"I want to meet him."

"It's sweet of you to take an interest, darling, but there's no need—"

"Will you make the arrangements, or shall I?"

A blush swept over Pauline's skin, whether from guilt or anger he couldn't tell. "You sound so *accusing*. Don't you believe I'm telling the truth about the baby?"

"I believe this 'accidental' pregnancy has been damned convenient for you," he said curtly. "And I think it's time we stopped playing games."

"I've never played games with you—"

"Haven't you?" he interrupted with a jeering smile.

Abandoning her kittenish posture, Pauline sat upright. "I refuse to discuss anything with you when you're so cross!"

He stared at her coldly. "I want you to arrange for me to see Dr. Chambers."

"You can't order him about like a servant—or me either, for that matter."

"I believe I've paid for the privilege."

Making an enraged sound, Pauline threw a gold-embroidered cushion at him. It landed on the floor near his feet. "You needn't act so superior. It wasn't my fault that you made me pregnant, or that you're saddled with a wife you can't seem to locate. Have you made any progress on that score?"

"That isn't your concern."

"I have the right to know whether my child will be born a bastard!"

"I told you I would take care of you and the baby. I intend to keep that promise."

"That's a far cry from marrying me!"

"I was forced into a marriage of convenience by my father. I'll go to hell before I let you or anyone else do the same to me."

"So this has become an issue of what's been done to *you*?" Pauline asked, her voice rising. "What about what's been done to *me*? I was seduced by you, made pregnant, and now it seems you're planning to abandon me—"

"You were hardly an innocent girl from the schoolroom." A sardonic smile crossed Damon's face as he recalled Pauline's outrageous pursuit of him, the wiles she had used to lure him into her bed. And now she was going to claim that *she* had been seduced? "You're a wealthy widow with a history of liaisons dating back to before your elderly husband's death. I wasn't your first protector, and God knows I won't be the last."

"You're a cold bastard," she said, her lovely face twisting with a sneer. "Get out. Leave this very moment! I'm certain it's harmful to the baby for me to become this angry."

Damon complied with a mocking bow and left the volatile, perfumed atmosphere of the bedroom, wondering how he had ever allowed himself to become entangled with Pauline.

Realizing it was nearly time for him to meet with two stewards regarding concerns about his various estates, Damon went to his carriage and told the driver to take him to his London home. He didn't want to be late, having always prided himself on being punctual and responsible— qualities his gambling-obsessed father had never possessed. Although he tried to keep his mind on the business before him, thoughts of Pauline and her pregnancy kept intruding.

Damon trusted his instincts, which told him that the "baby" was merely an invention to entrap him . . . but he had to allow for the possibility that Pauline was telling the truth. He was swamped with resentment. Other men casually accepted the fact of having children with their mistresses, even joked about it, but for him it wasn't a matter that could be treated lightly. The child would be a lifelong responsibility.

Damon groaned and rubbed his eyes wearily. "There is no baby," he muttered in a mixture of hope and frustration. "She's lying—she has to be."

When he arrived at his home and walked through the front door, the butler informed him that the stewards were already waiting for him in the library.

"Good," Damon said brusquely. "Send in some tea, and a tray of sandwiches. I expect the meeting will last a while."

"Yes, my lord, but . . ." The butler reached for a small silver tray upon which a sealed note was poised. "You may want to read this. It arrived not long ago, delivered by a messenger who seemed in a great hurry."

Frowning, Damon broke the lopsided seal and recognized the hasty scrawl as that of his younger brother, William. His gaze moved rapidly over the page.

Damon—

In real trouble this time, I'm afraid. Have gotten myself into a duel to be held on the morrow. Request that you act as my second and give some much-needed advice. Please come to War-

*wickshire at once and save the skin of your only
brother.*

William

Damon's nerves were suddenly stretched taut
with worry. He was accustomed to William's
scrapes and mishaps, but nothing had ever come
close to this. "God, Will, what have you done
now?" A thunderous scowl settled on his face.
"Dammit, my brother must be the last man in
England to know that dueling is out of fashion."
He glanced up to see a glint of sympathy in the
butler's usually implacable eyes. "Apparently
William's done it again," he growled. "This time
he's been challenged to a duel."

The butler showed no surprise. The younger
Savage's reckless streak was well-known to
everyone in the household. "May I be of some
assistance, my lord?"

"Yes." Damon nodded in the direction of the
library. "Tell those two that I've been called
away on an urgent matter. Have them reschedule
the appointment for next Monday. In the meanwhile, I'm going to write a note to be delivered
to Mrs. Jessica Wentworth, of Somerset Street.
She is to receive it this afternoon, without
delay."

A cool, misty September breeze swept
through the tiny garden in the back of Julia's
house. Her loose hair was ruffled and disordered
by the wind, and she pushed it over one shoul-

der. Surrounded by the heady scents of rosemary, wild peppermint, and other fragrant herbs, she sat on a small white bench and opened the letter that lay in her lap.

Dear Julia—

Unfortunately my plan to see you tonight has been altered. I must leave immediately for the Savage estate in Warwickshire to take care of an urgent piece of business concerning my brother, Lord William. I will visit you immediately upon my return to London.

> *Yours,*
> *Savage*

Almost as an afterthought, a last sentence had been added to the bottom of the page.

I have no regrets about what happened between us—I hope you feel the same.

Troubled by the tersely worded note, Julia reread it and frowned unhappily. A sense of uneasiness crept over her. Certainly that last had been intended as some sort of reassurance, but she didn't know if it had the effect of causing her relief or dismay. She began to crumple the letter, but instead found herself holding it tightly against her midriff.

Lord William Savage, the brother-in-law she had never met. She wondered if the lad were really in trouble, or if he served as a convenient excuse for Damon to avoid seeing her. Despite his words to the contrary, it was possible he *did* regret spending the night with her. Perhaps it was the conventional thing to tell a woman one had no regrets, even if the opposite were true.

Flushing with shame and uncertainty, Julia wondered if she had displeased him somehow, if he had found her to be less passionate and exciting than Lady Ashton. She hadn't known what to do or how to satisfy him. Perhaps he considered the experience disappointing or, worse, amusing. Damon must have expected to go to bed with an experienced lover, not an awkward virgin.

Julia grimaced and silently berated herself. She had to remind herself that she wanted an annulment, that she could never give up her career and her independence, and live under the thumb of a strong-willed man. It would be a good thing if she *had* displeased him—that way he would agree to end their marriage with no qualms.

The pale golden walls of the Warwickshire castle, looming high and serene over the countryside, gave no clue to the turmoil within. The sun was just setting in the sky, casting long shadows across the ground and striking off the glittering diamond-paned windows of the medieval structure.

Damon had lived here most of his life, forgoing the pleasures a young man could find in London in order to stay with his mother during her final years. She had suffered the long, painful death of a consumptive, and he had suffered with her. He still remembered the many times he had glanced up from a book or paper he had been reading aloud to her, and found her anxious gaze on him. "Take care of your brother and

father," she had entreated him. "They will need
your guidance and protection. I'm afraid you are
all that will keep them both from utter ruin."
During the five years since her death, he had
done his best to keep his promise, although it
hadn't been easy.

Striding through the great hall and into the
large first-floor parlor, Damon discovered his
brother sprawled on a damask-upholstered
couch with a glass of brandy in his hand.
Judging from his bloodshot eyes and disheveled
appearance, it appeared that William had
spent most of the day there, nursing his sorrows
with the help of a healthy portion of strong
drink.

"God, I'm glad you're here," William said
fervently, struggling up on the couch. "I half-
thought you'd stay in London and leave me to
my fate."

Damon regarded him with wry affection.
"Not likely, after all I've invested in you."

Moving over to make a place for him, William
let out a morose sigh. "I've never dueled before.
I wouldn't care to start now."

"I don't intend for you to." Damon frowned.
"What was Father's reaction?"

"Everyone has conspired to keep him from
finding out. With his health so precarious, it
would finish him off for certain if he were to
hear of it."

Damon shook his head in disagreement.
"Aside from his bad business sense, Father's no
fool. He would rather know the truth than have
everyone tiptoe around and keep secrets from
him."

"You tell him, then. I can't bring myself to heap such worry on the head of a dying man."

Rolling his eyes, Damon sat beside his younger brother, plucking the glass of brandy from his hand. "Leave off the spirits," he advised. "It won't do any good for you to get drunk." He looked around for a small table to deposit the half-finished brandy. Finding none conveniently close, he downed the last few swallows himself, closing his eyes at the smooth, pleasant glow of the liquor.

"That was mine," William said indignantly.

Damon gave him a warning glance. "I needed refreshment after my journey. Now why don't you tell me what the hell you've done to get in this mess? I had better plans for tonight than having to come get you out of another predicament."

"I don't know exactly how it happened." Bemusedly William dragged his hands through his rumpled black hair. "It was such a little thing. Last night I went to a dance held by the Wyvills, a simple country affair . . . I waltzed with young Sybill, and we slipped out into the garden . . . and the next thing I knew, her brother George was challenging me to a duel!"

It wasn't difficult for Damon to read between the lines. The Wyvills, a well-landed and titled family of Warwickshire, were notorious for their bad dispositions. From what he recalled, Sybill couldn't be more than sixteen or seventeen. Any offense to her would be taken as a mortal affront to the family honor. "What did you do, Will?" he asked in a threatening tone.

"All I did was kiss her! It was nothing—hardly worth risking my neck over, I can assure you! George and I have never gotten along. I suspect he was spying on us merely to have an excuse to challenge me—the hotheaded bastard—"

"Let's save the name-calling for later," Damon interrupted dryly. "The only way to solve this is to approach old Lord Wyvill. He rules the family with an iron fist, and he's the one who can put a stop to the whole affair if he chooses."

William's blue eyes widened hopefully. "Will you talk to him, Damon? If you could convince him to make George withdraw the challenge—"

"First I want the truth. Are you certain all you did was kiss Sybill?"

William didn't quite meet his gaze. "For the most part."

Damon scowled. "Dammit, Will, with all the doxies and barmaids between here and London, why did you pick a sheltered girl to molest?"

"I didn't molest her! She was staring at me all soft and doe-eyed, inviting me to kiss her, and when I did, she most definitely reciprocated . . . and then George came leaping out of the bushes like a madman."

"And Sybill, not wanting to earn the censure of her family, claimed complete innocence and said you had lured her out there and attempted to seduce her."

William nodded vigorously. "Yes, that's exactly what happened. And don't look at me as though you were never tempted by a pretty young innocent before! Hell, you probably did the same thing at my age."

"At your age I was trying my damnedest to keep the family from sinking beneath a mountain of debt. I had little time to dally with girls like Sybill Wyvill."

His brother crossed his arms defensively. "I may not be as saintly as some, but I'm not as bad as others."

Damon smiled darkly. "An appropriate family motto for the Savages."

After washing and changing his clothes, Damon went to the Wyvill estate, located just a few miles from the castle. In spite of a substantial fortune, the Wyvills lived in a quaint country manor half-buried in a grove of silver birch and rhododendron bushes. Wearing an appropriately sober demeanor, Damon asked the butler to give his regards to Lord Wyvill and perhaps allow him a few minutes to visit. The butler disappeared and returned shortly thereafter, then took him to the library.

Lord Wyvill, who was only a little older than Damon's father Frederick, was seated in a large leather-upholstered chair before a small fire, his feet extended toward the crackling blaze. Having met Wyvill many times before, Damon knew that he was an ambitious, self-important man with boundless pride in his children. Sybill was his only daughter, and he had made no secret of his plans to secure a splendid match for her. Only a duke or an earl would suffice, not to mention a man with a fortune as impressive as his bloodlines. Damon doubted that William was what Wyvill had in mind for a son-in-law.

Wyvill lifted a pudgy hand in a gesture for Damon to sit in the chair beside him. The firelight danced in a wavering gleam over his balding head. "Savage," he said in a deep voice that sounded incongruous coming from a man of such short stature. "I see your brother—the insolent scoundrel—has summoned you to protect him. Well, this is one time you won't be able to spare him. He has acted dishonorably, and he must answer for it."

"I understand your feelings, sir," Damon replied gravely. "It appears that William has indeed gone too far. However, in the interests of your daughter's welfare as well as your son's, I came to ask you to stop the duel. George will withdraw his challenge if you demand it."

"And why would I do that?" Wyvill asked, his round mouth pursed with anger. "My precious Sybill, a naive and innocent girl, has been ruined, her reputation *besmirched*—"

"By one kiss?" Damon asked, raising one brow. "Isn't that putting it a little too harshly? A beautiful girl, a moonlit garden . . . surely anyone can understand how William lost his head."

"He should never have been alone with my daughter in the garden, insulting her on my own estate, no less!"

"Yes, I know. I give you my word that William will make amends in any way you choose, if you will convince George to withdraw his challenge. Surely we can come to some other arrangement. I'm certain you are as reluctant as I to have bad blood between our families. Moreover, if the duel takes place tomorrow, Sybill's reputation will suffer. What is only a small, easily forgotten incident at the moment will become a scandal. Rumors will follow her wherever she goes." Damon carefully watched the other man's face as he spoke, seeing with satisfaction that he had scored a point. If Sybill were the focus of a scandal, it would become much more difficult for her to marry well.

"What kind of 'arrangement' do you have in mind?" Wyvill asked suspiciously.

Damon hesitated and met the other man's gaze. "That depends on what would satisfy you. Would it solve the matter if William were to offer for Sybill?" It was a suggestion he felt safe in making, knowing that Wyvill had greater ambitions than to marry his daughter to a second son.

"No," Wyvill said, his double chin wagging as he shook his head. "Your brother has neither the means nor the character I am seeking in a son-in-law." He paused for a long moment, and a crafty look came over his face. "However . . . I have an alternative to suggest."

"Yes?" Damon watched him intently.

"As far as I'm concerned, honor will be satisfied if *you* marry Sybill."

Damon felt his eyebrows crawl up to his hairline. He had to clear his throat several times before he could reply. "I'm flattered," he said hoarsely.

"Good. I'll call for Sybill, and you may propose to her at once."

"Lord Wyvill, I . . . have something to confess." All at once Damon was struck by the humor of the situation, and he felt a treacherous laugh rising in his throat. Somehow he managed to keep it from erupting. "Sybill is a lovely girl, I'm certain, and in any other circumstances . . ."

"But?" Wyvill prompted, scowling like a bulldog.

"I can't marry your daughter."

"Why not?"

"I'm already married."

For a long time there was no sound except for the small, snapping fire. Both men stared into the dancing flames, while Wyvill mulled over the extraordinary statement. After a while he spoke, his voice heavy with suspicion. "This is the first I've heard of it."

"It's been a well-kept secret for quite some time."

"Who is she?"

"Lord Hargate's daughter, Julia."

"*Hargate*," Wyvill repeated, his short brows arched like two question marks. "I heard she was sent to a school in Europe—either that or dispatched to a convent. What has been going on all this time? Been hiding her in your attic or dungeon, have you?"

"Not exactly."

"Then why—"

"I'm afraid I can't explain the particulars, sir."

Looking sourly disappointed, Wyvill accepted the statement with as much grace as possible. "Pity. You would have done well to marry my Sybill."

Damon did his best to assume a regretful expression. "I'm certain of that, Lord Wyvill. But as for William—"

The other man waved the issue away disdainfully. "I'll tell George there will be no duel. Let's just say that you owe me a favor to be determined at some future date."

Damon let out a barely perceptible sigh of relief. "Thank you, sir. In the meantime, I'll remove William from Warwickshire to defuse any remaining tensions.''

''That would be appreciated.''

They exchanged a cordial goodbye, and Damon left the room with a sense of relief. As he crossed the threshold, he heard Wyvill mutter to himself, *''Hargate . . .* no daughter of his could ever *hope* to equal Sybill.''

After telling William the good news, Damon was tempted to go immediately to his room and fall asleep. It had been a long day, and he needed some private time to rest and reflect. However, there was still a duty he had to attend to. Squaring his shoulders, he headed to his father's suite of rooms. He hoped that the duke had already retired for the evening, but as he neared the bedroom door, he saw a light burning from within, and heard a woman's voice reading aloud from a novel.

Knocking lightly on the half-open door, Damon pushed his way inside. Although his father, Frederick, had suffered from a series of brain hemorrhages that had left him partially disabled on his right side, he had retained much of his vigor. He had the coarsely handsome looks of a philanderer, a man who had enjoyed more than his share of worldly pleasures and had never regretted a moment of it. He loved to recount stories of his past debauchery to the many friends who still came to visit him regularly and reminisce about their youth.

Propped up on a pile of luxurious pillows, a glass of steaming milk in his hand, the duke seemed entirely comfortable. It was difficult to tell which he was enjoying more, the novel or the charms of the attractive young nurse who sat at his bedside. The woman paused in her reading, and the duke looked up expectantly.

"I've been waiting," his father said, his voice slightly slurred from his physical condition. "Why didn't you . . . come earlier?"

"I had something to take care of." Damon paused and added darkly, "A matter involving William."

"Again?" The duke always enjoyed listening to tales of his youngest son's escapades, clearly feeling that he and William had a great deal in common. "Tell me." He gestured for the nurse to vacate the chair she occupied.

As the nurse left the room, Damon sat by the duke. "You look well," he commented.

"Yes, I'm quite well." Frederick reached behind his pillow, withdrew a silver flask, and poured a liberal amount of brandy into his hot milk.

"You never change," Damon said ruefully, shaking his head as his father offered the flask to him.

The duke seemed momentarily disappointed by his son's refusal of the brandy, then shrugged in resignation. "Neither do you." He downed a large swallow of brandy-flavored milk and smacked his lips. "Now . . . about William?"

As matter-of-factly as possible, Damon enlightened him on the events of the past two days. As Damon had expected, the account seemed to entertain Frederick vastly. At first he seemed mildly displeased, but that was soon replaced by a misplaced sense of masculine pride.

"Foolish, self-indulgent boy . . ." the duke said, chuckling. "William has the morals of a tomcat."

Damon scowled. "Is his behavior any surprise, after the example you set for him all these years?"

"Ah . . . here it comes," Frederick said resignedly, gesturing with his half-finished milk. "Try to lay this at *my* door, will you?"

It had always infuriated Damon that his father was so unrepentant, so completely unwilling to accept responsibility for his actions. "I'm concerned that William is following in your footsteps," he muttered. "He appears to have the same tastes for whoring and gambling as you."

"And if he does? What is the worst that could happen to him?"

"He could end up being shot in a duel, or owing a fortune in debt."

His father regarded him with maddening indifference. "I shouldn't worry about debt. The money always comes, one way or another."

"How well I know." Damon was filled with bitter sarcasm. "It came easily enough to you eighteen years ago, didn't it? You brought the family to the brink of poverty and gave Lord Hargate the perfect opportunity to sail in with the offer of a large dowry. All you had to do was marry your seven year-old son to his daughter, who was barely out of nappies at the time."

Frederick sighed and set his empty glass on the bedside table. "You may blame me for anything you wish . . . including William's predicament and your own dissatisfaction with life. I have no doubt I wasn't the father I should have been. But the fact is, I did what I had to do. Why must you dwell on the past instead of looking toward the future?"

"Because for years I've had to dispose of your messes, and now it appears I'm to do the same for William—and I'm damned tired of it!"

"I suspect that in a way you rather like it," the duke said mildly. "It makes you feel superior to conduct your life with all the propriety and responsibility that William and I never seem to attain." He yawned and settled back against the pillows. "Heaven help poor Julia when you do find her. I'm afraid no wife will ever be quite straitlaced enough to suit you, even if she is a Hargate."

Damon opened his mouth to argue, but shut it suddenly as an echo of Julia's voice ran through his mind. *What could possibly come of a relationship between us? . . . I've turned myself into someone who is completely unsuitable . . . You would want me to give up everything I've worked for, everything I need to be happy . . .*

The duke smiled slightly as he saw the troubled expression on his son's face. "You know I'm right, don't you? Perhaps what you need is to take your example from William. A man should have a few weaknesses . . . otherwise he becomes a deadly bore."

Seeing that his father appeared to be tiring, Damon stood and slanted a look of exasperation at him. There were few times in his life when the duke had actually bothered to dispense some advice to him, and none of it had ever made sense. "I'll visit you again in the morning before William and I leave."

Frederick nodded. "Send the nurse in to attend me." He paused and added thoughtfully, "You know, you remind me of Lord Hargate in his youth. He was just as self-controlled, and every bit as determined to make everyone else conform to his notions of what was right."

Damon was momentarily outraged, revolted at the idea that any similarity could be drawn between him and Lord Hargate. But at the same time, he couldn't help but wonder if there were any truth to it. Even more disturbing was the possibility that Julia would agree. Was he so rigid and domineering that she feared he would make her life into a repetition of her childhood?

All of a sudden he was fiercely impatient to return to London and make Julia understand that he wouldn't try to change her, or take anything away from her . . . but was that true? He couldn't guarantee that he would easily accept her career, the theatrical world she occupied, or her stubborn independence. Perhaps the best thing was to set Julia free . . . but that seemed to be the most impossible choice of all.

Chapter 7

❧ ❧

The opening night of *My Lady Deception*, Logan Scott's newest play, had attracted a crowd of stunning proportions. Aristocrats had sent their servants to obtain and hold seats for them hours before the performance was scheduled to begin. The house nearly burst at the seams with the eager crowd. In the shilling gallery, where the cheaper seats were located, people argued and erupted into fistfights to defend their territory against determined encroachers.

Safely removed from the pandemonium below, Damon and William watched from one of the private boxes on the third-circle tier. A female singer employed to entertain the house labored to make herself heard above the din. "What a mob," William commented. He regarded Damon with a curious half-smile. "It's not like you to insist on coming to the opening night of a play. Why now?"

"I'm a patron of the Capital," Damon replied neutrally. "I want to see how well my investment was used."

"The word is that this play is very good," William assured him. "But I wish you had allowed me to bring a female companion or two. It seems a pity to waste the pair of empty seats in our box. I happen to know the most delightful twin sisters, both of them redheads—"

"Haven't you done enough skirt-chasing for one week?" Damon interrupted, shaking his head ruefully.

A grin spread across William's face. "I thought you knew me better than to ask such a question." When his older brother didn't return his smile, William's expression softened with concern. "Thinking of Pauline?" he asked. During their trip to London, Damon had told him all about the supposed pregnancy and his demand to have Pauline's condition confirmed by a physician. "I wouldn't worry," William said pragmatically. "It's a safe bet that Pauline is lying. She knows that if she can make you believe she's pregnant, you're the kind who'll feel honor-bound to marry her."

An ironic smile twisted Damon's lips. "I'm not as honorable as you may think."

"You've never done a selfish thing in your life. You've made sacrifices for the well-being of the family that I would never—"

"Whatever I've done, it's been for purely selfish reasons. It's all been for my own gain, my own protection, so that I would never again be forced to do anything I didn't want."

William sighed and nodded. "It always comes back to that damned marriage to Julia Hargate, doesn't it? Let's try to forget about her for one night, brother, and enjoy the play."

"I'm afraid that's not possible. The reason I insisted on coming here tonight is to see her."

"To see whom?" William shook his head as if he hadn't heard correctly.

Damon didn't bother to elucidate, only stared at him with the shadow of a smile on his lips.

"Do you mean . . . Julia is *here . . . tonight?*" William laughed incredulously. "No, you're trying to make me look the fool—"

"I've found her," Damon replied calmly, enjoying the astonishment on his brother's face. "I know where she's been hiding and exactly what she's been doing these past two years."

William raked his hands through his black hair, disheveling the thick black locks. "My God, I can't believe . . . how did you find her? Have you spoken with her yet? Why didn't she—"

Damon lifted his hand in a silencing gesture. "Wait. You'll understand soon."

Spluttering, shaking his head, William stared at the crowd around and below them, as if he expected Julia Hargate to leap out of her seat and announce herself.

The female singer concluded her performance, curtsying in thanks at the scattered applause she received. After she left the stage, the orchestra was silent for a minute as the musicians readied their next piece. They broke into a lively melody that heralded the beginning of the play. Gradually the house lights on the sides of the theater were dimmed. Waves of excitement rolled through the pit and galleries, while the applause and cries of anticipation spread to the boxes and proscenium seats.

Damon imagined Julia waiting in some offstage area, listening to the eager roar of the crowd, knowing what they desired and expected of her. It filled him with a strange mixture of pride and jealousy as he realized that the audience of nearly two thousand, rich and poor alike, were all clamoring to see his wife. Mrs. Jessica Wentworth had been the subject of songs, poetry, paintings, and engravings. Everyone was enchanted with her talent, her face and form. Men wanted her, and women fantasized about what it would be like to be her, a beautiful and acclaimed actress with all of London at her feet.

He wondered if Julia would ever be willing to give up such universal adoration for the quieter rewards of marriage and family. What could he offer that would be preferable to this? Wealth meant nothing to Julia—she had proven that by relinquishing her own family fortune in favor of her freedom. And the love of one man must pale in significance to the love of thousands. Troubled by his thoughts, Damon sat frowning at the stage even as the curtain parted to reveal a spectacular oceanside scene. The backcloth was painted to resemble a sparkling blue sea, and delicately painted flats had been erected to resemble an elegant home on the shore.

A single figure strode onto the stage, a slender woman swinging her hat by its ribbons as she stared dreamily at the rippling water. It was Julia—Jessica—steadfastly remaining in character despite the tumultuous applause that greeted her. Other actresses might have acknowledged the wild response of the house with a pretty curtsy or a wave, but Julia continued to maintain the illusion, waiting patiently for the noise to subside. She was ethereally beautiful in a light blue dress, her blond hair falling in long curls down her back.

"Ravishing creature," William said enthusiastically. "What I wouldn't give to sample her charms!"

"Not while I live," Damon muttered, sliding him a meaningful look. "She's mine."

William seemed startled by the comment. "Do you mean you've made her your mistress? Don't you think it would have been wise to get rid of Pauline first?"

"No, she's not my mistress. She has a greater claim on me than that."

"I don't understand. Damon, she's not . . ." As William stared at his older brother, a strangled laugh of disbelief escaped him. "My God, you're not implying that *she* . . . no." He shook his head. "*No*," he repeated in wonder, glancing rapidly from Damon's face to the woman on the stage. "She couldn't be . . . Julia Hargate? How is that possible?"

"Her father disowned her when she left home and turned to a life on the stage. She reinvented herself as Jessica Wentworth."

William spoke in a rapid undertone, his gaze locked on the stage. "By God, I think you're the luckiest bastard who ever lived. And furthermore, you should kiss Father's *feet* for arranging a marriage with her—"

"Things aren't that simple," Damon said grimly. "Do you suppose I'm in a position to claim her as my wife and drag her off to the castle in Warwickshire?"

"Well, there is the matter of Pauline to consider—"

"Pauline is the least of it. Julia has no desire to give up the life she has made for herself."

William was mightily puzzled. "Are you saying that Julia wouldn't want to be your wife? Any female in her right mind would aspire to marry a man with your title and fortune—"

"From all appearances, she already has what she wants."

"A life in the theater?" William asked skeptically.

"She's an independent woman with a successful career."

"A woman preferring a career to marriage?" William said, looking offended at the very idea. "It's unnatural."

"Julia wants to make decisions for herself—hardly surprising after being managed and manipulated by Lord Hargate all her life."

"I could understand it if she were a bluestocking or a hag . . . but a woman with her looks and breeding . . ." Confounded, William concentrated on the scene unfolding before them on the stage.

More characters made their entrances, a heavyset old man who garnered many laughs as Julia's socially ambitious father, and a small curly-haired woman as her personal maid. Soon a tall, blandly handsome suitor also appeared. He was intent on courting the aristocratic miss and also winning the approval of her father. A light conversation ensued, laced with charm and social satire.

Julia, in the character of Christine, exuded a mixture of sweetness and loneliness, clearly desiring more than the narrow confines of her life allowed. The next scene showed her in search of an adventure, daring to pose as a housemaid and venturing into town without a chaperone. Another skillfully painted backcloth and several set pieces were revealed, simulating a bustling seaside community.

Seeming lost amid the busy street merchants and townspeople, Christine wandered across the stage until she accidentally bumped into a tall, mahogany-haired man. Even before Logan Scott turned to reveal his face, the theater audience knew who he was, and burst into wild applause. His reception was as fervid as the response Julia had garnered, the shouts of approval and clapping hands lasting for a full minute or more. Like Julia, Scott chose to stay in character, waiting until the sound faded.

There was a tangible attraction between the two as they spoke. Every line of Julia's body was tense with wariness and curiosity. Logan Scott described himself as a servant to a local lord, but an appreciative laugh ran through the audience as they suspected that the identity was a ruse. Inexorably drawn to each other, the two made tentative plans to meet again, in secret. From then on the story took on a brisk momentum, at once romantic and lighthearted.

Glancing at his brother, Damon saw that William was watching the play with rapt attention. The skill of the actors made it nearly impossible to think of anything else. The supporting cast was strong, and Logan Scott was as talented as always, but Julia was undeniably the heart of the play. She was like a flame dancing across the stage, mysterious and vibrant. Every gesture seemed miraculously natural, each rise and fall of her voice filled with poignant meaning. She was the woman every man imagined himself falling in love with someday, desirable and infinitely difficult to possess. If Julia hadn't been a renowned celebrity before tonight, this performance would have ensured it.

It made the back of Damon's neck prickle with jealousy as he watched Julia and Logan interact as two lovers. He gritted his teeth each time they touched. At the moment they kissed, the theater was filled with wistful and envious sighs, while Damon longed to leap onto the stage and tear them apart.

During the temporary lull of a scene change, William turned to Damon with a speculative expression. "Do you suppose that Julia and Mr. Scott—"

"No," Damon snapped, fully aware of what he was thinking.

"It certainly *seems* as if they are."

"They're actors, Will. They're supposed to behave like two lovers—that's the point of the story."

"They're very good at it," came William's dubious reply.

The remark fanned the flames of Damon's jealousy, and he struggled to keep it under control. This was what it would be like, married to an actress. There would be doubts and resentment, and constant incentives to argue. Only a saint could withstand it—and God knew he was far from that.

Julia was filled with excitement and a calm sense of purpose as she waited in the wings for her next entrance. Gingerly she blotted the mist of sweat from her forehead with her sleeve, careful not to smear her makeup. The play was going wonderfully well, and she sensed that she was accomplishing everything she had hoped to in the part of Christine.

The laughter and enjoyment of the audience were invigorating, lending the performances of all the actors an extra sparkle. One of her favorite scenes was approaching, the one she and Logan had performed at the Brandons' weekend party. She and "James" would discover their true identities, with a blend of comedy and longing that she hoped would make everyone in the house laugh, and would touch their hearts at the same time.

Sensing a presence behind her, she turned and saw Logan nearby, his face crossed with shadows in the dimly lit wings. She smiled at him, arching her brows in silent question, and he winked at her. He hardly ever winked. "You must be pleased," Julia said dryly. "Either that or there's something in your eye."

"I'm pleased that you haven't let your personal problems interfere with your acting," he murmured. "You're giving a fairly decent performance tonight."

"I never said I was having personal problems."

"You didn't need to." Logan turned her to face

the expanse of stage that lay just beyond the wings. "But *that* is the only thing that matters. The stage will never fail you, as long as you give yourself to it completely."

"Don't you ever tire of it?" Julia asked softly, staring at the long wooden boards, weathered from thousands of foot marks and scuffs left by scenery. "Don't you ever want something you can't find here?"

"No," Logan said at once. "That's for conventional people—something you and I are not." Hearing his cue, he moved past her and strode onto the stage in character. Frowning, Julia held a fold of a soft velvet curtain and stroked its worn softness. She stepped forward to gain a better view of the scene in progress, and saw Arlyss waiting in the wing opposite her. They exchanged a grin and a little wave, both of them sharing pleasure in the play's success.

There was a hot, pungent smell in the air, the familiar scents of paint, sweat, and the calcium flares used to light the stage. But there was a new, nearly undetectable addition to the mix. Frowning curiously, Julia looked past Arlyss to the backcloth and flats. Nothing seemed out of the ordinary, but a sixth sense told her that something was wrong. Troubled, she turned to some of the crew nearby, a group of scene shifters and carpenters preparing for the next change of sets. She wondered if they too had the sense that something was off-kilter, but they seemed unperturbed.

All of a sudden, Julia caught a whiff of smoke. A throb of panic went through her body. Wondering if it was her imagination, she inhaled more deeply. The smell was stronger this time. Her heart slammed in her chest, and her thoughts turned into chaos. Fire had destroyed the theaters in both Drury Lane and Covent Garden eighteen years before. The death toll was frequently heavy in such situations, not only from the fire and smoke, but also from the panic that ensued in a crowded building. People would be crushed and trampled, even if the fire was quickly brought under control. Her cue was approaching—she had to tell someone—but where was the fire if she couldn't see it?

As if in answer to her silent question, the flat on stage right erupted into flames. It must have been overheated by a carelessly positioned lamp or flare, the blaze traveling greedily across the paint-coated surface. The actors on stage froze in sudden awareness of the disaster, while screams shot through the audience. "My God," Julia whispered, while members of the crew shoved past her with a volley of curses.

"Sweet Jesus," William exclaimed, staring spellbound at the blaze that had begun on the side of the stage. "Damon—we have to get out of here!" The boxes above, below, and around them were bursting in pandemonium as the audience realized what was happening. People fought frenziedly, pushing and shoving each other in the savage battle to escape the potential deathtrap. Women screamed in horror, while men brawled and pummeled to forge a path through the riot.

Damon stared at the blaze onstage, realizing it would be a miracle if they contained it. The water reservoirs built above the stage appeared to be of little use, despite the crew's frantic efforts to douse the fire. Red flames snaked along the painted flats and shot across the backcloth, sending scraps of scenery curling and blazing to the stage. Through the smoke and the rain of fire, Damon could see Julia's slender form arching and bending as she plied a water-soaked cloth to beat back the flames. He was filled with terror and fury. She had remained behind with the male cast and crew to combat the fire. "Damn you, Julia!" he shouted, the sound lost in the frightened roar of the crowd. All conscious thought was consumed in the need to reach her.

Running from the box, he made his way to one of the twin grand staircases that led to the main theater hall on the first floor. The stairs were packed with the writhing, screaming mob. William was at his heels, following him as he launched himself into the melee. "Let's try the side entrance," William panted. "Less crowded than the front."

"You go that way," Damon said over his shoulder. "I'm heading back inside."

"For *what*? For Julia? She's surrounded by a dozen people who are perfectly capable of taking care of her. By the time you reach the stage, she'll be outside . . . and you could very well be trapped!"

"She won't leave," Damon said hoarsely, staying close to the railing and shoving his way down a few more steps.

William grunted with the effort to follow him. "Anyone foolish enough to stay in that furnace deserves what they get!" He swore as he realized

Damon wasn't listening to him. "I'll be damned if I go with you! Unlike you, I don't have a heroic bone in my body."

"I *want* you to leave."

"No," William said in outrage. "With my luck you'll perish in the fire . . . and then *I'll* have to be the responsible eldest son . . . Hell, I'd rather take my chances in here."

Ignoring his brother's complaints, Damon continued to the bottom of the stairs, vaulting over the railing when there were only a few feet left. William followed him into the swarm, toward the doors that led to the pit and orchestra seats. It was nearly impossible to make way through the violent flow of the crowd, but they managed to travel a few feet at a time until they were in the middle of the bedlam. The air was rife with wholesale panic.

Leaping over rows of seats in an effort to reach the stage, Damon caught a glimpse of Julia. She was beating out flames with a vengeance, trying to stop them from spreading to the curtains. Crew members worked nearby to remove flammable ground pieces and collapse the flats before the blaze could reach the frontispiece of the stage and the scaffolding above. Yearning to throttle his wife for placing herself in such danger, Damon scrambled around the orchestra pit and hoisted himself onto the stage.

Half-blind from smoke and fumes, Julia beat at the yellow flames that tore across the scenery, while bits of burning ash stung her arms. Her breath burned in her raw throat, escaping in angry sobs of denial. The theater must not be destroyed—it meant more to her than she had realized. She was dimly aware of Logan nearby, working desperately to save the only thing that mattered to him. He wouldn't survive the loss of the Capital—he would stay there even if it burned to the ground.

Her arms trembled with exhaustion, and she felt her body swaying as it was engulfed in blasts of heat. She heard warning shouts from somewhere nearby, but she didn't pause in her battle to smother the flames that had begun to eat at one of the side curtains. Suddenly she was hit hard around the middle, her waist and sides compressed by a force that drove the breath from her. Flinching from pain and shock, she couldn't make a move to defend herself as she was dragged across the space of several yards. There was a cracking, whooshing sound in her ears, mingling with the heavy throb of her pulse.

As she pushed a lock of sweat-soaked hair from her eyes, Julia realized that the crew had collapsed the flat on stage right. She had been standing directly in its path. Someone had pulled her out of harm's way, the same person who was now beating at her skirts, his hand descending with bruising *thwacks* against her thighs and calves. Coughing, struggling for air, she tried to evade him before realizing with a thrill of horror that bits of burning residue from the backcloth had set her costume on fire.

When the material of her skirts was extinguished, her rescuer stood up, his face looming dark and furious over hers. Silhouetted against the background of fire and smoke, he looked like the devil. His bronzed face gleamed with sweat, his broad chest lifting as he took in deep, gulping breaths.

"Damon," she said, her lips feeling numb as they formed his name. He seemed ready to kill her. His hands clamped around her, and he began to yank her off the stage in spite of her protests.

"Jessica?" She heard Logan Scott's voice from nearby. He paused in his efforts to contain the fire, his eyes narrowed to slits as he glanced from her to Damon. "For God's sake, get her out of here!"

"My pleasure," Damon muttered.

Wincing at her husband's painful hold on her, Julia allowed him to usher her offstage to the greenroom. "This way," she managed to say, before she was overtaken by a spasm of coughing. She led him through the back of the theater, pausing only when she sensed that someone else was with them. She turned to get a hasty glance of a man who bore a startling resemblance to Damon. It could only be his brother. "L-Lord William?" she stammered.

"Yes, it's William," Damon said impatiently. "There'll be time for introductions later. Let's go."

Scowling at his high-handedness, Julia went to the door opening onto the street. She nearly collided with a small figure bolting back inside. It was Arlyss, bubbling over with relief and panicked excitement. "Jessica!" she exclaimed thankfully. "When I realized you weren't outside, I had to come back and find you . . ." She paused as she saw the two tall, dark-haired men behind Julia. A droll smile lit her face. "It seems you've already been rescued. Now I see that I should have stayed inside the theater and waited for help myself!"

William stepped forward, gallantly offering his arm to escort her. "I admire you for having the sense to leave immediately, Miss . . ."

"Barry," she said. Her bright gaze missed no detail of his elegantly tailored clothes and dark, handsome looks. "Arlyss Barry."

"Lord William Savage," he said, introducing himself with a flourish. "At your service, Miss Barry."

Rolling his eyes, Damon pulled Julia outside into the cool, fresh air. Annoyed by his rough treatment, she jerked away from him as soon as her feet touched the pavement. "There's no need to haul me around like a sack of barley," she snapped, heedless of the other people who milled around the small back street.

"You'll be fortunate if I don't do worse to you. Putting yourself in danger for no reason—"

"I wanted to stay!" she said heatedly. "I had to offer what help I could. If that theater burns, I'll have nothing!"

"You'll have your life," he pointed out, his tone scathing.

Another fit of coughing precluded a reply, but she managed to glare at him with watery, stinging eyes.

Staring at Julia's reddened face, her cheeks streaked with sweat and soot, Damon felt much of his anger fade. He had never seen anyone look so valiant and vulnerable at the same time. Managing to locate a handkerchief inside his coat, he went to her and began to wipe the grime and paint from her face. "Hold still," he murmured, sliding an arm around her when she tried to pull back. After a moment, he felt the rigid shape of her spine begin to relax. She lifted her face a few inches to allow him better access. Carefully he used a fresh corner of the linen square to blot her eyes.

"William," he murmured, aware of his brother's attempts to flirt with the curly-haired actress nearby, "try to locate our driver at the front of the theater, and tell him to bring the carriage back here."

"It would make more sense to hire a hackney," William said, clearly reluctant to leave Arlyss's company. "The street out front is probably crammed full of people, horses, carriages—it would be a miracle if I found—"

"Just do it," Damon said curtly.

"All right. All right." William looked down at Arlyss with a hopeful smile. "Don't go anywhere. Don't move from this spot. I'll be back soon."

Giggling in reply, Arlyss pretended to salute him, and watched admiringly as he strode away.

Julia looked up at her husband's expressionless face. "I didn't know you would be here tonight." Her nerves seemed ready to snap after the ordeal inside, yet even with the danger she had been in, and the sick worry about what was still happening inside the theater, she felt strangely comforted. There seemed to be no safer place in the world than there in Damon's arms.

The soft handkerchief continued to move over her face in gentle strokes. "I had no time to send a message," he said. "I collected William from Warwickshire and returned to London as soon as possible."

She shrugged in a show of indifference. "You could have stayed in the country. It didn't matter to me when you returned."

"It mattered to me. I wanted to see you—especially on your opening night."

Her lips twisted bitterly. The play was in ruins, and what would have been a significant step in her career had been obliterated by the fire. Worst of all, the theater—and all the dreams it had housed—might burn to ashes before the night was through. "Quite a show, wasn't it?" she said wearily.

"More than I bargained for," he admitted, a smile touching his lips. He seemed to understand what she was feeling, the fear and the aching awareness that life held such treacherous twists in store. It wasn't fair that after her hard work and sacrifice, everything could be destroyed so easily.

Julia stared up into his silver-gray eyes, struck by his calmness and strength, and the sense that he wasn't afraid of anything. He had saved her life tonight, or at the very least had kept her from harm. Why had he put himself at risk for her? Perhaps he felt he owed her his protection because she was technically his wife. "Thank you," she managed to say. "Thank you for . . . what you did."

He traced the trembling curve of her jaw with his thumb and the tip of his forefinger. "I'll never let anything happen to you."

His fingers seemed to burn her skin. She tried to lower her face, but he wouldn't let her. Emotion and sensation uncoiled inside, her body all too ready to respond to his touch. He was going to kiss her. It shocked her to realize how much she wanted it, how tempting it was to relax and yield to him. She had always been wary of strong-willed men, but in this moment it was a blessed relief to let him take care of her. "You have quite a sense of duty," she whispered. "But it's not necessary—"

"It has nothing to do with duty."

A new face emerged from the theater door. "Miss Barry! Thank God! I've been looking everywhere for you. Are you all right? Are you hurt in any way?"

Julia twisted to see Michael Fiske, the scene painter, rush toward Arlyss and impetuously take her by the shoulders. He was dirty and smudged, his shirt torn at the shoulder. Altogether, his appearance was exceptionally dashing.

"I'm perfectly fine," Arlyss told him, looking surprised and vaguely pleased at being the object of such fervent attention. "You needn't have worried, Mr. Fiske—"

"I couldn't live with the thought that you might have been harmed!"

"Mr. Fiske," Julia said, unable to keep from interrupting, "how is the theater? What is happening inside?"

Fiske kept his arm around Arlyss as he replied, and Arlyss seemed to be content with the arrangement. "The fire is under control now, I think. It looks as though some people have been hurt during the rush from the building, but so far I haven't heard of any deaths."

"Thank God." Julia was overwhelmed with relief. "Then after a few repairs, the Capital will be open again?"

"More than 'a few repairs,'" the scene painter replied ruefully. "Months of work, more like—and the devil knows where the money will come from. We're finished for most of the season, I'd say."

"Oh." Julia felt strangely disoriented, cut adrift from all sense of security. What would happen next? Would Logan decide to discontinue the actors' salaries for the rest of the theater season? She had some savings, but it might not be enough to last as long as she needed.

William's cheerful voice broke into her thoughts as he reappeared on the scene and addressed Damon. "The driver is going to bring the carriage 'round, brother. As for me, I'd rather not wait. I'm in the mood for a strong drink and a pretty wench to fill my arms." He glanced at Arlyss speculatively, reading the indecision in her face and the sudden wary defiance of the young man who held her.

"Miss Barry isn't that kind of woman," Michael Fiske said stiffly, keeping a protective arm around Arlyss.

The thoughts were clear on Arlyss's face as she looked from one man to the other . . . Fiske, so earnest and hopeful, and Lord William Savage, devilishly handsome and irresponsible. Slowly she worked herself free of Fiske's hold.

Julia felt a sinking dismay as she realized what Arlyss was going to do. The petite actress had never been able to resist a handsome lord, even when he clearly wanted nothing more than a night's entertainment from her. Silently Julia willed her friend not to make the wrong choice.

William arched a black brow as he stared at Arlyss, his blue eyes gleaming with wicked invitation. "Would you like to accompany me on an evening's revels, my pretty maid?"

Arlyss needed no further encouragement. With a regretful glance at Michael Fiske, she approached William. A saucy smile curved her lips, and she placed her hand on his arm. "Where shall we go first?" she asked, and William laughed. He murmured a farewell to Damon and took Julia's stiff hand in his, bending over it in a show of gallantry. "My deepest regards, Mrs. . . . Wentworth." He said the name in a way that let Julia know he was well aware of her real identity. Annoyed by his impudence, she did not return his smile.

Michael Fiske was expressionless, his gaze fixed on Arlyss as she walked away with William in search of a hackney to hire.

"I'm sorry," Julia said quietly.

Fiske nodded and summoned a brief, hopeless smile. A frown creased Julia's forehead as she watched him head back inside the building. She glanced up at Damon accusingly. "You could have said something to your brother. He should have left Arlyss in the company of a decent man who obviously cares for her!"

"The girl was free to make her choice."

"Well, she made the wrong one. I strongly doubt your brother has honorable intentions toward her!"

"I would say that's a safe assumption," Damon said dryly. "There's only one thing on William's mind—and your little friend made it clear that she was ready and willing to accommodate him." Catching sight of his carriage approaching, he nodded toward it in a decisive motion. "The driver's here. Come with me."

Automatically she shook her head. "I must go back inside and see—"

"There's nothing you can do here tonight. Come—I'm not leaving without you."

"If you're planning on having a repeat performance of the other night—"

"The thought had crossed my mind," Damon said, his eyes glinting with amusement. "But I wasn't going to insist on it. If you prefer, we'll merely have a drink and talk. I'll open a bottle of twenty-five-year-old French Armagnac—the best brandy you've ever tasted."

The offer was appealing, to say the least. It wasn't the brandy that tempted her, but rather the alarming need for his company, and the comfort he offered. She wasn't certain she could trust herself around him, especially not in her present mood. "I shouldn't."

"Are you afraid of being alone with me?" he asked softly.

Now it was more than an offer; it was a

challenge. Julia held his direct stare and felt the pull of recklessness inside. The night was in shambles, and she would face tomorrow when it came. For now, a bracing drink and the company of Lord Savage were exactly what she wanted.

Slowly she went to him. "I'm sure I'll regret this later."

He smiled and took her to the carriage, helping her inside. After a brief murmur to the driver, he climbed into the vehicle, occupying the space next to her. The carriage rolled away with a gentle sway, and Julia relaxed against the velvet seat cushions with a sigh.

She closed her eyes momentarily, but her lashes soon lifted as she sensed Damon's intent gaze on her. He was staring at the wrinkled, charred remains of her costume, a pale green dress that laced up the front with gold cords. Noting the way he lingered over her snugly fitted bodice, she frowned in reproval. "Must you stare at me that way?"

Reluctantly he dragged his gaze to her face. "What way?"

"As if you'd just sat down to supper and I was the entree." As he laughed, Julia crossed her arms defensively over her breasts. "One would think you'd be satisfied after the other night!"

"That only whetted my appetite for more." As Damon studied her, reading her discomfort, the hint of playfulness disappeared. He relaxed against the seat with deceptive casualness. "I know I hurt you that night," he said quietly. "It's always that way the first time."

A hot blush spread over her face. In a flash,

she remembered their naked bodies twisting together, the pain of their joining, the burning pleasure of being possessed by him. She had known what to expect, more or less, but she had never realized how closely such intimacy would bind them. It was unfathomable that some people could regard such an experience as casual . . . an experience that seemed to have changed her in a hundred indefinable ways. "It's all right," she murmured, unable to look at him.

"It will be better the next time."

The blush seemed to cover her entire body now. She knew he could see the warm color traveling over the soft skin of her throat and breasts. "There won't be a next time," she said breathlessly. "It would be wrong."

"Wrong?" he repeated, perplexed.

"Yes! Or have you forgotten all about Lady Ashton and her unborn child?"

His expression became closed. Even so, Julia sensed the frustration that welled up inside him. "I'm still not convinced there is a child," he said. "I'm trying to find out the truth. But even if Pauline *is* pregnant, I can't marry her. If I did, I would end up killing her."

For the first time Julia experienced a pang of sympathy for him. He was a proud man—he wouldn't take well to being manipulated by anyone, especially not a woman like Lady Ashton. Resisting the urge to touch him in consolation, she remained where she was, wedged in the corner of the carriage seat. "It must be difficult, dealing with such a situation—"

"I don't want to talk about Pauline tonight,"

he said abruptly. In a moment the hard look left his face, and there was a self-mocking twitch at the corner of his mouth. He fished inside his coat for something, and withdrew a small velvet pouch. "Here—I have something for you."

Julia stared at the gift, but she didn't move to take it. "Thank you, no," she said uncomfortably. "I don't want a present—"

"It's yours by right. You should have had it long ago."

Hesitantly she took the pouch and loosened the drawstring. Reaching in with two fingers, she withdrew a hard, cool lump from inside. Her breath caught as she beheld a magnificent ring, a rose-cut diamond set in a heavy gold band. The stone was at least four carats, almost blue in color, its facets flashing with unearthly fire.

"You never had a wedding ring," Damon said.

"I couldn't—"

"Try it on."

Julia longed to see how the diamond looked on her finger, but she didn't dare. The ring—and all it signified—was forbidden to her. Their marriage would not last. Their vows had been meaningless, the obedient mouthings of two children who had no idea what they were saying. She looked at Damon helplessly, both touched and appalled by his gesture. "Take it back," she said in soft pleading.

His mouth twisted wryly, and he reached for the ring. Before she could stop him, he caught her wrist and slid the diamond on the fourth finger of her left hand. It was only a little too loose.

Julia stared down at the glittering jewel in hypnotic fascination.

"It belonged to my mother," Damon said. "She would have wanted you to have it."

"Are you trying to bribe me?" Julia asked, lifting her hand to examine the huge stone.

"I'm trying to tempt you."

"And what will you demand in return?"

He was suddenly all innocence as he returned her gaze. "Consider it compensation for all you've had to endure because of our 'marriage.'"

"I'm not *that* naive," she said, sliding the heavy band from her finger. "You're not the kind of man to give something for nothing. Thank you, but I can't accept the ring."

"If you give it back to me, I'll toss it out the window."

She gave him a frankly disbelieving glance. "You wouldn't."

Damon's eyes were filled with a diabolical gleam, making her realize that he was indeed willing to cast the priceless stone into the street. "It's yours now. Do with it what you wish." He extended a hand, palm up, to receive the ring. "Will you throw it, or shall I?"

Alarmed, she closed her fingers around the priceless jewel. "I won't let you throw something this beautiful away!"

Satisfied, he lowered his hand. "Then keep the damned thing. Just don't give it to your mother." He laughed at the guilt in her expression, and watched as she slid the ring back onto her finger.

Julia was annoyed by the suspicion that her newfound husband was becoming adept at managing her. "You'll want something in return," she said pertly. "I know you well enough to be certain of that."

"I only want what you're willing to give." He drew closer, his gaze flickering over her. "Now . . . tell me what kind of relationship you envision for us, Mrs. Wentworth."

She damned the sudden awakening of her senses, the way her body jolted into acute awareness of him. He was so purposeful and confident, qualities she had always admired in a man. The fact that he wasn't part of the theater world made him all the more intriguing. There was nothing permanent in the life of a theater person. Like the Gypsies, they shared a superficial existence in which one production was always ending and another beginning. Until now she'd had little to do with a man like Damon.

"I suppose . . . we could try a sort of . . . friendship," Julia said tentatively. "There's no need for us to be at odds. After all, we both want the same thing."

"And what is that?"

"To be free of each other. Then I'll be able to continue my life in the theater, and you can fulfill your obligations to Lady Ashton."

"You keep mentioning her name . . . why is that?"

"I'm concerned, of course—"

"I don't think so. I think you're doing everything you can to put a wall between us."

"What if I am?" Julia parried, her voice unsteady. He was much too close, his hard thigh settled next to her own, his forearm braced on the upholstery above her head. It would be so easy to crawl into his lap and pull his head down to hers, to surrender to the pleasure of his hands and mouth. She took a deep breath and tried to still the nervous quivering inside. "Is it wrong to want to protect myself?"

"You don't need to be protected from me. Have I ever forced you to do something you didn't want?"

She laughed shakily. "Since we've met, I've been coerced into having dinner with you, given you my virginity, even accepted this ring in spite of my wishes not to—"

"I can't help it if you have a weakness for jewelry." He smiled as he saw the frustration in her face, and his voice lowered. "As for taking your innocence—that was a gift I never expected. I value it more than you know."

Julia closed her eyes as she felt his lips travel across her forehead, lingering on the fragile bridge of her nose. There were feather-soft touches on her eyelids and cheeks, and the brush of his mouth at the corner of her lips. Her own mouth tingled, and it took all her strength not to turn fully toward the light pressure, inviting the full, deep kiss she craved. "You were so sweet that night," Damon whispered. "And so beautiful. I've never experienced anything like it before. I can't stop remembering, and wanting you again."

Julia moistened her dry lips before she replied. "Just because you want it doesn't mean it's right."

"The last I heard, it wasn't a sin for a man to

sleep with his own wife." He drew his fingertips across the exposed skin of her chest, causing goosebumps to rise across the fine surface. Julia's breathing turned rapid and shallow. It seemed that all she could do was wait in suspended silence, her body taut with anticipation of what he might do. "So," Damon remarked softly, "you'd like to try a friendship with me. I have no objections to that." He pulled at the gold cord that held her bodice together until it gave way, the garment parting several inches in front. "In fact, I think we could become very close . . . friends." His warm mouth descended to her throat, while his hand slipped past her bodice and beneath the thin white chemise that covered her naked flesh.

Julia closed her eyes and gasped as she felt his long fingers curve over her breast, stroking, teasing until her nipple ached and hardened. Her body was flushed with heat, nerveless and weak with yearning. She murmured in protest as she felt herself being lifted, pulled into his lap, but any feeble objections were quickly silenced by his mouth. Hungrily she opened herself to his kiss, abandoning all shame, wanting more of the pleasure he offered.

The sway of the carriage broke their lips apart, and Julia sought another kiss, but he resisted. His mouth wandered in a new quest along the tender surface of her neck, down to the madly pulsing hollow of her throat. He found the exposed valley between her breasts and nuzzled deeply, while his fingers tugged at the fabric that covered them. A faint cry escaped Julia's lips as she felt him bite softly at the peak of her breast.

Her hands came to his head, holding him there, her fingers curling into his thick black hair. His tongue stroked and swirled over the sensitive point of her nipple, again and again, until she arched up to him with a moan. Moving to her other breast, he toyed with her leisurely, seeming to relish the small, helpless sounds she made.

When they were both breathing fast and hard, desire pounding through their bodies, Damon pulled her upright, his mouth at her ear. "Tell me you don't want this," he whispered fiercely. "Tell me you can see me, talk to me, without thinking about this . . . without needing me as much as I need you. And then tell me you want nothing more than friendship."

Trembling, Julia leaned against him, her naked breasts pressing into the fine linen and wool of his clothes. Her mind was strangely slow to form thoughts. "I do want you," she said with a small sob, afraid of her own needs, and the heartbreak that awaited her if she gave in to them. She must not let herself love him, or depend on him. That would give him the power to strip away all her strength and self-reliance. It would be worse than all the years of living with her dictatorial father. This man would own her very soul.

Damon pushed her long hair aside, kissed her bare shoulder, and clasped her close enough that she could feel the stiff shape of his arousal beneath her. Shivering, she pressed herself down on the hard length, fitting her softness against him until he groaned against her hair.

"Don't . . . or I'll take you right here." He

kissed her roughly, exploring her mouth in a storm of passion, and she answered his demand with one of her own.

The carriage stopped, and Julia realized that they had arrived at his estate. Tearing herself away, she retreated to the opposite seat and fumbled with her bodice. Her fingers were clumsy as she pulled the fabric together and tugged at the gold cord to tighten the lacing. When she had managed to restore a semblance of modesty, she looked up to find Damon's steady gaze on her.

"Come inside with me," he said. There was a tautness about his face and a banked glow in his eyes that made it clear what would happen if she accompanied him.

No, she cried inwardly, but somehow the word wouldn't come out. She wanted to be with him, wanted him to soothe the physical ache of her body, and give her the same peace and fulfillment she had experienced before. One more night with him . . . would it cause any more harm than had already been done? Ashamed of her weakness, overcome with temptation, she struggled with her feelings.

Damon made the decision for her, opening the carriage door and reaching inside. Her hand was caught in his, and she let him tug her from the vehicle. The footman rushed ahead of them to open the front door of the mansion, and they crossed the threshold into the quiet entrance hall. It must have been the servants' night off—there was no one in sight, and the place was dimly lit.

As soon as the door closed, Damon turned her

in his arms and kissed her, his mouth urgent as it descended over hers. Julia shuddered in pleasure and stood on her toes to fit herself against him, wrapping her arms around his broad shoulders. Damon moved his lips to whisper at her ear, something tender and erotic . . . but Julia stiffened as she saw a movement beyond him. Startled, she pushed at his chest and stared wide-eyed at the intruder. Turning his head, Damon looked as well.

A woman was coming down the stairs in a slow, deliberate saunter, her hips swaying gracefully. The folds of her thin gown, fashioned in transparent layers of peach, moved about her thighs and ankles like liquid. It was a seductive garment intended to ensnare a man's attention. She was barefoot, as if she had just arisen from bed and come to welcome unexpected guests.

"Pauline," Damon muttered, sounding stunned.

Julia eased away from him, unconsciously smoothing her skirts. Even with the hard look in her eyes, Pauline was extraordinarily beautiful, her hair dark and silky as it tumbled down her back, her eyes slanted like a cat's.

"I thought to surprise you, darling," Pauline said softly, seeming to be in utter command of the situation. "Little did I know that I would be the one surprised. I didn't expect that with everything so unresolved between us, you would be entertaining another woman tonight." She reached the bottom of the stairs and folded her arms, causing her cleavage to swell enticingly. Her cool, amused gaze fell on Julia. "What has happened to you, my dear? You look terribly bedraggled . . . and the two of you reek of smoke."

"A mishap at the theater," Julia replied shortly.

"Ah." Pauline looked back at Damon, arching her fine brows. "You've become quite a devotee of the theater lately, haven't you?"

"What the hell are you doing here?" he asked in a hard voice.

She looked wounded at his tone. One slim hand came to her stomach, reminding him of her delicate condition. "I thought we needed to talk . . . and since you wouldn't come to me, this seemed to be my only choice." She looked once more at Julia. "Do run along, won't you? Damon and I require some privacy. I'm certain you can find some other man to satisfy your needs tonight."

Julia's blood turned cold with fury and humiliation. She kept her face blank. "Certainly," she replied in a controlled voice. "I'd like to get as far away from both of you as possible."

"Wait," Damon said, reaching for her arm, but she jerked away.

A satisfied smile crept across Pauline's face. It appeared that she couldn't resist one parting shot. "Mrs. Wentworth . . . perhaps you think you're becoming quite close to Lord Savage, but there's much about him you don't know. I suspect that among the things he has omitted to tell you is one very relevant fact—he is already married."

Julia paused at the front door. "Yes, I know that," she said calmly.

Pauline seemed surprised, and then her face wrinkled with disdain. "My God, you have the morals of a cat in heat. To throw yourself at a man who is married to one woman and has made another pregnant . . . you're the most shameless creature I've ever encountered."

"Pauline—" Damon said in a murderous tone, but Julia interrupted evenly.

"Shameless? *You're* the one parading around a married man's home dressed in nothing but a peignoir." She burned to tell the other woman the truth, that *she* was the wife in question, and that Pauline certainly had no right to pass judgment on anyone.

Somehow managing to hold her tongue, Julia strode to the front door and tugged it open. She paused to give Damon a backward glance, but he appeared to be ignoring her, all his attention focused on Pauline. Jealousy shot through her. She couldn't decide if she was more angry with him or with herself.

Hurrying outside, Julia called to the footman. "Tell the driver to bring back the carriage immediately. I wish to leave now." As he hurried to obey, she rubbed her bare arms and began to shiver from the cool breeze. She thought of going home, but rejected the idea at once. There was someone she needed to see right now, the only person in the world who could restore her sanity and anchor her in reality.

Damon was silent for a long time, staring hard at Pauline until her victorious smile dimmed and she began to look uncomfortable. She spoke smoothly, making an effort to seem at ease. "I suppose I can't blame you for your dalliance with her, darling. She is rather attractive, albeit in a cheap, obvious way—"

"You shouldn't have come here." Until this moment he had never actively disliked Pauline. He had been suspicious, exasperated, angry with her, but he had never felt anything that bordered on hatred before. She seemed like a millstone around his neck, clinging with ruthless determination, dragging him down to a very dark, cold place. She brought out the absolute worst in him. He stiffened as she came to him, pressing her perfumed body against his.

"I couldn't stay away from you," Pauline murmured. "I've missed you so."

"Have you spoken to Dr. Chambers yet?"

Her elusive gaze darted from his. "Not yet, but I plan to very soon." Her silky arms began to wind around his shoulders. "In the meanwhile—"

"Then I'll make the arrangements." He pushed her back a step or two, breaking her hold on him. His handling of her was not rough, but neither was it gentle.

Pauline looked annoyed and alarmed. "You can't do that!"

"Why not?"

"Dr. Chambers is a very busy man—you can't order him about like a servant. And he won't discuss my condition with you unless I give my consent."

"You're playing games with me," he said with dangerous quietness. "I won't tolerate it."

She drew back, looking offended. "There's no need to be so threatening. I've never seen this side of you before, and I find it quite disagreeable."

"Disagreeable?" he repeated thickly. "There aren't words to describe the side of me you're going to see if I discover you've been lying."

She met his gaze directly. "I've told you the truth."

"Then produce a doctor for me soon, Pauline—one who'll stake his reputation on the fact that you're breeding. That's the only chance you have of keeping me from wringing your neck."

"You're in an ugly mood because I've thwarted your plans to bed that little theater whore tonight—"

"Not one word against her." A bolt of fury caused his voice to shake.

Although enraged, Pauline recognized the sincerity of his unspoken threat. For several moments she struggled to control her emotions.

"I understand that you want her," she finally said. "Perhaps as much as you once wanted me. But I will not step aside to make things easy for you. I will have what I want, what I am *owed*." She stared into his granite-hard face and softened her voice, her expression changing from sullen to cajoling. "It's not exactly a torment to be with me, is it? You've enjoyed my company in the past—that doesn't have to change. If our games in bed have begun to bore you, I'll invent new ones. I'll satisfy you in ways that most women would never dare—"

"It's over," he said coldly.

Her dark eyes widened. "Exactly *what* is over?"

"Our relationship—at least the way it has been."

"What about the child?"

"If you produce a baby within the next nine months, I'll decide what my responsibility is. If not, there will be no doubt that I'm *not* the father—because I'm not going to bed you, I'm not going to touch you, and God willing, I won't even have to see you."

"There is a baby," she said, each word snapped out like a whiplash. "You'll eat your words, Damon. You'll regret that you treated me this way."

"Perhaps." He took her by the arm in a painful grip and began to usher her upstairs. "In the meanwhile you're going to dress yourself and get the hell out of my house."

Chapter 8

"**T**ell the butler that I wish to see Mr. Scott," Julia said to the footman, stepping down from the carriage. "Tell him I regret that the hour is late, but this is an urgent matter."

"Yes, Mrs. Wentworth." The footman strode rapidly to the front door and alerted the butler inside to their arrival.

Julia followed slowly, her courage evaporating with each step she took toward Logan Scott's luxurious house in the quiet court suburb of St. James Square. The house was three bays wide and fronted with massive fluted columns that seemed designed to intimidate curious visitors such as herself. She had never been here before—Logan had all but forbidden the actors and crew of the Capital to set foot on the property.

As far as Julia knew, Logan rarely entertained at home. The few who had been privileged to visit hadn't breathed a word about the house or its occupant, respecting his wishes for privacy. It was his exclusive domain, this small estate, and it seemed to be covered by an invisible shroud of mystery. But she wanted to see him, and it didn't seem possible to wait until morning.

Logan was the closest thing to a mentor she had, and the problem she faced was too over-whelming to deal with on her own. There was no one else she could trust for sound advice. She wondered if Logan would eject her from the house at once, if he would be surprised at her unexpected appearance, or angry, or both. It was possible he would be amused by her dilemma, and mock her. She winced at the thought but forced herself to continue walking.

The tall footman who had preceded her was talking to the butler, who disappeared and re-turned shortly. The butler's training was evident in the complete lack of expression on his face, even when confronted with the sight of a shiver-ing young woman in a charred stage costume. "Mr. Scott will see you, Mrs. Wentworth," he murmured.

After dismissing the footman, Julia followed the butler inside. She hoped that she hadn't awakened Logan after he had already retired for the evening. Surely not—she couldn't imagine him sleeping after everything that had hap-pened that night. Her thoughts were distracted as she wandered through the house, hardly able to believe she was finally getting a glimpse of Logan Scott's private world.

The decor of the rooms was Italianate, with pieces of intricately carved furniture, painted frescoes on the ceilings, and pale marble busts. An air of lushness pervaded the place, every-thing polished and velvety and quietly understated. The upholstery and window hangings were all in rich shades of blue, gold, and plum.

They came to an intimate parlor where the furniture was piled with silk and velvet pillows, and small inlaid tables were laden with novels and books of engravings. Logan Scott rose from a chaise longue as Julia crossed the threshold. "Mrs. Wentworth," he said, his voice slightly hoarse. "How are you? No injuries from the fire, I hope?"

"I'm very well," Julia assured him. Her gaze traveled to the other occupant of the parlor, one of the most exotically beautiful women she had ever seen. She had creamy golden skin, straight black hair, and striking pale green eyes. The heavy silk robe she wore was belted tightly at a slim waist, revealing the shape of a lithe, long figure. Julia was fascinated by her. So this was the mysterious woman who was living with Logan. Was she more than a mistress to him, or merely a convenience?

The woman smiled at Julia and came to stand by Logan's side. "I will leave the two of you to talk," she said tactfully, and smoothed her hand over Logan's hair in a proprietary sweep before taking her leave.

Logan stared at Julia speculatively. His eyes were reddened from exposure to smoke, making the blue irises seem more unnervingly bright than ever. "Have a seat," he said, indicating a cushioned chair nearby. "Would you like a drink?"

"Yes, anything," Julia said gratefully, settling into the comfortable chair. He brought her a glass of pale amber liquid, which she identified as watered-down whiskey, smooth and slightly sweet. After pouring himself a glass of straight spirits, Logan sat nearby and stretched out his legs. Like her, he hadn't yet changed from his costume. It was in poor condition, stained with sweat and smoke, the shirt ripped in places, the trousers torn at the knee.

"How is the theater?" Julia asked hesitantly, sipping her whiskey. It wasn't a drink she particularly enjoyed, but she welcomed its bracing effect.

His face was shadowed with a frown. "It wasn't destroyed, but there are many expensive repairs to make. We'll have to cut half the number of shows I planned for the season, and take the rest on tour in the provinces. In the meanwhile, I'll travel back and forth to oversee the work being done on the Capital."

"Oh." Julia hated touring, the late hours, the poor food and dirty rooms. In the past they had taken a few shows on limited tours to places such as Bristol, Leicester, and Chester. It was tiring to deal with the crowds that usually waited outside her lodgings, and to bear the close scrutiny she received no matter where she went.

In spite of his obvious weariness, Logan smiled at her lack of enthusiasm. "No complaints," he murmured. "I'm not fit for sparring tonight."

Julia managed a wan smile in return. "Neither am I." Looking down at her costume, she toyed with a fold of her skirts. "The play was going splendidly tonight before the fire broke out. I'm certain it would have been well-reviewed."

"We'll take it to Bath next week."

"So soon?" Julia asked, raising her brows in astonishment. "But the backcloth and set pieces that were destroyed—"

"I'll have Fiske and the others improvise something. They can alter the sea-and-shore pieces we saved from *The Merchant of Venice,* and some of the cloths we used in other productions." He rubbed the bridge of his nose with his thumb and forefinger. "The fact is, we can't afford to delay our touring."

"Perhaps some benefit shows will raise extra funds to repair the theater," Julia suggested.

"I'll worry about the money. In the meantime . . ." He stared at her steadily. "Why are you here, Jessica?"

She sipped furtively at her whiskey. "I . . . need your guidance."

Logan waited for her to continue, exhibiting a patience that was unusual for him.

Julia inhaled and let out a long breath. "I'm having personal problems," she blurted out.

"I already guessed that. Go on."

"I'm not behaving at all like myself, I'm making choices that I know are wrong, and yet I can't seem to help myself. I'm afraid my work will suffer, but most of all I'm afraid of what I might do next—"

"Wait," Logan murmured, sorting through the babbling statements. "This has something to do with a man, I surmise. Is it Lord Savage by chance?"

"Yes."

"Of course." Sardonic amusement glinted in his eyes. "He's turned your life inside-out . . .

and now you think you're beginning to fall in love with him."

Julia disliked the way he put it, as if her feelings were merely a cliché and her distress unwarranted. Logan didn't understand the huge, cold knot in her chest, the loneliness that was driving her toward disaster. But she considered his statement seriously. The things she felt for Damon, the powerful physical attraction, the yearning for his company, the sense that they understood each other . . . A deep tremor went through her as she forced herself to face the truth. Yes, she was in love with Damon. Her eyes prickled with tears, and she hastily downed more of the whiskey until her throat stung.

"It's not something I want to feel," she said, coughing slightly.

"Of course not." Logan ruffled his mahogany hair and tugged absently at a gleaming forelock. "Have you slept with him?"

"That's none of your business!"

"You have," he said dispassionately, reading the answer in her affronted expression. "That explains a great deal. You're not the kind to give your favors easily. No doubt you have trouble distinguishing love from passion—and that's dangerous. Never indulge in an affair unless you're in complete control of it. If Savage seems to be more than you can manage, break it off with him. No matter how painful it seems at the time, it's the only wise choice."

"It's not that easy," Julia said.

"Why not?"

"Because . . . I happen to be married to him."

Were she not so miserable, Julia would have

enjoyed the sudden blankness of her employer's face. She hadn't expected that Logan, so worldly-wise and sophisticated, would have been quite so shocked by her revelation.

Choking on his drink, Logan required a moment to recover himself. "For how long?" he asked dazedly.

"Eighteen years."

Any attempt at self-possession was drowned in a fresh tide of bewilderment. "Jessica, you're not making sense—"

"We were married as children."

Looking fascinated and appalled, Logan set his drink aside. "Go on," he said softly.

Words came tumbling out as she told him about her past and the marriage that had burdened her for so long. She felt his unblinking gaze on her as she spoke, but she couldn't bring herself to look at him. It felt odd to be confessing the truth after two years of keeping her secret, but relief unfurled inside her as she confessed everything, leaving out only the part about Lady Ashton's pregnancy. For some reason that seemed too personal to tell him, leaving both her and Damon open to mockery.

At the end of Julia's monologue, Logan appeared to have composed himself somewhat. "Now that you've revealed all this, what do you want from me?"

"I suppose I want someone to tell me what to do. And don't say that I must make these decisions by myself, because I don't seem to be able—"

"Does Savage want to make a go of the marriage?"

"I'm not certain," Julia said cautiously. "I think . . . perhaps he might."

"I'll tell you my opinion. It's no good, Jessica . . . Julia. If you stay with him, you won't want to make the sacrifices he'll ask of you."

"I know," she whispered sadly.

"Moreover, I don't believe in love. At least not in the grand, passionate emotion we create for people on stage. That's an illusion, one that never lasts. People are intrinsically selfish. When they're in love, they make false promises to each other in order to get what they want. And after the love fades or is destroyed, all that is left are lies and disillusionment . . . and memories that keep you awake at night."

Julia was mildly surprised at the depth of his cynicism. "You seem to be speaking from experience."

Logan smiled without amusement. "Oh, I've had experience. Enough to understand the risks of trusting another person with your heart. It's never advisable, Jessica, especially for a woman."

"Why do you say that?"

"The obvious reason. In essence, marriage is nothing more than a business transaction. Law, religion, and society all dictate that you are your husband's property. Poetry and romance are a way of making it seem palatable, but only the young and the foolish are deceived by such things. You may decide that you love Savage enough to surrender your body and soul to his keeping . . . but I wouldn't advise it."

"What would you do if you were in my position?"

"I would consider finding a magistrate who will invalidate the marriage. That is, if it was legal in the first place. I'm certain it was based on a license obtained by perjury." A sudden smile crossed his face. "A remarkable pair of fathers the two of you have—almost Shakespearean in their greed."

"You can't imagine," Julia said dryly. She considered Logan's advice, so uncompromising and realistic. She had hoped that after talking to him everything would be clear . . . but she had just as many doubts as before. He seemed to be advocating a life of independence and complete self-sufficiency, but there was a price to pay for that. She didn't want to be alone forever.

"This is all very confusing," she said, more to herself than to him. "I don't want to leave the stage, and I value my freedom. But part of me longs to have a husband and a family, and a proper home—"

"You can't have everything."

Julia sighed. "Even as a child, I wanted the things that weren't good for me. In our parlor we used to have a silver box filled with sweets, and I was allowed to take only one on special occasions. But the sweets kept disappearing mysteriously, until my father began to accuse the servants of stealing them."

"It wasn't the servants," Logan guessed.

"No, it was me. I would sneak downstairs at night, and gorge on them until I was ill."

Logan laughed. "It's always that way with worldly pleasures. One taste is never enough."

Julia tried to summon an answering smile, but she was overcome with worry. She had never felt so uncertain of her own judgment, fearing that the life of pleasure and ease Damon could offer her would be too tempting to refuse. And then when she discovered her mistake, it would be too late. She would be bound to him forever. She would come to blame him as well as herself for her eternal discontentment.

"Perhaps it's not a bad thing for me to go on tour," she said. "I need to be away from here—from *him*—in order to think clearly."

"Go to Bath early," Logan suggested. "Leave tomorrow, if you like. I won't tell anyone where you are. For the next few days you can spend some time alone, sit in the Pump Room and take the waters, visit the shops on Bond Street . . . whatever you fancy. Take some time to contemplate your decision."

Impulsively Julia reached over to touch the back of his long-boned hand, slightly roughened with reddish-brown hair. "Thank you. You've been very kind."

His hand didn't move beneath her fingers. "I have an ulterior motive. You would be difficult to replace at the Capital."

Julia pulled back and smiled. "Have you ever loved anyone the way you love that wretched old theater, Mr. Scott?"

"Only once . . . and that was enough."

The interior of the Capital Theatre was damaged by the combined effects of fire, smoke, and water, but it wasn't nearly as bad as Damon had expected. Pushing past some broken seats that blocked his path, he walked from the back of the theater toward the stage. There were at least a

dozen men working beneath the ruined frontispiece, some of them perched on ladders to
remove tatters of charred scenery, others sweeping and clearing out rubble.

In the midst of the action, Logan Scott labored
to unroll a backcloth that must have been used
in a previous production. "Hold that while I
have a look at it," he ordered the scene painter
and a nearby assistant. Standing back, he
viewed the piece critically, folding his arms and
shaking his head.

Alerted to Damon's approach, one of the
crew members walked over to Logan Scott and
murmured in a quiet undertone. Scott's head
snapped around, and he regarded Damon with
a piercing gaze. His expression was at once
guarded and affable. "Lord Savage," he said
easily. "Is there something I can help you with?"

"I'm looking for Mrs. Wentworth." Damon
had been driven to come here after being informed by Julia's servants that she had left
London and would not be returning for a while.
They had refused to reveal more than that, in
spite of the bribery and outright threats he had
used.

"You won't find her here," Scott said.

"Where is she?"

Jumping down from the stage, Scott approached him with a cool, polite smile. He
lowered his voice as he spoke. "At present Mrs.
Wentworth doesn't want to be found, my lord."

"That's too damned bad," Damon said
evenly. "I'm going to locate her with or without
your help."

Scott's features could have been chiseled from

stone. He took a deep breath. "I have a fair idea of what's going on, Savage. It's not my right to disapprove. However, I've invested a great deal in Jessica—and the company needs her talents now more than ever. I hope you'll choose to respect her need for privacy."

Damon would be damned if he discussed his private life with Julia's employer. But the discomforting truth was that Scott had known Julia far longer than he had. She seemed to trust Scott, and she was grateful to him for having given her the opportunity to work at the Capital. Although she had indicated that their relationship went no deeper than that, Damon couldn't help but be suspicious. How could Scott not be attracted to a woman like Julia?

"Could it be that you have some other interest in keeping her away from me?" Damon asked with a sardonic smile. "Or do all theater managers exhibit such personal concern for their actresses?"

Scott was expressionless. "I consider Mrs. Wentworth to be a friend, my lord. And I will lend her my protection whenever it appears to be necessary."

"Protection against what? A man who could offer her something besides a life of spinning fantasies in front of an audience?" Damon cast a contemptuous glance at the scorched walls and singed curtains of the theater. "She needs more than this, whether or not either of you wants to admit it."

"Can you give her everything she wants?" Scott murmured.

"That remains to be seen."

Scott shook his head. "Regardless of the rights you seem to think you have over Jessica, you don't know her. Perhaps you intend to remove her from the world of the theater and give her substitutes, but she would wither like a cut flower."

"Spoken as a concerned friend?" Damon asked with deceptive idleness. "Or as a manager worried about his profits?" Although Scott didn't react visibly to the taunt, there was a sudden rigidity to his posture that told Damon he had hit his target.

"She means more to me than profits."

"How much more?" When met with silence, Damon laughed shortly. "Spare me your hypocritical concern over Mrs. Wentworth. Just don't interfere in my relationship with her . . . or I'll make you wish to God you'd never set eyes on me."

"I already do," Scott muttered, standing like a statue as he watched Damon leave.

The city of Bath had first been built by the Romans around a series of natural hot mineral springs. In the early 1700s, the area was developed by the Georgians into a fashionable resort, with sedate promenades and tall, elegant Palladian terraces. Now in its maturity, Bath was available not only to the *ton* but to the middle classes as well. They came to improve their health by drinking and bathing in the medicinal waters, and to renew cherished social acquaintances. Settled along the river Avon among a cluster of lush limestone hills, the city offered entertainment, shopping, and lodgings that ranged from merely comfortable to luxurious.

Walking toward the bath house and thermal spring near her inn, Julia watched the last of the sun's pink and lavender rays disappear behind the New Theatre. It was an elegant building that housed a fine stage and three tiers of boxes, all magnificently adorned with crimson and gold. Julia had been in Bath for a week, and during the last two days she had seen shipments of boxes filled with stage equipment arrive in preparation for the opening of *My Lady Deception.* Some of the crew and cast had also come to town. Logan had sent word that everyone must be fully assembled for tomorrow's rehearsal in preparation for the first performance on Thursday.

During her shopping expeditions and visits to the Pump Room, a magnificent building with Corinthian columns set within and without, Julia had overheard the local gossip concerning the play. Some claimed it was jinxed, and nothing would make them attend. Others expressed eager interest in the production. There was a fair amount of speculation about Mrs. Wentworth, which amused Julia as she sat nearby with a veil concealing her face.

It was necessary to keep her identity a secret. Years ago Julia had learned that she would never satisfy the expectations people had of her. Invariably they wanted her to be like one of the heroines she had played, complete with sparkling dialogue and flamboyant gestures. Even Logan Scott had complained that women desired—and sometimes demanded—that he play the romantic lover for them, just as he did onstage. "It's a common problem for actors," he had informed her. "People are always disappointed when they find out we're as human as they are."

When she reached the bath house, Julia entered the small building with its simple Grecian design, and nodded to the attendant who waited inside. Julia had made prior arrangements with the elderly woman that no one else would be allowed in the bath during her evening visit. It was the only way for Julia to enjoy an hour of peace without having to deal with gossip and questions and prying stares of curious women. Conveniently, few people ever wanted to visit the bath house during the unfashionable evening hours. It was believed to be more healthful—not to mention socially desirable—to bathe in the morning.

Julia left the antechamber and went through a warped wooden door into the bathing room. The surface of the water was as smooth as glass, reflecting the light of a single lamp mounted on the wall. Steam drifted from the pool and spread an acrid mineral scent through the air. The heated water would be a wonderful contrast to the cool air outside. Sighing in anticipation, Julia removed her clothes and piled them on a wooden chair. She used two pins to secure her hair in a knot on top of her head.

Carefully she descended the worn steps leading into the water. Warmth lapped against her calves and traveled to her hips, her waist, and then her shoulders as she reached the bottom of the pool. She shivered in pleasure at the pene-

trating heat, letting her arms float in the buoyant
water, splashing it languidly against her throat.

As her body relaxed, her mind drifted from
one thought to another. She wondered how
Damon had reacted to her sudden disappearance, if he had tried to find her . . . or if he had
been too busy dealing with Lady Ashton to give
her a thought. Her imagination conjured a picture of him with Pauline, their bodies entwined
in the act of love. She shook her head to clear
away the image. It troubled her profoundly, the
question of what had happened after she left
Damon's home the night of the theater fire. Had
Damon allowed his mistress to stay? Had they
argued? Made love?

"I don't care, I don't *care*," Julia muttered,
rubbing her wet hands over her face. But that
was a lie. Despite all her denials, fear, and
stubbornness, she couldn't help but feel that
Damon was *hers*. After all she had suffered
because of their marriage, she had certainly
earned the right to love him. On the other hand,
if there was a baby . . . she wasn't certain she
could live with the thought that she had influ-
enced Damon to abandon his responsibilities.

Just as she splashed her face again, she heard
the bath house attendant's chirruping voice.
"Mrs. Wentworth?"

Wiping her blurry eyes, Julia looked toward
the doorway where the elderly woman stood.

The gray curls pinned on top of the old
woman's head bobbed cheerfully as she spoke.
"Mrs. Wentworth, there's a visitor for you. One
you'll be quite happy to see, I've no doubt."

Julia shook her head emphatically. "I told you

that no one is to come into the bath while I'm here—"

"Aye, but you wouldn't turn away your own husband, would you now?"

"Husband?" Julia asked sharply.

The attendant nodded until her pinned-up curls were in danger of toppling. "Aye, and a fine, handsome man he is."

Julia's mouth sagged open in disbelief as Lord Savage pushed past the woman. "There you are," he said pleasantly, his gaze falling to Julia as she sank deeper into the steaming pool. "Have you missed me, darling?"

Recovering quickly, Julia gave him a slitted glare. "Not at all." She longed to fling an armful of water over his immaculate trousers and white linen shirt.

The bath attendant giggled at what she perceived as their playfulness. Damon turned to favor her with a charming smile. "My deepest thanks for reuniting me with my wife, madam. Now if you wouldn't mind allowing us a few minutes of privacy . . . and keeping other visitors away . . ."

"Not a soul will cross the threshold," the woman vowed, winking at him as she departed. "Good evening, Mr. Wentworth!"

The name elicited a scowl from Damon. "I'm not Mr. Wentworth," he muttered, but the attendant had already gone. When he turned back to Julia, she was still glaring at him.

"How did you find me?"

Casually Damon removed his coat and draped it across the back of a chair. "Your friend Arlyss told me that the acting company was preparing to tour in Bath. After investigating a few hotels and inns, I discovered where you were staying. The proprietor of the inn told me it was your habit to come here in the evenings."

"He had no right—"

"I was very persuasive." His gaze fell to the white tops of her breasts, gleaming in the wavering lamplight.

"Oh, I have no doubt of that," Julia said sarcastically. She came closer to the wall of the pool, concealing her body from him. Perhaps it was because of the heat of the water, but her heart had picked up a rapid beat. No one else looked at her the way he did, his gray eyes warm and appraising, filled with possessiveness.

Damon crouched near her, balancing his arms on his bent knees. "Keep running from me," he said softly, "and I'll keep finding you."

"You won't spend a single night with me at the inn. And I suspect that nearly every lodging in Bath is completely full. If you don't care to sleep in the street tonight, you'd better return to London without delay."

"I own a terrace house at Laura Place."

"Why?" she retorted, trying to cover her discomfort. "You're not exactly the kind of man to make the social rounds in Bath—"

"I bought the house for my father. He likes to come here when his health permits the journey. Would you like to see it?"

"Hardly. In case you hadn't noticed, I've been trying to avoid you." Her head jerked back as Damon reached out to brush some drops of water off her chin. "Don't touch me!"

"If you're angry because of what happened with Pauline the other night—"

"It doesn't matter in the least. I don't care if you arranged for her to be there or not. And I'm more angry with myself than anyone else."

"Because you wanted to be with me?" he murmured.

The silence would have been complete, except for the gentle sloshing of water in the pool. The relaxed feeling the bath had given Julia was now gone, replaced by a tension that stretched through every part of her. She stared at Damon's tautly honed face, the alert gleam of his eyes, and she realized the extent of his hunger. He was here because he wanted her—and he would not let her go easily.

"You shouldn't have followed me to Bath," she snapped. "You won't get anything from me, especially not the kind of welcome you seem to expect."

Rather than argue, he raked her with a thorough glance. His gaze fell to her slender hand, her fingers stiff against the slippery stone that edged the bath. "You're wearing the ring I gave you," he observed.

Julia's hand clenched, and she lowered it into the water, submerging the sparkling diamond. "It doesn't mean anything, except that I happen to like it. And if you presume that my favors can be bought—"

"I'm presuming nothing." A smile crossed his lips. "You seem to expect that I'll pounce on you at any moment. I'm almost inclined to think you'll be disappointed if I don't."

"Let's not play games," she said pertly. "You're here because you want to bed me again."

"Of course I do," he replied in a level voice. "And you want the same thing. As I recall, it was a mutually enjoyable experience—or will you try to claim you were only acting?"

Reddening in frustration, Julia drew her arm back in open threat. "Leave, or I'll throw enough water on you to ruin those very fine clothes."

Damon's smile remained. "Then I'd have no reason not to join you."

Slowly her arm relaxed. "*Please* leave," she said through her teeth. "I've been in the bath long enough. My skin is beginning to wrinkle."

He extended a solicitous hand to her. "I'll help you out."

"No, thank you."

"Shy?" he asked with a mocking lift of his brows. "I've seen you naked before. Once more will hardly make a difference."

"I won't get out until you've left!"

A taunting smile curved his lips. "I'm not leaving."

Irritated beyond bearing, Julia kept her features expressionless and extended a hand to him. "Very well," she said coolly. "You may help me out of the bath." Obligingly Damon reached in for her, and she took hold of his wrist with both hands. Before he could brace himself against her forward pull, she used all her weight to tug him into the water. With a muffled curse, he lost his balance and plunged headfirst.

Julia yelped in triumph and retreated to the opposite side of the bath. She couldn't help sputtering with laughter as Damon emerged with his black hair plastered to his head. Through the water-spiked frames of his lashes, his gray eyes promised retribution. "You little devil," he muttered, and lunged for her.

Laughing with a mixture of enjoyment and alarm, Julia fought to evade him. Damon caught her around the waist and pulled her against his body, the soaked layers of his clothes crushed between them.

"You needed a medicinal dunking," she informed him, still shaking with giggles. "The water will cure all your ills."

"There's one problem it won't cure," he said meaningfully, and cupped his hands over her naked buttocks, pressing her hard against him.

Julia's laughter dissolved as she felt the swelling shape of him wedged intimately high between her thighs. Her body drifted in the hot water until she anchored herself to him, holding on to his shoulders, allowing her legs to wrap around his hips. Their breath mingled in irregular bursts as they stared at each other. Although they were both perfectly still, Julia had the sensation of being tumbled over and over in the onslaught of an incoming tide, caught helplessly in the pull of the churning waves.

Gently she pushed the locks of water-soaked hair from his forehead, her fingers passing from his temple to his ear. Her thumb brushed his jaw, and then she touched the soft place just beneath the bone of his chin. She was enthralled by the scratchy-slick feel of his skin, the movement of muscle as he swallowed.

Suddenly Damon hoisted her higher against

him, his movements effortless in the buoyant water. His large hands hooked underneath her arms, holding her steady as he bent his head to her breast. Julia squirmed in protest until she felt his mouth slide across the tender curve of her breast and fasten onto a flushed nipple. The flicker of his tongue caused an achingly sweet response, the soft peak contracting in his mouth. He tugged and stroked her with his mouth, making her gasp and arch in his arms. Greedily her hands clawed at the thin linen film of his shirt, craving the feel of his bare skin.

Lowering her back into the water, Damon slid his hand over her hip and across the taut skin of her belly. His touch glided between her thighs, reaching into the velvet patch of hair until he found the most sensitive part of her. Julia shuddered in growing desire, wanting more of the pleasure he offered. But an awareness of where they were, a public place, kept her from abandoning herself completely.

"We can't," she gasped against his mouth. "Not here."

"Do you want me?" he whispered, and kissed her deeply, tasting the sweet warmth of her mouth.

Julia trembled against him, her body slick and weightless in his arms. Through the blur of her wet lashes, she saw his face next to hers, his skin gleaming like bronze, his gaze promising erotic fantasies.

At her silence, Damon lowered his mouth to her neck, kissing and nibbling the sensitive path that led up to her ear. "All you have to do is tell me," he murmured. "Just one word, Julia . . . yes or no."

A small moan escaped her. She was drowning in sensation, wanting what she had forbidden herself, knowing how wrong it was . . . but that didn't matter. It seemed that nothing and no one existed outside this small room. Her hand came to the water-soaked hair at the back of his neck, gripping feverishly. "Yes," she whispered.

Damon pried at the buttons on his shirt, smiling as Julia tried to help him, their fingers slipping and tangling beneath the surface of the pool. When his chest was bared, Julia drew her hands down the smooth expanse, as hard as wet marble. The tips of her breasts brushed against his skin, and she breathed faster in excitement. "Hurry," she urged, spreading kisses over his face and neck.

Damon paused in the difficult act of unfastening his wet trousers, one brow raised sardonically. "I've never disrobed under water before. It's not as easy as you might think."

"Try harder," Julia whispered, kissing him. Her tongue entered his mouth, tempting and teasing, until he gave a laughing groan and yanked more roughly at his trousers. The fastenings finally gave way, allowing his rampant erection to spring free. Julia's hand closed around the hard silken length, gently gripping and sliding.

He said her name, his voice ragged in her ear, his fingers digging into her hips as he guided her body over his. He held her steady and pushed inside her slowly. She whimpered and clung to him, shivering in delight. Damon nudged deeper, wanting to thrust rapidly but restrained by the sloshing water to a torturously slow rhythm. Their bodies flexed together in a teasing, sliding friction that promised to last an eternity.

Quivering, Julia wrapped her arms around his shoulders and buried her face against his wet throat. She felt the powerful force of his breath expanding in his chest. It seemed that they had become one being, sharing the same rhythms of pulse and nerves. The pleasure climbed sharply, shocking her with its intensity. She lost all awareness except the driving movements inside her, the sensations that overflowed until she could bear them no longer.

Damon smothered her cry with his mouth, feeling the convulsive shudders of her body as she climaxed. Her inner muscles rippled tightly around him, sending him to his own forceful release. He closed his eyes, while his senses shattered and his blood was set on fire. "Julia," he gasped against her tautly arched throat. "I'll never let you go . . . never . . ."

Somehow Julia heard him above the chaotic rushing of her own blood. While part of her rebelled against the ownership in his voice, another part of her gloried in it. She owned him too; she took the same deep pleasure in their joining . . . and despite her inexperience she knew that she would never find this with anyone else. Weak and fulfilled and despairing, she sagged against him in the water. His hands slipped over her body, traveling softly from the nape of her neck to her hips.

"Let me stay the night with you," he murmured.

Julia saw no point in objecting. It would be hypocritical after what had just happened. She gave him a small nod and wriggled away, feeling him slip from her body.

Glancing back at Damon, she choked on a sudden giggle as she saw him fishing at the bottom of the pool for his shoes. When he resurfaced and held up the ruined leather articles in triumph, Julia shook her head slowly. "Do you intend to walk to the inn dressed in wet clothes? You'll catch a chill, or worse."

Damon drew her out of the bath, his gray eyes caressing as he glanced over her flushed, naked body. "You can warm me when we reach your room."

Chapter 9

❧ ❧

Filled with vitality and a sense of lightness, Julia stood on the stage of Bath's New Theatre and surveyed the activity around her with satisfaction. The fire in London didn't seem to have daunted the spirits of the cast and crew. Busily they assembled new scenery, rehearsed bits of dialogue and stage blocking, and exchanged jokes about the hardships of touring.

"Bloody boring little city," Arlyss murmured, resting her hands on her hips. She made a comical face at Julia. "Not a healthy young man in sight. Nothing but desperate old maids and invalids."

Julia smiled wryly. "I thought we were here to perform *My Lady Deception*, not to look for men."

"The day I stop looking . . ." Arlyss began, and suddenly stopped with an odd expression on her face.

Following her friend's gaze, Julia saw that Mary Woods, one of the company's minor actresses, was flirting openly with Michael Fiske. The scene painter seemed more than a little interested in the pretty young woman and her ebullient smile.

"What is she doing, taking up Fiske's time when she should be rehearsing her part?" Arlyss demanded, a scowl pulling at the bridge of her slim nose.

Julia repressed a smile as she heard the distinct note of jealousy in Arlyss's voice. "Mary has only a few lines. I'm sure she knows them to perfection by now."

Arlyss's scowl remained. "Mr. Fiske has enough to do without entertaining the likes of her."

"You could have had Fiske, had you wanted him," Julia said matter-of-factly. "But as I recall, you were more taken with Lord William Savage."

"Well, he was no better than any of the others," Arlyss retorted. "Although William is divine in bed, he apparently has no interest in me outside of it. I'm finished with him. With *all* men, at the moment." Crossing her arms over her chest, she pointedly turned her back on the sight of Michael Fiske and Mary Woods. Just then Julia saw Fiske take a surreptitious glance at Arlyss. So he was trying to make her jealous, Julia thought, and her lips twitched with sympathetic amusement.

"Let's talk about *your* paramour," Arlyss suggested, turning impish. "Lord Savage came to see me in London—he was trying to find you. All I said to him was that the company was going to begin touring in Bath. Did he come here? Have you seen him?"

Julia hesitated and nodded, while warm color burnished her cheeks.

"Well?" Arlyss prompted. "What happened?"

Shaking her head, Julia gave a self-conscious laugh. Even if she were inclined to tell her, no words could describe last night. After leaving the bath house, they had walked to the inn. The brisk night air had felt refreshing to Julia, but she had been aware of the shivers that ran up and down Damon's frame as his wet, chilly garments clung to his body. When they reached her room, Julia had stirred a fire in the grate, and they had hung his garments to dry.

After climbing into the small but cozy bed, they had pressed their naked bodies together until Damon's skin had turned as warm as her own. He had made love to her wordlessly, using the tender brush of his fingertips, the heat of his mouth, and the movements of his body to communicate his feelings. Remembering the ecstasy she had found in the fire-touched darkness, Julia felt her blush deepen. This morning Damon had been slow to awaken, yawning and stretching and grumbling . . . pulling her against him when she tried to leave the bed. He had taken her once more, plunging into her body with slow thrusts that had driven her senseless.

Somehow Julia pulled her mind away from the lurid thoughts. "It's nothing I would feel comfortable discussing," she murmured.

Arlyss leaned closer in conspiratorial delight. "I'm so happy for you, Jessica! I've never seen you look this way before. You must be in love. It's been a long time coming for you, hasn't it?"

"Don't tell anyone, please."

"Oh, I won't . . . but they'll guess anyway. You know how gossip is. Besides, you can't hide when you're in love—it comes out in a hundred different ways."

Julia was spared from replying by the arrival of Logan Scott, who had been detained by a bevy of local politicians, clergy, and townspeople, all of them eager to make his acquaintance and welcome him to Bath. His vivid blue eyes took in the activity onstage, and he gave a short nod of approval. As people gathered around him with questions, he held them off with a murmur and strode toward Julia.

"Mrs. Wentworth," he said briskly, "how are you?"

She held his gaze and smiled slightly. "Perfectly well after a week's rest, Mr. Scott."

"Good."

Sensing that her presence was *de trop*, Arlyss promptly headed toward Michael Fiske, who was still occupied with Mary Woods.

Logan didn't remove his penetrating gaze from Julia's face. "I've heard that Savage is here in Bath," he remarked. Though the words were toneless, Julia felt as if she had been accused of something.

"Yes," she said in a way that could have been taken either as confirmation or as question.

"Have you seen him yet?"

Julia couldn't bring herself to answer, but he read her expression easily. "Gorging on sweets again?" he asked.

Julia flushed at his reference to their conversation at his London home. Her shoulders inched upward defensively. "It's not my fault if he chooses to follow me."

One russet brow curled in derision. "Isn't it?"

"If you're implying that I've offered him encouragement—"

"I don't give a damn what you've offered him. Just make certain your work isn't affected. The first morning you arrive late to rehearsal because you've been lolling in bed with—"

"I wasn't late this morning," Julia interrupted, her voice touched with frost. "*You* were, Mr. Scott."

Giving her a chilling glance, Logan turned and walked away, snapping out commands right and left.

Julia felt disturbed and slightly puzzled. It was the closest they had ever come to an outright argument, and she wasn't certain why. If they had been any other two people, she might have speculated that Logan Scott had been motivated by jealousy. But that was ridiculous. He certainly had no romantic feelings for her—and even if he did, he would rather die than break his strict rule about never having a relationship with any of the actresses in the company.

Was Logan worried that she might abandon her career in favor of marriage? *You would be difficult to replace at the Capital*, he had told her last week. Perhaps that was true, but it wouldn't be impossible. There were always new and talented young actresses on the rise, and Julia had no illusions that she was irreplaceable.

As they conducted a full run-through of the play, the company was relieved to discover that aside from a few minor pacing problems, the production was nearly flawless. Logan, however, seemed far from satisfied, stopping the rehearsal several times to deliver terse lectures to the cast and crew. As the afternoon lengthened, Julia wondered how hard he intended to push the actors. Rebellious murmurs ran through the group until the rehearsal was finally concluded in early evening. "I want everyone to be here at nine o'clock tomorrow morning," Logan said. Grumbling beneath their breaths, the assemblage dispersed quickly.

"You should be pleased at how well it went," Julia dared to say to Logan as he stood in the middle of the stage. The lines of his face were set in harsh angles. "Instead you're behaving as if the rehearsal were a disaster."

He gave her a threatening glance. "When someone appoints you as manager of the company, you can decide how to run things. In the meantime, kindly leave that responsibility to me."

Julia was surprised and stung by his foul temper. "I wish we could all be as perfect as you, Mr. Scott," she said sarcastically, and strode away. After snatching up her cloak and hat from one of the theater seats, she made her way to the entrance, forgetting in her haste that there would undoubtedly be a crowd outside. Now that the townspeople in Bath were aware of the acting company's presence, they would gather to catch a glimpse of Logan Scott or the other Capital players.

As she opened the door and began to step outside, she was immediately pushed back by a horde of people trying to enter the locked theater. "It's her!" someone cried. "Mrs. Went-worth!" There were eager cries from both men and women, and frantic hands reaching for her. Startled, Julia wedged all her weight against the door and managed to close it, but not before two men had forced their way inside.

Gasping with effort, Julia stepped back and regarded the pair. One was heavyset and middle-aged, and the other tall, scrawny, and much younger. The portly one removed his hat and regarded her with an obvious leer. The tip of his red tongue edged over small, puffy lips. When he spoke, the scents of tobacco and liquor wafted heavily from his mouth.

He introduced himself as if he expected her to be impressed by his title. "Lord Langate, my dear, and this is my companion, Lord Strathearn." He removed his hat, revealing a sparse patch of pomaded and cologned hair. "Let me say you are even more delectable at close range than at a distance."

"Thank you," Julia said warily. She positioned her small hat on her head and pinned it to the neatly coiled hair at her crown. "If you'll excuse me, gentlemen—"

They crowded closer to her, backing her against the door. Langate's pebblelike eyes gleamed greedily as he glanced over her slender figure. "Being familiar with the city and all its delights, Strathearn and I decided to offer our services to you for the evening."

"That's not necessary," Julia said in a clipped voice.

"We'll take you for an excellent meal, madam,

and then a tour in my carriage. You'll find it quite enjoyable, I assure you."

"I have other plans for tonight."

"No doubt you do." Langate licked his thick lips and smiled, revealing tobacco-stained teeth. "But surely you could be persuaded to change them for a pair of gentlemen who admire you so greatly."

"I'm afraid not." Julia tried to push past them, only to be crowded against the door once more.

Langate's hand came to her shoulder, then spread over her chest. "Perhaps you need a little inducement."

To her shock, she felt him fumble at her bodice, his short, pudgy fingers depositing a small wad of bills into her cleavage. Shuddering in revulsion, she jerked back and fished the money out of her dress. Her face turned scarlet as she opened her mouth to call for help.

Before she could make a sound, however, a dark whirlwind descended on them. Julia blinked and froze while swift movement took place around her. The two men who had crushed her against the door were suddenly gone, plucked away as if by some gigantic Olympian hand. The wad of money dropped from Julia's fingers and scattered over the floor. Dazedly she stared at her rescuer. It was Damon, his face a cold mask, his eyes lit with murderous fury. He had pinned the hapless lords against the wall like a pair of yapping terriers. It didn't seem that he heard their babbling apologies and explanations. They both fell silent as he spoke to them, words hissing between his teeth.

"If you approach her again, I'll rip you to pieces . . . and I won't stop until you're scattered from one side of Bath to the other."

Langate's blubbery face turned purple. "We weren't aware she was spoken for," he managed to say.

Damon released Strathearn and focused all his attention on Langate. His fingers tightened on the man's throat. "Touch her, speak to her, even look at her . . . and I'll kill you."

"No need . . ." the man gasped, choking for air. "Please . . . I'll go . . ."

Abruptly Damon let go, and Langate collapsed against the door. Strathearn went to him immediately, looking cowed and pale as he lent a supporting arm to his companion. Together the pair made their way through the door, back into the eager throng that waited outside.

Damon turned to Julia, his eyes still glittering with rage.

"How . . . ?" she asked breathlessly.

"I came through the back entrance of the theater. There's a crowd waiting for you there as well."

"And for the other actors," she said with a flicker of returning spirit.

"Mostly for you." He gave her a hard smile. "You seem to be considered public property, Mrs. Wentworth."

"I'm no one's property."

"I can produce a certificate of marriage that states otherwise."

"Your certificate is worth *this*," she retorted with a snap of her fingers. "Our marriage is of questionable legality, as you're well aware. Any court would set it aside with no hesitation, considering the fact that neither of us was of an appropriate age."

After a long moment Julia's gaze fell, and she wondered why they were suddenly so angry with each other. She softened her voice considerably. "Thank you for getting rid of those buffoons."

Damon didn't reply, his features still tense.

"I'll have to wait here until the crowd begins to disperse," Julia commented.

"That won't be necessary," he said grimly. "I'll escort you to my carriage."

She shook her head and drew back. "No, thank you. I don't think it would be wise to spend another evening with you."

"Not even to share supper? As far as I know, you haven't eaten today."

"I don't object to sharing a meal with you, it's just . . . afterward . . ."

As Damon saw how flustered she had become, he turned strangely gentle. He reached up to her hat and adjusted it a half-inch, his fingers smoothing back a few soft wisps of blond hair. "I didn't come to Bath merely to chase you around the bedroom—though the idea does have merit."

"Then why are you here?"

"I want to spend some time with you. I want to know more about the life you lead, and why it holds such attraction for you. And I want you to know more about me. The fact is, we're still strangers. Before we discuss how to end our marriage, it wouldn't hurt to become more familiar with each other."

"I suppose not," Julia said cautiously, looking up at him. She made a move to unroll the black veil from the crown of her hat. He did it for her, carefully arranging the netting over her face.

"Then have supper with me tonight at my terrace. I'll deliver you to the inn afterward, completely untouched. You have my word."

Julia considered the offer. The thought of having a meal by herself at the inn, or with other people in the acting company, sounded none too appealing at the moment. "I suppose anything your cook prepares will be better than the fare at the inn," she said.

Her grudging acceptance provoked a smile from him. "You have my word on that as well." He pulled her hand into the crook of his arm. "Let's go, madam, before your public become even more unruly."

It had always been necessary for Julia to fend off overeager suitors and admirers by herself. It was a pleasant change to walk out on a strong man's arm, letting him assume control of the situation. She made no protest as Damon slid a protective hand onto her slender back and guided her through the crush of inquisitive strangers outside. Immediately she was assaulted by eager questions and hands plucking at her hat, veil, and cloak.

Startled, Julia felt her hat being pulled off her head. Smarting tears came to her eyes as the anchoring pin tugged sharply. Turning away from the slew of excited cries, she clung to Damon until they reached the carriage. She managed to smile and wave at the crowd before entering the vehicle. Damon wasn't nearly so forgiving, shoving the people at the front of the mob to keep them at bay, ignoring their protests.

Tucked safely inside the carriage, Julia sighed in relief and rubbed her sore scalp. "I thought they might pluck my hair out by the roots," she exclaimed as the carriage pulled away.

Damon's gaze was imperturbable. "Basking in public adoration, pursued by everyone . . . it must be what every actress wants."

Julia considered the remark and replied carefully. "I suppose I like knowing that people are pleased with what I do . . . and their approval means that my position at the Capital and my salary are secure."

"Their approval means more to you than that."

Annoyed by the derisive note in his voice, Julia opened her mouth to reply. But she closed it abruptly. He was right, although she hated his perceptiveness, not wanting anyone to read her with such apparent ease. She did like the feeling of being admired by the public, who seemed more than ready to give her all the attention and affection her father had always denied her.

"Leading an ordinary life must pale in comparison," Damon remarked.

"I wouldn't know," she said with an edge of sarcasm, pulling down her disheveled hair. "Tell me what an ordinary life is like . . . oh, but I forgot. You wouldn't know either."

"I lead the life I was intended for."

"So do I," she said defensively.

There was a sardonic twist at the corner of his mouth, but he chose not to argue. He watched her steadily as she used one of her tortoiseshell combs to straighten her hair before twisting it back up again.

The terrace house was as elegant as one would expect of an address in posh Laura Place. The gleaming oak floors were covered with pale English hand-knotted carpets, upon which were scattered handsome pieces of polished rosewood furniture and urns filled with lush plants. Pale yellow and green curtains covered the long windows, while sheets of ornately framed mirror glass gave the rooms an airy, open appearance.

Relaxing in the luxurious candlelit atmosphere of the small dining room, Julia applied herself hungrily to the meal. The array of French dishes included chicken and truffles in champagne sauce, veal scallops stuffed with herbs, and vegetables glistening with a hint of butter. A plate of wine-soaked fruit was brought out for dessert, as well as tiny almond tarts heaped with raspberries and meringue.

"After such a large meal, I won't be able to fit into my costumes," Julia said, biting into a tart and making an appreciative noise.

"You barely do now."

Julia smiled at the touch of jealousy in his voice. "Compared to other actresses, my costumes are extraordinarily modest." She picked up a raspberry that had fallen to her plate and consumed it daintily.

The shadow of displeasure remained on his face. "I don't like it that other men are able to see so much of my wife. I know exactly what they think when they look at you."

Amused by his possessiveness, Julia leaned her chin on her hand and stared at him. "What do they think?" she prompted.

On the pretext of pouring more wine for her, Damon stood and walked to her side of the table. Half-sitting on the edge, he refilled her glass and looked down at her. Julia didn't move, even when his warm gaze traveled to her breasts and back to her face. Lightly he caught the fragile edge of her jaw in his fingers, and tilted her head back.

"They imagine what your skin feels like, and if it could really be as soft as it appears." His forefinger traced the curve of her cheek and grazed the tender corner of her lips. "They wonder how you taste . . . they think about loosening your hair and letting it fall over your body . . . arranging it over your breasts . . ." His hand moved in a slow caress down her throat, and then the backs of his knuckles passed once, twice over the peak of her breast.

Julia's breath quickened, and her fingers grasped the edge of her chair as she fought for composure. She wanted to stand and press herself into the lee of his thighs, to welcome the warmth of his hands on her skin. Damon continued to toy with her leisurely, his silver-gray eyes locked on every nuance of her expression. "They want to make love to you," he murmured, "and lock you away somewhere for their private pleasure." His fingers slid beneath the edge of her bodice, dipping close to the tingling bud of her nipple.

Shivering, Julia caught his hand. "You said you would return me to the inn untouched."

"So I did." Gradually his fingers withdrew from her gown. His lips hovered above hers, his breath warm and sweet against her skin. "There's a bit of meringue at the corner of your mouth."

Automatically Julia reached with her tongue and found the touch of stickiness, letting it dissolve in her mouth. Damon's gaze didn't miss the flicker of movement. His hand, still caught in hers, was as hard as steel.

Slowly Julia let go of him, and happened to glance at the sparkling diamond on her own finger. The stone was extraordinarily beautiful in the candlelight, glittering in constantly shifting patterns. She felt guilty for having accepted it from him, for wearing something she wasn't entitled to keep. "You should take this back," she said, removing the ring and offering it to him.

"I have no use for it."

"It doesn't belong to me."

"It does," he contradicted quietly. "You're my wife."

Julia frowned, holding the ring in her palm. "This is a symbol of a marriage that never existed—and never will."

"I want you to keep it. No matter what happens in the future, you'll look at that ring and know that once you were mine."

Julia hadn't realized that he considered the ring a sign of ownership. She set it on the table, forcing herself to let go of the beautiful diamond. The ring came with a price she wasn't certain she was willing to pay. "I'm sorry," she said, unable to look at him.

Although she couldn't see his face, she sensed a change in the atmosphere . . . the fierce will of a warrior in battle, the urge to conquer and dominate. Aware of his violence barely kept in check, Julia remained very still. She kept her face turned away and listened to his breathing, until the deepening movements of his lungs became calm once more.

"You'll ask for it back someday."

Startled, Julia made the mistake of looking at him. His face was very near, his eyes gleaming like a well-sharpened knife blade. It took all her self-control to keep from shivering in alarm. In this moment it was easy to see how he had singlehandedly pulled his family from poverty to wealth, with pure force of will. "No," she said softly. "Even if I were to fall in love with you, I wouldn't accept the ring and become your property."

"Property," he repeated, his tone infused with the sting of a riding whip. "Is that how you think I would treat you?"

Rising from her chair, Julia stared at him face to face, while he remained half-seated on the table. "If I were your wife, would you let me go wherever I chose, do whatever I pleased, with no questions or recriminations? Would you make no protest while I continued with my profession, attending rehearsals in the mornings, coming back from performances at midnight or later? And what of your friends and peers?—the sneers and nasty comments they would make about me, their assumptions that I was little more than a prostitute. Would you find a way to accept all that?"

His face turned a few shades darker, confirming her suspicions. "Why does the theater mean so much to you?" he asked curtly. "Is it such a damned sacrifice to give up the life of a Gypsy?"

"I've never been able to depend on anything else. It's the only thing I'm certain of. I don't want a title and an endless round of social events, and a quiet estate in the country—that's the life my father would have chosen for me."

Damon caught her hips in his hands, imprisoning her between his thighs. "Part of you wants that life."

Twisting, pushing at his hard chest, Julia tried to free herself, but his grip only tightened. He pulled her closer until her struggles created an intimate friction between them. Abruptly she froze, realizing the effect her movements were having on him. The rigid proof of his arousal pressed against her abdomen, eliciting an immediate response from her body. "I want to leave now," she said breathlessly.

Damon released her, but with his intent gaze fastened on hers, she couldn't seem to move away. "I won't make it easy for you. You're not going to avoid me—or get rid of me—without a fight."

Julia stared at him with a mixture of fury and longing. It was difficult enough, denying herself what she wanted so badly. There were dreams she still harbored deep inside, of having her own family and home, falling asleep each night in the arms of her husband, spending leisurely hours playing with her children. Now those faceless images had taken clear shape in her mind . . . she wanted to be Damon's wife, and bear his dark-haired offspring. The dreams were now a possibility, and giving them up would be the hardest thing she had ever done.

Suddenly she remembered Logan Scott's cool, mocking voice as he said, *You may decide that you love Savage enough to surrender your body and soul to his keeping . . . but I wouldn't advise it.*

Stumbling back, Julia turned away and held her hands to her pounding chest. She took several deep breaths, willing the emotions inside her to uncoil. Damon came up behind her, close but not touching. His voice was flat as he spoke somewhere above her head. "I'll accompany you to the inn."

"You don't have to . . ." she began, but he ignored her and went to ring for a carriage.

They were silent as they traveled to the inn, the atmosphere strained between them. Their thighs rested close together, brushing occasionally as the wheels of the vehicle bounced over uneven places in the street. Julia tried to move away, but it seemed that she kept sliding against him. She would die before moving to the opposite seat, especially under the focus of his cool, jeering gaze. Finally the miserable ride was over, and he helped her from the carriage.

"I'll go up to my room by myself," Julia said, sensing that he intended to accompany her.

Damon shook his head briefly. "It's dangerous. I'll see you to the door."

"I've stayed here alone for more than a week, and I've been perfectly fine without your protection," Julia pointed out.

"For God's sake, I'm not going to touch you. If I had seduction in mind for tonight, you'd be in bed with me right now. All I want is to see you safely to your room."

"I don't need—"

"Indulge me," he said through his teeth, looking as though he were going to strangle her.

Throwing up her hands in exasperation, Julia preceded him into the building, past the proprietor's table and the vacant dining room, toward the stairs that led to the second floor. Damon followed at a slower pace, his black brows drawn together in displeasure. They progressed down a long, poorly lit hallway until they reached her room. Extracting a slender key from the reticule slung around her wrist, Julia turned her attention to the lock. The key turned far too easily.

Realizing that she must have forgotten to lock her room when she had left that morning, Julia made a show of rattling the key against the metal catch. She'd had enough to deal with tonight, without being accused of carelessness and incompetence. Turning the knob, she paused and looked back at Damon. "You've done your gentlemanly duty," she informed him. "I've been delivered safely to my door. Good night."

Taking the unsubtle cue to leave, Damon stared at her with sullen gray eyes before turning his back on her and striding away.

With a sigh, Julia entered her room and fumbled for a box of matches. Carefully she struck a match and applied the tiny yellow flare to the oil lamp on the dresser. She replaced the glass globe and adjusted the wick until a gentle glow filled the room. Her mind was consumed with thoughts that made her head ache. She was oblivious to her surroundings, lost in worry . . .

but as she glanced in the cheval glass, she saw a flicker of movement in the corner of the reflective surface. At the same time there was an odd scraping noise on the floor.

She was not alone. A bolt of fright went through her. Whirling, Julia managed a half-scream before the sound was extinguished by a man's hand crushing hard over her mouth. She was hauled back against a skinny but inexorably strong frame. Nostrils flaring, eyes wide, she stared at the heavyset form of Lord Langate as he approached her. She was being held by his companion, Strathearn. They were the two men who had pestered her at the New Theatre earlier in the day. It appeared that they had bolstered their courage with a great deal of liquor, both of them stinking and sour-breathed, and insufferably smug.

"You didn't expect to see us again, did you?" Langate purred, smoothing his chubby hand over the greasy strands of hair combed across his balding head. His gaze slid appreciatively over her writhing form. "What a prize wench you are—the smartest bit of goods we've ever seen. Isn't that right, Strathearn?"

The tall man nodded and chortled in agreement.

Langate's small mouth opened in a grin as he spoke to Julia. "There's no need to be frightened. We'll take our ease with you, and we'll pay you nicely for it afterward. You'll be able to purchase any bauble you like. Don't look so outraged, my dear. I'll wager you've entertained many eager gentlemen of our sort between your pretty thighs." He came closer and caught one of

Julia's flailing hands, forcing it to his swollen crotch. A leer of anticipation creased his round face. "There," he crooned. "That isn't so bad, is it? I think you'll enjoy—"

But his sentence was never finished. Julia heard the sound of the door bursting open, and she was abruptly released. Unable to find her balance, she fell forward, her hands and knees striking the hard floor. Crawling to the corner, she pressed her back hard against the wall. A lock of hair fell over her face, obscuring her view of the action before her. She heard the dull, meaty sound of fists impacting flesh in repetitive blows, and the howls of pain that filled the room.

Scraping back her wayward hair, Julia realized that Damon had come back, and he seemed intent on killing her attackers. After sending Strathearn crumpling to the floor in a heap, he turned his attention to Langate, beating the older man until he was whimpering for mercy. Through her shock and fear, Julia realized that Damon was indeed ready to commit murder. "Please stop," she gasped. "I'm all right. If you don't stop, you'll kill him . . . *Damon* . . ."

At the sound of his name, he paused to glance at her with eyes as dark as coal. Whatever he saw in her face seemed to recall him from the murderous rage that had overtaken him. He stared down at the quivering man beneath him, and shook his head to clear away the haze of blood-lust. After wiping his bloodied fists on Langate's coat, he stood and crossed the room to Julia. Langate and Strathearn took the opportunity to leave immediately, groaning and cursing as they made their escape.

Knowing she couldn't stand on her own, Julia reached up to her husband, her hands shaking visibly. Damon bent and scooped her up as if she were a child, lifting her high against his chest. She clung to him tightly, trying to comprehend what had happened. "Thank you," she gasped, her throat working hard. "Thank you . . ."

Damon sat on the bed and held her in his lap, smoothing back her tumbled hair. She felt him brush away the wetness on her cheeks with his fingers. Through the thunder in her ears she could hear the sound of his voice as he soothed her with quiet assurances that she was safe, that no one would hurt her.

Julia kept her eyes closed, focusing all her will inward, trying to keep from bursting into renewed tears. If Damon hadn't come back, Langate and his companion would have raped her. The thought of being subjected to such brutality was terrifying.

"Why . . . why did you come back?" she finally managed to ask.

The stroke of his hand on her throat was exquisitely gentle. "I reached the end of the hall and thought I heard you cry out. At the risk of seeming a fool, I decided to check on you once more."

Her hand came up to his, and she squeezed his fingers hard. "You always seem to be rescuing me."

Damon urged her chin up, not allowing her to

turn away as he stared into her eyes. "Listen to me, Julia . . . I won't always be able to reach you in time. It was a stroke of luck that I was here tonight—"

"It's over now," she interrupted, sensing the sudden departure of tenderness, the new note of censure in his voice.

"It's not over," he said roughly. "It will only get worse from now on. There will be more like Langate, wanting a piece of you, doing anything to be close to you. If you want to continue your acting career, you'll need protection day and night, and that's a position I don't intend to apply for."

Unceremoniously he dumped her onto the bed and stood up, his gaze pitiless. "If this is the life you want, so be it. I would hate to deprive you of such enjoyment. But take my advice and hire someone to safeguard you from your legion of 'admirers.' And lock the damned door when I leave."

Julia remained on the bed, silently watching him stride from the room. She wanted to beg him to stay. *Don't leave me . . . I need you . . .* But the words remained locked inside her, and she kept her mouth clamped shut. The door closed sharply behind him. Julia's fist curled around a pillow, and she hurled it with all her strength. There was no trace of satisfaction in hearing the soft *thwack* as it hit the doorjamb.

How dare he sound accusatory, as if she had asked for what had happened! Did the fact that she earned her living on the stage give anyone the right to attack her? Why was it mandatory for a woman to live under a man's protection?

Leaping up from the bed, she went to the door and locked it against Damon and the rest of the world, enclosing herself tightly in the small room. She rubbed her palms roughly over her face, finding her cheeks still moist with the residue of tears.

For some reason she hadn't realized until now just how bitterly Damon disapproved of her career. They were at an impasse. He would make her choose—he would never tolerate a compromise. The acting profession exposed a woman to censure and risk, and it didn't allow for the needs of a husband and family.

Miserably Julia wandered about the room, hugging her arms around her middle. She would find someone else, perhaps a few years from now . . . a man who had none of the full-blooded demanding arrogance of Lord Savage. He would be softer in character, more accepting of her independence, and he would have nothing to do with the strange, impossible past she had shared with Damon.

But it would always bind them, their past, no matter how they tried to ignore it. She and Damon had been shaped by the same forces, tempered by years of secret awareness of each other. It had been a mistake to avoid her husband, hoping against all reason that he would miraculously disappear, changing her own name and her life to ensure that they would never meet. She shouldn't have run away—she should have confronted him long before now.

Unfortunately it was too late for that. She knew that the kinship they shared, the blaze of passion between them, the pure simmering delight in each other's company, would never be found with anyone else. If she chose him over everything else she valued, there would be ample rewards to compensate her. But to sacrifice her profession would be like amputating a part of herself, and she would eventually resent him for not being able to fill the empty space that was left behind.

Leaning against the window, Julia pressed her forehead against a small, cool pane, her vision blurred by subtle waves and distortions in the glass. Lady Ashton would be better for Damon, she thought. Pauline wanted nothing more than to be his wife and bear his children—and she would not ask him for compromises he wasn't able to make.

After a sleepless night, Julia dressed herself wearily and walked to the New Theatre, her veil draped across her face. At this early hour of the morning, there wasn't a curiosity-seeker in sight. She entered the theater and saw Logan Scott standing alone on stage. His face was turned toward the newly painted backdrop as he scrutinized it. Something about his posture betrayed that he was preoccupied with other matters, his mind lingering on thoughts that no one would ever be privileged to know.

Hearing Julia approach the stage, Logan turned to face her, seeming unsurprised by her early arrival. He helped her up to the boards easily, his grip hard and reassuring before he released her hand. "You look like hell," he said.

"I couldn't sleep." Julia forced a tired smile to her lips. "My conscience was troubled."

"You'd do well to dispense with your conscience altogether," Logan advised. "I did years ago, and I've slept like a babe every night since."

"You must tell me how you did it," she said, only half-jesting.

"Some other time. I have some news." His expression was inscrutable. "A message was sent to the Capital for you and forwarded here. Apparently there's an illness in your family."

"My mother," Julia said automatically, while her heart beat out a worried staccato.

"Your father, I believe. I'm not aware of the particulars."

"My father . . ." Julia shook her head in confusion. "That can't be true. He's never ill, he . . ." She fell silent, staring blankly ahead, all words sputtering into silence. There must be something terribly wrong. Eva would never have sent for her otherwise. It was impossible to imagine her father ill, confined to his bed. Throughout her childhood, she had never seen him afflicted with so much as a head cold.

"Are you planning to go to him?" Logan asked without inflection.

"I can't . . . there's no time . . . not with the play opening tomorrow night . . ."

"I'll cancel tomorrow night's performance. We'll open the following Tuesday evening."

Bewildered, Julia looked into his vivid blue eyes. Logan never canceled a performance—it was one of his strictest codes. "Why?" she asked softly.

He ignored the question. "Will you be able to return by Tuesday?"

"Yes, I think so." She was touched by his

unexpected kindness. "Most managers in your position wouldn't let me go. I never would have expected this."

Logan shrugged casually. "If I forced you to stay, you'd be in no condition to give a decent performance."

"You could give the part to Arlyss," Julia suggested. "She knows all of my lines. There's no need to cancel the play tomorrow night."

"The role is yours. No one else could play it as you do."

"Thank you, but—"

"Go to your father. Try to make peace with him. And come back soon . . . or I'll dock your salary."

"Yes, sir," Julia said obediently, though she wasn't deceived by Logan's attempted callousness. She gave him a small, grateful smile. "I've just realized that underneath everything you're a kind man. But don't worry—I won't ruin your reputation by telling anyone."

Chapter 10

As Julia undertook the half-day journey to the Hargate estate in Logan Scott's wine-red lacquered carriage, she debated with herself about whether she should have informed Damon that she was leaving Bath. She was troubled by the nagging feeling that she should have confided in him. Was it wrong of her to want his comfort? More than anyone else, Damon would understand her complicated feelings toward her father.

The recollection of their bitter parting made Julia wince and set her jaw stubbornly. Damon wouldn't offer comfort; he would probably make some scornful remark and tell her she was welcome to shoulder her burdens alone. It would be hypocritical of her to make grand statements about her freedom and independence, and then turn to him for help at the first sign of trouble.

As the carriage and accompanying outriders traveled across the hilly countryside and approached the Hargate estate, Julia's urgency changed to apprehension. She realized she was afraid of what she might find at her childhood home, afraid of seeing her father ill, and certain that he would order her off the estate as soon as he saw her. The tall house perched among the hills like a hawk, dark and magnificent with its towers stretching toward the sky.

The vehicle stopped before the front entrance. A pair of footmen helped Julia from the carriage, while other servants came to take the horses and show the driver to the stables and carriage house. Before Julia had reached the top step, the massive door opened and the butler was there to welcome her inside.

In a matter of moments Eva appeared, wordlessly enfolding Julia in her arms.

"Mama," Julia said in surprise, her cheek crushed against the pleated blue linen of her mother's gown. Although Eva's health had always varied greatly, she had never appeared as well as this. Somehow her mother had summoned a strength and sense of purpose she hadn't displayed in years. She was still far too thin, but the bones were no longer starkly prominent in her face, and there was a gleam of tranquillity in her brown eyes. It appeared that Eva took well to the unusual situation of being needed by her husband. For once *he* was the invalid and she was the head of the household.

"I'm glad you came," Eva murmured. "I was afraid your schedule wouldn't allow a visit."

"How is he?" Julia asked, walking with her through the entrance hall to the stairs. It seemed that a shroud had been pulled over the house; everything was unnaturally quiet and still.

Eva replied calmly, her face tense with worry. "Your father took to his bed with a fever several days ago. It was a very bad one—the doctor says it weakened all his organs. We weren't certain he would live, but now it seems the worst has passed."

"Will he recover fully?"

"The doctor says he'll never be quite the same. The fever was enough to have killed a lesser man. It will take some time for Edward to regain his strength."

"He won't want to see me," Julia said, her insides drawn as tightly as violin strings.

"That's not true. He's been asking for you."

"Why?" she asked warily. "If he wants to express his opinion that I've ruined my life and disgraced the family, I'm already aware—"

"Give him a chance," Eva murmured. "He's been through an ordeal, Julia, and he wants to see his only child. I don't know what he wishes to say to you, but I entreat you to go to him in the spirit of forgiveness."

Julia hesitated before replying. "I'll try."

Eva shook her head ruefully. "If you only knew how like him you are. I believe you love him in spite of everything, but you won't set aside your pride long enough to admit it."

"I do love him," Julia admitted defiantly, "but that doesn't erase the things that have been said and done. Love doesn't keep people from hurting each other."

They were both silent as they ascended the stairs together. "Would you like to freshen up in your room?" Eva asked.

"I'd prefer to see him right away," Julia replied. She was too nervous to wait, and her tension built with each minute that passed. "That is, if Father is strong enough."

Eva accompanied her to Edward's room. "Julia . . ." she said gently, "you must allow for the fact that people can change. Even your father. It's frightening to come so close to dying. I believe it made Edward face some events in his past that he has tried to ignore for years. Please be kind to him, and listen to what he has to say."

"Of course. I'm hardly going to rush into his sickroom and start hurling accusations, Mama."

Julia stopped at the doorway, waiting as Eva entered the room. Her mother's slender form was silhouetted against the strip of sunlight that had managed to slip through the lemon-colored window curtains. Bending over the lean form stretched out on the bed, Eva touched Edward's hair and murmured quietly.

As she watched the scene, Julia was troubled by her own lack of emotion. Her heart was blank and numb, unmarked by grief or even anger. She couldn't seem to summon any feeling for her father, and it bothered her profoundly.

Eva looked up and gestured for Julia to enter. Slowly she crossed the threshold and approached the bed, where her father lay shadowed beneath the chintz canopy. All at once a rush of feeling came, a tide of remorse and sympathy that overwhelmed her. Edward had always been a powerful figure, but he seemed small and solitary as he lay in bed with the covers pulled to his shoulders. The robust quality he had possessed in abundance had fled, leaving him immeasurably older. There was a waxen look about his skin, the result of having recently been bled by the physician.

Carefully Julia sat on the edge of the mattress. She took his hand, feeling the skin move too easily over the long bones. He had lost weight. She pressed his hand as hard as she dared, wishing she could impart some of her vitality to him.

"Father," she said softly. "It's Julia."

A long time passed, and his pale lashes lifted His eyes were as bright and acute as always as they took measure of her. Julia had never known her father to experience a single moment of awkwardness—he was always in command of any situation. Strangely, however, he seemed to share her uncertainty, searching in vain for words.

"Thank you," he said, his voice alarmingly thready. His hand twitched, and for a split second Julia thought he meant to draw it away. Instead his fingers closed more firmly over hers. It was the most affection he had shown to her in years.

"I thought you might have me ejected from the house," Julia said with a self-conscious smile.

"I thought you might not come." Edward sighed, his chest moving in a shallow rise and fall. "I wouldn't have blamed you."

"Mama told me how ill you've been," Julia murmured, retaining his hand. "I could have told her and the doctor that you were too stubborn to let a mere fever get the best of you."

Laboriously her father tried to prop himself up in bed. Eva moved forward to assist him, but

Julia was already pushing a nearby pillow behind him. Edward gave his wife an enigmatic glance. "My dear . . . I would like to speak to Julia alone."

Eva smiled faintly. "I understand." She disappeared from the room with wraithlike grace, leaving father and daughter to confront each other.

Withdrawing to a nearby chair, Julia stared at Edward with a perplexed frown. She couldn't imagine what he wanted to tell her, after all the arguments and bitter feelings between them. "What is it?" she asked quietly. "Do you wish to talk about my professional life or my personal one?"

"Neither," her father said with an effort. "It's about me." He reached for a glass, and Julia filled it with fresh water from a small porcelain pitcher. Carefully he sipped the cool liquid. "I've never told you about my past. There were . . . details about the Hargates that I failed to mention."

"Details," Julia repeated, her fine brows quirking. The history of the Hargates was basic and uncomplicated. It was a family of moderate prestige and considerable wealth, ambitious to gain the high social status that could only be gained by intermarriage with blood even bluer than their own.

"I told myself it was necessary to protect you from the truth," Edward said, "but that was pure cowardice on my part."

"No. There are many qualities I would ascribe to you, Father, but cowardice is not one of them."

Edward continued resolutely. "There are things I've never been able to talk about because I find them painful . . . and I've punished you because of them." His rusty voice contained a poignant regret that astonished Julia. It was a revelation, albeit a discomforting one, to see that her father was capable of such emotion.

"What things?" she asked softly. "What is it you want to tell me?"

"You've never known about . . . Anna." The name seemed to leave a bittersweet taste on his lips.

"Who is she, Father?"

"She was your aunt . . . my sister."

Julia was amazed. She had never known anyone in her father's family except a pair of uncles who had each married and chosen to live quietly in the country. "Why has no one ever mentioned her? Where is she now, and what—"

Edward lifted his hand to stop the flow of questions. Slowly he began to explain. "Anna was my older sister. She was the most beautiful creature on earth. If not for Anna, I would have had the most barren childhood imaginable. She made up games and stories to entertain me . . . she was a mother, a sister, a friend . . . she was . . ." Failing to find an appropriate word, he paused helplessly.

Julia listened intently. Her father had never spoken to her like this before, his face softening in reflection, his steely eyes turning hazy with memories.

"Neither of our parents was fond of children," he said. "Not even their own. They had little to do with us until we had reached maturity, and even then we held little interest for them. Their only concern was that they had fostered a sense of discipline and duty in us. I can't say I had a fondness for them either. But I loved Anna . . . and I knew she was the only person in the world who truly loved me."

"What was she like?" Julia asked in the silent interlude that followed. It seemed that Edward found it difficult to continue the narrative, memories entangling him in their fragile threads.

His gaze was unfocused, as if he were staring across a great distance. "She was wild and fanciful, very different from my brothers and I. Anna didn't care about rules or responsibilities. She was a creature of emotion, completely unpredictable. Our parents never understood her—she drove them mad at times."

"What happened to her?"

"When Anna was eighteen, she made the acquaintance of a foreign diplomat who held a position at an embassy in London. He must have seemed the embodiment of all Anna's dreams. My father disapproved of the man and forbade Anna to see him. Naturally she rebelled and took every opportunity to sneak away and be with him. She fell in love as she did everything else . . . wholeheartedly, committing herself to him body and soul. But she had chosen unwisely. She . . ." A shadow came over Edward's face, and it seemed that he wanted to stop. He had said too much, however. Having come this far, he would follow the narrative to its painful conclusion.

"Anna conceived a child," he said, strangling briefly on the words. "Her lover abandoned her after explaining that he was already married and had nothing to offer. My family abhorred any kind of scandal, and cast her out of our midst. It was as if she had suddenly ceased to exist. My father disinherited Anna, leaving her nearly destitute. She decided to leave for Europe to bear the consequences of her shame alone.

"Before she departed, she came to me. She didn't ask for money or any kind of help . . . only my reassurance that I still loved her. And I couldn't give it to her. I turned my back on her. I wouldn't even speak to her. And when she persisted in calling my name and trying to put her arms around me, I . . . called her a whore and walked away."

Edward began to weep openly, the tears seeming to drain what strength he had left. "That was the last time I saw her. Anna went to France to stay with a distant cousin. Later we learned that she had died in childbirth. I managed to put her out of my mind for several years—it was either that or go mad thinking about her. Just when I had almost forgotten that she had ever existed, you were born."

He blotted his face with a handkerchief, the stream of moisture from his eyes refusing to abate. "You looked so much like her that it shocked me every time I looked at you. I thought it a cruel twist of fate to see her in your face, your eyes . . . you were a constant reminder of my cruelty to Anna. And worse, you had her spirit, her way of looking at things. You were my sister reborn. I didn't want to lose you as I did her. I thought if I could make you more like me . . . sensible, serious, completely without imagination . . . then you would never leave me. But the more I tried to mold you, the more you resisted . . . the more like *her* you became. Everything I thought I was doing for your good was a mistake."

Julia wiped a trickle of tears from her own cheeks. "Including the marriage to Lord Savage."

"Especially that," Edward agreed in a choked voice. "I thought it would leave you no choice except to become exactly what I wanted you to be. But you rebelled just as Anna did. You discarded your name and took to the stage, and worse, you became successful. I tried to punish you by disinheriting you . . . but that didn't seem to matter."

"You're right, the money didn't matter," Julia said, her voice unsteady. "All I wanted was for you to love me."

Her father shook his head, the movement resembling the wobble of a broken toy. "I didn't want to love you if I couldn't change you. I couldn't bear the risk."

And now? Julia longed to ask, questions hovering on her lips. Was it too late for them? Why had he brought himself to tell her all this? She was afraid to hope that he would want her back in his life, that he might try to accept her as he hadn't been able to in the past. But it was too soon for questions. For now, understanding was enough.

She stared at her father, seeing the exhaustion in every line of his face. His eyelids drooped, his chin dipping toward his chest. "Thank you for telling me," she whispered, and leaned over him to arrange his pillows. "Sleep now—you're tired."

"You'll . . . stay?" he managed to ask.

She nodded and smiled tenderly. "I'll stay until you're better, Father."

Although her father's confidences had left her too stunned to be hungry, Julia mechanically consumed a small plate of chicken and boiled vegetables from a tray sent to her room. She had told Eva all that had been said, and her mother had reacted without much surprise. "I knew about poor Anna," Eva had admitted, "but none of the Hargates were inclined to talk about her. Your father never told me that you reminded him so strongly of his sister. I suppose I should have guessed. It explains so many things . . ."

"Why did he tell me now?" Julia had wondered aloud. "What did he mean to accomplish?"

"He was trying to tell you that he is sorry," her mother replied softly.

It was strange to be sleeping beneath her parents' roof once more, listening to the subtle creaks of the house, the sound of the wind whipping against the windows, the night noises of the countryside beyond. All of it was acutely familiar. Julia could almost believe she was a little girl again, and that she would wake in the morning to spend the day studying her lessons and seeking private places to read piles of books.

Staring open-eyed into the darkness, Julia saw images of her childhood pass before her in a slow parade . . . her father's iron-fisted rule of the house, her mother's timid presence, her own elaborately wrought fantasies . . . and as always, the shadow of Damon. Throughout her adolescence he had been the focus of her curiosity, fear, and resentment. He had been an invisible burden she had yearned to cast off. And when she had met him, she discovered that he was not so much torment as temptation, luring her dangerously close to a betrayal of her hardwon freedom.

Damon had shown her what she would miss if she spent her life merely interpreting roles on the stage, going home each night to an empty house and a solitary bed. She loved him now in spite of her will to resist; how much more she could love him if she let herself! She wanted him even despite his entanglement with Lady Ashton. Beneath his controlled exterior Damon was a passionate flesh-and-blood man, one who struggled with questions of desire and honor and responsibility. She admired his relentless pursuit of his goals, his efforts to shape the world to his will. If she had met him before she became an actress, how might it have changed her life?

When she finally slept, there was no respite in her dreams. Images of Damon and the sound of his voice filled her mind, tormenting her sweetly. She awoke several times during the night, reshaping her pillow, constantly changing positions in the effort to get comfortable. "Will you send for him?" her mother had asked earlier in the evening. The question still plagued Julia. She couldn't help wanting him . . . she ached to feel his arms around her. However, she would not send for him. She would not depend on anyone but herself.

For the next three days, Julia spent endless hours at her father's bedside, helping to care for him, entertaining him by reading aloud from novels. Edward listened with rapt attention, his gaze locked on her face. "I'm certain you must be an accomplished actress," he said at one point, surprising her into silence. For a man who was so bitterly opposed to her career, it must have been a difficult admission. "When you read, you make the printed word come alive."

"You might come to see me at the Capital someday," Julia said, her tone more wistful than she had intended. "That is, if you could bear the idea of watching your daughter on stage."

"Perhaps," came Edward's dubious reply.

Julia smiled. Merely allowing for the possibility was more than she ever would have expected from her father. "It's possible you would enjoy it," she said. "I'm known as a fairly proficient player."

"You're known as a great actress," he corrected. "I can't seem to avoid every mention of you in the papers. It seems that you are a favorite subject of the gossips—most of it highly discomforting for a father to hear, I might add."

"Oh, gossip," Julia replied airily, enjoying the experience of actually conversing with him. "Almost all of it is false, I assure you. I lead a very quiet life in London—no affairs or scandals to boast of."

"You're often mentioned in the same breath as your theater manager."

"Mr. Scott is a friend, nothing more." Julia

met his gaze directly. "The theater is his only true love, and no other passion could come close to it."

"What of Lord Savage? Your mother seems to think you may have some feelings for him."

Julia looked away, her brow wrinkling. "I do," she admitted reluctantly. "But nothing can come of it. He's too . . . uncompromising."

Edward seemed to understand the wealth of implications in the word. He regarded her silently, his gaze reflective.

"No doubt you would still like me to take my place as his wife and become a duchess someday," Julia said.

A dry laugh escaped him. "As you've so clearly demonstrated over the years, the choice isn't mine to make."

"What if I have the marriage annulled?" she asked. "Would you disown me once again?"

"No," he said after a brief pause. "I will abide by your decision, whatever it happens to be."

Gratitude welled inside her, and she found herself reaching out to him. Her hand closed tightly over his. "Thank you," she said, her throat constricting. "You'll never know what that means to me."

To Julia and Eva's relief, Edward's return to health was slow but steady, his color and strength improving a little each day. As Julia prepared to return to Bath, she took pleasure in the new beginning she had made with her family. Edward's attitude had softened toward her, his autocratic manner now tempered with tolerance and even occasional signs of affection.

He seemed to be more considerate of Eva as well, perhaps realizing how much he had taken his wife's devotion for granted throughout their marriage.

On Monday morning, when the last of her bags had been packed, Julia went to her father's room to say goodbye. It was imperative that she reach Bath in time to prepare for tomorrow's rehearsal and performance. To her surprise, Edward was not alone. He had been meeting with a lawyer who had been in the Hargates' service for at least a decade. "Come in, Julia," Edward said. "I was just concluding some business with Mr. Bridgeman."

Exchanging a polite greeting with the lawyer, Julia waited until he had left the room before turning to her father with a questioning glance.

Edward's expression was solemn, but there was a glint in his eyes that betrayed his satisfaction. He gestured for Julia to sit by him. "I have a gift for you."

"Oh?" Julia made her reply deliberately light and flippant. She settled in the bedside chair. "Dare I hope that I'm back in the will?"

"Yes, you've been reinstated. But I've included something else in the bargain." He extended a packet to her, a sheaf of papers enfolded in parchment.

"What is it?" she asked, hesitating.

"Your freedom."

Cautiously Julia received the packet and held it in her lap.

"Enclosed is your marriage contract," Edward said. "In the meanwhile I will undertake to have the clergyman who performed the rites remove the entry from his register. There will be no sign that the ceremony ever took place."

Julia was silent. Apparently desiring a demonstration of gratitude, Edward frowned at her. "Well? You must be pleased. It's what you claim you've always wanted."

"What I've always wanted is never to have been married in the first place," Julia murmured, trying to rouse herself from her bewilderment. She wasn't certain how she felt . . . perhaps like a prisoner who had been unceremoniously tossed the keys by the jailer. It had come without warning, leaving her no opportunity to prepare herself.

"I can't change that," her father replied. "However, I can try to make amends."

In his own way he was admitting that he had made a mistake—he was doing his best to return what he had taken from her. He was right, the past couldn't be changed. However, they each had control over the future, and they were free to shape it as they wished. Lifting the packet to her lips, Julia regarded him over the edge of it, and summoned a smile.

As Edward saw the crinkling of her eyes, he smiled in return. "In your view, I have done the right thing, then."

She lowered the packet and ran her fingers over the smooth, dry surface. "You've given me the power to navigate my own course. Nothing could please me more."

Her father shook his head slowly as he stared at her. "You're an unusual woman, Julia. I suspect it would be easier for everyone if you were more like your mother."

"But I'm not," Julia replied, a faint smile lingering on her lips. "I'm like you, Father."

The amusements of Bath had quickly begun to pall for Damon. He had little interest in shopping or social amusements, and God knew he had no need of the mineral waters and their vigorous effects on the digestive organs. That left nothing to do except wait for Julia's return, an occupation that bored and frustrated him mightily. He had a busy life awaiting him in London, business and personal affairs that required his immediate attention, and here he was languishing in Bath.

It had been a carefully considered decision to remain in the city rather than follow Julia. Having coaxed the particulars of the situation from Arlyss and a few talkative members of the acting company, Damon knew that Julia had left Bath because of a family illness, and she would likely return by Tuesday. He guessed that Eva had taken a turn for the worse, moving Edward to send for his daughter against all inclinations.

Julia had chosen to go to her family alone, wanting no outsider's support. That was her right, and Damon would not force himself into the Hargates' private family gathering. Besides, he would be damned if he trotted after Julia like a puppy dog.

The second day after Julia's departure, as he returned from a two-mile walk to the nearby village of Weston and back, Damon was surprised to discover that his brother had arrived at the Laura Place terrace house. William was in his usual fine form, stretched out on a Grecian-style couch in the library with a brandy in his hand. He looked up as Damon entered the room, and grinned in welcome.

"Taking your exercise?" William commented, noting the ruddy touch of color in his brother's cheeks and the crisp scent of leaves and autumn air that still clung to him. "Don't tell me you've exhausted all other possibilities for a fine afternoon in Bath. If nothing else you could find some fairly attractive old maid to dally with—the city is full of them. They're quite underrated, old maids. I find that an abundance of gratitude and willingness makes up for a lack of beauty—"

"Spare me your theories on women," Damon said wryly, pouring himself a drink and sitting in a heavy leather armchair.

William sat up and regarded him amiably. "How is your wife, dear brother?"

"Julia's fine, as far as I know." Damon paused and added curtly, "She's left Bath."

"Oh?" William's head tilted to the side, in the manner of an intrigued parrot. "When will she return?"

"Tuesday, most likely. She didn't tell me."

Regarding his brother's grim expression, William suddenly burst out in irrepressible chuckles. "My God," he gasped. "I find it ironic that with the scores of women angling for you, and Lady Ashton's pursuit, all Julia seems to want is to escape you."

"Go on and laugh," Damon said, a reluctant smile intruding on his scowl. "Someday she'll see my charms in a new light."

William continued to snicker like a schoolboy on holiday. "Knowing you, I can guess what the problem is. Let me give you some advice, brother—"

"I'd rather you didn't," Damon said, but William continued.

"Women don't look for honesty in a man. They want to be charmed, deceived, seduced . . . and above all, they don't want to be certain of a fellow. Women like to play games. And before you give me that superior look, reflect on the fact that I've always gotten every woman I made a play for."

Damon smiled sardonically. "Barmaids and actresses are easy conquests, Will."

William dropped his boastful facade, looking vaguely offended. "Well, it shouldn't be difficult for you to make a conquest of Julia. Being married to her ought to give you some advantage over the competition!"

Damon watched his brother steadily. As entertaining as William seemed to find the conversation, there was a barely discernible thread of tension in his expression. He knew his brother well enough to be aware that something was on his mind. Abruptly he changed the subject.

"Why have you come to Bath, Will?"

"To see *My Lady Deception*, of course. I can't stand not knowing the end of a story." William produced a lopsided grin, which faded quickly. A spasm of cringing discomfort crossed his face. "And . . . there's something else."

"I thought so," Damon said dryly. "Are you in trouble again?"

"Not really. The truth is . . . *you're* the one in trouble, and I seem to be caught up in it."

"Explain."

William winced and downed a healthy portion of his drink. "Pauline came to see me in London at my private apartments," he said bluntly. "She said she wanted to become better acquainted with me, as we would be related soon. She said there was no reason we couldn't become 'friends' and support each other as brother and sister do."

"What kind of 'support' did she want?"

"She didn't say exactly, but . . . considering the gown she was wearing, and the way she kept touching me, I think she was trying to seduce me! I swear I did nothing to encourage her, Damon, I would *never* encroach on your territory. For God's sake, we're brothers—"

"It's all right," Damon interrupted calmly. "Tell me what else Pauline said."

"She flattered me like hell, and said that she and I had a lot in common, and that I might be interested in discovering just how much. I pretended not to understand, of course, and did my best to shove her out as soon as possible . . . but not before she said that she was lonely when you were away from London, and she hoped she could call on me for help if it was ever necessary."

Damon considered the situation and let out a long breath as relief washed over him. "Interesting," he murmured. William's information was the confirmation of his greatest hopes. Now there was no doubt in his mind: Pauline was not pregnant. The only surprise was that she would sink low enough to try to seduce his own brother. It made sense, however. If Pauline could succeed in conceiving a child by William, the family resemblance would be incontrovertible . . . and as one of the guilty parties, William would never want to reveal the nasty little secret that his brother's heir was actually his own bastard.

"You're not angry?" William asked, seeming vastly relieved.

"Far from it." Damon lifted his glass in a toast to his brother, and a smile flashed across his face. "Thank you, Will."

"For what?"

"For coming to me with this so quickly. And for your self-restraint. I'm sure many men would have found Pauline's offer too tempting to refuse."

"Please," William said indignantly. "Even I have standards."

"Sometimes," Damon reflected aloud, "I actually think there's hope for you."

"Does this mean I've repaid you for the Sybill Wyvill affair?"

"Almost," Damon said. "If you could see your way clear to help me with one last matter involving Pauline . . ."

William leaned forward, his blue eyes dancing with anticipation. "What do you have in mind?"

* * *

Upon Julia's return, the cast and crew of *My Lady Deception* assembled at the New Theatre on Tuesday morning. To everyone's gratification, the rehearsal was lively and smooth. Even Logan, the relentless perfectionist, couldn't conceal his satisfaction. After bestowing a few words of praise on the assemblage, he dismissed them early, giving them ample time to rest and prepare for the opening performance that night.

Julia couldn't help but notice that something had happened to Arlyss during her absence. There was a sparkle and an air of youthful eagerness about the petite actress. While Arlyss waited in the wings for her cues, she made eyes at Michael Fiske and flirted indiscreetly with him. For his part, Fiske seemed to have completely lost interest in Mary Woods, all his attention focused on Arlyss. Whenever the two were near each other, the air crackled with romantic tension.

As soon as the rehearsal was over, Julia cornered Arlyss and regarded her with an expectant smile. "Well?" she demanded. "Something has occurred between you and Mr. Fiske in my absence, and I must hear about it."

Arlyss's face glowed with a self-satisfied grin. "I've decided you were right. I deserve to be with a man who appreciates me. I went to Michael after the company shared a late supper at the hotel, and whispered a few sweet words in his ear . . . he melted like butter. He loves me, Jessica! To Michael it doesn't matter who I am or what I've done . . . and when I ask him how he could feel that way, he says he's loved me from the first moment he saw me. Can you believe a man would tell me such things?"

"Of course I can," Julia replied in genuine delight. "You deserve to be loved, Arlyss. I'm glad you finally had the wisdom to choose someone who won't take advantage of you." She paused and regarded Arlyss closely. "But what of your infatuation with Mr. Scott?"

"Completely gone." Arlyss leaned closer and said conspiratorially, "If you ask me, Mr. Scott is a cold fish. He'll never give his heart to anyone." Her gaze happened to fall on Michael Fiske as he adjusted a piece of scenery, and her expression brightened. "This afternoon Michael and I are going to shop among the bookstalls, and then we'll stop at a pastry shop for gingerbread. Come with us, Jessica—you look as though you need a bit of fun."

The idea of browsing among stacks of books was definitely appealing. "Thank you," Julia said with a dawning smile. "Perhaps I will."

"Mrs. Wentworth, I want a word with you." Logan interrupted the conversation in his usual brusque manner, taking her aside for a private conversation. Arlyss smiled and went to Fiske, resting her hands on her hips and swaying them saucily.

Julia gave Logan an inquiring glance. He had surprised her earlier in the day with his terse greeting, not even bothering to ask about her father's health. They had launched immediately into the business of the rehearsal, and she had assumed that Logan was either too busy or didn't care to hear about her personal life.

The bright theater lighting struck glints of fire in Logan's auburn hair and made his blunt features seem more angular than usual. "How is your father?" he asked without preamble.

"Much better, thank you."

"And the differences between you? Were any of those resolved?"

For some reason she hesitated before answering, feeling as if the subject were too intimate to discuss openly. But she had confessed her secrets to him before, and she knew him to be a trustworthy confidant. "Yes, actually. My father seems to regret what he has done. He expressed the desire to make amends. He even gave me the means to procure an annulment, if I so choose."

His eyes flickered with interest. "What will you decide?"

Julia thought of facing Damon again, and her stomach tightened with a strange, almost pleasurable tension. "I don't know." A frown etched itself deeply across her forehead. "Part of me wants nothing more than to go to him and tell him how much I love him, that he's worth any sacrifice . . . and the other part wants to cling so tightly to the theater that everything else will be lost. I never imagined that making such a choice would be so difficult."

"There are other options," Logan said, his expression enigmatic.

"Such as?"

"Perhaps we'll discuss them someday."

Perplexed, Julia stared after him as he left, and a short laugh broke from her lips. It was so like Logan to cast out a mysterious statement and then leave. He was a consummate showman, knowing exactly how to capture the attention of any audience and keep it.

Moving slowly among the open-air bookstalls, Julia enjoyed the scent of crisp air mingling with leather and book dust. Some volumes were new, some used, all of them containing the tantalizing promise of new worlds to escape into. Her collection of purchases grew until it had become an ungainly tower of books that wobbled dangerously in her arms. Arlyss and Michael seemed far less interested in the reading material than in each other. They exchanged giggling whispers, meaningful glances, and occasional fondles that they thought no one else could see.

Although Julia had decided she had selected enough books, one more with a scarlet and gold-embossed cover caught her eye, and she opened the thick volume. As she glanced through the first few pages, she heard a vaguely familiar voice nearby. Alertly she listened, and watched through the screen of her veil until she saw the speaker.

Julia's heart lurched as a tall, dark figure came into view a few stalls away, a man with raven-black hair and a striking hard-edged profile. *Damon*, she thought immediately . . . but it wasn't her husband; it was his younger brother, Lord William. He appeared to be less than enthralled by the piles of books around him, complaining to an unseen companion that it was time to leave. "I had better things in mind than hunting for *books*," he said irritably. "Haven't you seen enough of the damned things by now, brother?"

So Damon was here. Julia's gaze darted around the scene, and she found him immediately, his broad-shouldered form unmistakable. Somehow the intensity of her stare must have betrayed her, for he turned in a sudden fluid movement and looked directly at her. An immediate gleam of recognition shone in his eyes. Blindly Julia turned back toward the table of books, while her heart knocked clumsily inside her chest. She held the heavy stack of volumes close to her body, waiting with her eyes half-closed, wondering madly if he would come to her.

Gradually she sensed him standing behind her, close but not touching, his breath stirring the veil that flowed from the narrow brim of her hat. He spoke in a near whisper that undercut the bustle of the bookstall crowd, the softness of his voice recalling the intimate conversations they had shared the last night they had spent together.

"How was your visit to Buckinghamshire?"

Julia wanted to face him, but her feet seemed rooted to the ground. Words threatened to burst from her lips in a nervous flurry. Somehow she managed to contain them and answer calmly. "My father was ill with a fever. I went to him as soon as I found out."

"Your father," he repeated, surprise coloring his tone. "I assumed it was Lady Hargate—"

"No, she's very well, actually. She's nursing Father, and he seems much better now. He and I have come to a sort of . . . truce." Julia felt his hand on her arm, turning her to look at him. She complied, still clutching the pile of books. The luminous gray of his eyes was visible through her veil, his expression remote.

"I'm glad for you," Damon said quietly. "It was a long time coming. No doubt it was a relief to him as well as to you."

"Yes," Julia said, feeling out of breath as she stared at him. Why did he have to be so devastatingly attractive? Why did he have to look serious and brooding? Why was it such an unholy temptation to coax the firm set of his mouth into the passionate softness she remembered so well? She wanted to drop the load of books and reach for his large, warm hands, and pull them to her body. She wanted him, she was starved for him . . . and he gave no clue as to whether he felt the same. "I . . . I'm sorry I didn't tell you I was leaving, but there was little time—"

"It doesn't matter," he said casually, reaching for the books in her arms. "May I take these for you?"

"No, thank you." She withdrew a step, holding her burden tightly.

Damon gave a short nod, as if her refusal was what he had expected. "I have something to tell you," he said matter-of-factly. "I'll be leaving for London tonight. There are matters I've left unattended for too long."

"Oh." Julia managed an indifferent smile, thankful that she was wearing a veil. It wouldn't do for him to see any sign of her sudden deflation, the hollow feeling that seeped through every nerve and fiber. "Will you be seeing Lady Ashton?" some inner devil prompted her to ask.

"I expect so."

The brusque reply did not invite further comment. Questions brimmed inside her, and Julia was seized in the grip of gnawing anxiety. What would occur between Damon and Lady Ashton? Perhaps he would attempt some kind of reconciliation. Pauline would accept, of course. She would welcome him back eagerly, and they would begin to make plans for the life they would share with their baby.

Trying to banish the rankling images from her mind, Julia asked quietly, "Will you be returning to Bath?"

He hesitated while his gaze held hers. "Is that what you want?"

Yes, her heart cried, but she was paralyzed with indecision. All she could do was stare at him mutely.

"Damn you," he muttered. "What do you want from me, Julia?"

Before she could reply, she heard Arlyss's pert voice nearby, half-accusing, half-teasing. ". . . surprised you still remember my name, my lord . . . you made it clear I was only a passing fancy."

To Julia's dismay, William had seen Arlyss among the bookstalls and had wasted no time in approaching her. Turning, Julia watched the scene unfolding before them . . . William eyeing the small actress with roguish appreciation, Arlyss's posture of saucy challenge, and Michael Fiske, all bristling masculinity as he strode toward the pair. It was likely there would be a fight. Julia hated the thought of what such a scene might do to Arlyss's budding romance with Fiske.

"Please," Julia said, instinctively looking to

Damon for help, "don't let your brother cause trouble."

Damon seemed unsympathetic. "There won't be, unless your featherbrained little friend offers William encouragement."

Julia cursed beneath her breath. William and his randy impulses were going to ruin everything for Arlyss. He would soothe Arlyss's wounded pride by making blatant advances to her, and he would leave her again when the seduction was over. And Michael Fiske would want nothing more to do with her.

William grinned at Arlyss, his blue eyes sparkling with irresistible charm. "Of course I remember your name, my sweet. I remember that and a good deal more. I came to Bath because I missed you and your considerable charms."

It was clear Arlyss couldn't resist such blatant flattery. "You came to Bath just to see me?" she asked warily.

"Of course I did. There's no other attraction here."

Michael Fiske joined the conversation, glaring fiercely at his rival in the manner of a handsome mutt challenging a polished thoroughbred. "Arlyss is with me now. Go now, and don't bother her again."

Seeming amused, William addressed his reply to Arlyss. "Am I bothering you, sweetling?"

She stood between the two men, her mop of curls bobbing as she looked from one to the other. Tentatively she inched toward Michael Fiske. "I'm with Mr. Fiske now," she murmured, in a tone that was far from certain. It was a small step, but it was all that Fiske required.

Seizing the meager encouragement, he jerked Arlyss close and planted a bruising kiss on her lips. As Arlyss laughed at the blatant display, Fiske hoisted her in the air and slung her over his shoulder. Feminine shrieks and uncontrollable giggles resulted, causing everyone in the market-place to turn and stare at the pair as Fiske carried Arlyss away.

"Now see here . . ." William protested, beginning to follow them. He was brought up short as Damon caught him by the arm.

"Will . . . find some other pigeon to amuse yourself with."

William hesitated, staring after the departing couple. "You know how I enjoy a challenge," he said wistfully.

"Let this one go," Damon said. "You've caused enough trouble. Besides, you're leaving for London with me tonight . . . remember?"

William grumbled and nodded. Quickly recovering his former high spirits, he cast a roguish glance at Julia and back to Damon. "Just remember *my* advice to *you*," he said, winking broadly before taking his own leave.

Julia turned to Damon. "What was his advice?"

"He told me that women like to be charmed and seduced."

Her mouth twisted wryly. "Your brother has a great deal to learn about women."

"It appears your friends have left you. Would you like to be escorted somewhere?"

Murmuring a refusal, Julia shook her head. "It's only a short walk back to the inn."

"You push me away with one hand and beckon me closer with the other. Some would say you are a tease, Mrs. Wentworth."

"Is that what you think of me?"

"I think you're the most maddening woman I've ever known." His gaze caressed her even as his mocking voice stung her ears. "Make up your mind about what you want, Julia. Soon. My patience has its limits." He left her standing there among the bookstalls, her delicate face drawn in a scowl beneath the veil.

In spite of the reports of the bad luck *My Lady Deception* had experienced in London, every seat in the New Theatre was occupied, the building filled to overflowing. It seemed that everyone of note in Bath was attending, the audience infected with enthusiasm as they waited for the play to begin. Julia came to the wings to wait for her first entrance, smiling briefly at the encouragement the crew offered as they passed her in the semidarkness.

She made an effort to concentrate on the work ahead of her, making the play as successful as it deserved to be. However, it was difficult to push the events of the last few days from her mind. Her mind kept dwelling on the peace offering her father had given her, the scene with Damon today, the knowledge that she could free herself from him at any time. Damon was right; she would have to make a choice soon, if only for her own peace of mind.

Despite the hardships of her profession, she loved being an actress, loved the excitement and fulfillment of it. The idea of giving up the stage for good was unthinkable. But never to see

Damon again . . . or, worse, to see him marry someone else, while her own life was devoid of companionship . . . that was equally repugnant.

"You're not thinking about the play," a voice said behind her, and Julia glanced over her shoulder at Logan Scott.

"A thousand other things," she confessed. "How could you tell?"

"You're so tense that your shoulders are at your ears."

Julia made a face at him and relaxed her shoulders. She took a deep breath, held it for a moment, and let it out slowly. When she looked back at Logan, he seemed reassured.

"That's better."

Thoughtfully Julia looked out onto the stage, the shadowy outlines of scenes and props barely visible behind the lowered curtain. She had always loved this moment just before a play began, anticipation coursing through her body. But for some reason the feeling was tainted with sadness now. She felt almost as if she were a little girl who had opened a brightly wrapped package and found it empty. "How long will my life on the stage last?" she asked, speaking almost to herself. "Will I have another ten years? Even twenty?"

Logan came to stand beside her and viewed her critically. "You'll have a long run, I would say. As you age, you'll have the talent to mature into other kinds of roles, including substantial character parts."

A bleak smile touched her lips. "Will that be enough for me, I wonder?"

"You're the only one who can answer that question."

Together they waited in silence for the curtain to be drawn, for real life to be banished and the illusions to begin.

The performance flew by with lightning speed. For two hours one scene flowed into another, blending into a seamless whole. When Julia wasn't onstage or changing costumes, she waited impatiently in the wings, riveted on the action that kept the audience enthralled. When she was on the boards, speaking her part, she felt as if she were pulling magic from the air. She sensed the way the crowd hung on every word, their gazes following each gesture, every tilt of her head.

Julia knew she had never acted so well with Logan, their scenes resonant with emotion, filled with sparkling humor and yearning. For a while she ceased to exist as herself. There was no other thought in her mind but the play, no feelings inside her except those she manufactured to entertain the audience. As the final curtain fell, she knew that she had fulfilled the expectations others had of her, that she had played the part to the best of her ability. Triumphantly she let Logan pull her in front of the curtain to receive a thunderstorm of clapping and cheers.

Her face glowed, and she sank in a curtsy to acknowledge their appreciation. The applause endured for long minutes until she drifted toward the wing in an effort to slip away. Logan wouldn't let her leave, catching her hand and bringing her forward as the cries of appreciation rose even higher. Flowers and small gifts were thrown to the stage, piling in heaps. Bending to scoop up a white rose, Logan handed the blossom to Julia. She closed her fingers around the long stem and curtsied once more before walking to the wing despite the multitude of voices that entreated her to stay.

The cast and crew backstage erupted with congratulations, making her laugh self-consciously. Her maid Betsy accompanied her to her private dressing room. "There's a pitcher of lemonade for you," Betsy pointed out, and headed to the door, knowing Julia liked a few minutes of privacy after a performance. "I'll be back soon to collect your costume."

"Thank you," Julia said, sighing in relief at the peace and quiet of the small room. She stood before the looking-glass, beginning to unlace the front of her dress. Now that the exhilaration of the performance was fading, she was exhausted. There were blotches of sweat beneath her arms, and the bloom of paint on her cheeks was beginning to streak and fade.

As she contemplated her reflection, she saw a dark form slip into the room. Startled, she whirled around, a faint exhalation leaving her lips as Damon stood before her. She hadn't expected him to be here tonight. Whatever he had thought of the performance, it wasn't delight or pride he felt. A flush colored the tops of his cheeks and the bridge of his nose, and his gray eyes were brilliantly hot. He was angry with her . . . and she wasn't going to be spared the biting lash of his fury.

Chapter 11

Staring at her husband in silent wonderment, Julia didn't resist as he approached her in two strides, crushing her back against the looking-glass. One large hand gripped her arm, and the other came to her face, his fingers wrapping around her jaw.

"I thought you were leaving for London to-night," she managed to say.

"I had to see you first."

"You saw the play—"

"Yes, I saw. I saw the pleasure you took in your acting. I saw how much it meant to you and everyone else in this cursed place."

Julia shook her head, confused by his anger.

Damon's fingers tightened on her jaw, almost hurting her. "You're going to choose this, aren't you?" he said through his teeth. "You won't be able to give it up. Tell me the truth, Julia."

"Not now—"

"Yes, now. I need to hear the words from you before I leave."

"How would *you* react if I asked you to sacrifice everything for me?"

307

"Is that your answer?"

"I'm not even certain what the question is," she cried, trying to pull free.

"I want you," he muttered.

"But only on your terms."

"Yes, on my terms. Taking my name, living in my home, sleeping in my bed each night. I want you to be mine with no limits . . . every part of you . . . every thought, every word you speak . . ."

Julia's struggles ceased suddenly as she felt his mouth on hers, the heat of his lips and tongue robbing her of breath. It seemed that he was trying to brand her with his kiss, imprint her very soul with the force of his jealous passion. His arms were hard as they closed around her. Roughly his hands gripped the curves of her body, his head bending over hers until she arched against him. She didn't want to respond, but the wildness rose inside her until she submitted with a sob of despair.

Her hands reached around his neck, fingers clenching in his dark hair to hold him close. Damon made an urgent sound in his throat and cupped his hands over her buttocks, lifting her high against him. "You are mine," he said against her throat, teeth and bristle scraping her soft skin. "You'll never be free of me, no matter what you do."

She only half-heard the words, her body straining desperately against his, seeking the pleasure that only he could give her. His palms slipped up to her bodice, catching the edges of the fabric and spreading them wide until the laces slid free. Pushing her chemise down, he sought her breasts. His warm fingers curved beneath their tender weight, his thumbs passing over her nipples. Gasping, Julia offered herself to him, her mouth open beneath his, her breasts impelled into his hands.

He urged her against the dressing table and lowered his head to her breast, drawing the tight peak past his lips, against the flat of his tongue. Holding on to him for balance, Julia clasped his taut body between her thighs, her arms locked around his waist. Damon turned his attention to her other breast, licking and tugging at the rosy crest. Julia was trapped between desire and denial, knowing that the closeness she craved so desperately would be her ultimate undoing.

"Please stop," she said between the rasping breaths that were torn from her throat. "Please . . . I don't want this."

At first Damon seemed not to hear her, his attention focused on the ripening promise of her body, his mouth moving hungrily over her skin. She pushed at his chest and head, tentatively and then with greater force, until the embrace was broken. His gaze bore into hers, hands coming up to hold her head steady. "I'm going to London," he said thickly, "and then I'm coming back for you."

"No—"

"I'll never let you go. Not until you can look into my eyes and tell me that you don't love me . . . that you can spend the rest of your life without needing this . . . without wanting me."

Her lips trembled, but she couldn't make a sound.

The opening click of the door, as quiet as it

was, made them both start in surprise. The maid, Betsy, stood in the doorway with a basket of clothes. "Oh," she said, her eyes round as she beheld Julia's visitor.

Damon moved in front of Julia to hide her from view while she fumbled with the laces to her bodice. "Excuse me, Mrs. Wentworth," the maid murmured, and disappeared at once. The door shut firmly behind her.

Flushing, Julia continued the effort to restore her clothing, while Damon watched intently. "Please don't come back for me," Julia said, avoiding his gaze. "I can't see you for a while. I need time to think."

"You mean you want time to convince yourself that things can go back to the way they were before we met. It won't work, Julia. You'll never be the same . . . and neither will I."

"You'll make it impossible for me to act. I won't be able to concentrate on anything."

"I'll return soon," he insisted, "and we'll settle things once and for all."

Julia didn't move as Damon left. She leaned against the dressing table for support and let out an unsteady breath. It seemed that she had finally lost the tight control she had maintained over her life ever since leaving home. She thought of the papers her father had given her, the key to her freedom. Did she have the courage to use them? She hated the paralysis that had come over her, the fear of losing Damon almost as great as the fear of giving herself to him.

Slowly she undressed, letting her costume drop to the floor in a heap. "Mrs. Wentworth?"

came Betsy's voice, accompanied by a timid knock.

"Yes, come in."

The maid's face was stained with a blush. "I'm sorry about interrupting before, ma'am, but I didn't know—"

"That's perfectly all right," Julia said evenly. "Just help me with my clothes."

The maid helped Julia to dress, fastening a row of buttons on the back of her green silk gown. After pinning her hair tightly on the crown of her head, Julia washed her face and checked her appearance in the looking-glass. Her lips were soft and swollen, her cheeks were flushed, and there were betraying bristle marks on her throat. Carefully Julia arranged the high ruched neckline of her gown to cover the marks. She paused as she heard Logan Scott's deep murmur beyond the dressing room.

"Mrs. Wentworth, I desire a word with you."

Julia motioned for the maid to admit him inside. Logan had also changed his clothes and washed, the residual dampness turning his gleaming hair the color of cherry wood.

Picking up her basket of clothes, Betsy said good night and left them alone.

"Were you pleased with the performance tonight?" Julia asked, "or have you come to deliver a critique?"

Logan smiled. "You exceeded every hope I had for you. You made everyone in the cast shine in your reflected glory, including myself."

The lavish praise was so unexpected that Julia was disconcerted. She gave him a tentative smile and turned to straighten the articles on her dressing table.

"I saw Lord Savage coming backstage," Logan remarked. "From his expression, it was obvious he didn't intend to congratulate you."

"No, he didn't." Julia's hands went still on the dressing table, fingertips pressed on the smooth surface until they turned white. She took care that her reflection gave no clue as to what had happened.

Logan regarded her thoughtfully and gave a short nod, as if coming to a decision. "Come with me, Julia. I want to talk to you about an idea I've been considering lately."

She turned toward him, unable to hide her surprise. "The hour is late."

"I'll deliver you to the inn by midnight." His wide mouth curved in a smile. "I have a proposition that concerns your future."

Julia was intrigued. "Tell me."

"In private." Logan clamped a gentle hand over her arm and drew her from the dressing room.

"Where are we going?" she asked, picking up her cloak as they left.

"I have a house near the river."

Mystified, Julia accompanied him without further questions. She was puzzled as to why he would allow her to see yet another of his residences, inviting her a step further into the private world he guarded so jealously.

After making their way through the crowd waiting outside the theater, they took a carriage ride to a small, elegant villa situated amid thickly wooded grounds. Like Logan's London home, it was Italianate in flavor, with a luxurious but quiet atmosphere.

Sitting in the parlor with a glass of wine in her hand, Julia relaxed against the upholstered back of an Empire-style sofa. She stared at Logan expectantly. He fiddled with a few objects placed artfully on a marble-topped pier table: a Chinese meiping vase, a green malachite box, an ebony Louis XIV bracket clock. He slid her a sidelong glance, appraising her mood.

"You look as if you're preparing to talk me into something," Julia commented.

"I am," he said with disarming frankness. "But before I make the attempt, tell me how things stand between you and Lord Savage."

Julia occupied herself with removing a minuscule bit of cork from the inside of her glass. She finally looked up at him with an uncomfortable smile. "May I know the reason you're asking?"

"I don't want to interfere in your relationship . . . your marriage."

"There can be no real marriage," she said, her voice dull and flat. "It's clear to me that we would both be better off with an annulment. Unfortunately Lord Savage doesn't agree . . . and he's rather overwhelming when it comes to getting what he wants."

"And he wants you," Logan said quietly.

"He wants a traditional wife." Julia took a swallow of wine. "He wants me to become Lady Savage and leave all traces of Jessica Wentworth in the past."

"That won't be possible. Not for someone with your talent."

"If only I were a man," she said bitterly.

"Then I could have everything . . . my work, a family, freedom to decide things for myself . . . and no one would disapprove. But I'm a woman, and no matter what I choose, I'm going to be unhappy."

"For a while, perhaps. The pain of losing something—or someone—fades in time."

Logan was so matter-of-fact, so self-possessed, as if his heart was encased in steel. Julia wasn't certain if she was envious or appalled by his coolness. "You said you had a proposition for me?" she asked.

He came to the sofa and sat at the other end. His tone was brisk and businesslike. "During the next few years I'm going to make some changes at the Capital."

"Oh?"

"I'm going to build the company into the most renowned group of actors in the world. I need you to be part of it."

"I'm flattered that you think so highly of my work."

"I never flatter anyone, Julia—certainly not someone I respect. You must understand by now that you're an invaluable asset to the company. I intend for you to be a cornerstone of its success. I'm willing to offer you a share in the Capital's profits to ensure that you'll stay."

Julia was silent with astonishment. She had never heard of Logan making such an offer to another actor.

"I will do whatever is necessary to protect my investment in you," he continued, "and to make a difficult choice easier for a friend."

She tilted her head, considering the words

with a perplexed frown. "It sounds as if you're offering a sort of . . . business partnership?"

"You could describe it as such. But the partnership would involve more than business."

More than business? Julia stared at him closely. There was nothing predatory in his expression, nothing that would lend a sexual intent to his words. What could he possibly mean? Finding it inconceivable that she was having this conversation with Logan, she gave him a questioning look. "Perhaps you should explain."

Absently Logan tugged at a lock of his ruddy hair. "I've told you before that I don't believe in love. However, I do believe in friendship—the kind that involves respect and honesty. I would never marry for love, but I would choose to marry for practical reasons."

"Marry?" she repeated with an astonished laugh. "Are you possibly suggesting that you and I . . . but I could never marry a man I didn't love!"

"Why not?" he asked calmly. "You would have all the benefits of marriage . . . protection, companionship, mutual interests . . . and none of the liabilities. No false promises, no emotional entanglement, nothing but the security that two friends could offer each other. Consider it, Julia. Together we could build an acting company like nothing the world has ever seen. We're more alike than you think, both of us existing on the fringe of a society that looks down their noses at us—and at the same time they need what we have to offer."

"But is it necessary for us to *marry?*"

"As my wife, you would accompany me to social events in London, Paris, and Rome. You could devote as much time as you wanted to your acting, choose roles for yourself, develop plays for the theater . . . I don't know of any woman who has had such influence in this profession."

"The last thing I expected was to receive another proposal," Julia said dazedly.

"There's an important difference. Savage wants to marry you in order to keep you all to himself. I'm offering to marry you in order to make us both successful, financially and artistically."

Agitated, Julia finished her wine and set aside the glass. She stood and wandered around the room, repeatedly smoothing the long sleeves of her green gown. "What about . . . sleeping together?" she asked without looking at him. "Would that be part of the arrangement?"

"If the idea becomes mutually agreeable, I don't see why not. However, in the meantime we would pursue our separate interests. I don't want to own you, Julia. I want no rights over you—and you would have none over me."

Gathering her wits, Julia turned and faced Logan squarely. He lounged on the sofa, looking utterly relaxed, as if he had proposed afternoon tea rather than marriage. "Why me?" Julia asked bluntly. "There are a score of other women you could marry, including a daughter of some titled family that would welcome a man of your means."

"I don't want some clinging vine or social-minded miss. I want someone with whom I share common goals. As an actress, you have potential beyond any I've ever seen. As a person . . . I happen to like you. I believe we would get on well together." His intense blue eyes focused on her pale face. "Moreover," he added softly, "it would help you out of your dilemma, wouldn't it? If you became my wife, Savage would never bother you again."

As she returned his gaze, Julia was suddenly not staring into blue eyes but silver-gray ones. The sound of Damon's voice filled her mind. *You are mine . . . You'll never be free of me, no matter what you do.*

This was the only sure way to guarantee that the threat Damon posed to her independence and her acting career would be extinguished. If she didn't accept Logan's protection, she knew in her very marrow that she wouldn't be able to resist Damon's insistent passion. She would let herself be seduced, persuaded, convinced . . . and face a lifetime of regrets afterward. She loved Damon, but she couldn't change herself into the kind of woman he wanted.

She was filled with misgivings, but in the mass of contradictions she waded through, there seemed to be no other choice. When she spoke, her voice sounded faint and far away. "I . . . I'll need to take care of some things first."

"Of course." There was a glimmer of satisfaction in Logan's eyes. "When would you like me to arrange the wedding?"

"As soon as possible," Julia said stiffly. "I would like this to be done right away."

Logan approached her, his bluntly attractive features softening with concern. "Julia, if you want to change your mind—"

"No," she interrupted, squaring her shoulders. "This is the right decision."

"I agree." He reached out and took hold of her upper arms, squeezing gently. "You'll find I'm a good friend, Julia. I wear well over time."

She nodded and smiled in spite of the heavy feeling inside, as if a block of granite were lodged in her chest.

The next morning Julia received a note at the Bath Inn from her old friend and teacher Mrs. Florence. The elderly actress had come to town for reasons of health and social amusement, and was full of praise for Julia's performance in *My Lady Deception.* Mrs. Florence extended an invitation to meet in the Pump Room during the fashionable morning hour, and Julia didn't hesitate to comply. It had been several months since she visited the elderly woman in London, despite the fact that they lived on the same street. Time had a way of slipping by much too quickly, and Julia felt guilty for not having made a point of going to see her friend.

When she arrived at the Pump Room, Julia was pleased to see that Mrs. Florence appeared as vibrant as ever, her faded red hair arranged in stylish coils on top of her head, her face filled with keen intelligence. She wore her age gracefully, like a marble statue that had been gently weathered and mellowed by time. Seated at a small table with a glass of mineral water before her, Mrs. Florence listened to the music provided by a nearby string quartet. As soon as she saw Julia, her eyes brightened expectantly.

"Mrs. Florence," Julia exclaimed, sincerely glad to see her. It was providential that her mentor should have come to Bath at precisely the moment she needed her. She sat in the chair beside her, and took the elderly woman's soft, finely wrinkled hands in hers. Mrs. Florence's fingers were adorned with a collection of substantial jewels, and a slim rope of pearls and garnets was wrapped around her wrist. "You look wonderful, as always."

"It's been a long time since you came to call," Mrs. Florence said in friendly reproof. "I finally realized I would have to travel to Bath to see you."

Julia began to sputter with apologies and explanations, and gave her a lame smile. "I've been *very* busy. You can't imagine—"

"Oh, I believe I can," Mrs. Florence interrupted dryly. "I'm not so old that I can't remember the demands made on a popular actress." She regarded Julia fondly. "You may remove your veil, child. I can keep all of the admirers and curiosity-seekers at bay."

Julia obeyed, lifting the veil from her small hat, aware of the sudden wave of interest that passed through the room and the gazes that fastened on her. A pair of plump women with excited expressions immediately rose to approach the table. Expertly Mrs. Florence lifted her cane, which had been hooked around the back of her chair, and raised it as if to poke them away. "Another time," she told them firmly. "My young friend and I are having a private conversation."

Cowed, the women retreated and muttered complaints under their breath, while Julia suppressed an admiring laugh. "You're a tigress, Mrs. Florence."

The elderly woman waved away the praise. "I blessed the day when I could finally be rude to people and have them excuse me because of my age." She returned Julia's smile. "You're maturing into a splendid actress, Jessica. I was so pleased and proud to see you on stage last night, and to think that I might have had some small part in your success."

"I owe everything to you, for your advice and guidance, and for the way you encouraged me to join the Capital players."

"It seems you've achieved everything you dreamed of," Mrs. Florence remarked with a vaguely quizzical look. "Why is it that you don't look happy, my dear?"

Ruefully Julia realized that her friend knew her too well to be fooled by facades. She settled back in her chair and sighed. "Do you remember the conversation we had years ago, when you told me that you hadn't married the man you loved because he wanted you to leave the theater? You implied that I might someday face the same dilemma, and I didn't believe you."

"And now you do," Mrs. Florence said, immediate understanding gleaming in her eyes. "It gives me no satisfaction to be proven right, Jessica. I wouldn't have wished this for you—it's a very peculiar sort of pain, isn't it?"

Julia nodded, suddenly unable to speak. Her chest and throat felt unbearably tight.

"I assume he proposed to you," Mrs. Florence remarked. "What was your reply?"

"I . . . broke off our relationship. And then last night I received a proposal from another man . . . from Mr. Scott."

Mrs. Florence looked intrigued. "Is he in love with you?"

"No, it's nothing like that. He described it as a marriage of convenience."

"Oh, I see." Mrs. Florence laughed softly. "Your Mr. Scott's ambitions know no limits, do they? If you left the Capital, there would be a difficult vacancy to fill. However, with you as his wife, he could build his acting company into something extraordinary . . . and he's willing to marry you in order to ensure it. The question is, are you willing to sacrifice the other man—the one you love—for the sake of your profession?"

"*You* did," Julia pointed out.

Mrs. Florence pinched her nose shut and took a sip of bitter mineral water. "I also told you that I regretted my actions," she said, using a lace handkerchief to dab at the corners of her mouth.

"If you could make the choice all over again—"

"No," Mrs. Florence interrupted gently but firmly. "Once the decision is made, it won't do to look back. Proceed in the direction you've chosen, whatever it may be, and tell yourself it's all for the best."

Julia threw her a pleading glance. "If only you would advise me, as you've done so often before—"

"I'll dispense all the advice about acting you could ever require, but not about your personal life. I can't make such a decision for you. And I don't care to think about what I might have done differently. The past can't be changed."

Julia made a face, realizing just how much she had hoped that Mrs. Florence would tell her what to do. "There's only one thing I'm certain of," she said glumly. "It will be safer to follow my head rather than my heart."

"Indeed." The older woman regarded her with a mixture of amusement and sympathy. "At all costs we must be safe, mustn't we?"

William strode into the parlor of his St. James terrace apartment, where his butler had just shown Lady Ashton. It was no surprise that Pauline had come to call at this late hour in the evening. Immediately upon William's return to London, he had made it known among the appropriate social circles that he would be staying at his town residence for a while. In addition, he had hinted broadly that he was at a loss for sorely needed female companionship. Like a fly to honey, Pauline had wasted no time in descending on him.

Pauline was standing at the window, expertly displaying her spectacular silhouette. In a practiced move, she turned to face him with the hint of a smile on her red lips. She was strikingly beautiful in a burgundy velvet dress that blended in rich harmony with the masculine colors of the room. The bodice was cut very low, revealing an inch or two more of her smooth white breasts than was tasteful. The effect was stimulating, to say the least.

"Lady Ashton . . . what a surprise," William murmured, crossing the room to her out-stretched hands.

"Lord William," she purred, wrapping her fingers around his. "I had to see you right away. I hope you don't mind. I'm so terribly dis-traught."

He looked into her face with a show of con-cern. "But why, Lady Ashton?"

All of a sudden there was a glimmer of moisture in her dark eyes. "You must call me Pauline. Surely we've known each other long enough for that."

"Pauline," he repeated obediently. "Won't you sit down?"

Reluctantly she released his hands and went to the sofa, spreading her skirts across the slick damask.

"A drink?" William offered. At her nod, he went to pour each of them some wine, and sat on the other end of the sofa. Pauline held the wine glass in her long fingers, toying with the shape of it, delicately tracing the stem and the rim.

"I hope I haven't interrupted your plans for the evening," she said, staring at him intently.

"Nothing to interrupt," he assured her.

"You look lonely, poor boy." Her voice sof-tened to a throaty whisper. "I happen to be lonely as well." Her sleek head came to rest on his shoulder, causing him to shift uncomfort-ably.

"Lady Ashton . . . Pauline . . . please don't

think I'm unsympathetic, but to someone with a suspicious mind, this situation would seem rather compromising. I owe my brother a certain amount of loyalty—"

"Your brother is the reason I'm distraught," she interrupted, smoothing the fabric of William's coat before settling her cheek on his shoulder. "I can't bear to talk of what is owed to *him*, when he apparently thinks nothing is owed to *me*. There is no one I can trust with my innermost feelings, except you. You wouldn't be so heartless as to turn me away, would you?"

William squirmed uncomfortably. "I can't interfere in the relationship between you and Damon—"

"I don't want you to interfere," she said, her hand beginning a slow stroking of his chest. "All I want is a friend. Is that too much to ask of you, William? Your brother hasn't been very kind to me of late. Can you imagine what it is like to be a woman in my position? I need some companionship."

"Surely you can get that from someone other than me."

"No one is able to offer me what you can, William."

"But my brother—"

"Damon is gone for now. He doesn't care what I do in his absence, as along as I'm available when he wants me. And he's made no claim on me . . . you know that. Come, William, you're a man of the world. There's nothing wrong with two friends spending time with each other in private."

Before he could reply, she leaned over him

and crushed her red lips on his. Her small hands swarmed hungrily over his body, while her exotic scent surrounded him in an invisible cloud.

"Pauline," he yelped, flinching as she sought between his thighs with tightly grasping fingers.

"It's all right," she muttered, levering her body over his. "We won't tell anyone. Haven't you wondered what it would be like with me, William? I'll give you pleasure beyond anything you could imagine. Don't worry about your brother. You must be jealous of him—anyone in your position would be. He's the firstborn, he has all the money and influence. You deserve a taste of what he's had . . . and I'm going to give it to you." Aggressively she pulled his hand to her breast. "Yes, touch me," she purred. "Touch me everywhere . . . take me to your bedroom . . . oh, William . . ."

As she twisted herself around him, a shadow crossed Pauline's face, and her heavy lashes lifted a fraction. Suddenly her eyes flew open, and she turned white with astonishment as she beheld Damon standing before them. His eyes were cold, his expression as hard as marble.

The moment was fraught with tension until Pauline shoved William away in a decisive motion. She jerked at her bodice in a futile effort to cover her ample breasts. Her gaze returned to Damon's, and her voice trembled as she spoke. "I'm sorry you had to see this, darling. It must pain you to witness your younger brother trying to take advantage of me."

A cynical smile touched Damon's lips. "I heard everything, Pauline."

William leaped from the sofa and pulled at his cravat and coat, looking for all the world like an outraged virgin. "I was wondering how damned long you were planning to let it go on," he said, giving Damon a dark frown.

"You planned this?" Pauline asked in building fury, looking from one to the other. "The two of you conspired to trick me?" She confronted Damon with her fists clenched. A wrathful flush covered her face. "You have no decency! I will not be manipulated or deceived, you bastard!"

Suddenly Damon burst into uproarious laughter. "*You* won't be manipulated?"

"That's right. You owe me for all the months we spent together, for the use of my body and the way you misled me—"

"I paid for the use of your body, overpriced as it was," Damon informed her, a gleam of laughter lingering in his eyes. "As for your being misled . . . you'll have to explain, since it's not precisely clear to me."

"You let me believe that you would take responsibility for this baby!"

"There is no baby, though not for your lack of trying."

"I was doing it for *us*," she said vehemently. "You know we're a good match, Damon. You know I'm the best you'll ever have, and that we're right for each other—"

"I know you were planning to foster my brother's bastard on me," Damon said softly. "That was a master stroke, Pauline, though hardly flattering to William or me."

"I would have succeeded. I only miscalculated how much under your thumb he is." She cast a baleful glance at William. "You have no will of your own, do you?" she asked spitefully. "You'll spend your entire life living in your older brother's shadow—"

"That's enough," William said, coming forward to take her by the arm. "Damned if I have to be insulted under my own roof." He bundled her out of the room, while she spat and hissed like an enraged feline.

When William returned, he looked harassed and exhausted, and there was a distinct slap mark on his right cheek.

"Is she gone?"

"Yes, after giving me a parting shot." William rubbed his cheek reflectively. "My God, she must be a tigress in bed. It's a wonder you weren't eaten alive. You're a better man than I, brother—I prefer my females a little more accommodating than that."

"Thank God I'm finally rid of her," Damon said, dropping into a chair and stretching out his legs.

William smiled as he beheld the weary relief on his brother's face. He went to the sideboard and poured two brandies. "I assume you're going to tell Julia right away?"

"Yes—although it's not going to solve the problems between us."

"What problems could you possibly have now?"

Frowning, Damon took the drink that William offered him. "The last time I saw Father, he told me that no woman would ever be straitlaced enough to suit me. He was right. I've made it clear to Julia that I want her to play yet another role . . . the properly dependent and devoted wife, existing only to serve my needs."

"I don't see what's wrong with that."

Damon shook his head and groaned quietly. "Julia isn't like any other woman I've ever met. Unfortunately the very things that make her unique are also the obstacles to a peaceful marriage between us."

"You want her to leave the theater for good," William said rather than asked.

"I can't see any other way. God knows I can't live with the idea of my wife flaunting herself on stage in front of thousands of people. I've tried to imagine it—" Damon stopped and rubbed his temples. "I can't," he said gruffly. "But neither can I stop wanting her."

"Perhaps in time that will fade," William said with an effort at diplomacy. "There are other women in the world, some of them every bit as beautiful and accomplished as Julia—and they would leap at the chance to sacrifice whatever was necessary in order to marry the future Duke of Leeds."

"I don't want anyone else."

"You and your women . . ." William shook his head and grinned. "You always pick the complicated ones. Thank God I'm a man with simple tastes. I assure you, my barmaids and lightskirts never give me the problems you've been having."

Damon went to his London residence, intending to leave for Bath in the morning after a good night's rest. However, he was awakened in the predawn hours by his butler, who knocked with quiet insistence at the bedroom door until he sat up in bed. "What is it?" he grumbled.

The door opened a crack. "My apologies, my lord, but one of the footmen from Warwickshire was dispatched to bring you a letter. The matter is of some urgency. I assumed you would want to know immediately."

Damon shook his head to clear the haze from his brain. "Know what?"

Entering the room with an oil lamp in hand, the butler set it on the night table and handed a sealed letter to Damon.

Blinking in the yellow light, Damon broke the wax seal and scanned the letter quickly. It was from his father's doctor. "Damn," he said softly, and to his surprise, the parchment trembled in his hand.

The butler averted his eyes, though he wore a look of quiet understanding. "Do you wish to notify your brother, Your Grace?"

After a week of rapturously received performances of *My Lady Deception*, the play's success was being touted all over England. Theaters from Bristol to York were clamoring to be included among the Capital players' tour destinations. Critics had begun to call the character of Christine one of Jessica Wentworth's signature roles, one that only she could play with such artless perfection.

Julia found it ironic that the success she had dreamed of should prove to be far less fulfilling than she had expected. She felt alive only in the glow of the stage lighting, while every moment off the boards seemed flat and anticlimactic.

Now she understood exactly how Logan felt about the theater. Because she had sacrificed everything else of value in her life, the illusions of the stage were all she had left.

Logan had offered to give Julia a grand wedding, but the thought of it made her uneasy. She asked him instead to arrange a private ceremony, and to keep their plans secret. She wasn't yet ready to offer explanations or face the surprise of friends and family when they learned of her decision to marry Logan. Not being the sentimental sort, Logan had readily agreed. In the meanwhile Julia had consulted with a lawyer who had confirmed everything her father had said. Any day now, Damon would receive the letter requesting the return of her dowry.

After the next-to-last performance of the play in Bath had been concluded, Julia sat in her dressing room and removed the paint and sweat from her face. Dully she stared into the looking-glass, wondering how to take away the numbness she felt inside.

"Jessica!" Arlyss burst into the dressing room without warning, her face glowing with excitement. "I had to see you at once. You'll be the first to know."

Julia turned to her with a wan smile. "The first to know what?"

Arlyss's smile turned shy, and she extended her hand. "Michael just gave this to me."

Still seated, Julia leaned close and looked at Arlyss's fourth finger, where a small diamond glittered on a narrow gold band. "Oh, my," she breathed, and glanced up at her friend's face. "Does this mean—"

"Yes!" Arlyss beamed at her.

"It's very soon, isn't it?"

"It may seem so to others, but not to me. Michael is the only man who will ever love me like this, and I love him the same way." Arlyss stared proudly at the ring and tilted her hand to make it glitter. "Isn't it pretty?"

"It's beautiful," Julia assured her.

"He also gave me this." Arlyss showed her half of a broken silver coin. "It's a tradition in the Fiske family to break a coin when a couple becomes engaged. Michael is keeping the other half. Isn't it romantic?"

Taking the coin from her friend, Julia looked at it closely, and her mouth curved in a bittersweet smile. "You're very lucky, Arlyss. It's a rare thing to be able to marry someone you love."

Seeing the wistfulness on Julia's face, Arlyss leaned a hip against the dressing table and stared at her sharply. "What's the matter, Jessica? Are you having problems with your lover? Is it Lord Savage?"

"He's not my lover. At least not anymore. I've . . ." Julia hesitated and chose her words carefully. "I've made certain the relationship is over."

"I don't understand why. He's handsome, rich, and he seems to be a gentleman—"

"I've realized that I have no future with him."

"Even if that's true, why can't you just enjoy the affair while it lasts?"

"Because I'm going to . . ." Julia stopped abruptly, knowing that it would be extremely unwise to confide anything in Arlyss if she wished to keep it private. But she felt driven to tell someone. The unspoken words seemed to burn on her lips.

"What is it?" Arlyss asked, frowning in concern. "You can tell me, Jessica."

Julia lowered her head and stared at her lap. "I'm going to marry Mr. Scott."

Arlyss's eyes widened. "I can't believe it. Why in the world would you do that?"

All Julia could manage was a lame shrug in reply.

"You don't love him," Arlyss continued. "Anyone can see that. Are you having financial troubles? Are you doing it for your career?"

"No, it . . . just seems the best choice."

"You're making a mistake," Arlyss said with certainty. "You don't belong with Mr. Scott. When were you planning to marry him?"

"The day after tomorrow."

"Thank God there's still time to call it off."

Somehow Julia had thought that telling a friend about her decision might ease some of the depression and heaviness inside. Her hopes deflated rapidly as she realized that no amount of sympathy or well-intentioned objections would change the situation. "I can't do that," she said softly, and gave the silver half-coin back to Arlyss. She picked up a damp cloth and wiped it over her cheeks, erasing the last smudges of rouge.

Arlyss contemplated Julia while her nimble mind raced from one speculation to another. "Oh, Jessica . . . you aren't pregnant, are you?"

Julia shook her head, her throat squeezing hard against an upswell of emotion. "No, no, it's nothing like that. It's just that I can't have the man I want, for too many reasons to explain. And if a life with him isn't possible, I might as well marry Mr. Scott."

"B-but," Arlyss spluttered, "you're the one who's always telling me to choose a man for love and no other reason! You told me—"

"I meant every word," Julia said, her voice slightly hoarse. "Unfortunately some dreams aren't possible for everyone."

"There must be something I can do to help."

Reaching out to touch her friend's hand, Julia smiled at her fondly, her eyes glittering suddenly. "No," she murmured. "But thank you, Arlyss. You're a dear friend, and I'm happy for you."

Arlyss didn't reply, a preoccupied expression stealing over her face.

There was an unreal quality about the Duke of Leeds's private funeral, attended by only a few relatives and close friends. It was difficult for Damon to understand that his father had finally been laid to rest, that there would be no more of the endless arguments and frustrations and amusements his father had provided over the years. Glancing at his brother's tense face, Damon sensed that William was experiencing the same mixture of sadness and bewilderment.

After the coffin had been lowered into the cold autumn ground and the shovels of dirt landed on its glossy wooden surface, the mourners left to return to the castle and partake of refreshments. Damon and William followed at a slower pace, their long legs matched in a leisurely stride.

A breeze whipped through Damon's hair and cooled his face as he stared at the gray-green landscape around them. He took comfort in the familiar sight of the castle, serene and stalwart as always, and he felt a flicker of pride that through his own efforts the estate had been kept in the family. Frederick had nearly lost everything for the Savages. Still, despite the duke's selfish whims and dangerous habits, there was no trace of satisfaction in his passing. Damon knew that he was going to miss his father . . . in fact, he already did.

"Father had a hell of a good time, didn't he?" William murmured. "He did whatever he pleased and damned the consequences. If he hasn't made it to heaven, I'll bet he's managed to tempt old Lucifer into a grand game of cards by now."

Damon almost smiled at the image.

"I'm too much like him," William continued bleakly. "I'll end up exactly as he did, alone and chortling over my past debaucheries, trying to pinch the housemaids as they pass by."

"You won't," Damon assured him. "I wouldn't let that happen."

William expelled a deep sigh. "Precious little you've done to stop me so far. I have to take stock of my life, Damon. I've got to do something besides chase after lightskirts and spend my allowance on drink and clothes and horses."

"You're not the only one who has to change."

Upon hearing Damon's grim tone, William turned a surprised gaze on him. "Surely you're not referring to yourself? You're conscientious, responsible. You have no bad habits—"

"I'm overbearing as hell. I try to make everyone else fit into the patterns I've devised for them."

"I've always assumed that's part of being the elder son. Some people would make a virtue of it."

"Julia isn't one of those people."

"Well, she's not the usual sort of female, is she?" William glanced at the castle before them, its dignified lines and great stone arches reflected in the silver lake below. "Can you imagine her living so far removed from the amusements of London?"

As a matter of fact, Damon could. It wasn't difficult to picture Julia riding with him through the hills and woods that surrounded the estate, her blond hair wind-tousled . . . or acting as hostess at a dance in the great hall, her slender figure illuminated by the massive chandeliers . . . or twining with him in the enormous bed in the east-facing bedroom, waking together as the sun rose.

Damon's mind was still filled with images of Julia as he and William entered the castle. Bypassing the crowd that was milling in the parlor and dining room, they headed to the library, where Mr. Archibald Lane awaited them. Lane was a lawyer Damon had employed for years to help oversee his affairs. Although somewhat retiring in manner and appearance, Lane was acutely intelligent. He was only slightly older than Damon, but his thinning hair and glasses gave him an appearance of quiet maturity.

"My lord . . . I mean, Your Grace . . ." Lane murmured as he shook Damon's hand. "I trust all is well with you? That is, as well as could be expected?"

Damon nodded and offered the lawyer a drink, which he declined. "I assume there are no surprises in my father's will," Damon remarked, nodding at the neat sheaf of papers on the desk nearby.

"Nothing that appears to be out of the ordinary, Your Grace. However, before we attend to that, there is something . . ." An uneasy expression crossed Lane's narrow face. "Recently I received a copy of a letter which pertains to the matter of Mrs. Wentworth and the circumstances of your, er . . . marriage."

Damon stared at him alertly.

"It seems that the union was invalid from the beginning," the lawyer continued, "It should be regarded in the light of a betrothal that was never fulfilled. As such, Lord Hargate has requested the return of the dowry that was paid to the Savages."

Damon shook his head, trying to comprehend what Lane had said.

"According to Hargate, his daughter Julia considers the both of you free of all obligations from now on."

"I have to talk to her," Damon heard himself mutter. Julia wanted to end all hope of a relationship between them. He had to convince her otherwise. "Damn her . . . she's my wife." Although he knew that wasn't really true, he couldn't think of her in any other way. He loved her . . . he needed her.

"Your Grace," the lawyer said, "you have no wife. By any legal definition, you never did."

You have no wife. The words seemed to ring in Damon's ears, quiet and yet dizzying in their intensity. *You have no wife . . .*

William chose that moment to intercede. "Damon . . . this may be fate's way of telling you to make a new beginning. Father's gone, and you're a free man now. There is no reason you shouldn't begin to enjoy some of the things in life you've always denied yourself."

"After all this time . . ." Damon said. "After all the years I spent trying to find her, she dances away to the nearest lawyer and sends a letter like this. By God, when I reach her—"

"You should thank Julia," William interrupted. "In my opinion, she's done the sensible thing. It's clear that you're not right for each other, and she's wise enough to know . . ." His voice trailed into silence as he found himself the focus of a chilling glare.

"You don't know what the hell you're talking about," Damon snarled.

"You're right, I don't," William said hastily. "There are times when my mouth seems to work independently of my brain . . . damned inconvenient. I think I'll go upstairs now." He wasted no time in retreating from the room, after throwing a warning glance to the lawyer that made Lane fidget nervously.

"Your Grace, if you wish I can return at a later time when it is convenient for you to discuss your father's affairs—"

"Go," Damon said.

"Yes, Your Grace." The lawyer disappeared even more quickly than William.

It took Damon a long time to think past the

flood of anger. He found himself sitting at his desk, a drink in one hand and a bottle of brandy in the other. The smooth fire of the alcohol began to dissolve the cold lump in his stomach.

Julia didn't want him, or the life he had offered her. He wished she were here at this moment, a readily available target for the derisive words he wanted to hurl at her. She was a fool for preferring a life on the stage to that of a duchess. Surely anyone would tell her that— even she must know it, despite her insistence on keeping her damned career.

Thoughts of revenge danced before him. He wanted to throttle her, bully her into accepting what he wanted . . . but she would never yield to him. She was too stubborn for that. Perhaps he would take some fresh-faced, blushing daughter of a peer as his wife, and bring her everywhere that Julia was certain to see her. He would make Julia jealous, flaunt his pretty young wife before her until Julia was eaten up with envy and regret. He would make her believe that the sham-marriage had meant nothing to him, that he considered himself well rid of her.

Pouring another glass, Damon drank in a search for oblivion that seemed just out of reach. The bitterness faded a little, and he stared at the papers before him until the words and letters were a jumble of foreign markings. Julia's voice drifted through his mind.

You would want me to give up everything I've worked for, everything I need to be happy . . .

If I were your wife, would you let me go wherever I

chose, do whatever I pleased, with no questions or recriminations? . . .

Don't come back for me.

And the memory of Logan Scott's sardonic question, which stung even now. *Can you give her everything she wants?*

He thought of Julia in all her different guises. He had never met a woman who was so fascinating. For the first time he began to understand that to imprison Julia in the gilded cage he had planned would be intolerable for her.

"Damon?" William's brusque voice heralded his entrance. Walking uninvited into the library, he flipped a sealed note onto the desk. "This just arrived from Bath."

Damon stared at the letter without reaching for it. "Is it from Julia?"

"Oddly enough, the letter appears to be from her friend Arlyss Barry. I thought I would bring it to you before you're too drunk to read."

"I already am," Damon muttered, swilling from his glass once more. "You read it."

"Very well," William said cheerfully, "although you know how I hate to pry into other peoples' affairs." Breaking the wax seal, he scanned the letter. The gleam of amusement left his eyes, and he shot Damon a wary glance.

"What does our Miss Barry say?" Damon asked, his voice surly.

William scratched the nape of his neck and shook his head doubtfully. "Considering your present state of mind, it might be better to discuss it later."

"Tell me, damn you!"

"Very well. Miss Barry writes that although

it's not her place to interfere, she feels compelled to inform you that she has learned of Jessica Wentworth's plans to marry Logan Scott . . . tomorrow.''

William flinched as Damon's half-full glass of brandy shattered against the wall behind him, sending a spray of amber drops and crystalline fragments everywhere. Damon lurched to his feet, breathing heavily.

''What are you going to do?'' William asked gingerly.

''I'm leaving for Bath.''

''I think I should go with you.''

''Stay here.''

''Damon, I've never seen you like this before, and it scares the hell out of me. You should let me . . .'' But before the last word had left William's lips, his older brother had departed the room with purposeful strides.

Chapter 12

❦ ❦

There was usually a little extra magic in the air during a play's last performance. The actors were touched with a special glow as they went through their paces. The Bath audience was generous with its laughter and applause, becoming intensely involved in the story of *My Lady Deception* from the opening scene to the last.

Julia couldn't help but feel removed from the play tonight. Although she knew her performance was adequate, she couldn't seem to lose herself in the part as usual. Perhaps it was because she would marry Logan Scott tomorrow, linking her future to his in a permanent, if impersonal way. Her mind lingered on that fact even as she spoke and laughed and acted on-stage.

By now Damon must have received the letter. What had he said? How had he felt? She wondered how it would be the next time she saw him, when she introduced herself as Logan Scott's wife. It was better for both of them, she thought . . . but practical reasons didn't ease the

341

pain and worry she felt inside. If only things were different, if only . . .

The play concluded with long swells of applause, while the actors took their bows and acknowledged the flood of appreciation. Relieved when Logan finally led her off the stage, Julia pulled at her perspiration-dampened bodice and sighed.

Logan cast an assessing glance at her. "You look a bit fashed. Get a good night's rest," he advised, knowing that the cast would try to persuade her to join them in an evening of lavish drinking and eating. "We'll take care of the ceremony tomorrow morning, before we leave for Bristol."

Julia managed a wan smile. "More touring, more performances . . . it's not the usual sort of honeymoon, is it?"

He looked at her as if the thought hadn't occurred to him before. "Would you like a honeymoon?"

For a split second it was tempting to say yes. She would like to go somewhere exotic, a place she could relax and allow herself to forget everything, if only for a little while. However, the idea of going somewhere alone with Logan was unnerving. Besides, he would resent having to interrupt their schedule of touring for any reason, especially when he desired to oversee the reconstruction of the Capital Theatre.

"No," Julia murmured. "Now isn't the time. Perhaps someday, though . . ."

"Rome," he promised. "Or Greece. We'll go to a festival in Athens and watch plays in an open-air theater."

Julia smiled and murmured good night, smoothing her hair as she headed to her dressing room. Passing a number of people who were crossing through the dark backstage area, she found herself squeezed to the side, where she waited for the crowd to pass. "Mrs. Wentworth?" came a low voice beside her. She recognized one of the stagehands. He and a male companion stood on either side of her, forced together by the crush of people around them.

"Yes," Julia said uncomfortably. "It's very crowded, isn't it?" She waited until she found an opportunity to leave, and walked away from the stagehand and his friend. To her surprise, they went in the same direction, following her closely. An uneasy feeling crept over her, and she quickened her pace until she had almost reached her dressing room.

Before Julia had reached the threshold, she was grabbed from behind, her sudden scream muffled by a cotton gag, her arms bound efficiently behind her. Terror exploded inside her. She writhed in vain as they threw a cloak over her, its hood flapping down to conceal her face. The two men ushered her away with rapid strides, their hands gripping her arms and holding her upright.

"Sorry, Mrs. Wentworth," one of them muttered, "but there's a gentleman waiting outside who paid us to bring you to him. He says he only wants to talk to you for a few minutes . . . that's not too much to ask, is it?"

Stiff with fear, Julia was half-dragged, half-carried to the back of the theater, and loaded into a waiting carriage. The hood obscured her view completely. Blindly she waited with her arms bound and imprisoned between the seat and her back. Her breath came in hard bursts. There was nothing but silence in the vehicle. It started with a lurch, and began to move away from the theater.

Sweat trickled in icy droplets down Julia's neck and between her breasts. Just as she surmised that she was alone in the carriage, she felt someone move to the space beside her. Cringing, she lowered her head as a hand grasped the edge of the hood and yanked it back to reveal her face. Slowly she looked up with wide eyes and beheld the face of her husband—*former* husband—Lord Savage.

Her first reaction was a blaze of fury, but that died quickly as she stared at him. She felt her face blanch beneath the streaks of her makeup. It was Damon as she had never seen him before, disheveled and reeking of brandy.

He spoke in a barely recognizable drawl. "Good evening, Mrs. Wentworth. So kind of you to allow me an hour or two of your valuable time. I would have fetched you myself, but it seemed easier this way." His hot fingers came to the side of her jaw and stroked the soft edge. Julia jerked her head back and glared at him, silently demanding that he remove the gag from her mouth.

"No," he muttered, reading her thoughts. "I don't need to hear what you have to say. You've made yourself clear by cutting me loose and agreeing to marry Scott. Yes, I know about that . . . you should have known better than to trust Arlyss with your secrets."

He pulled the cloak from her shoulders and stared openly at her body, at the mounds of her breasts thrust forward by the pressure of her arms behind her back. Julia inhaled sharply, her spine as rigid as steel.

"Have you taken him as your lover yet?" Damon asked. "You haven't the look of a satisfied woman . . . the look you wear after I've made love to you. Did you enjoy his hands on you, his mouth on yours? How does it feel to lie with a man you don't love?"

Julia wanted to shake her head in denial, but she kept stubbornly still, her eyes fixed on his brooding face. Damn him for doing this to her, the selfish bastard! He wanted retribution . . . he wanted to scare the wits out of her. There was something different about his appearance tonight, a coarseness that obliterated his handsomeness and gave him the appearance of a satyr. Tonight it seemed as if he would be capable of anything . . . as if he were a wounded beast who would take pleasure in hurting anyone and everyone within reach.

"He doesn't love you," Damon said. "I wouldn't either, if I could help it. I would do anything to drive thoughts of you out of my head . . . your face, your sweet body . . ." He touched her breast, gently at first, then closed his fingers around the swelling curve and gripped until Julia made a small sound of discomfort. "This is mine," he said, his breath wafting against her face and throat. "You're still my wife. That will never change. No law of God or man will take you away from me."

Outraged, Julia tried to move away from him,

but he pinned her against the seat. Her mind reeled as he bent over her body with an incomprehensible murmur, his lips seeking her throat, his hands fondling her with clumsy but passionate intent. She closed her eyes and fought against her own response, but nothing would stop the sudden thrill of her nerves, the rise of her nipples against his palms, the goosebumps that swept over her skin. Her body relished the familiar smell of him, the crisp brush of his hair against her cheek as his mouth wandered from her neck to her cleavage.

Damon licked the trace of salt on her skin, his breath burning like steam against the moist path his mouth had made. At the sound of her faint whimper, he raised his head and stared at her in triumph. Julia knew that her face was flushed and her pulse was racing, that the signs of her arousal were clear. Roughly he pulled the gag from her mouth and crushed his lips over hers, sending his tongue deep in an ardent search.

As soon as he lifted his head, Julia glared at him and fought to steady her nerves. "Untie my hands," she said on a suffocated breath.

"Not until we've settled a few points."

"I won't discuss anything with you while you're drunk."

"I'm not drunk—but I have been drinking. It was the only thing that kept me sane during the trip to London."

"What are you planning to do?" she asked. "Abduct me? Prevent the wedding somehow? It doesn't matter, you'll only delay the inevitable."

"I'm going to ruin you for any other man." His

hands brushed over her fragile throat and down to her breasts. "You may choose him, but you'll never have what I can give you."

"Are you resorting to rape now?" she asked coldly, ignoring the flaring response of her body to his touch.

"It won't be rape."

Julia was infuriated by his selfish arrogance. "You're going to make me regret everything that has ever happened between us."

"You will. You'll regret having known what it's like to be loved by someone, when you're lying in bed next to a man who doesn't give a damn about anything but his profession."

"It's what I want. And I haven't slept with Logan—our marriage will be one of convenience."

He snorted at the idea. "Eventually you'll end up in his bed. You're too beautiful for him not to desire you. But you'll awaken beside him wanting me."

"Don't you think I know that?" she demanded, her voice suddenly breaking. "Do you believe it's been easy for me to accept the offer of a loveless marriage rather than stay with the man I . . ."

The words died away, but Damon pounced on the unfinished sentence. "The man you *what*? Say it, Julia. You owe me that much, at least."

She clamped her trembling lips together and stared at him with glittering eyes.

His breath caught as he looked at her. "By God, I'll make you admit it before the night is through."

"What good would that do?" she asked, while a tear dropped from one of her eyes and slid down her cheek.

Damon traced the wet path with his thumb. "I have to hear the words. I need to know that you understand what you're doing." His face was very close to hers, his disheveled black hair falling over his forehead, his eyes bloodshot. His arms slid around her and she felt his fingers working at the bonds around her wrists. When her arms were free, she pushed hard against his chest, but he continued to crush her close, his mouth at her ear. "I know what you want," he said roughly. "The very thing you're most afraid of . . . to be loved by a man, to give yourself to him without holding anything back. But you're too damned afraid to trust me. You think I'll use your feelings against you, just as your father did to your mother."

"And what about you?" she demanded, writhing against him. "You must have everything *your* way, at *your* convenience, regardless of what I must sacrifice in order to please you!"

"It doesn't have to be like that."

They were both still, locked together like two warriors in battle. The carriage stopped, and Damon dragged Julia from the vehicle despite her protests. They were at the Savage house at Laura Place. A pair of perplexed footmen tried to perform their duties as their employer hauled an obviously unwilling woman into the residence. Julia thought of screaming at the house servants for assistance, but Damon cut her short with a curt statement. "Don't bother. They won't help you."

Julia continued to struggle as he hauled her toward the staircase, until he stopped and slung her over his shoulder. After a shriek of surprise, she had a dizzying glimpse of the stairs passing beneath Damon's feet. Finally they reached his bedroom, furnished with a massive bed covered by a royal blue canopy. After depositing Julia on the mattress, Damon went to the door and locked it. He turned to face her and tossed the key to the carpeted floor.

Julia scrambled off the bed, her muscles stiff with outrage. "Is this approach effective with Lady Ashton? Because I assure you, it's not going to work with me."

"I've broken off my relationship with Pauline. She's not pregnant. She has no claim on me."

Julia refused to show any reaction to the news, although her heart gave an unwanted skip of gladness. "How ironic. You're bereft of a wife and a mistress all at once."

"I'm glad we're not married."

"Why is that?" she asked, managing to stand her ground as he approached her.

Damon stopped a few feet away and removed his coat. He dropped it to the floor and began unfastening his shirt buttons. "Now it's just you and me. The past is no longer between us, and everything our parents did is over."

"Have you told your father about the letter?" Julia asked, not yet having brought herself to tell her own family about what she had done.

A strange, stiff expression crossed his face. "No," he said curtly. "He died before I found out about it."

"What?" Julia asked in bewilderment, staring at him blankly until the meaning of his words sank in. "Oh," she said faintly. "That's why you didn't come back to Bath. I . . . I'm sorry—"

Damon cut her off with an impatient shrug, clearly unwilling to discuss it. "He was ill for a long time."

Pity and regret crept through the tumult of emotions inside her. If she had been aware of the situation, she certainly wouldn't have chosen to send the letter at the same time the duke had died. "I suppose my timing wasn't very considerate—" she began contritely.

"I don't want your consideration." He pulled his shirt free of his trousers. The white linen gaped open to reveal the ridged muscles of his abdomen. "I want you to take your clothes off and get into bed."

Julia's mouth went dry, and she could feel the frantic rush of blood in her veins. "You can't really mean that."

"Would you like me to assist you?"

"Have you gone mad?" she asked, her voice controlled except for the slight gasp that punctuated her question.

"I'm very close to it." Although there was a sardonic twist to his mouth, Julia realized with a chill of fear that he was in earnest. "I have been since the moment I met you," he continued. "I wondered why I couldn't have fallen in love with someone else . . . a woman who wanted the life I could offer. But there has never been a choice for me.

"I loved you long before I realized you were my wife. Finding out that you were Julia Hargate was a stroke of luck I never expected. I hoped it would bind you to me . . . but as you once pointed out, the marriage was never a real one. I couldn't hold you to the vows you were forced to make as a child. And you were hell-bent on having your way, just as I was. I'm afraid neither of us is very proficient at the art of compromise. And neither of us can force the other to change. So . . . I'm left with just one desire. For once in my life I want to make love to you and hear you admit that you love me."

They stared at each other, aware of the leap of tension in the air, the flicker of unwarranted hope. In the taut silence came the disruption of a man's voice echoing up the stairs, making threats and demands as the servants tried to dissuade him.

"Savage! I want to know where the hell Jessica is! You damned coward . . . I want to see her now!"

Julia was more than a little startled. It was clearly Logan's voice, but she had never heard him shout in such a manner except on stage. He must have worked himself into a rage upon discovering her abrupt disappearance from the New Theatre. With her gaze still locked on Damon, she called out in a strained but steady voice.

"I'm all right, Logan."

His voice was louder as he ventured up the stairs. "Where are you?"

Julia shot a wary glance at Damon, who didn't move. Evidently the prospect of facing an enraged Logan Scott did not bother him in the least. "I'm in the suite to the right of the stairs," she answered. Tentatively she moved toward the key that lay gleaming on the carpet, wondering if Damon would prevent her from unlocking the door. Before she reached it, the door vibrated with an explosive thump, and then another, its hinges squeaking in alarm. Two more devastating blows, and the door burst open.

Logan stood there with a grim expression, his mahogany hair in wild disarray. Rapidly his gaze moved over the scene; Julia's bedraggled condition, the discarded coat and key on the floor, Damon's open shirt. A contemptuous snarl distorted Logan's wide mouth. "You'll learn to stay away from her after I'm finished with you."

Dark pleasure cast a frightening shadow over Damon's face. "She's not yours yet."

"I'm perfectly all right," Julia said to Logan, breathless from the aura of hatred that filled the room. "Please take me away from here, and we'll settle this later like adults—"

"The only place you're going is to my bed," Damon said thickly. "Right after I throw your fiancé out of my home."

That was clearly the last straw for Logan. He launched himself forward with lightning speed, his broad fist swinging in a wide arc, impacting with a sickening thud against Damon's face.

"No," Julia gasped, darting toward them, then stopping short as Damon hurled himself on his rival. The two men fought violently, pummeling each other in spite of Julia's shrieks for them to stop. With a grunt of effort, Damon shoved Logan back several steps, and they faced each other with murderous gazes.

Immediately Julia took the opportunity to rush between the two men. After one glance at the unreasoning fury on Damon's face, she went instead to Logan and placed a restraining hand on the center of his chest. He looked down at her with hot blue eyes, his nostrils flaring with each breath he took.

"Please," she said quietly, "this isn't necessary."

"Leave with me now," Logan muttered.

Julia thought of complying, but something inside her resisted the idea. She could only manage a stammer. "I . . . c-can't."

"After what he's done?" Logan asked sharply. "One of the scene movers saw you being abducted from backstage. I knew at once that it was Savage. God knows I wasn't surprised by his behavior." He took hold of her shoulders, his fingers digging into her soft flesh. "He believes he owns you, Julia. Walk away from him now, and finish this damned mess."

Her gaze dropped. She couldn't look into his face any longer. "Not yet," she said under her breath. "Things aren't settled. Please try to understand."

"Oh, I understand," Logan replied coolly. Julia felt his fingers loosen, and then his hands fell away. "Shall I wait downstairs for you?"

"No, but . . . thank you for coming here. It means a great deal that you would want to protect me."

"If only I could protect you from yourself," he said with an ironic edge to his voice. Exchanging a glance of loathing with Damon, Logan turned and left the room, making a mocking show of closing the ruined door behind him.

Julia turned to face Damon, only to find that he had apparently lost all desire for her company. "Get out," he said, using his shirt sleeve to blot his bloodied nose, ruining the exquisite white linen.

Her mouth tightened with exasperation. Going to the washstand, she found a linen towel and moistened it with water from the porcelain pitcher. Damon sat on the edge of the bed and jerked his head back as she tried to dab at his face.

"Is your nose broken?" Julia asked, persisting until she had removing the blood from his upper lip.

"No." He took the cloth from her. "You can stop playing the ministering angel. I don't need you."

Julia shook her head slowly, feeling an overwhelming rush of love for him . . . the obstinate, arrogant, foul-tempered man. She pushed back the skeins of hair that had fallen across her face, and sat beside him. Gently she slid her hand over his smooth-shaven cheek and urged him to look at her. His face was like granite.

"I need *you*," she said softly.

Damon didn't move, but she felt the hardening of his cheek beneath her hand. "You were right," she continued. "I am afraid to trust you. But if I don't, then I'll never be able to trust anyone. It scares me to death to think that you'll want more than I can give. However, if you're willing to accept what I'm able to offer . . ."

Damon battled silently with the remnants of his jealous rage. The madness that had possessed him ever since he had discovered that she intended to become Logan Scott's wife began to ebb a little. As he looked at Julia, he saw the signs of strain about her face.

Her hand was soft on his cheek, and her blue-green eyes were filled with an emotion that made his heart constrict painfully. He wanted her so badly he was suffocated with it, wanted her any way he could have her. There were still too many words left unsaid, sorely needed explanations, issues to resolve . . . but he ignored them all and reached for Julia in a move that took her by surprise.

She didn't protest as he covered her mouth with his, kissing her hungrily. Her lips parted, and her arms slid beneath his open shirt, her hands coming to rest on his back. How many nights had he dreamed of Julia this way, soft and willing in his arms, pressing close against him.

He turned her, pushed her back onto the mattress until her hair spilled behind her head in a golden torrent. Bending over her, he kissed her throat and chest, moving down to her breasts. The tips hardened and rose against the fabric of her costume, and she made a soft sound in her throat as Damon bit gently through the bodice.

It seemed miraculous, Julia's lack of resistance, the way she accepted his touch . . . he realized that tonight she would allow whatever he wanted, and his heart hammered in a furious rhythm of need. With unsteady fingers he unlaced her bodice and pulled the dress from her shoulders and down to her waist. She lifted her

hips and helped him strip away the costume
completely, leaving only her linen undergar-
ments. In a lithe movement she rose to her knees
and pulled the chemise over her head, revealing
the enticing curves and shadows of her body.
Damon touched the delicate roundness of one
breast, brushing his knuckles over the taut crest.
Raising his gaze to Julia's luminous face, he saw
a tenderness that devastated him.

"Do as you promised," she said, her voice
hushed. "Make love to me tonight . . . and let
me tell you how much I love you."

"And in the morning?" he couldn't help
asking.

She smiled as if the question were foolish, and
leaned forward to kiss his mouth. "Turn down
the lights," she whispered.

Damon went to extinguish the lamps, leaving
only a small flame burning in one of them, and
returned to the bed. Julia's body was almost
ghostly in the dimness, sleek and silvery as she
stretched across the bed. The silken sheen of her
stockings and the ridges of her garters were all
that remained to cover her. Damon removed his
clothes and lowered himself onto the mattress,
his senses reeling as he pulled her naked body
against his, fire igniting everywhere their skin
touched.

Julia's teasing hands moved over his back and
hips, traveling down to his taut buttocks. She
was bolder than she had ever been before, her
mouth and fingers maddeningly inventive as she
explored him, a playful nymph bent on torture.

Damon fought to keep from taking her immediately, wanting to make the pleasure last. He removed one of her garters and unrolled her stocking, kissing each inch of newly revealed skin until he had worked his way from her inner thigh to the arch of her foot. Julia purred in response and offered him her other leg, wantonly drawing her silk-covered toes across his midriff. He removed that stocking as well, making her squirm at the tickling sensation of his mouth behind her knee. When the task was completed, he rolled her beneath him.

"Tell me," he commanded, nuzzling the curve of her jaw.

Julia's eyes opened, and he saw the coquettish gleam that betrayed her utter enjoyment. "Tell you what?"

"What you promised to say to me."

"Later," she said, and clasped his stiff erection in her hand, guiding him between her thighs. Damon resisted and frowned down at her, wanting the words she withheld. Artfully Julia tried to coax him closer, murmuring erotic promises, clasping her slender thighs around him. An unwilling laugh was torn from his throat. He stroked and kissed her, savoring her response . . . the rush of her breathing, the trembling that took hold of her. "Take me now," she said breathlessly. "Now, now . . ."

"Do you love me?" he asked, smoothing his hand over her stomach, dipping his finger into her navel.

"Yes," Julia finally gasped, opening her thighs. "Don't make me wait any longer." She scalded his ears with a litany of love and threats and pleading, until at last he relented and slipped his fingers inside her, sliding them in a rhythmic motion that brought her quickly to release. She arched upward, pressing the thatch of soft curls into his hand, and climaxed with a groan and an endless shiver.

A long time later her lashes stirred, and she responded to his kiss, her tongue twining with his. He brought his hips to hers and fused their bodies in a thrust that made her whimper in pleasure. He pushed inside her, his movements long and unhurried, and she clutched at his back and hips to draw him even deeper. Catching her wrists in his hand, he pulled them over her head, pinning her heavily against the mattress.

Julia felt his mouth at her throat, lips moving with unspoken words. His hands slid from her breasts to the place of their joining, softly tormenting until she could no longer breathe. Just as she thought she would faint, the sensations flowed over her, inundating every nerve. She trembled violently, her hips tilting upward to receive him as he released a flood of lust and longing inside her body.

When they could both move, they turned to their sides. Julia smiled drowsily as she felt his long legs tuck up beneath hers, his chest pressed against her back. "I like being abducted," she murmured, drawing his hand over her waist and up to her breast.

"I didn't know what else to do. I've been insane ever since this morning." His fingers traced her nipple in gentle circles. "Julia . . . are you going to marry Scott tomorrow?"

"Are you offering an alternative?"

Damon's hand cupped her breast until he could feel the rapid beating of her heart. He was silent for a long time, until she thought he wasn't going to reply. "Marry me," he said gruffly. "This time for real."

Julia closed her eyes and took an unsteady breath. "And your conditions?"

"No conditions. I won't ask you to leave the theater."

"What if people mock you for marrying a notorious actress?" she asked softly.

"To hell with them."

So it had finally come to this. He loved her enough to make the greatest concession of all. She had never imagined that Damon, the proudest and most demanding man she had ever met, would put aside his own desires in deference to her own. She knew that she owed him the same unselfish consideration. "I could limit my involvement with the theater," she said hesitantly. "I'll choose only the roles that interest me most . . . and I'll stop touring."

"Will Scott allow that?"

"He'll have to, if he wants me to stay at the Capital."

"Your career won't ever be the same."

"That won't matter as long as I have you."

Carefully he turned her to face him. Although Julia was brimming with hope and happiness, there was no answering smile on Damon's face. "I'll want children, Julia." His voice was low and scratchy, and she could only guess at the emotions that moved him.

"Yes, so will I." She shrugged helplessly. "I don't know how we'll manage, but . . . we'll find a way. It won't be easy."

"Easier than living apart."

Julia nodded and kissed him gently.

"What of your feelings for Scott?" Damon asked when their lips had parted.

"There is no love between us. He'll understand why I can't marry him. Besides, I was never meant to be anyone's wife but yours."

"Good. Because I've been your husband for too long to imagine anything else."

She smiled and stroked his chest. "How strange that we both wanted to be free of each other for so long . . . and just when we are, all we want is to be together again."

"Then you'll take the ring back."

"The ring, and all that comes with it."

Damon caught her hand and held it so tightly that she winced from the pressure. Bringing her palm to his mouth, he crushed a kiss within the soft cove. Emotion left him wordless . . . love and joy that mingled inside him . . . fear that this was a dream, and that the woman beside him was a fantasy spun from the loneliness and longing he had felt his entire life.

Slipping a hand behind his head, Julia pulled him over her once more, inviting his kiss and returning it without restraint.

As Logan welcomed Julia into his Bath villa early the following morning, there was no expression on his face, save for a slight crease between his auburn brows. His gaze searched her face, taking note of the flush on her cheeks and the gleam of happiness in her eyes.

"Good morning," she said breathlessly. He nodded, understanding at once that there would be no wedding that day. The plans they had made would never be mentioned again.

Sitting with Julia in the parlor, Logan seemed relaxed as a servant poured coffee into gold china cups and brought it to them. Logan motioned for the servant to leave, and threw Julia a resigned glance. "You're making a mistake," he said flatly.

A smile tugged at the corners of her mouth. "Perhaps I am. Marrying Damon could prove to be a disaster. But I would never forgive myself if I didn't try."

"I wish you luck."

"Aren't you going to warn me about what I'm doing? Aren't you going to point out all the sensible reasons that the marriage won't work, and tell me—"

"You already know my opinion on the subject of marrying for love. My only concern is how your actions will affect my acting company. It's obvious things will have to change."

"Yes," Julia said, trying to match his matter-of-fact tone. "I would like to remain as one of the Capital players. However, I won't be able to tour . . . and I'll have to limit the number of plays I'll be able to perform in."

"You can stay with the Capital as long as you like. Only a fool would refuse to have an actress like you in the company, even in a limited capacity."

"Thank you."

"I wanted more for you than this," he said abruptly. "You haven't even begun to reach the limits of your skill. You could have been the most acclaimed actress of the English stage—"

"Instead I'll be happy," Julia interrupted. "All the acclaim and fortune in the world wouldn't keep me from being lonely. I want to be loved, I want laughter and companionship . . . I want more than the pretend life I've had in the theater."

"Are you certain Savage will allow you to continue with the Capital?"

"Oh, yes." An impish smile crossed her face. "He may not like it, but he's willing to tolerate my career for the sake of having me as his wife." She sipped the coffee, glancing at him over the rim of her cup, and her smile turned rueful. "You think I'm a fool, don't you? You can't imagine making any sort of compromise that would take you away from the theater."

"No, I can't," Logan said evenly, and for the first time there was a friendly glint in his blue eyes. "But I don't think you're a fool. In a way I almost envy you. And don't ask me why—God knows I can't explain it even to myself."

Epilogue

They held a small wedding without fanfare at the castle chapel in Warwick, attended by family and a few close friends. Julia's mother, Eva, took an obvious delight in the fact that her daughter was marrying Damon. It was obvious from Lord Hargate's expression that he took a more ironic view of the proceedings, but he expressed his pleasure in the match regardless.

In the months that followed, Julia assumed her place as Damon's wife with an ease that surprised both of them. If there were any thoughts in Julia's mind that life as the Duchess of Leeds would prove dull and dignified, they quickly evaporated. Damon indulged Julia as no one ever had, spoiling her with extravagant gifts and stealing every possible moment of her time away from the theater.

Unlike her, Damon was an outdoors enthusiast, and she found herself accompanying him on long walks and rides through the countryside. Occasionally she participated in the shooting and fishing he enjoyed, and while she couldn't profess any great love of such sports, she admired his skill.

As Damon fished a trout stream on one of his estates, Julia lounged on a small bridge that crossed the water. Enjoying the sunshine, she hiked up her skirts and let her bare legs dangle over the edge. Silently she watched her husband cast toward the overhanging bank where a large brown trout hovered warily in the water. Standing on the opposite bank, Damon worked with the unhurried grace of an expert fisherman. Each cast rolled out in a steady rhythm, the line pulling back and flowing forward.

"Don't move," Damon said in a low voice as he noticed the flash of Julia's pale legs, but it was too late. Alerted by the unfamiliar glimmer, the wily trout disappeared, too unnerved to feed near the surface of the water. Damon scowled. "Dammit!"

"Did I frighten him?" Julia asked apologetically. "I find it amazing that a mere fish could be so sensitive. You know I never can sit still for long." Lifting her hands in a resigned gesture, she lay back on the bridge and sighed. "Very well, I won't come with you next time."

Less than a minute later she sensed Damon standing over her. "You won't get out of it that easily."

Julia smiled, keeping her eyes closed. "You'll fish better without distractions."

Damon lowered himself beside her, his hand sliding over her bare knee. "I happen to like distractions," he murmured, and pressed his lips to her sun-warmed throat.

To please Julia, Damon willingly escorted her

to endless rounds of balls, soirées and musical evenings. She was delighted to discover that her husband was an excellent dancer and had the unflagging energy to stay up all night if she desired. Best of all were the dark evening hours after their social events, when he would dismiss the maid and undress her himself, and make love to her until she fell asleep in pleasurable exhaustion.

Damon was the companion Julia had never dared to dream of, listening to her opinions with interest, debating the points on which they didn't agree, taking pride in her intelligence whereas most men would have been threatened by it. Julia soon realized that she could turn to him with any problem, no matter how insignificant, and he would treat it seriously. When she needed comfort, she would crawl into his lap and rest her head on his shoulder until her troubles had assumed their proper perspective. Sometimes it almost frightened her to realize how quickly she had come to depend on him.

"I never expected to feel this way about anyone," she told him one night as they lay together in bed and watched a fire burn in the grate. "Least of all a man like you."

"A man like me?" Damon repeated, amused.

"Yes, with all your business speculations and investments and your talk of tenants and farming—"

"It must seem dull in comparison to the theater."

"You must admit, we have very different interests."

Damon laughed and pulled the covers down

from her shoulders, until the cool air caused her nipples to rise into points. Her skin was dappled with firelight and shadow, and he drew his hand slowly over the silken surface. "In some ways, yes," he said, bending his head to her throat. "But we also have a few important things in common." He smiled as he felt her shiver in response to his touch. "Would you like me to elaborate?" he asked, nibbling at the sensitive side of her neck.

Julia slid her arms around him and arched upward, eager as always for the pleasure he offered.

Damon was a generous lover, sometimes lingering over her body for long, sweet hours, sometimes taking her with a rough passion that filled her with excitement. Julia gained the confidence to seduce him when it took her fancy, wearing provocative gowns and teasing him until he snatched her in his arms and gave her exactly what she asked for. When they were together, she could let the worries of her profession slip away, and she became a new person entirely, filled with contentment and ease.

As September drew near and rehearsals for the upcoming season increased, Julia traveled back and forth from the Savages' London residence to the Capital. At first the members of the company had seemed uncomfortable with her new status as the Duchess of Leeds, but that was all quickly forgotten in the work before them. Arlyss was clearly happy in her marriage to Michael Fiske and satisfied with her continuing popularity as a comic actress.

Logan Scott, for his part, was the same as

ever—demanding, arrogant, and obsessed with making his theater the most spectacular draw in London. With each bit of renovation that was completed on the Capital's interior, his spirits seemed to rise.

"Your one great love," Julia commented laughingly as she saw him inspecting the freshly gilded proscenium one day after rehearsal. "How many women would give anything to have you look at them that way! Just bear in mind that a mere building will never love you back."

"You're wrong," Logan informed her, throwing her a smiling sideways glance. His large hand drifted over the intricate carving of the proscenium. "She gives me far more than any flesh-and-blood woman ever could."

"Can a theater be a she?"

"How could it be anything else?"

Julia folded her arms across her chest and regarded him in a speculative way, thankful to her very marrow that she hadn't married him. Logan was—and would probably always be—extremely limited when it came to matters of the heart. Something in him wouldn't allow the trust and intimacy that were necessary to love a real person, to surrender to the risk that a relationship required.

When the theater season began, Julia found herself inundated with hordes of admirers, some respectful, some intrusive. To ensure Julia's safety, Damon made certain that she was accompanied to and from the theater with outriders and armed footmen, and that she had a capable escort whenever she went to shop or pay calls.

At first Julia thought the extra security measures were overdone, but she soon realized they were necessary. As she left the Capital after a performance, her ears were filled with screams of "Mrs. Wentworth!" or "Duchess!" and she was assailed by people trying to snatch a bit of lace from her gown or even a few hairs from her head.

Logan was openly pleased by Julia's popularity, knowing it was one of the reasons for the spectacular revenues being drawn in by the Capital. "Marrying Savage may not have been such a bad decision," he said reflectively, after witnessing the crowds gathering to await Julia's exits and entrances to the Capital. "The public likes the idea of a duchess performing for their entertainment. It makes me wish I'd been born with a title—just think what heights I would reach."

"I'm so glad you can find some benefit for your theater in all of this," Julia replied sourly. "That makes this inconvenience worthwhile."

Logan grinned at her sarcasm. "You're the one who chose to marry a duke over a mere thespian," he pointed out. "It's not my fault if the Capital has profited through your actions."

"Yes . . . but must you *gloat* over it?" Julia asked, her reproving look dissolving into a wry laugh.

Recently there had been some tension between the two of them. At a social gathering the previous week, Logan had tried to demonstrate that although Julia was the Duchess of Leeds, she was also an employee who was required at least part of the time to do his will. When called upon to entertain the guests, Logan had gestured to Julia, who was standing nearby with her husband. "Perhaps Her Grace would care to perform with me?" he suggested.

Julia gave Logan a discreet glare, having told him earlier that she would not help with any scenes that evening. She was there as Damon's wife, not as an actress Logan could trot out to solicit donations for his theater. The guests at the party urged her to come forward, but she stayed by Damon's side.

"I'm certain Mr. Scott can perform something with no assistance from me," she said, a fixed smile on her lips.

Logan's gaze met hers in a battle of wills. "Come, Your Grace. Don't deprive everyone of the enjoyment your talent provides."

Damon interrupted then, his face an expressionless mask. "My wife knows of my wish to have her exclusive company this evening. Perhaps you may prevail on her some other time."

Logan addressed his next comment to the room in general. "Evidently the duke isn't aware that it's unfashionable for a man to be jealous of his own wife."

Damon slid his arm around Julia's slender waist. "But it's entirely understandable with a wife like mine." He glanced down at Julia's distressed face and smiled reassuringly. "Go play the scene, if you wish."

She nodded briefly and returned his smile. "For you I will."

Later that evening Julia had snuggled beside

Damon in bed and kissed him gratefully. "Logan's behavior was appalling," she said. "He never gives a thought to anything except what will profit his theater. You were very understanding. Thank God you're not one of those possessive husbands who might have caused a scene!"

Carefully Damon turned her face toward his. "I want you all to myself," he said, his eyes utterly serious. "I always will. I'm as jealous as hell of every minute Scott spends with you in that damned theater. It's only because I love you that I won't stand in the way of what you want. Don't ever make the mistake of thinking I'm not possessive."

Julia nodded contritely. She leaned over to kiss him, trying to show him how little need there was for jealousy.

Jane Patrick was one of the plays that launched the new season at the Capital. The story was based on the life of a flamboyant writer and the many triumphs, failures, and disastrous love affairs that made her one of the most complex figures in the literary world. Logan had expressed his doubts about whether Julia was too delicate in appearance to play a woman who had been famed for her robust figure and masculine quality.

Gamely Julia tackled the role of Jane Patrick, making up for her lack of physical stature by adopting an outsize personality, until Logan was satisfied with the result. Logan played one of Jane's closest friends, a man who had been secretly in love with her for three decades but had never consummated the relationship. They found an agreeable balance onstage, with Julia emphasizing her character's bold arrogance and Logan giving a carefully restrained performance.

The production was both popular and critically acclaimed, and as the second week began, Julia was pleased to see the house filled to overflowing. She would be glad when the play finished its scheduled month-long run. It was exhausting playing a woman so different from herself. She returned home each night almost too weary to eat or make conversation, falling asleep as soon as she crawled into bed.

On the night that Damon attended *Jane Patrick*, Julia strove to give her best performance. She knew her husband was seated in a private box on the second tier, along with his brother, William, and a few friends. Filled with determination, Julia gave the part everything it required, as she delivered passionate tirades and quips of devastating wit, and swaggered across the stage as if she owned it. The audience reacted with laughter, gasps of surprise, and absorbed silences until the first act was nearly over. They reached a scene in which Julia and Logan erupted into a violent argument, as Jane's friend attempted to take her to task for her irresponsible life, and she reacted with a furious outburst.

A sweat of exertion broke out on Julia's face as she began one of her speeches. She was aware of feeling clammy beneath her costume, of cold trickles down her neck and bodice. Focusing on Logan's face, Julia continued the scene in spite of a wave of dizziness. Realizing that something wasn't right, she wished desperately for the scene to end soon. If they could finish the first act, she could sit somewhere and drink a glass of water, and calm the pounding in her head.

To Julia's horror, she felt the boards sway beneath her feet like the lurching of a ship. Logan's voice sounded far away, even though she knew he was standing right next to her. His face blurred, his blue eyes becoming distant points of color in the gray mist that hovered over her. Nothing like this had ever happened before. *I'm going to faint,* she thought in panicked wonder, even as she felt her legs crumple.

Instantly she was grasped and held upright in Logan's hard grip. She was vaguely aware that he was improvising lines, saying something about her character being intoxicated, and then he lifted her in his arms and carried her offstage. The audience, unaware that the faint had not been planned, burst into applause as the curtain fell.

Drenched with moisture, Julia was silent in Logan's arms, unable to answer his questions as he brought her to her dressing room. Sitting her carefully in a chair, Logan snapped out orders to the members of the company who hovered around them. "Bring some water," he growled to one of them, "and the rest of you stop crowding." Obediently the onlookers left the room. Logan stood before Julia, chafing her cold hands in his. "Tell me what's wrong," he said, forcing her to look at him. "You're as white as a sheet. Have you eaten today? Would you like some tea? A drink?"

"Nothing," she murmured, holding a hand over her mouth as the suggestions elicited a pang of nausea. Logan's eyes narrowed at the gesture, but he kept silent, his gaze sharp and speculative.

Someone else entered the room, and Logan moved aside. "She's all right," he said curtly.

Julia glanced up at her husband's dark, implacable face, and her mouth wobbled with a smile. Damon didn't return the smile as he sank to his haunches before her. His warm hand slid beneath her chin, and he surveyed her face. "What happened?" he asked.

"I fainted," Julia said, at once surprised and sheepish. "I was dizzy. I . . . I'm much better now." She risked a glance at Logan. "I'm well enough to finish the play."

Before Logan could reply, Damon interrupted quietly. "You're going home with me."

"Isn't that a decision for Julia to make?" Logan asked.

Damon's gaze locked with Julia's, and his hand fell away from her chin. "Let your understudy finish it. Or do you want to risk fainting again?"

"I've never left a performance before it was over," she murmured, shocked at the idea.

"You've probably never collapsed in the middle of a scene either." Although Damon's manner was controlled, Julia sensed the mixture of anger and concern beneath his facade. "Come with me, Julia. You don't look well."

Slowly Julia stood to glance in the mirror, discovering that she was still unsteady on her feet. Damon was right—she looked sick and clammy. The thought of finishing the play, and the emotional and physical exertion it would require, seemed an impossible notion.

Apparently Logan realized that she was incapable of going on. He dragged both hands through his hair. "Go," he muttered. "I'll take care of things here." He paused and added to Damon, "Send word about her condition in the morning."

In spite of Julia's protests, Damon carried her out to the back of the theater, where he had instructed the driver to bring the vehicle. She leaned against him as they went home, taking comfort in the support of his arm around her. "I don't know what's wrong with me," she murmured. "I'm just exhausted, I suppose . . . the role is very draining."

Damon didn't reply, stroking her hair and blotting her moist face with his handkerchief.

The doctor left the room and paused to speak briefly to Damon, who had been waiting just outside the door. Sitting up in bed, Julia watched as a comical array of expressions crossed her husband's face, joy and concern among them. She managed a smile as he came into the bedroom and sat beside her on the mattress. He took her hand as if it were too frail to bear more than the lightest pressure.

"You didn't suspect anything?" he asked, his voice hoarse.

"I wasn't certain," she admitted with a faltering smile. "I thought I would wait another few weeks before mentioning anything. Are you pleased about the baby?"

"God, Julia . . . that you should even ask . . ."
Damon leaned forward and captured her mouth
in a reverent kiss. Julia responded eagerly, tangling her fingers in his black hair.

Withdrawing, Damon stared into her eyes.
Julia sensed the questions that hovered on his
lips, knowing it required all his restraint to keep
them locked inside.

"I've been considering some things lately,"
she told him, drawing her hands over his chest.

Damon was silent, waiting for her to continue.
It was important for her to choose the right
words, to make him understand the revelations
that had come to her.

Because she had never known the security of
her father's affection and approval, she had
never been able to completely trust anyone, to
rest secure in the knowledge that their love
would not fade or be withdrawn. But Damon
had changed that. He had made her believe that
his feelings for her were everlasting . . . and that
would give her the courage to loosen her tight
grip on her acting career. She wanted to explore
other sides of herself. She wanted to give herself
to love as freely as she had given herself to
ambition.

She had always been so self-protective, avoiding everything that posed a threat to her independence. In a way she had built a prison
around herself, and now the walls were crumbling to reveal a view she had never considered
before.

It filled Julia with a sense of adventure, the
thought of what might await her if she finally
dared to let go of the past. Tentatively she pulled

Damon's hand to her flat stomach, pressing it over the tiny life beginning within her. She imagined Damon as a father, and the thought brought a smile to her face. How strange that the things she had once feared would rob her of her precious freedom, a husband and a child, had given her more freedom than she had ever dreamed of. They would be her source of strength. And she would be theirs.

"I've decided that I would like to leave acting for a while," she said. "I've come up with an alternative that I believe will suit me better . . . at least for now. I would like to make a financial investment in the Capital Theatre, a substantial one, in order to have my name put on the company's charter. That would make me a partner of Mr. Scott's . . . a minor partner, but one with some influence nonetheless."

"What purpose would that serve?"

"I would be able to help manage the Capital, consult with writers who are developing plays; oversee the painters, musicians, and carpenters; work in the business office and assist in scheduling, casting, costuming . . . oh, there are a thousand things I could attend to that Mr. Scott never has enough time for! It would allow me to do as much or as little as I wished, and yet I wouldn't have the burden of being in the public eye. Don't you see what a perfect compromise it would be? I would still have the theater, but I would also have more time to spend with you and the baby. I would be here every evening instead of returning home late after a performance."

"You'll want to act again," Damon said, looking down at her hand as he played with the diamond ring on her finger.

"Perhaps every once in a while . . . if a role proves to be irresistible."

"How do you think Scott will react to the idea? Could he tolerate the idea of a woman as a business partner?"

"For enough money, he'll tolerate anything," Julia assured him with a sudden grin.

They stared at each other for a long while, until a reluctant smile spread over Damon's face. Carefully he pulled her down to the mattress and lay beside her. His hand played over her body and lingered on her stomach. "I want you to be happy," he said, his lips brushing her cheek.

Julia tangled her legs with his. "How could I not be? You've given me so many things I never thought I would have . . . love, a home, a family . . ."

"Tell me what else you want." Damon cupped her face in his hands and pressed a fierce kiss on her lips. "Tell me, and I'll get it for you."

"All I want is you," she said, her eyes gleaming. "Forever."

"You've had that since the beginning," he whispered, pulling her close and kissing her once again.